AMERICAN INDIAN LITERATURE
AND
CRITICAL STUDIES SERIES

Gerald Vizenor and Louis Owens,
General Editors

JOSANIE'S WAR

Other books by Karl H. Schlesier

Nonfiction

The Wolves of Heaven: Cheyenne Shamanism, Ceremonies, and Prehistoric Origins (Norman, 1987)

Plains Indians, A.D. 500–1500: The Archaeological Past of Historic Groups (Norman, 1994)

JOSANIE'S WAR

A Chiricahua Apache Novel

by
Karl H. Schlesier

UNIVERSITY OF OKLAHOMA PRESS
Norman

Though some historical materials with notes are included, this is a work of fiction. Names, characters, places, and incidents are either the product of the author's imagination or are used fictitiously, and any resemblance to actual events, locales, or persons, living or dead, is entirely coincidental.

Library of Congress Cataloging-in-Publication Data

Schlesier, Karl H.
    Josanie's war : a Chiricahua Apache novel / by Karl H. Schlesier.
        p.   cm.   — (American Indian literature and critical studies series ; v. 27)
    ISBN 0–8061–3065–2
    1. Chiricahua Indians—Fiction.   I. Title.   II. Series
PS3569.C5128J67   1998
813'.54—dc21   98–6212
                                                                        CIP

Josanie's War: A Chiricahua Apache Novel is Volume 27 in the
AMERICAN INDIAN LITERATURE AND CRITICAL STUDIES SERIES.

The paper in this book meets the guidelines for permanence and durability of the Committee on Production Guidelines for Book Longevity of the Council on Library Resources, Inc. ∞

1   2   3   4   5   6   7   8   9   10

To Iszánádle-sé and Tóbáshi-scinén, who may still be listening, even if I misspell their names. And for Claire.

The white man makes two wars. One to kill us.
And one to make sure no one will remember.

Black Kettle, Cheyenne chief, 1867

INTRODUCTION

On May 17, 1885, five small bands of Chiricahua Apaches left their camps on Turkey Creek, seventeen miles southwest of Fort Apache, Arizona, and fled the reservation. Three of these bands were of the old Chokonen division of the tribe, led by Chihuahua, Naiche, and Geronimo. The other two bands were of the old Chihenne, or Warm Springs, division of the tribe, led by Nana and Mangus. Together they numbered 35 men, 8 boys tagged by reservation officials as subadults capable of bearing arms, and 101 women and children. Charles F. Lummis, a journalist who accompanied the commanding officer of the Department of Arizona, Brigadier General George Crook, during some of his attempts to recapture or kill these Apaches, called them "the deadliest fighting handful in the calendar of man."

These Chiricahua men, women, and children were the same who had surrendered to Crook in the Sierra Madre of Mexico on May 20, 1883, after they had been worn down by constant warfare against them on both sides of the border. For two years they had lived without fear of imminent death, but they had paid a heavy price for it. With the surrender they relinquished any hope of ever keeping for themselves a fraction of the great and wealthy country that they had held and defended for many generations, through the Spanish and Mexican periods and into the American period.

Originally mountain people, they had been imprisoned on sun-drenched, disease-infected desert lands that were foreign to them. They had been subjected to rules considered unlawful anywhere outside the reservation boundaries. Every aspect of their culture and religion had been assaulted by civilian and military authorities. Corrupt reservation officials had become rich by defrauding them. They had seen many of their people die of European-introduced diseases and of starvation. None of the solemn promises made by the government had been kept. Slowly, life on the reservation had become intolerable; the human spirit was dying.

When they broke away from bondage and misery once again, they knew what storm their flight would cause. Within days every trail above and below the border with Mexico would be examined by Indian scouts guiding cavalry and infantry regiments in order to find and destroy them. The only other beings that inspired a similar hatred on the mining and cattle frontier were the wolf and the grizzly bear. It is true, of course, that these and the Chiricahua Apaches belonged to a world as the Creator had made it and had meant it to remain. That is how the world is explained in sacred Chiricahua ceremonies.

This is the story of one of the Chokonen bands, that of Chihuahua and Josanie. Chihuahua, a renowned warrior and leader, was the band's chief. Josanie, his older brother, was the band's established war captain.

JOSANIE'S WAR

ONE

In the east, a black cloud stands upright.
There, his home is made of black clouds.
The Great Black Mountain Spirit in the east,
he is happy over me.
My songs have been created.
He sings the ceremony into my mouth.
My songs have been created.
The cross made of turquoise,
the tips of his horns are covered
with yellow pollen.
Now we can see in all directions,
drive evil and sickness away.
My songs will go out into the world.

*Gahé song. Song of the mountain spirits, recorded
by Jules Henry in 1930.*

TWO

There was a wind. It came from the southwest, across the high broken country south of the Gila River, and brushed gently through the canyon of Eagle Creek. It carried the smoke of fires upstream from camps huddled closely under the great cottonwood trees, on dry sand and gravel bars, hidden behind two sharply curved bends about a mile from the creek's mouth. A huge moon stood directly above on a cool, cloudless night, creating light-flooded surfaces on open, exposed ground and long, dark niches along the rock walls. At about four o'clock in the morning most of the fires had died down but a few still glowed brightly in the moonlight. Around them people lay asleep, bundled up in tight clusters. On benches along the swift-running, narrow stream, horses moved slowly, cropping the new grass.

This was the second night camp. Two days ago they had ridden away from Turkey Creek in the early afternoon of a balmy Sunday, when a baseball game was being played at Fort Apache between two teams of Fourth Cavalry troopers stationed at the post. First to leave were Mangus's, Naiche's, and Geronimo's bands. Chihuahua and Nana left last. They had ridden hard on the trail east toward Black River and Eagle Creek. On the first day they covered about eighty miles and camped late at night in the canyon near Cottonwood Spring. The rocky terrain had exhausted the horses even though they had changed gaits often after reaching Eagle Creek, switching from a lope to periods of walking.

At first light the men searched the spring and Cottonwood Canyon for horses but found none. They found cattle and killed three amber-colored steers noiselessly, with lances, and butchered them quickly and roasted thin slices of meat on the coals. Not to ruin the horses, the men rode only fifty miles on the second day and made camp a short way above the Gila. Naiche's scouts, sent ahead to reconnoiter downriver and upriver and into the grassy plain below the mining town of Clifton, as far as the Arizona and New Mexico

Railroad, reported no unusual movements and believed that they had gone unnoticed. Chihuahua's scouts, covering the back trail, had not yet come in.

There was the sudden wailing of a baby in Chihuahua's camp, a series of piercing cries that cracked the stillness of the night. Some of the sleepers lifted their heads and looked around. The baby's mother quickly muffled the infant and laid it against her breast. A few more sobs, quiet again. There was a sound from upstream. A horse moving toward the camp, hooves on soft ground, a clanking on cobblestones. A horseman rode up, a rifle held out at his side. Chihuahua and Josanie stepped away from their blankets and walked toward the rider. It was Zele, one of the two scouts who had stayed on the back trail.

His horse stood weakly, glinting with sweat. "They are coming," Zele said.

"Where is Galeana?" Josanie asked.

Zele slid off the horse's back. He untied the blanket that served as a saddle and loosened the double knot that held the bridle over the mare's lower jaw. He patted her on the rump, and she walked stiffly away toward the creek. "Galeana is still back there." He pointed with his thumb. "We stayed about half a mile in front of them."

"How far away are they now?" Chihuahua asked.

"If they keep going the way they have, they will be here at first light. They are tired, but they are coming."

"How many?" Josanie asked.

"Sixty. Seventy. Maybe more. They have a mule train with them."

"How many scouts?"

"Maybe ten. They are just ahead of the soldiers. They could be White Mountain. I don't think they are our people."

Nana had come up from his camp. "They are coming," Josanie said. "They will be here in two hours, maybe earlier."

Nana nodded. "We'll leave soon. We must have a brief meeting . . . with Mangus and the others." In the sky the white moon walked west unhurriedly, lengthening the shadows in the canyon. Around the fireplaces people were getting up, sensing that something was happening. Josanie called softly to one of the men to bring the other band leaders.

They sat around Chihuahua's fire, Chihuahua with his brother Josanie next to him, then Nana, Naiche, Geronimo, and Mangus. Behind them men of their bands formed a tight circle. Chihuahua searched for Zele and pointed at him with his chin.

"I just came in," Zele said. "They are behind us. Maybe two troops of cavalry. A mule train. Ten scouts, maybe. I and Galeana think that they are White Mountain. One white man is with them, Gatewood. They stick close to the soldiers. They have been riding all night."

There was a silence. Then Mangus spoke. "I'm going south, to the Sierra Madre. We will never be safe north of the border. They will come at us from everywhere."

"We already have decided to do the same," Naiche said. He nodded toward Geronimo, who sat beside him. "We should all go there. Split up and meet there, in the Blue Mountains. Help each other. Stay there together."

Silence again. Nana spoke slowly. "I want to see my old country again, the Black Range. I hunger for it. My heart aches for it. I can't stay there anymore, but I want to go there for some time." He paused. "We'll go north, up the San Francisco River. I have one good cache in the mountains east of the Silver City road. I want to get some of the things from there."

"You can get more in Mexico," Geronimo said.

"We'll go with Nana," Chihuahua said. "Then to the mountains around the headwaters of the Gila. Wait there. See what happens. This is our country up there, where we were born." He touched his brother's arm. He looked across the fire into Geronimo's eyes. "You, too," he said. "You were born there, too."

Geronimo nodded. He opened his hands in a gesture of helplessness. Wings of a bird, fluttering in despair. "It is true," he said. "But it is not safe there. They will find you there. The soldiers won't, but the Apache scouts will. Come with us."

They sat in silence. The dark circle of men stood without stirring. All had heard. Now was the time to speak, but no one spoke.

Finally Chihuahua said, "So it is decided." He looked along the faces of the men who had said that they would go south. "If we come later, where in the Sierra Madre do we find you?"

"In the mountains east of Nacori Chico," Naiche said. "If we move from there, we'll leave signs for you, tell you where we have gone."

Nana spoke again. "My heart is heavy," he said. And after a pause: "We must leave here. Maybe we see you down there."

They left the canyon as they had camped. The three bands going south were in the lead, Nana and Chihuahua following. They let the horses walk until they reached the flats along the Gila. When they turned upstream, they pushed the horses into a slow, space-consuming lope.

Josanie and a screen of eight men rode point for Nana's band and his own. Nana and a few men rode with the women and children, while Chihuahua brought up the rear with another handful of men. At first light they passed across the wide floodplain at the mouth of the San Francisco, splashing through the cold waters of the stream sneaking through gravel fans, and when they reached the Hot Springs trail, one man of the rear guard saw a single rider far behind them.

They slowed the horses to a walk and let Galeana come up. His horse was covered with foam. Binoculars hung on his chest on a blue calico shirt, and he carried a .44–40 Winchester on a rawhide rope on his back. His face, painted with a white stripe across the cheekbones and the saddle of his nose, was tired, the eyes glittering in deep sockets. He had not slept for two days. He was solemnly greeted and fell in with them.

"I need a fresh horse," he said. "They are fifteen miles behind me, but they won't catch up. Their horses are gone, too. They can hardly walk."

When the point riders reached the Safford road in the rolling plain, Josanie brought his horse to a halt and called out. The bands ahead looked back and halted. He raised his arm and men there raised theirs. Then they turned and rode on, back toward the Gila, southeast, on the long trail to Mexico. Josanie and the men with him stood their horses and watched the others go. They crossed a ridge and were gone, the plain empty under the sun peering over the rim of the mountains to the east. Josanie swung his horse north, and the last two bands followed on the road to Clifton. There was a railroad to cross and a telegraph line to cut and at least two ranches to hit for fresh horses. Josanie and his outriders ran off eighteen horses and left their own exhausted mounts and moved on, around the grimy mining town sitting over the river and the filthy tailing heaps. The men slipped into the stream channel of the San Francisco cut deep into the mountains. When they caught another bunch of horses in the cottonwoods and green grass of a river bend, they were seen by two riders high on a bluff, but passed without a shot fired.

From the place where Ash Spring ran into the river from the high peak to the east, the bands took their time and when they reached the Blue, they turned into the canyon and rode north through the cottonwoods, along the winding stream, to a hidden place across the mouth of Horse Canyon. Twice they had passed grizzly tracks, and the prints of deer and elk and wolves were etched in the fine sands and on gravel bars. There were weary cattle with a triple X brand. Nitzin, expert handler of the old-time silent weapon and one of the three men of the combined bands who carried one, lanced two fat young steers. There was enough meat to last a couple of days.

That evening the fires burned free. They built a small altar from stones arranged in a circle, and Chaddi, one of the medicine men, spoke a prayer to *Bikego I'ndan*, Him, the Master of Life, and sang a song to the mountain spirits and gave thanks for deliverance. The adults stood with bowed heads, and the children looked on shyly, but then there were only smiles and the good smell of roasting meat. They were at home and at ease, and on all sides beyond the canyon the mountains stretched into the sky. The air was cool with the fragrance of flowers and piñons and pines. In the morning they bathed in the cold, clear water running down from the high country and the last of the snowfields shrinking under the spring sun.

They lingered and let the children play a little, then moved upstream three miles, slipped into the canyon of Little Blue Creek that ran in from the northeast, and made camp at a spring seven miles farther up. Three of the older boys went out with bows to look for deer upstream, where the canyon walls came down below the Alma Mesa. There was a low saddle to the east that allowed easy crossing toward the San Francisco River and the mining towns of Alma and Cooney in New Mexico.

THREE

Sunday afternoon there was a baseball game between two post nines that I was asked to umpire while I was waiting at the post for a reply to my telegram. In the midst of the game, about four o'clock in the afternoon, Mickey and Chato came to me with the report that a number of Indians, they did not know how many, had left their camps and were on their way to Mexico.

I attempted at once to send a telegram to Captain Pierce advising him of this, but the operator found that the wires had been cut. It was not until the next day near noon that the break was found. The Indians had cut the line in the fork of a tree and tied it with a buckskin thong. My telegram then went through and was forwarded to the General.

Colonel Wade, in command of the troops at Fort Apache, immediately ordered them to prepare to take the field, but it was dark before they were ready.

With the troops from Fort Apache we marched all night, my scouts and a dozen of Gatewood's White Mountain following the trail, a slow proceeding at night. A little after sunrise the following morning we came out on the crest of a ridge bordering a valley some fifteen or twenty miles wide. In the distance, on the opposite side of the valley, we could see the dust raised by the Indian ponies ascending another ridge.

Realizing that further pursuit by troops was useless and that we were in for a long campaign in Mexico, I reported to Captain Smith in command of the troops that I would return with my scouts to Fort Apache and wire the General again, asking for instructions.

Immediately on reaching Fort Apache I had all the Chiricahua and Warm Springs brought to my camp and counted them. Thirty-five men, eight tagged boys (those old enough to bear arms), and 101 women and children were missing.

Under the General's orders I enlisted a hundred more scouts, half of them Chiricahua, Warm Springs, and White Mountain, the other half San Carlos, Tonto, Yuma, and Mohave sent me by Captain Pierce. With a pack train of supplies I again took the field. The leaders who took part in the outbreak were Geronimo, Chihuahua, Nachite [Naiche], Mangus, and old Nana.

Statement by Lieutenant Britton Davis, Third Cavalry, who had been in charge of the Chiricahua and Warm Springs Apaches on Turkey Creek from the spring of 1884 to the summer of 1885.

FOUR

In early afternoon three men sat together on a patch of grass surrounded by wolfberry bushes, away from the small camp.

"I wonder where they are," Nana said. "If they went back or are still moving on. If they got fresh horses, they may still be coming."

Chihuahua looked thoughtfully at the old man. "They could follow the other trail south," he said at last. "It's easier on the horses than this one." And after a pause: "They are not going to split the troops and go after Naiche and them and after us. If they go on, they either come after us or go after the others."

Nana nodded, playing with a stem of grass between his teeth. "We'll know tonight or by tomorrow," Josanie said. "Galeana is back there." He pointed with his chin down the canyon.

Galeana rode in after dark, before the moon had climbed over the eastern rim of the canyon. A dozen fires were burning. He was quickly surrounded by men. His horse, a bay taken a day before from one of the ranches southwest of Clifton, was skittish, not yet used to the single lariat bridle tied over its lower jaw and to Apaches. Galeana held it tightly after dismounting.

"They have come after us," he said. "Same bunch. They are camped for the night at a spring a way downstream from where we were last night. I have counted the scouts. Twelve, White Mountain. The white man Gatewood is with them. They camp off by themselves. There are two troops from the fort. We know the main officer. Smith."

There was a silence. "They think us more dangerous than Geronimo and Naiche," Nana said with a chuckle.

"Is there a way to run off their horses?" Josanie asked.

"No. They camp in a narrow place, and they have guards posted. I could not get around them. I have tried. Their horses and mules are south of the camp."

The men stood quietly, considering everything. Finally Nana spoke: "There are good places on the Blue for an ambush. One is just a mile below where we camped last night."

Some men grunted in agreement. "I know the place," Josanie said. "The army scouts don't."

"I like you to go," Chihuahua said. "Stop them. Maybe turn them back."

"Hn, yes," Josanie said. And after a pause: "I take six men. With him," he pointed with his chin at Galeana, "and with Zele still down there we are nine men. Enough." He touched his brother's arm. Turning, he asked, "Who goes with me?"

Some men spoke their names. "It is good," Chihuahua said. "We leave this place at daybreak and move up to that low ridge on the east side. We go across and wait for you there. If we have to move, we cross the river south of the mining town and go into Whitewater Creek."

So it was agreed. Josanie and seven men rode out from the camp near midnight, under a fierce moon. They rode the eleven miles slowly, letting the horses choose the trail. They had stripped for battle, wearing only moccasin boots and blue calico breechclouts. They were painted with a white line across their faces below the eyes. Most wore blue headbands, but three had feathered war caps, tied under the chin, atop black, flowing hair. A few had medicine cords strapped diagonally across their torsos that held *godiyo*, holy power, for protection. Everyone wore a medicine pouch tied to his cartridge belt that contained *hoddentin*, sacred pollen, and small medicine objects. All carried rifles, half of them Springfield .45-70 single shots, army pattern, the others lever-action Henrys and Winchesters. Josanie rode with a .45-70 Sharps-Borchardt on his thigh. Only Tsach carried in addition a bow and arrow case. When they were still miles away, they could smell the fires of the soldier bivouac. Galeana led them to a secluded place where Zele's horse was concealed behind boulders.

They dismounted and left their horses there, without a guard. They walked silently downstream, past three ancient cottonwoods, and around a bench they found Zele waiting. They walked on and took up positions for the ambush. The enemy camp was behind another bend, out of sight. The moon moved on and the night turned toward morning.

The air was cold, but they ignored it. Josanie sat in a crevice in the rock wall twenty feet above the ground. Below him the canyon narrowed to a width of about fifty feet full of gravel, sand, and broken rocks through which a shallow stream wound its way. He could look over a rocky ledge into the small, oval valley beyond the tight curve of the canyon. On the valley floor under him he saw Tsach, Bish, and Nitzin, and he knew that the rest of the men were hidden on the far side of the stream, from where they could cover the approach through the valley.

With a flutter a kingbird alighted on a ledge ten feet away, blinked the dark pearls of his eyes from under his shale-colored cap, made his mournful call, once, and dropped away. Slowly the sky turned golden and the sun's rays came to rest on the western rim of the canyon.

Josanie pressed himself into the stone and peered over the ledge to where the river disappeared in an opening in the canyon walls. A lone gray pinnacle stood before it, a silent sentinel. Behind it appeared two riders, about a hundred yards away. Two more, then three. Six more. They came slowly, their rifles at the ready. The eighth rider was a white man; the others were Apaches. They had rubbed their white cotton clothes and red headbands with dirt for camouflage. They rode on, the first two looking at the tracks on the ground, the others studying the cliffs and tumbled rocks for hidden danger.

Josanie heard the hoofbeats, and when the first two scouts came into the gap below him, he saw the head of a cavalry column at the entrance to the valley, blue uniforms and yellow scarfs, the men riding in twos, keeping distance from the scouts. He looked down and saw that Tsach had unsheathed his bow and notched an arrow.

Josanie looked again at the approaching cavalry. When he looked down, he saw that the first two riders had passed the gap. Tsach raised the bow and released the arrow, and Josanie saw the second rider slump in the saddle as the arrow struck the ribs under his right arm. The point rider rose in the saddle and looked back, and Tsach hit him on the side of the neck with the second arrow. He slipped from the saddle, screaming, and was dragged away by the panicked horse.

The narrow space along the Blue exploded with deafening gunfire. Josanie heard screams and the hard slaps of bullets hitting flesh, the wild clatter of hooves when horses were racing back. He saw four or five of the scouts galloping away but raised the Sharps-Borchardt to fire at the packed ranks of the cavalry. He hit them before they broke up and turned away, trying desperately to reach the safety of the river bend. He kept firing fast with the long-range rifle. Someone else was shooting at the same targets. He saw horses fall and men lying still, some crawling away.

It was over. He climbed down from his perch. Four of the army scouts lay dead, and two, wounded, were finished off by his men when he got there. There were hard feelings because these Apaches had guided the whites to the camps of their own people and to slaughter, when the opportunity arose, and they were known to have taken part in it.

Josanie and his men took the scouts' army-issued Springfield rifles and ammunition boxes and belts and saddles and caught three frightened but healthy horses. They shot two crippled ones and walked away. Josanie stayed behind and took tule pollen from a pouch on the medicine cord on his chest. He held a pinch in his right hand and turned east, praying softly, then faced the remaining cardinal directions sunwise, finally offering the pollen to the above and the below worlds. He asked the spirits of the slain for forgiveness and marked with pollen a tiny line, between the dead and the living, on the ground. He joined the others, who had watched from a distance. They mounted and rode away knowing that they would not be followed for a little time. They felt good for the moment, but they knew there would be harder times coming.

It took them a bit more than an hour to reach the place where they had camped the night before. They passed it, and two miles farther up they saw where the tracks of the band left the floodplain and led east toward the low saddle reaching out below Alma Mesa. They climbed it and let the horses walk through the pines and shallow furrows cut by the water courses coming down from the mesa, and when they walked off the eastern slope of the saddle, they found their people waiting at the entrance to Keller Canyon. They had eaten cold food after arrival; there were no fires. Women, children, and old people lounged under the cottonwoods, but the horses, including the few packhorses, were kept ready to ride at an instant. Some men with rifles were at guard, but others were not in sight, scouting toward the river.

They all stood up and looked, missing nothing, when Josanie's party rode in. They saw that everyone had come back, no one wounded, and from the extra horses, rifles, and saddles they knew what had happened. There were only smiles, no welcoming songs as in old times—Apache songs, so strange to whites. They could be heard by someone who might bring packs of whites to descend on them.

The raiders dismounted. The bridles of their horses were eagerly grasped by young boys, who took the animals in their care. Josanie's young son, Nachi, proudly led his father's horse away. Chihuahua and Nana were the first to greet them.

"All of you are back," Chihuahua said, grabbing his older brother's arm. He looked in his face: hollow cheeks, hard, tired eyes under the rawhide war cap crowned with tail feathers of the golden eagle. "We are thankful, all of us." He made a wide gesture with his hand. "You have stopped them?"

Josanie nodded. "Yes. We killed six of the White Mountain scouts. Perhaps a few of the soldiers, maybe two or three. We've wounded some and crippled some of their horses. They will stay back for a while, I think. Maybe not for long."

"Yes," Nana said. "They will do what their officers tell them to do. They have no women and children to protect. They will follow us. We must find a safe place." After a pause he continued, "You did well, Josanie." Gently the old man touched the raider's shoulder.

"We better go on," Chihuahua said. From the winding canyon below four men rode in who had scouted ahead.

"There are two ranches in this canyon," Kezinne said, working with both hands on his blue headband. "The first one is about two miles away, the other five miles, not far from the river. They are small ranches. They have horses nearby. There are cows, too." He finished fastening the headband and shook his head. "We found one ranch in a side canyon, south." He pointed. "Eight horses in a corral. There was no ranch there the last time we were here."

The men nodded gravely. Some grunted in agreement. There was a silence. "It would be good if we could get twenty-five fresh horses," Chihuahua said. "Let's take them from those ranches. Eight men are enough. The old man and I," he pointed with his chin at Nana, "we will go with the women and children, south, then across the river and the road and into Whitewater Canyon. We wait for you there." He paused. "Agreed?" The men nodded.

They rode together past the first ranch, where their outriders gathered six horses and saw one white man gallop away. He would raise the alarm. They parted at the mouth of Beaver Canyon, the bands going southwest, below the shoulder of Sunflower Mesa, seven men riding ahead with rifles ready. Josanie and his men continued down Keller Canyon at a fast lope. They heard a few shots coming from behind them, from the direction of the ranch on the Beaver where Nana and Chihuahua had gone, and then nothing more, and they knew that their families had passed the white man's place and done what they had to do.

When they were about four hundred yards from the second ranch on Keller, they were fired on from the ranch house by at least four rifles. They pulled to a halt. There were a dozen horses between them and the ranch, bucking and running from the noise, and Josanie and Galeana rode out, low on their horses' backs, and rounded them up. Bullets zipped past and ricocheted among the rocks, but no one was hit. They surrounded the frightened animals and drove them up toward the Beaver.

FIVE

We have made diligent inquiry into the various charges presented in regard to Indian goods and the traffic at San Carlos and elsewhere, and have acquired a vast amount of information which we think will be of benefit. For several years the people of this Territory have been gradually arriving at the conclusion that the management of the Indian reservations in Arizona was a fraud upon the Government; that the constantly recurring outbreaks of the Indians and their consequent devastations were due to the criminal neglect or apathy of the Indian agent at San Carlos; but never until the present investigations of the Grand Jury have laid bare the infamy of Agent Tiffany could a proper idea be formed of the fraud and villany which are constantly practiced in open violation of law and in defiance of public justice. Fraud, speculation, conspiracy, larceny, plots and counterplots, seem to be the rule of action upon this reservation. The Grand Jury little thought when they began this investigation that they were about to open a Pandora's box of iniquities seldom surpassed in the annals of crime.

With the immense power wielded by the Indian agent almost any crime is possible. There seems to be no check upon his conduct. In collusion with the chief clerk and storekeeper, rations can be issued ad libitum for which the Government must pay, while the proceeds pass into the capacious pockets of the agent. Indians are sent to work on the coal-fields, superintended by white men; all the workmen and superintendents are fed and frequently paid from the agency stores, and no return of the same is made. Government tools and wagons are used in transporting goods and working the coal-mines, in the interest of this close corporation and with the same result. All surplus supplies are used in the interest of the agent, and no return made thereof. Government contractors, in collusion with Agent Tiffany, get receipts for large amounts of supplies never furnished, and the profit is divided mutually, and a general spoilation of the United States Treasury is thus effected. While six hundred Indians are off on passes, their rations are counted and turned in to the mutual aid association, consisting of Tiffany and his associates. Every Indian child born receives rations from the moment of its advent into this vale of tears, and thus adds its mite to the Tiffany pile. In the meantime, the Indians are neglected, half-fed, discontented, and turbulent, until at last, with the vigilant eye peculiar to the savage, the Indians observe the manner in which the Government, through its agent, complies with its sacred obligations.

This was the united testimony of the Grand Jury, corroborated by white witnesses, and to these and kindred causes may be attributed the desolation and bloodshed which have dotted our plains with the graves of murdered victims.

From the report of the federal grand jury of Arizona, published in the newspaper Star, *of Tucson, Arizona, October 24, 1882. As a result of this investigation, Indian agent J. C. Tiffany was dismissed from his post at San Carlos by the secretary of the interior, Carl Schurz.*

SIX

It was not yet midmorning when Josanie and his men passed the ranch Kezinne had mentioned. The corral was empty, the gate flung wide. In front of a rough log cabin a white man sat on the ground, wounded, and a woman was kneeling beside him. She was dressed in a long black gown and stood up and started to cry when she saw the remuda and the Apaches, but they only looked and rode on.

A mile farther up the canyon narrowed between bulging rocks for about a hundred yards before broadening out again. They rode through the winding cleft, and Josanie looked back and halted. He called out, and the others stopped. He turned his horse and faced the rocks and circled. He grinned and gestured with his right hand.

"Look at this place. It's a place to wait and see if anyone is following us. It's the best place for an ambush I have seen yet." And after a pause: "Three should stay here with the horses. The others come with me."

Nitzin, Nalgee, Galeana, and Kezinne walked with Josanie into the cleft and took up positions near the entrance, with a clear field of vision of the broken ground of the canyon beyond. Two men stayed on the ground, behind boulders, while the others searched for shooting posts on rock ledges higher up.

They sat and listened patiently. Nothing stirred and for a while there were no other sounds but the humming of insects and the calls of birds. High above in the blue sky buzzards circled. Then there was a distant tremor, which grew and grew into a vibrating thunder caused by the hooves of many horses running fast.

The first riders came into view about four hundred yards away, partially blocked from sight by clumps of pines and rock piles. They came into the open fifty yards closer, riding as hard as the ground allowed. A gush of men emerged, twenty, thirty men, more, still more, with a clanking of metal on metal, stirrups flapping, breaching the distance. This was a big posse of miners and cattlemen, short on Apache-fighting experience but feeling secure in their great numbers.

Among the warriors no command was required. They stood up from their hiding places; the rifles crashed at about the same moment, and the head of the column vanished as if it had run into a steel rope. Horses fell with their riders; some somersaulted and hit the ground with thudding sounds. Riders following behind, unable to avoid collision, plunged headlong into the melee in front of them. Into the tangle of bodies eighty to a hundred yards away, the warriors sent a stream of bullets. They stood out in the open, facing the enemy. Galeana, Kezinne, and Nalgee carried repeating rifles, and they fired as fast as they could work the levers. When the magazines were empty, they raised their rifles and let loose the bone-chilling war cry of the Chokonen warriors. The bulk of the posse was galloping away, but among the dead or injured horses were five dead men and a few wounded ones, lying still or trying to crawl away.

Josanie and the men went to collect weapons and ammunition belts, three revolvers with the rifles, saddles. When they loosened the gun belt from one of the wounded, he died with a sigh, his eyes wild. Perhaps he died of fright, expecting to be tortured, not knowing that Apache warriors mutilated a live enemy rarely, and only for special reasons, and abhorred scalping because they feared ghost sickness transmitted through the hair and skin of the dead.

They did not touch the dead or the wounded. They shot the injured horses but did not check one that stood alone and still a distance away. Josanie again prayed with pollen and marked a line between himself and his men and the dead whites. Perhaps even white men could punish with ghost sickness those who had killed them.

The Apaches made bundles with the acquired weapons and belts and saddles and packed them on three of the horses taken from the second ranch. From the sun's position they knew it was near midday. They followed Beaver Creek upstream for another two miles, then cut south across high, dissected ground to the foot of Webster Mesa and Pine Canyon. They followed the foot of the mesa past Park Mountain to the San Francisco River about four miles south of Alma. There they crossed the wide, gravelly floodplain and the river, the water not reaching higher than the horses' girth line. They passed under huge cottonwoods and crossed a winding dirt road above the eastern bank that connected Silver City and Fort Bayard with the mining districts of Cooney and Alma, the cattle town of Frisco, and the sheep town of Luna in the north.

They worked on the road to wipe out their tracks but knew that, despite their efforts, Apache scouts with the army would not be fooled. There would be much military traffic on the road soon. They rode into Whiteriver Valley of the Mogollon Mountains on the trail of the bands and turned east at the mouth of Little Whitewater Creek. There they found the bands' camp in a grove of aspen and mighty sycamores surrounded by Ponderosa pines and firs, with two men of Nana's band standing watch over the approach.

Kezinne, who had been riding point, reined his horse and let boys from the camp head the captured horses into the glade along the creek. They were milling nervously, and some had to be hazed out of the trees. They were contained and moved upstream and into the trees where the herd was grazing.

The people had formed two lines, and the raiders rode through them slowly, touched by the outstretched arms, in silence. They dismounted at the edge of the camp, and their horses were quickly taken away. There were no fires. Next to the temporary shelters, near the massive trunk of an ancient sycamore, was an uneven grassy surface large enough for the people of the two bands to sit.

Chihuahua embraced his brother and pointed to it. When they sat down with Nana, they were joined in a circle by the fighting men of the two bands, twenty in all, including the chiefs, Nana and Chihuahua, not including the two guards downstream. The women and children and two old men formed a second circle behind the men, numbering fifty-three. Nana, although about eighty years old, was still counted as a warrior.

The women brought cold meat and the last of the supply of mescal they had taken with them when bolting from Turkey Creek. When all the people had eaten, Chaddi rose and walked to the center of the circle. He spoke a prayer and sang to the mountain spirits. Starting with the east, he addressed the leader of the black mountain spirits, then, sunwise, the blue chief of the south, the yellow chief of the west, and the white chief of the north, the guardians. He ended with a low note and walked to his blanket and sat down.

After a few minutes of silence, Chihuahua stood up. Fifty-seven years old, with blue-gray eyes, unusual for an Apache, he looked along the two circles of people, taking in everyone. He spoke with a firm, clear voice.

"Today we are happy. We are back in our mountains. We had a hard time getting here. These are the mountains of our peoples, Chokonen and Chihenne. They were given to us by the Creator, and by White Painted Woman and the mysterious child, Child of the Water. They taught us what we know, the way we live, the way we used to live."

He paused, struggling with his emotions.

"When we come here now, we find the land occupied by strangers. There are more and more of them. Where three years ago there were none or a few, there are many now. Everywhere," he pointed in the cardinal directions, "east, south, west, north, there are new mines, new towns, new ranches, and cattle and tame sheep are run in our mountains. Maybe there are more tame sheep here than there are deer. Is this still our land, or is it theirs?"

He paused, and in the silent circles people stirred.

"When we leave the reservation, the dead ground where they starve us and kill us, we have to fight our way out. Coming to these mountains, we have to fight our way in. They make us fight all the time. When we are here, we have to hide like thieves. But we are not thieves. They are thieves. They have taken most everything from us. They want us dead so our voices are silent in the earth, so we can no longer speak the truth. These whites, they are worse than any enemy we ever had."

There was a strong murmur of approval. A baby cried out but was quickly silenced by its mother, laid inside her dress, and nursed.

"I say this is still our land," Chihuahua continued, "even if whites seem to have taken it. We know the special places, the homes of the mountain spirits, the secret power places. They speak to us but do not recognize them. They are strangers here and will always be strangers. They are nothing and nothing speaks to them. Nothing, that's what they are."

He fell silent. Finally he looked up and slowly his face shone.

"We must be happy today. Our men fought two times today against many. They fought well, and no one of ours was lost. Because of them we are safe. We are grateful to them."

He paused. "I want my brother to speak." He sat down.

Josanie got up slowly. Fifty-nine years old, his slim figure stood relaxed. "We fought two times," he said simply, "and today our enemies gave themselves to us. They ran into our guns as if they were crazy. The second bunch surely did. They were blinded."

He searched briefly along the line of the seated men and made a sign, and Kizenne and Galeana got up and carried bundles in and sat down.

"There are eight rifles and three handguns we took from the second bunch," he said. "Saddles. Ammunition. Whoever wants a gun should take it. The ammunition must be divided among all of us."

So it was done. The two guards were called up, some of the men inspected the rifles, and four picked one. The others went to the women, along with two handguns. The ammunition was separated into three piles, .44 caliber rimfire and .44-40 and .45-70 calibers centerfire, and evenly distributed.

Nana raised his hand and talk ceased.

"We had a good day today," he said. "Thanks to our men. The spirits were good to us today." He paused. "Where do we go from here? I want to go up and cross over to the fork of the big river, to where the cliff houses of the old people are, then to the Black Range. It is safer for us to split up. What will you do?" He spoke to Chihuahua, but nearly everyone heard him.

"I want to stay in these mountains," Chihuahua said. "Live like we used to live. Hunt elk and deer and bighorn sheep. There are many springs here. Maybe in the fall, before the snow comes, we should meet at the place of the cliff houses east of here. Maybe, if everything goes well, we can spend the winter together in the high grassland and forest northwest of the cliff houses."

He looked around, and his men nodded in agreement.

"Yes," Nana said, "let's do that. We will try that. We will go with you for two more days."

So it was decided. They spent the night in the grove on Little Whitewater Creek and moved out at sunrise. They climbed into the great stillness of the Mogollon Mountains on the old Chokonen trail that left the narrow path above the creek and wound north toward Nabours Mountain, passed just below the small plateau of its summit, nine thousand feet high, and then crossed east toward the headwaters of the big Whitewater Creek to Rock Spring. Sometimes they could see clear across the valley and the mountain range to the west, all the way to Bear Mountain in Arizona, forty-five miles away.

SEVEN

If the Government would lift the Apaches from the slough of ignorance and loathsome degradation in which they now wallow, compulsory education must be resorted to. Under the strong hand of the law of force they must be taught to labor systematically, and when it becomes necessary to educate the rising generation in the mystery of books, force should compel them to accept the situation.

Force is the one law the Indian recognizes and respects; it is his law, and when he fails to enforce it the power is lacking to sustain him. No argument will serve to convince him that the white man stays his hand for any other reason. Overcome in battle, deprived of his arms and trodden remorselessly beneath the heel of the conqueror, he bows with humility to the power that has subdued him, and submits without murmuring to the will of his master. Under such conditions the Apaches can be trained to a knowledge of steady industry, and induced to submit their children to the guidance of the white man for such development of their mental faculties as may be possible with this fast disappearing and seemingly doomed race.

P. P. Wilcox, United States Indian Agent, Report of the Secretary of the Interior, *San Carlos Indian Agency, Arizona Territory, August 9, 1883.*

The health of the Indians has not been affected by unusual conditions of sickness; the ordinary diseases common to hot climates, miasmatic bottom lands, impure water and unrestrained license in social life, have prevailed unaided in the work of extermination.

P. P. Wilcox, United States Indian Agent, Report of the Secretary of the Interior, *San Carlos Indian Agency, Arizona Territory, August 15, 1884.*

EIGHT

It was hard climbing and often the riders walked, leading the horses. On slopes there were aspen thickets surrounded by firs and stately Ponderosa pines. The air was cool with a southwest wind, under a cloudless sky. They made camp in the triangle of a hollow between the spring and the crack in the rock from which the first trickle of the middle fork of the Whitewater emerged.

Two men and the older boys went out to hunt with bows and brought in two elk cows and one deer, with the meat left from the Blue River cattle enough food for the night. They lit fires only after dark, with dry wood that made little smoke. On the second day they killed one of the horses for food. On the morning of the third day Nana and his little band left.

The old man embraced Chihuahua and Josanie. His wrinkled face looked sad, and the obsidian eyes under the old, beaded war cap had no smile. "Be well, friends," he said. "Be watchful."

He turned quickly and grabbed the horse's bridle that one of his men held out to him. They walked away without looking back. With Nana went four warriors and ten women and children, so pitifully few, so few left of the Chihenne from the time of Victorio, only five years before.

Chihuahua and Josanie watched them disappear in the trees, hearing the clatter of hooves, then quiet. "We should leave, too," Chihuahua said. They broke camp and moved west on another Chokonen trail. They traveled five miles over very rough terrain and came to a waterfall and a cave under a cliff on the eight-thousand-foot level.

They searched the ground but found only the tracks of deer and puma, porcupine and raccoon. There was no trace of humans. It seemed that no one had been here for some time. The waterfall, about fourteen feet high, had become a mere trickle, the result of the rainless season, but the small basin in the sheets of stone beneath it was filled with clear, cold water. Some of the men climbed over the rocks that had fallen in from the ceiling of the cave and the cliff above it, which screened most of the cave's entrance. A good place to hide in, a dangerous place to be trapped in. They searched the interior, about forty feet deep, but found on the soft surfaces of the floor only the prints of pumas, which seemed to favor the place.

White clouds drifted in from the southwest, and the people knew that they would have rain soon. They settled for a campsite nearby, along the tiny creek that started Shelton Canyon, and took the horses to Holt Gulch, less than half a mile away. In enemy country they never kept the herd close to the camp but held it instead in a secluded location. Should the camp be attacked, they would make an escape to the horses; if the horses were captured, the people would walk out and raid for horses later. Two guards were left with the horses to keep them together and to protect them from pumas and wandering grizzlies.

Men and boys went out with bows and arrows to hunt and watch for tracks of horses and men. The first hunters came in before midday, the last by late afternoon. They had worked within an area a little more than a mile around the camp and seen nothing suspicious. The catch was one bull elk and one deer. After dark fires were built from dry wood.

It was a still night filled only with the sounds of the mountains. Once wolves howled to the west. The fires burned down after midnight. At first light two men went over the trail to relieve the guards and others got up to prepare for another hunt. The camp was awakening.

The booming of the rifles split the quiet without warning. The narrow canyon was filled with the deafening sounds of gunfire coming from the top of the northern ridge. Heavy lead bullets struck like hail around people rushing and crawling to cover. The men fired desperately at the gun flashes high above them. Some of the women and children ran south, along the shelf toward the cave; most moved upstream in the lee of the slope, and among boulders, trying to escape the relentless guns. Chaddi alone sat on his blanket in the middle of the camp, oblivious to the carnage around him, painting himself and singing a spirit song clearly heard above the noise.

Bullets were falling all around him. Chihuahua stormed forward and dragged him away. There were broken bodies in the canyon. When the people fleeing upstream reached a saddle where the rifles no longer found them, the men followed, forming a protective shield behind them.

The firing ended. There were perhaps sixty or more riflemen on the ridge. Some men in blue uniforms tried to climb down toward the camp. They came under the Chokonen rifles and soldiers fell. Those who still could went back up and out of sight, and it was over. Suddenly there was a deadly quiet. The men remained behind when the women and children went over the trail to where the horses were hidden. The troopers did not follow the Apache retreat.

A brief burst of gunfire was heard from the direction of the cave. Josanie and a few men climbed around the shelf, came down on the south side of the cliff, and closed in on the waterfall and the cave. They found the old man José Second dead nearby, shot through the head twice. Unarmed, he had tried to draw the troopers away from the cave, but they had overtaken and killed him. There were hoofprints and blood on the ground, outside the cave and inside, and a number of spent shells. Whoever had tried to hide in the cave had been taken away.

In the ruins of the camp they found three women and a girl of seven dead. One of the dead was Chihuahua's old mother. Two wounded soldiers tried to sneak away near the crest of the ridge, but Nitzin climbed after them and stabbed them with a lance. These were Negro soldiers like those stationed at Fort Bayard, not white soldiers from San Carlos or Fort Apache. They died screaming. When the horses were brought in, the survivors were counted. Five women, including Chihuahua's wife, Coro, were missing, as were two boys, Chihuahua's son, Eugene, and Josanie's son, Nachi. They had last been seen running south. Many were lightly wounded, mostly from flying stone chips, but two of the men and one child had flesh wounds from bullets.

Josanie and a handful of grim warriors rode after the troopers but made no contact. They rode five miles down the canyon and came to where it opened into the valley. They saw the cavalry column draw near the little Mormon town of Pleasanton, three miles away on the Silver City road, at the edge of the floodplain of the San Francisco River. Looking through Galeana's binoculars, they saw that soldiers had slung the prisoners across their saddles in order to make a fast getaway. The men wanted to ride down on the enemy, but Josanie held them back.

"Too many guns for us," he said. "By the time we get to them, they have killed the prisoners. We will go after them some other time." So they turned their horses and rode back into the mountains.

They were watched by all when they rode into camp. Josanie looked to his brother and shook his head. They dismounted. The dead had been washed and cleaned and laid side by side. The wailing began, the sad, piercing song of bereavement. It flooded over the mountain slopes and ended with a cry like the call of the peregrine, harsh under the sky. The dead were wrapped in blankets and carried by kin closest to them. The bearers, accompanied by Chaddi, walked away from the camp. The bodies were placed in the niche in the rear of the cave, where the walls tumbled down, with some of their personal things beside them. The burial place was closed with rocks.

The work took some time. Chaddi had built a small fire outside, and when the bearers came out, he put a fistful of sage on the burning twigs, ghost medicine. They bathed their hands in the smoke and rubbed their bodies, from their moccasin boots to the tops of their heads, purifying themselves. In camp the long black hair of those who were kin to the deceased was cut short, to shoulder length. Jaccali, Josanie's wife, cut her husband's and Chihuahua's hair and her own.

Chihuahua spoke briefly. He called the true Chokonen names of the dead for a last time. They would not be spoken again. The dead wanted peace. If their names were breathed by the living, their spirits might come from the other world, called up by the word, and interfere in this world.

NINE

Before it got really light, my cousin [Josanie's son] and I asked our mothers for our bows and arrows and went down the ridge looking for rabbits. On our left was the canyon where the cave was, and not far from it the horses were concealed. If an attack should come, the men were to draw the cavalry away from the defenseless.

Suddenly, something buzzed by my ear. Then I heard a shot; then many shots. My cousin fell. When I tried to lift him blood ran down my hands. I could not get him on his feet. He told me to leave and save myself. Suddenly a woman came to us. She lifted my cousin to her shoulder and ran along the ridge with me following.

When we reached a place where a shallow trickle of water fell over the cliff, she stopped. The stones were slick. At the bottom I saw a man standing. She put the wounded boy down and pushed him over. The man, José Second, caught him and eased him to the ground; then she shoved me over. She followed, but because she was heavier both she and José Second fell to the ground. Carrying the wounded boy, he led the way to the cave where there were many women and children.

The cavalry did follow the men, but they left a Negro sergeant and troopers to find the women. They rode to the spring to water their horses, saw and followed our tracks, and dragged us out. Three women were wounded, one with a bullet hole through the calf of her leg. My mother was there. I looked for my grandmother, but my mother shook her head. Tears streamed down her face and I knew that my grandmother had been killed. Other women, too, were missing; whether they were dead or wounded we never knew.

The soldiers put my cousin on a pack mule, but he did not live to reach Fort Bowie. Not one of the women, not even the wounded, was permitted to ride. We were herded along like cattle. The one with the bullet hole in her leg limped along as best as she could. My mother signalled me and I left the line of march to get a good strong stick for her. With it she hobbled along with the rest. I don't know how long it took us to reach the fort, but when we did we were locked in a building. Some food was thrown on the ground for us as though we were dogs.

After a day or two the children were permitted to play outside and the women were put to digging latrines. . . . Picks and shovels! For the women, and even the wounded ones! They made those women do that digging. They forced the lame one to work with the rest. She bound the stick to her leg for support and worked. When she fell, a soldier prodded her with his rifle and kicked her till she scrambled to her feet. One day she fell and no kicking or prodding could rouse her. We knew that she had escaped and gone to the Happy Place, and we were glad.

Eyewitness account by Eugene Chihuahua, son of the band chief, of the attack on their camp in the Mogollons, on May 24, 1885, and its aftermath, as told to Eve Ball.

TEN

They packed the horses and rode away from the place of death. This time it was Chaddi who drew the line of separation on the ground. They rode eighteen miles, climbing most of the time, all the way to Apache Spring, ten thousand feet high, below the crown of Center Baldy Mountain. They made camp on the edge of a grassy plateau high above the surrounding green mountains, in the pines, in the mist of rolling clouds, in a soft rain, female rain, tears from the sky. No one ate. For a long time no one spoke.

They spent a wet night. The mountain itself seemed to have turned hostile to them. But the rain stopped before dawn and the clouds moved on, and they watched a brilliant sunrise, the great golden light coming into the world once again. They build large fires regardless of the smoke they were sure could be seen from a long way off. They dried clothing and blankets and cooked the meat that was left. Because of the death of his mother and the capture of his wife and son, Chihuahua and his young daughter, Ramona, had joined the camp of his sister-in-law. Jaccali and Ramona were serving the brothers food. The men sat with crossed legs and saw the grazing horses outlined against the sky and ate and looked along the campfires.

The two of us and fourteen men, and Zilahe, who is *dikohe*, not yet fully a warrior, thirty women and children and one old man, that is all of us, Josanie thought. Chihuahua looked at him; he seemed to know.

"Maybe we should give up."

"Surrender?" Josanie asked.

"Yes."

"We surrendered two years ago. And before that. We have tried. We can't live there, on that reservation," Josanie said.

"We can't live here either." Chihuahua made a gesture of helplessness with his hands. "I was wrong thinking that we could. It was my fault."

"No," Josanie said strongly. "It happened. We were careful, but it happened. It has happened like this before. There are too many of them. I don't know how they found us." He paused, shaking his head. "They did not come over the trail; they came from below. Perhaps they searched the mountains with their binoculars and saw one of our men hunting."

"I lost my mother, my wife, my son. Another son is a prisoner at Fort Apache," Chihuahua said bitterly. "Why should I go on? I don't want to be without them. I don't know if my wife and son are still alive."

There was a silence. Josanie played with a stick, scratching figures into the pale brown carpet of pine needles. "I found no bodies on the trail. We saw the prisoners among the soldiers. They are alive."

He paused. "I lost my son, too." He waited. "Bish's wife and little daughter were killed. Tsana's mother. Tsach's wife is a prisoner. Nalgee's second wife is a prisoner. Tisnol's and Parte's wives were taken. Parte's father was killed, the old man. We all suffered yesterday. Many are wounded."

Again he paused. "I'll go after them and bring them back some other time. I'm sure they will take them to Fort Apache. I'll go there and get them."

Again there was a silence. Softly, he continued: "You are *nantan*, chief, of this band, through our father. You cannot forget that. You must think of these people. Must I tell you?"

They sat silently. And then Chihuahua said, "You are right." And after a pause: "Naiche and Geronimo . . . they spoke true. I was blind. We will not be safe here. We have to go across the border."

Ramona was sent to call the men, and when they were gathered, Chihuahua told what he and Josanie had talked about. They sat gravely and listened. They had been surrounded by war and death since birth. They all had lost loved ones to war or to the white man's diseases, and they had seen the numbers of their people steadily diminishing. They grieved but did not show it. They would retaliate for the harm done to them, as so many times before, slashing like so many cornered grizzly bears.

They spoke slowly and carefully, weighing their words, and it was agreed by all that they would go into Mexico, into the Sierra Madre, and rescue the captives later, along with other members of their families still on the reservation. A plan was laid out, and they broke camp before midmorning. They rode over the rough trail east through the high country, then south into the canyon of Mogollon Creek. Galeana and Kezinne rode ahead. They could ignore the back trail because the rain had washed their tracks away.

On a meadow near Hobo Spring they found a dozen sheep, dead about two weeks, partly eaten. More fluffy white carcasses lay flung over the rocks of the slope below the small plateau where they had fallen, in panic. Near the spring stood the tattered green tent of a sheepherder. The decomposing body of a Mexican lay nearby, head and neck badly injured, right arm torn off. A dead sheepdog was lying close by.

Even from horseback it was easy to read what had happened here. A grizzly had rushed the sheep and killed a dozen while the flock stampeded. The man and the dog had tried to drive the bear away, but it had killed them, too. It had stayed for a few days and fed on the sheep carcasses. After the bear the coyotes and the buzzards had come.

"Even this high on the mountain they are running their sheep," Galeana said grimly.

"The mountain killed them," Chaddi said.

"The whites will say we killed them," Josanie said.

A mile east of Hobo Spring the band reached the head of Mogollon Creek and descended into the canyon. While traveling, the bowmen had shot two deer, and they made camp in the early afternoon on a spring below Lookout Mountain, with red and ochre and gray cliffs around them.

On the next day they continued south and reached the main channel of Mogollon Creek below Buds Hole. They were following it west to another spring when Galeana and Kezinne, who had scouted ahead, drove five red-colored steers that they had rounded up beyond the mouth of the canyon, a mile away. Chihuahua and Josanie decided the band would stay at the spring. The women butchered the steers to provide food for the dash south to Mexico. The meat, cut in thin strips, was sun dried and then smoked over fires at night.

Some of their horses were in poor condition, and many had lost their shoes. Traveling over the hard trails of the mountains, their hooves were worn, and a few limped painfully. To make it to the Sierra Madre, the Chokonen needed some fresh stock. They also needed to divert attention from the route they planned to take and to maneuver military units and posses waiting for them to search in the wrong places.

It was agreed that Chihuahua and seven warriors would stay with the camp in the present location for two days. On the third day they would move west to Little Dry Creek and across the Silver City road and wait at the two springs in the canyon near the San Francisco River.

Two raiding parties would go out. Josanie and Tsach, each with three men, would work south, ten to twenty miles apart. Josanie would strike along the Silver City road and a stretch of the Gila River valley to the west; Tsach, through Bear Creek valley to the edge of Pinos Altos, the mining town north of Silver City, place of many skirmishes in the past. Both parties needed to bring horses and were to meet the camp at the place of the two springs on the afternoon of the third day. In case the camp could not get there, the raiders should watch for signals made with hand mirrors.

The two raiding parties rode out of the mouth of the canyon at sunrise, on the best horses left among the camp herd. The men wore blue calico shirts and from a distance could have been mistaken for army scouts. Where Rain Creek ran into Mogollon Creek from the north, they split. Tsach and the warriors with him raised their right arms in greeting and followed the broadening valley south, toward the Gila and Bear Creek. Josanie and his men raised their arms and turned west. They climbed Rain Creek Mesa, the third in a string of mesas that rose in five successive layers, one on the other, eastward from the valley floor to the high Mogollon Mountains. They rode the few miles to the coulee through which Sacaton Creek flowed south and climbed down and rode in its shelter until they were a mile from the road. Galeana went up on a knoll with a clear view in both directions and watched with binoculars. The road was empty.

They came out on a small flat where the Sacaton joined Duck Creek. It ran northwest to southeast, and the road meandered along it on higher ground. They crossed the gravel bars and the small trickle of water, and Josanie and Galeana dismounted and walked up to the road. This strip of dirt road was the major link among cattle towns, mining districts, and military installations from the plains of San Agustin along the Tularosa and San Francisco Rivers to Silver City and Fort Bayard and the railroad towns farther south, Lordsburg, Separ, and Deming. It was also one of the known outlaw trails to and from Mexico, traveled by white rustlers and cutthroats.

They studied the tracks. Cavalry and freighters, a number of wagons drawn by mule teams, had gone south three days before, but since the rains no one had passed. Fear of us has closed the road, Josanie mused. The rains had obliterated some of the imprints. Since then the sandy soil had hardened under the sun. This was the road on which the captured women and boys had been taken away. Josanie and his men searched and found marks of moccasined feet. The prisoners had been made to walk, and one had limped badly.

The raiders rode on with grim determination, along Duck Creek to where a hollow came in from the west. The road dipped into it, and they went through the water of a rivulet and crossed the road without leaving a trace. They walked the horses through the hollow until they passed a series of low hills running almost parallel to the road, less than a mile away. They turned south, letting the horses lope.

They rode past some widely scattered bunches of red-colored cattle and circled some swampy areas before crossing the Gila River ten miles below the Sacaton. Three miles to the east the cluster of buildings of the huge Lyons-Campbell ranch sat above the Gila, an arrogant claim to stolen property. Tsach would pass it on the east side. If he did not get horses elsewhere, he might run them off this ranch, despite the large number of cowhands and workers. To sack the place would be impossible even if the two parties joined forces. Josanie and his men continued west of the road, and near the place of many springs (Mangus Springs), near the ruins of the soldier fort where, about twenty years before, the Mimbres Apache chief Mangas Coloradas had been tortured and killed, they ran into three prospectors who had come out of the Burro Mountains.

When they rounded a tongue of pine-clad land, the four horsemen came face to face with the prospectors, less than a hundred yards away. These were the men who scoured the Chokonen and Chihenne mountains, scratching in the earth, hammering on rocks for gold and other metals, and bringing after them thousands of others like them. Here they were sitting on the ground, resting, returning from some place that was not theirs and going to another place that did not belong to them. Near them were two heavily loaded mules.

The warriors' reaction was instantaneous. While Josanie and Nalgee headed straight for them, Galeana rode to flank them on the left, Kezinne on the right. One of the prospectors ran; the other two tried frantically to get to the rifles tied up on the mule packs. One was able to fire a shot, wildly, when the long blade of Nalgee's lance caught him in the armpit. Josanie shot the second man from a few yards away, and they heard the three shots with which Galeana killed the running man.

They caught the bawling mules, which had run away from the shots, unhitched the pack saddles, and let them go. They searched the packs. There was nothing they needed but two boxes of .44-40 shells, the ammunition Galeana's and Nalgee's rifles used. They did not touch the dead, and Josanie once again drew the pollen line on to the ground. Not wanting to be burdened with extra weapons, they cached the rifles, handguns, and one box of ammunition in a small hollow under the roots of a pine tree, marked the place with a strip of blue cloth, and rode on. They went south in the Mangas Valley for another twelve miles, then doubled back and followed the road to Silver City, marking in their minds two places they would hit the following day. They had not yet been seen by living eyes. Five miles west of Silver City they slipped into Wind Canyon and found a place to camp for the night. They knew the canyon from a raid made in April 1883. There were a cover of pines and willows, good water, and grass for the horses. After dark coyotes barked and whined farther up in the canyon.

The following morning, on May 28, three miles out of Silver City, they came on a dreadful scene. A man and a young woman lay dead by the road, the woman raped, her skirts pulled up to her waist, the lower part of her body naked and bloody. Off to the side were a toddler boy, his head bashed in, and a girl of five hanging on a meat hook from a tree branch, her blond hair encrusted with freshly dried blood.

The horses shied from the smell of death and had to be held fast. The warriors sat like stone sculptures, stunned by what they saw. There was a light four-wheeled carriage near the road, but there were no horses. They looked at the ground and saw the boot impressions of five men. The carriage had come from the direction of the town, and five riders had followed and overtaken it, forcing the occupants out. After the raping and killing, they had plundered the carriage and left open trunks on the road, with clothing strewn around. The killers had unharnessed four horses and ridden west.

"They do to their own people what they do to us," Nalgee said in wonder.

Josanie looked at the little blond girl and for a moment thought that she was still alive, but she was not.

"Those who killed them . . . ," he said, "they are bad spirits come into this world. Witches." Without dismounting he took a small pouch from his medicine cord and threw four pinches of hoddentin, sacred tule pollen, toward the dead.

"Let us ride. This is a bad place. The spirits of the dead are traveling. I don't want them to see us."

He turned his horse. "These men . . . they are on the road ahead of us. I wish we meet them," he said, darkly.

But they did not.

ELEVEN

Some particulars of the killing done by Geronimo's [sic] band near Silver City to-day are learned. . . . The family consisted of Phillips, wife and two children, aged 3 and 5 years. This morning Geronimo's band attacked him and his family, killing the entire family excepting the oldest child, a girl, whom they hanged on a meat-hook. The hook entered the back portion of her head, in which position she was found, still alive, by a rescuing posse of citizens and brought to Silver City, but only lived a few hours. The citizens think this is pretty rough, occurring within sight of a ten-company military post, and at present departmental headquarters.

Silver City (New Mexico), May 28, 1885, newspaper dispatch.

TWELVE

The raiders burned one ranch near the Silver City road and, to the west, another ranch in Mangas Valley. They made sure that the smoke plumes were thick and black and could be seen over a long distance. In both places people ran away and wisely did not interfere with the raiders. Riding north, they passed the place where the bodies of the prospectors lay prone in the grass. The buzzards had found them, but no one else had. The mules had disappeared. They left the weapons cache intact; it might be needed at some other time. A little farther up they turned west into Mangas Creek and followed it to the northern spur of the Burro Mountains and went down into the valley of the Gila. They rode slowly through the cottonwoods, along the winding stream, under the bluffs. They passed one broken-down, empty cabin and some bunches of mixed-color cattle, and in midafternoon they came on a ranch on the west bank of the river, across from the mouth of Rough Canyon.

They took the horses into cover and studied the ranch with binoculars, shading the lenses with their hands so that sunlight would not be reflected in the glass. They saw a one-story ranch building with a veranda in front, a bunkhouse sitting at right angle to it, a small blacksmith workplace, two sheds, a barn. Below the bunkhouse was a pole corral with three horses in it. A clothesline with laundry was strung near the back of the ranch house. Down the valley horses could be seen grazing on the flat by the river.

While they watched, a woman came out of the house with a small child, gathered laundry in a basket, and took it into the house. A German shepherd dog walked to the corral and lay down. Early in the evening two men went from the bunkhouse to the main building. Some time later one man came out and went to the corral, saddled one of the horses, and left downriver. He drove fourteen horses up and corraled them, unsaddled his horse, and left it tied up on the outside of the corral.

"Two men," Josanie said. "I think, three. A woman and a child."

"And a dog," Galeana said.

"Yes."

They watched until nightfall. No one had left the ranch, and no one else had come. The warriors went to their horses and found a place to sleep on a grassy knoll beside the river, out of sight for anyone passing by, under the brilliant canopy of stars. They did not build a fire. Shortly before midnight a wolf pack howled across the bluffs to the south.

Josanie woke up before first light. He walked to the jumble of trees on a gravel bar and urinated, then went to the water's edge and bent and drank deeply. He brushed his face and hair with water. He stretched and, at his sleeping place, rolled his blanket up and sat down. From a rawhide saddlebag he took a small pouch and painted his face, a white line across his cheekbones and the bridge of his nose. He took a piece of dried meat from another pouch, put both pouches back into the saddlebag, tied it closed, and started to chew. Around him the men got up, went for water, and folded their sleeping blankets. Josanie went for his horse, a chestnut mare, and threw the saddle blanket over its back and rocked the saddle into place. He pulled up the latigo, fastened the backcinch, and waited. The horse breathed out, and Josanie pulled the strap and buckled it. He mounted.

At first light there were still deep shadows in the valley. The warriors crossed the river and approached the ranch four abreast, rifles ready. Nalgee had hooked the lance to his back, to the cartridge belts, one he carried around his waist and one he wore diagonally across his chest and back. The upper half of the shaft was painted blue; the lower half, red. A bunch of hawk feathers was tied below the long steel blade made from a Mexican cavalry officer's saber. The tip of the fearsome weapon stood high above him, with fluttering feathers.

The black-backed dog ran out and started barking, but the warriors rode on, with an easy walk. There was no response from the ranch buildings. When they were about forty yards away from the ranch house, Josanie shot the dog squarely in the upper chest, the heavy bullet slamming the body back and to the ground.

Unhurriedly he opened the Sharps-Borchardt's breech block and inserted a fresh shell.

He rode toward the ranch house and held in front of the veranda. Someone opened the door and quickly closed it again. Josanie held the rifle ready but gave no indication that he intended to dismount. Nalgee sat his horse in front of the bunkhouse, the Winchester half raised, but no one came out. Without dismounting Galeana untied the horse at the pole corral and pulled it after him. He opened the gate, and Kezinne rode into the corral, hazing the horses out. They shouldered their way through the gate and bunched and rolled their eyes, Galeana rode point and the herd followed, and Kezinne closed in behind and rode drag when the remuda ran on the grassy flat, under the broad cottonwoods, upstream along the river.

Josanie raised his arm, and Nalgee turned away from the bunkhouse. Josanie covered him with his rifle in case someone came through the door or shot through a window, but no one did. They rode off together, picking up speed, and followed the remuda. Once Josanie looked back and saw three men and a woman in a long white dress standing on the empty ground below the ranch house, their faces white and rigid, staring after them.

They drove the herd fifteen miles until they reached the place where they had crossed the Gila two days before, then turned northwest, nearly parallel to the road. Josanie had studied the length of the road in both directions with binoculars but had seen no movement on it. They passed a place where wolves had killed a steer a day before, the rib cage like so many bloody spikes, and the buzzards working on the entrails. They rode another twelve miles, with an easy gait, and past the Sacaton they entered the canyon of Fivemile Creek that ran into Duck Creek from the northwest. They took their time moving up toward the Mule Mountains, and after leaving the head of the canyon on an old trail, they slipped into Eliot Canyon, which took them, by midafternoon, to where their camp was waiting, at the place of the two springs below the San Francisco River.

The valley of Little Dry Creek was about half a mile wide there, with serrated edges of low bluffs on both sides. The horses that Josanie's men had brought in were added to the herd grazing on grassy benches below the bluffs. Two dozen or more horses were tethered between clusters of people sitting on the ground. Saddles and packs were piled around them. Men and women formed two lines once again and touched Josanie and the men with him with outstretched arms as they rode through, in silence.

Among the women and girls, in their long, vividly colored calico skirts and hip-length overblouses, Josanie searched for his wife, Jaccali, and their eyes met. She squeezed his arm when he passed her, and he nodded, with a somber face. He was thinking of their son, Nachi, now a prisoner somewhere on an army post or perhaps dead. It was another boy who took Josanie's horse when he dismounted.

Chihuahua stood there and touched his brother's shoulder. The younger man was dressed in his war shirt, and his usually skeptical face showed a broad grin. "I'm happy you are back. Tsach is back, too."

They walked side by side to a sandy stretch of even ground near the creekbed, and Chihuahua made a sign with his hand to sit down. The warriors joined them one by one; and the women and children sat behind them. Jaccali and two women brought cold meat and passed jars with creek water. They all ate. Jaccali sat at Josanie's back. She watched when he loosened the strap under his chin and removed the buckskin war cap with the painted spirit figures in black, blue, yellow, and white, and four golden eagle feathers tied on top.

The men sat cross-legged, rifles across their knees. The women sat sideways on the ground, legs together. When Chaddi stood up and prayed to Bikego I'ndan, Master of Life, and sang to the mountain spirits, all bowed their heads. A silence followed. They thought of those they had lost five days ago, of others who had stayed behind on Turkey Creek, and of those whose dead bodies lay in silent places spread over a thousand miles of mountains and grasslands and deserts.

"Cuchuta and Antonio . . . I don't see them," Josanie said, looking along the row of warriors.

"Cuchuta is back there, toward the road," Chihuahua said, pointing east with his chin. "Antonio is down there, toward the river." He pointed west. "They are watching."

He addressed the assembled people. "We have plenty of good horses now. Tsach brought twenty-three; Josanie, seventeen. I thank them." He paused. "We should have enough to take us into Mexico." There was a murmur of approval.

"Now I say they should tell us what happened, what they did." He looked at his brother.

Josanie gave a short talk. He did not think that they had done anything special. When he described how they had found the murdered white family, the little girl hanging on a meat hook, there was a gasp from the listeners.

They all knew about white men's cruelty. The torture of warriors taken alive. The scalping of Apache heads, even of the smallest children, for bounty money, dollar or peso. The selling of captured Apache women into slavery in Old Mexico and in New Mexico, long after the war between the whites in the east was over. The whites were even using former Negro slaves as soldiers to kill Apaches, as they were using Apache relatives for the same purpose.

When Josanie spoke of the killing of the prospectors, the burning of the ranches, and the taking of the horses on the Gila, the listeners responded with a strong murmur of satisfaction. He ended, saying, "This is all."

There was a pause. Tsach cleared his throat. Thirty-seven years old, he was Chaddi's son and a medicine man himself. Measuring about six feet, he was the tallest man in the band. He had removed his war cap but still wore a fringed buckskin war shirt with painted figures and the sun and moon and mountain symbols on it. His taut face was grim under the blue headband. He spoke slowly.

He looked at Josanie. "I already told them." He pointed with his chin at Chihuahua and around the circle. "We killed seven miners in a canyon north of Bear Creek. Arrows and knives. We did not fire a gun. We couldn't make a noise—we were too close to that big ranch on the Gila. We waited until they were cooking food . . . surprised them." He paused. "Bish and Tsana, they insisted that we kill them, take revenge."

He nodded. "We did. We killed their mules and cached their rifles. We couldn't take the mules. It happened on the first day out."

He paused again. "The next day we rode close to Pinos Altos. We burned three places and took all their horses. One man took shots at us and crippled two of the horses, and Bish went back and killed him."

He searched along the circle of warriors for the three men who had been with him. "We drove the horses over rocky ground and camped for the night in a canyon in the hills east of here. Bish stayed on the back trail, but no one tried to follow us." He breathed in deeply. "This morning we rode north until we struck Chihuahua's trail and followed it here. This is all."

Again the listeners murmured with approval and satisfaction.

"It is good," Chihuahua said. He made a sign with his right hand. He turned to his brother. "We arrived here a while ago. Tsach was closely behind us." He paused. "When we crossed the road we saw only old tracks—three or four days old. But Antonio found fresh tracks on the river, going downstream. Five ponies."

He paused again. "We think they are scouts for soldiers. If they belong to the bunch you stopped in the river canyon, they are Apaches. If they belong to soldiers we don't know about, they are maybe Navajo."

He made a gesture of contempt. "In any case, there are soldiers to the north of us. We don't know where they are or who they are. They are looking for us but don't know where we are. We have to move."

There was a silence.

"We should do what we planned," Josanie said. "Go south through these mountains to the Gila, near their town of Duncan. Then into the Peloncillos and south. After we burned those places east and west of the road to Siver City, soldiers must have blocked the valley southeast of here. That's what we wanted."

He paused. "They are blocking the San Francisco River farther down, hoping that we come out that way. If their scouts would find us, the soldiers would try to push us against the other soldiers. If we get around them, we have to deal with the soldiers and scouts waiting for us along the border."

He paused again. "The only trail open to us now is through these mountains here. That's what we expected." He looked at the faces of the warriors. They nodded.

Chihuahua touched Josanie's arm. "Yes," he said. "We already talked about it. This is what we thought."

So it was decided. They saddled up and loaded the packhorses, leaving worn-out and lame horses behind. They brought the two scouts in who had watched to the west and east and moved out. Galeana and Zele rode point. Josanie and Chihuahua followed with a few warriors, and Chaddi came with the women, who brought up the packhorses and the small herd of extra mounts. Tsach with a handful of warriors formed the rear guard.

They knew the trail. Under a bright sun they rode into the fold in the gentle hills that was Burnt Stump Canyon and climbed past the pine-covered shoulder of the Mule Mountains. Then they descended into the grassy dell of Cienega Creek and went south and made camp below Bear Mountain, on a creek between wide slopes covered with spring grass that reached up to the bellies of their horses.

THIRTEEN

Lt. Davis with sixty scouts is seeking to ferret out the enemy women and children among the mountains east of Duck Creek on the Upper Gila. Maj. Van Vliet with five troops of 10th Cavalry and thirty Apache scouts, is moving north of Bayard towards Datil Range. Capt. Chaffee with one troop 6th. is in vicinity of Cuchillo Negro. Maj. Van Horn with Cavalry from Fort Stanton and Mescalero Scouts is scouting each bank of Rio Grande to prevent Indians crossing. Capt. Madden with two troops 6th. Cav'y is west of Burro Mtns. Capt. Lee with three troops 10th Cav'y is moving across Black Range between Smith and Van Vliet. Maj. Biddle followed trail of ten or fifteen Indians which crossed railroad near Florida Pass beyond Lake Paloma, Mexico. Troops are now moving into positions near all known water holes between railroad and Mexico to intercept Indians going south. Capt. Lawton with three troops 4th. Cav'y and Lt. Roach's scouts is in Guadelupe Canyon near boundary line. Maj. Beaumont with two troops 4th. Cav'y is in Stein's Pass.

Report by General George Crook, commanding officer of the Department of Arizona, June 2, 1885.

FOURTEEN

The valley, situated at about six thousand feet, was half a mile wide and five miles long, north to south, and sat, an island of grass, below surrounding mountains wrapped in pines and firs. Four deep draws cut through its western slope and fed the creek with waters running off Tillie Hall Peak. The valley's opening in the north led to Buckhorn Creek, the one in the south narrowed to a canyon that wound southwest, climbing steadily toward the Summit Mountains astride the Arizona–New Mexico line.

At first light in the chilly morning, two men who had guarded the horses during the night gathered them up and loose-herded them toward the camp. People who were not yet awake were roused by the drumming hoofbeats. At Jaccali's camp, she and Ramona had already packed their bedrolls and went with bridles to catch their mounts. Josanie and Chihuahua were rolling up their sleeping blankets when Chaddi walked up. He stood quietly, and Chihuahua pointed to the ground by the cold fireplace. The three men sat down.

They wore fringed buckskin shirts because of the frigid air. Josanie and Chihuahua had their cartridge belts on, but Chaddi was unarmed. He looked away toward the creek, where mist was rising like smoke. He turned his head and looked at them. He touched the four-stringed medicine cord he wore diagonally across his chest.

"This is the Valley of Mother's Sibling," he said. He used the honorary term for grizzly. It was bad taste to call a bear by its regular name; the grizzly might hear it and come after the person who had spoken it.

Josanie and Chihuahua nodded.

Chaddi opened his shirt and lifted a grizzly claw he wore hidden on a string. "This is one of my medicines. You have seen it before. We have nothing to fear from the sibling." He slipped the claw back and closed his shirt. He nodded, searching for their eyes.

"This is the valley where my mother was born," he said. "I haven't been here for a long time. Once we are in Mexico, we might not get back here, perhaps never again. I think we should stay here for a few days, so we remember."

There was a pause.

"Here is good grass, good water. Deer and elk, plenty. And there are plenty of prickly pears here for food and for dressing wounds."

Josanie nodded.

Chihuahua said, "Yes." He paused. "My wife was born here, too." There was a silence. "She can't see the valley now. I see it for her." He paused again. "Perhaps we should stay for a few days." Turning to Josanie, he said, "What do you think?"

Josanie looked across the camp where the horses were milling around, snorting, shifting, and stepping. Men and women were walking between them, talking softly, stroking them, slipping halters over their necks, and leading them away.

"We should go on," he said. "We know that their scouts are searching for us. They found us in the mountains east of here when we thought we were safe. They could find us here. Some of them may know this valley."

He paused. "We'll only be safe when we are across the border." He laughed grimly. "Perhaps not. Two years ago they followed us way into the Sierra Madre." He paused again. "We are safe nowhere."

He played with a blade of grass. "Let's not make it easy for them. I'm for riding."

He looked at his brother. "You decide."

Chihuahua shook his head. "We'll ask the men."

He got up and called for the men to join them. They came one by one, fully armed, and stood behind the three men sitting. To carry weapons at all times had become a way of life.

Chihuahua explained what they had discussed and asked the men to speak. Each spoke in turn. A majority felt that they could stay for a few days but that they should watch out and not be surprised again.

Chihuahua stood up. "I have heard you all," he said. "We'll stay in the valley for four days. Maybe it's a last time." He paused. "This is one of the old camping places of our people. We'll have scouts watch the back trail and the trail toward Arizona."

When they moved out, Galeana and Zele rode ahead, and Tsach and Tsana went back to guard the entrance to the valley, toward Buckhorn Creek Canyon. They rode slowly under an early sun. They passed two old Chokonen campsites indicated by remains of wickiup frames and brush windbreaks, the ground surfaces, with fireplaces and camp debris, overgrown with grasses. At each of the sites Chaddi placed four pinches of hoddentin on the ground as boundary markers in case ghosts were lingering there, looking at the living. And a little farther on they came on the animal after which the valley was named.

It was a grizzly mother with two two-year-old cubs. They were feeding on grasses on the slope west of the creek, about a hundred yards above it. Their coats were light to dark brown, with silvery tips, and their throats and bellies and upper forearms were golden. When the column of riders approached, the mother bear rose on her hind legs, facing them, moving her huge head slowly from side to side.

Chaddi raised his right arm, and the column halted. The herd of extra horses galloped away; some of the others bucked and stepped and had to be calmed and held tightly by the riders. Chaddi dismounted and crossed the creek. He walked a little way up the slope and, facing the bears, raised his arms horizontally, hands spread out.

He addressed them formally, then started to sing in a low, soothing voice. The words were in the sacred language used only in ceremonies, in hunting, and in war. He sang the praises of the great bears, the mountains, and the spirits who lived there. The bears listened, and then the mother grizzly came down on her front paws and turned and walked away slowly, the cubs trailing her. Chaddi ended the song and knelt and touched the ground four times with hoddentin between thumb and index finger of his right hand, creating a magical fence that protected the Chokonen and their horses from the grizzlies and the grizzlies from the humans.

Chaddi's wife, Chie, held his horse, and when he was mounted again, the Apaches rode two more miles, past a third old campsite, and settled for flat ground behind a knee in a creek large enough for a camp and all their horses. If they had built wickiups, the simple round and dome-shaped lodges with skins or blankets draped over a light frame made from shoots and tree branches, it would have been like old times. But they slept in the open and built fires only at night and kept the horses close. They bathed in the creek, and deer and elk came to drink during daylight, unafraid. Prickly pears grew in many places. Women went to collect the fruits. The pads were skinned from the soft inner flesh, which made a delicious food. It was also a healing agent. Raw fillets of prickly pear flesh were placed over injuries and bruises and tied on, removed, and replaced after a few hours. They absorbed fluid built up in the injury, softened the skin, and lessened pain. The scouts reported nothing suspicious. At sunrise every morning Chaddi sang the morning song across the camp.

Near midmorning on the fourth day three shots rang out a few miles away to the south. The sounds reverberated thunderously in the mountains. They would be heard a long distance off.

Silence followed. While the people quickly made ready to move, Josanie rode with a few warriors to the sound of the shots. Zele was waiting at the opening of a side canyon. They followed at a brisk trot over flat slabs of rock. The canyon widened to an almond-shaped meadow lined with pines. Galeana sat his horse in the middle of the clearing, looking at something on the ground. He held his rifle across the pommel of the saddle.

When the riders came closer, they saw a white man lying face down, his legs oddly twisted. He had two bullet holes in his back, and blood was oozing out from under his chest. He had dropped a rifle when he was hit. Two mules were tied to a pine trunk, and equipment was piled up nearby. There was a fireplace. Embers were still glowing, and a coffeepot sat on the coals.

"Prospectors," Galeana said. He pointed to a narrow cut in the rock wall. "One got away. He is in there. He has a rifle." After a pause he added, "We smelled smoke and came to look."

Josanie touched his arm and nodded. He rode forward and inspected the fissure into which the second man had disappeared. Too narrow, too deep, he thought. Only one way to get in. No way to get out. He turned his horse.

"We have to leave him in there. We have no time to smoke him out. If he walks out, it takes him days to get help."

He leaned over and picked up the rifle without dismounting. He handed it to Galeana. He took pinches of hoddentin from a pouch on his medicine cord and threw them toward the dead man. He prayed briefly. When he was finished, the warriors searched the prospectors' equipment and took what they could use. They untied the braying mules and dragged them along when they rode away.

They met with Chihuahua and a few warriors riding ahead of the women, the pack train, and the horse herd. Josanie told his brother what he had seen and with six warriors took the lead, Galeana and Zele riding point. Chihuahua and Tsach, with the remaining warriors, let the column pass and formed the rear guard. They rode into the winding canyon at the south end of the beautiful valley and climbed on a hard, boulder- and rock-strewn floor toward the Summit Mountains. No one looked back.

They arrived below the stony ramparts in the late afternoon. When they turned their horses into Bitter Creek, Nitzin, who rode a horse length behind Josanie, called out. Josanie turned in the saddle and saw. A huge, black plume of smoke rose to the northeast, about ten miles away as the raven flew.

Josanie halted the horse and looked into the distance. A signal of distress, anger, he thought. A message.

"The man we left behind, the one we didn't kill," he said. "He'll bring troops after us if there are any around."

That night they camped on Black Willow Spring in a somber mood. They had lanced one of the horses for food and started the cooking fires after dark.

Close to sunrise on the following morning, the horses saddled and the camp ready to move, there was a clatter of hooves from the trail behind them. Two horses, ridden as hard as the terrain allowed. Tsach and Tsana, who had spent the night on the back trail, came into view. They rode up to Josanie and Chihuahua, who were standing by their mounts.

"They are coming up the trail," Tsach said. "Apache scouts."

"We can hold them back," Josanie said. "Let the women escape down this creek and across the Gila."

Chihuahua looked up to the sky filled with light from the rising sun. He looked to the ground between his feet.

"Yes," he said. "I stay back with six men, hold them for a while." He touched his brother's arm. "You ride ahead with the others."

He paused. "We'll follow you. We meet at Horseshoe Canyon in the Peloncillos, the place where we fought the cavalry three years ago. Remember?"

They mounted up. Chihuahua waived, and a few warriors joined him, with Tsach and Tsana, and they rode down the trail and into the canyon. Josanie waived, and Galeana and Zele rode point as always, and the men followed, with Chaddi and the women and the packhorses close behind. They left on the campsite a dozen horses and the two mules, which might have slowed them down. They rode into the spiraling canyon of Bitter Creek that twisted southwest and down from the high mountains toward the Gila. When they were a mile into the canyon's rugged vastness, they heard behind them the reports of heavy gunfire.

They rode on steadily but tried to spare the horses. They rode twenty-two miles until they came out of the mountains and reached the flats along the Gila River. They turned south and rode along the river for another eight miles to the ford above the little town of Duncan. They halted and Josanie dismounted. He took four turquoise beads from a pouch on his medicine cord and walked to the riverbank. He knelt and tossed the blue beads into the stream. He prayed for a safe crossing.

Galeana, Zele, Kezinne, and Nalgee rode into the river first and swam their horses across. They spread out on the other side. The women followed, while Josanie and the remaining warriors waited until they were safely through, then crossed themselves. They formed up once again and, after passing over the tracks of the Arizona and New Mexico Railroad and halting briefly to cut the telegraph line, struck out south across the wide open plain of the Animas Valley toward the distant peaks of the Peloncillos. They went past the Lazy B ranch a few miles south of Duncan and rode on, the horses running for a few miles before walking to conserve their strength. All around the Apaches the country lay silent and empty under the afternoon sun.

They rode twenty miles in the plain before they climbed slowly rising ground that ended at treeless mountains jutting abruptly to a height of almost seven thousand feet. They approached the mouth of Horseshoe Canyon, which led west into the heart of the Peloncillos. Here they had fought Forsyth and six troops of the Fourth Cavalry to a standstill in April 1882. From here they could look clear across the Animas plain to the Gila and the mountains beyond. Later, with darkness coming on, way to the north through binoculars they made out dust and seven dots in the plain moving their way—Chihuahua and the men who had fought the government scouts.

FIFTEEN

To polish a diamond there is nothing like its own dust. It is the same with these fellows. Nothing breaks them up like turning their own people against them. They don't fear the white soldiers, whom they easily surpass in the peculiar style of warfare which they force upon us, but put upon their trail an enemy of their own blood, an enemy as tireless, as foxy, and as stealthy and familiar with the country as themselves, and it breaks them all up. It is not merely a question of catching them better with Indians, but of a broader and more enduring aim—their disintegration.

The invention of the breech-loading gun and the metallic cartridge has entirely transformed the methods and the nature of Indian warfare. It is not many years ago that the Indians were miserably armed, but all that has changed. They are no longer inferiors in equipment. Instead of bows and lances, they now have the best makes of breech-loading guns and revolvers. For white soldiers to whip the Chiricahuas in their own haunts would be impossible. The enormous country which they range is the roughest in America and probably in the world. It is almost utterly bare of anything upon which a white man could exist, but it supplies everything the Chiricahuas need to prolong life indefinitely. . . . He knows every foot of his territory, and can live through fatigue, lack of food and of water which would kill the hardiest white mountaineer. By the generalship which they have found necessary, they oblige us always to be the pursuers, and unless we can surprise them, the odds are all in their favor.

No, to operate against the Apache we must use Apache methods and Apache soldiers—under, of course, the leadership of the white soldier. The first great difficulty is to discover the whereabouts of the hostiles, and this can be done well only by Indian scouts. Their stronghold once located, the next thing is to reach it secretly. The marches must be made with the utmost stealth and by night. Fires and noise are absolutely prohibited. The

Indian scouts must be kept far enough in front and on the flanks to discover the enemy without being seen themselves, leaving no trail whatever, but slinking along from cover to cover. As soon as they locate the hostile camp, they noiselessly surround it if possible, meantime sending runners back to us. We make forced marches by night, come up and attack the hostiles, if they have not already flown. It is impossible to pursue them, for every rock may hide an Apache at bay, and with his breechloader he can kill as many pursuers as he pleases, himself secure. Then there is nothing for us to do but to return to our base of supplies, wait until the hostiles begin to feel secure again, and then repeat the same tedious operation. A single element of precaution neglected, and failure is certain.

General George Crook to Charles R. Lummis, correspondent for the Los Angeles Times, *April 1886, on why he used hundreds of Apache scouts in his campaigns against Chiricahua and Warm Springs Apaches.*

SIXTEEN

"Who were they?" Josanie asked.

"Fort Apache scouts, perhaps Chiricahuas among them," Chihuahua said angrily. "We saw the Fat Boy, the officer Davis, with them. Perhaps they were all from Turkey Creek."

"How many?"

"Maybe fifty, maybe more. We tried to ambush them a couple of times, but they were too wise."

He paused. "We fired a couple of times at them and they at us. Long distance. They never came close enough for us to do real damage. At least you got away with the women and children."

He paused again. "They did not follow us past Duncan. We watched. They stopped there for the night and went into camp. Maybe they had enough. Maybe their horses gave out. Tomorrow we'll see if they are still coming."

Galeana climbed high into the rocks before sunrise. He saw them through binoculars, a drawn-out column with a mule pack train. They were moving west on the road toward Ash Peak and the San Simon Valley. He watched them until they were swallowed by rises in the plain.

He reported to Josanie and Chihuahua, who sat at Jaccali's fireplace. "They are not coming after us," he said. "They are moving west. Perhaps they are going back to San Carlos."

"They may be going for supplies," Josanie said. "Maybe to Solomonville or to Fort Grant."

"Yes," Chihuahua said. "They'll come again. They are paid in silver dollars to hunt us. They get all the supplies they want for free."

The men felt badly, and they looked over the camp where the people were resting and the children were playing games among the saddles and packs with equipment and supplies. Beyond the camp the horses were grazing.

"I think we should give the horses some time to rest," Chihuahua said. "We still have a long ride."

He paused. "We should stay until early afternoon and then go into Little Doubtful Canyon. We have a choice then. We can go into West Doubtful Canyon or go east and south, through the alkali flats, across the railroad. What do you think?" He looked at Josanie.

Josanie sat in silence for a while. "I think we should go east and down through the Animas Valley," he said finally. "They might wait for us along the railroad, though. I think that West Doubtful Canyon is too dangerous. There might be troops in there. They might also be blocking the San Simon Valley, those from Fort Bowie."

He paused. "If they repaired the telegraph line we cut yesterday, they will know that we are close."

But the band stuck with Chihuahua's plan. The people filled the canteens from potholes in the creekbed and climbed a steep ridge and dropped into Little Doubtful Canyon in the early afternoon. They rode in the tested formation, with Galeana and Zele at point, Josanie and six men behind them, ahead of the women and the packhorses, and Chihuahua with the remaining six men serving as rear guard. They wound their way through that narrow fold in the Peloncillos and came out in an open space where West Doubtful Canyon led southwest and a widening gap in the rock walls emptied eastward into the Animas plain.

Galeana and Zele waited in the middle of the gap, not knowing which way to turn and waiting for the rest of the column to catch up. Suddenly there were the suck and whiff of bullets around them, the sounds of the shots lagging after. Small fountains of dust rolled out where bullets hit the ground and caromed off and sang away over the plain behind them. About two dozen rifles were firing at them from the entrance of West Doubtful Canyon, about five hundred yards away, the shots echoing back from the mountain walls.

Even before the reports from the first salvo reached them, the Chokonen had wheeled their horses and galloped away toward the plain, spreading out like scattering quail. The rifle fire was inaccurate, more so over the rapidly increasing distance, but a few bullets found marks. One packhorse and two riding horses went down. The riders, two women, were grabbed up by men who hardly broke speed.

Riding double, one woman, Tsana's wife, Magalena, started to wail. She tried to jump loose, but her husband struggled to hold her behind his back. Their baby, fourteen months old, was lost. Her cradleboard had been tied to the pommel of Magalena's saddle and went down with the horse.

Out of rifle range the Apaches halted the horses, calming them. Women rode over to comfort Magalena. The warriors looked back. No one followed.

"A posse," Josanie said. "Apache scouts would have waited until we were closer. Soldiers, too. These men were afraid and started shooting too early.

He paused. "It could have been worse."

"Yes," Chihuahua said grimly. He looked at the women surrounding Magalena. This was familiar to them. They joined in the wailing, the sad, piercing song that gripped their hearts.

"We can't go back for the child," Chihuahua said.

Tsana tried. Lying low on the horse's neck, he rode for the distant dots on the even ground in front of the desolate mountains, the dead or dying horses. Well before he reached them, dust flags were all around him, and then came the reports of the fusilade. They watched as he raced and feinted and circled and attempted to outrun the guns, but he could not. Finally he gave up. He and his horse were untouched, but he had tears in his eyes.

They felt for him and his wife and sadly rode on, the wailing like a cloud around them, past the abandoned station of the Butterfield Overland Mail. They turned southeast. With a space-consuming lope they rode by the two northern playas of the alkali flats, drainage basins that lay gray and white and muddy under the afternoon sun. There was some water in the playas from recent rains, and a few blue herons were standing out there like statues, looking quizzically at their own reflections.

They rode along the shores on the west sides of the playas, through the spare grass and over cracked platelets of dry mud. Below the second playa they turned east and followed the eastern shore of the large Kathrine Playa south and reached the railroad embankment ten miles west of Lordsburg. The tracks were empty. They rode over them and continued southeast without cutting the telegraph line; they did not want to mark the place where they had crossed.

The Animas Valley lay still and wide before them, the lush grasses stirrup high. They saw bands of antelope and once a pack of wolves, seven heads watching them pass. At dusk they came to a campsite they knew at a spring on the southern edge of the Pyramid Mountains. They searched the area but found no disturbing signs. They lanced one of the packhorses for food and started cooking fires after dark, in a piñon-covered depression where the light would not escape. The border of Mexico was fifty miles away.

During the night the wind shifted and clouds rolled in from the southwest. Morning brought a stone-colored sky without sun.

They sat in two circles, the women and children behind the men. Ramona sat at Chihuahua's back, Jaccali at Josanie's. Chihuahua cleared his throat.

"We lost a little girl yesterday," he said quietly. "All of us . . .we loved her. She made us happy in hard times." He paused. "We do not know if she is alive. Perhaps she has gone into the spirit world. I think she has."

He paused again. "That is good. She won't be alone. Many there she knows, more over there than here. We'll see her again. She is waiting for us."

He looked at a broken twig in his hand. There was a heavy silence. Finally he looked up and tried to smile. "We are still in this place and must decide what to do." People looked at him and nodded.

He stood up and scratched a number of lines on the ground. They combined to join for a rough but precise map of the region.

"We are here," he said, pointing with the stick. "South, a little southeast, is the valley of the big playa lake. Through there is flat ground all the way across the border to the Sierra Enmedio.

"South and west are the Animas Mountains, west of there the Peloncillos, and west of them San Simon Valley and the mountains named after our people."

He paused. "We could go through the valley of the big playa lake or through the Animas Valley. We don't know where troops are waiting. They will be in many places to prevent us from crossing.

"I think the most dangerous route is through the Animas Valley. One of the doors of Guadelupe Canyon is in there, on the west side, and I'm sure that they have closed it. Also, there may be soldiers in the pass in the Animas Mountains." He pointed at San Luis Pass. "They could block the valley and try to crush us between them.

"I think we should go through the big playa valley. But we must make sure that there are no soldiers there. If there are, we must trick them into leaving."

He peered around, searching faces. They were studying the marks on the ground or were looking at him.

After a moment Josanie spoke: "Yes. I think so, too. They expect us to cross west of here. It's the old trail, and we have crossed there before, many times. We must make them believe that we will do it again this time."

He paused. "I could do that. I could go west and make much damage there, burn places, draw troops there from everywhere.

"I could take six men. We would ride fast, hit places, and ride on. Let them think that we are more than we are. They should think it's all of us, the whole band. Confuse them."

There was a murmur of agreement.

"Yes," Chihuahua said. "How much time do you need?"

"Four or five days," Josanie said. "We should meet in six days in Mexico. You could stay here for four days, leave on the fifth day. On the sixth day we meet there. What do you think?"

Chihuahua nodded. "Yes. We should do it this way. I know the place where we meet. The spring in the little plain on the west side of the Sierra Enmedio. The spring where we fought with the cavalry from Fort Bowie three years ago. I don't think they expect us to go there."

He stopped and looked to the ground. There were many places as bloody as this one. In April 1882 they had fought an engagement at this spring with Tupper's Sixth Cavalry and two companies of Apache scouts and forced them to retreat. They themselves had withdrawn during the night toward the Sierra Madre. But at dawn, twenty-nine miles farther south, they had been caught in the Janos plain by Garcia's two Mexican cavalry columns and suffered heavy losses. All those who were around him had been in that desperate fight in the Arroyo a las Alisos, saved only by their bravery and a few rounds of ammunition.

He thought of those killed in the battle, others captured and tortured to death by Mexican militia, of women and children who had disappeared into slavery and never been heard from again. The memory lay over them like a blanket of sorrow. They thought of that day and others that had followed.

"I don't think they would look for us at that spring," Chihuahua said finally. He looked around the two circles of faces. "Is it agreed?"

There was no disagreement. The men and some of the women nodded. The plan was good. It would be no one's fault if something went wrong.

"Good. We meet there on the sixth day. How will you get there?"

"I don't know," Josanie said. "Somewhere through the San Bernardino and the San Luis Mountains. But wait for us not more than two days. If we're not there by then, go on."

"Yes," Chihuahua said. "But if we're not there . . . ?"

"I come looking for you." Josanie paused. "Where will you go from that spring?" Seven ravens flew over the camp, circled, called, and flew on. Josanie watched them go.

"West, through the mountains. About twenty miles southwest of the spring. Do you remember the trail?"

"We will find it if we have to. And whereto from there?"

"To the branch of the Bavispe River that flows south. We'll try to go into the Pinitos Mountains east of it. There are many good campsites. We have been there. I think of one northeast of Oputo. Do you remember it?"

"Yes," Josanie said.

"We would watch for you. Leave signs. There is good water, shelter, grass for the horses. From there we can go in any direction. Maybe wait for Nana. Go south, deeper into the Sierra Madre."

"When will you leave?"

Josanie raised his right arm. "Who goes with me?" Nearly all the men made signs with their hands. He pointed at six of them with his lips.

"We are leaving," he said with a smile.

The circles of people broke up. Jaccali had her arm around Josanie when they walked toward their camp. Nothing had to be said. They knew each other. They had been through this for many years. Josanie had always been the war captain of this band, Chihuahua its chief, nantan. Ramona brought his horse. He checked the dun mare's hooves and saddled her. He strapped blankets and equipment on and put the rifle in the scabbard. Jaccali held out the painted buckskin shirt. He put it on and took the war cap and placed it on his head, tying the string under his chin. Galeana and Kezinne rode by, looking at him over their shoulders.

Chihuahua walked up. He embraced his brother and turned away. Josanie closed his arms around his wife's slender figure, touching her bare neck with his mouth, breathing in the smell of her body. He let her go, looking once into her eyes. He mounted up and rode out.

Seven men gathered below the camp and pointed the horses west, no one looking back. In camp the people began to gather material to build wickiups as shelters from the approaching rain.

SEVENTEEN

Comment from Deming, New Mexico

The citizens of these territories are at last thoroughly aroused. Our local press without exception are publishing the storm of indignation against Crook and the War Department, and every paper contains offers of prominent citizens to arm and furnish men to exterminate the occupants of the reservation (6,000), be they good or bad. The government has been appealed to year after year to stop this annual butchery, but the War Department, on the strength of the representations of such Indian-fighters as Pope, Crook and Hatch, pigeon-hole the whole business, and wonder why the frontier folk are kicking up such a fuss over nothing! Haven't they got the army to attend to the Indians?

What the citizens demand is: That the scouts be discharged; that every hostile found off the reservation and captured shall be turned over to the civil authorities; that the Indians at San Carlos be completely disarmed, or that the reservation be abandoned. If not, the San Carlos reservation will be raided and thousands of good Indians made.

E. B. L.

Item in the Silver City Enterprise, *June 13, 1885.*

EIGHTEEN

Half a mile west of the camp the horsemen crossed a small creek that emerged from the south face of the Pyramid Mountains and meandered to the southwest. They rode hard through the gently rolling grasslands toward the sycamore and cottonwood trees that lined Animas Creek on its course north. Tall, blooming stalks of sotols rose here and there from the ground like so many lances. To the southwest a storm was approaching and the grasslands were turning dark under a dark sky, thin white wires of lighting diving into the dark blue mountains in the distance in utter silence. During the full gallop the men tore the shirts from their bodies and stashed them under the packs behind the saddles.

The rain came ripping across the land, the grass shifting in swirls and waves as an inland sea. They rode into a wall of water and were soaked instantly. They rode on without pause and made it to the cottonwoods and stood and held the horses and heard the rain hammer the branches and roar in the canopy above them. The storm passed quickly, and they stood shivering and listening to the water foaming in the creekbed.

They checked rifles and equipment and mounted. They rode slowly through the turbulent waters and trotted up a slow rise above the west bank. In the distance, to the south, they saw ranch buildings outlined against the sky. They rode on west. Before them the sky lit up slowly, the morning sun a brilliant disk in a fresh and shining world.

They left Animas Valley through a low section in the Peloncillo range and came upon the first ranch in San Simon Valley. It sat above the east bank of the creek, one main building, a bunkhouse, sheds, a woodpile, a pole corral with five horses. Smoke was coming from the chimney of the main building. There was a white sheepdog.

They rode forward slowly, in skirmish line, noiselessly in the tall grass. Kezinne notched an arrow on the string of his mulberry wood bow. When they were less than a hundred yards away, the dog ran to the front of the main building and watched them and started to growl. Kezinne shot it in the throat with an arrow, and it died without making another sound. Josanie and Kezinne went into the main building, while Bish held the horses, his rifle leveled. Galeana, Tisnol, Zele, and Nalgee surrounded the bunkhouse.

In the third room, the kitchen, Josanie came face to face with two women, one old, one young. They heard his catlike step and saw him standing in the door. They saw a slender, bare-chested Chiricahua Apache, sharp face and glittering eyes under a feathered cap, who was gripping a big-bore rifle pointed at them. In their long black dresses they stood like stone statues, their white faces ashen with terror.

Josanie saw it. He shook his head and walked away. Outside the warriors were coming from the bunkhouse. Galeana made a sign: nothing. Burn it, Josanie signaled. They smashed bunk beds and a table and piled straw mattresses on top. They lit the pile and watched the flames shoot high and reach the wooden beams of the ceiling. They took the five horses from the corral and drove south. Behind them a black billow of smoke rolled out and climbed toward the sky.

They rode through bunches of red-colored Mexican cattle and hit a second ranch four miles farther on. This time they were fired on by three rifles from a large wooden building with a veranda in front. Galeana and Nalgee went around to the back and put it to the torch, and Josanie and Kezinne shot the men when they tumbled out. In another building the raiders found a woman with three children, whom they left alone. They took some food, dry goods, ammunition, two rifles, and a double-barreled shotgun. They added seventeen horses to the band of six, four pulled from the corral, the rest hazed out of the sycamores along the creek.

They changed horses and rode on, Galeana at point, Kezinne at drag. To the west loomed the giant turtleback of the Chiricahua Mountains, its middle reaching up to ten thousand feet. Passing south, they reached the eastern foothills and crossed the road that led around Davis Mountain to the mining camp of Galeyville, a dirty place of tents, refuse, brothels, and bars that they had sacked twice in past years. Grimly they went on and tumbled with the remuda into another ranch, where they set fire to two buildings and left behind one cowhand dead and one dying. They added more horses to the remuda and pushed on.

They rode on like a wind, the red wind of war, of death, a whirlwind. Two more ranches were burned and men killed, and behind the ever-growing remuda, over a distance of thirty miles north to south in San Simon Valley, stood the black clouds of burning ranches, like banners waving in the shining sky. They turned southwest in the shadow of the Chiricahua Mountains, torching one more place at the foot of Squaw Mountain.

They raced on and in the evening came near the door of the canyon now called Tex Canyon. Josanie held when the remuda and the warriors rode between the towering walls. He dismounted and made marks with hoddentin against ghost sickness, then followed the others. They rode fifteen miles of a winding, rocky course before stopping for camp on Brushy Creek, in the heart of the Chiricahua Mountains, at the crossing of the canyon called Rucker that led to the western door of the mountains and into what is now called Sulphur Springs Valley.

They killed a colt for food and cooked meat over a blazing fire. They dried clothing and equipment still wet from the storm. They gorged themselves. They were home and alive, and they had burned a message into the ground that the whites would have to decode by themselves. During the night Josanie awoke and walked away from the fire into the dark, listening to the sounds of the mountains. The wind played among the trees, an owl called, and later wolves howled to the north.

At sunrise they were on their way. They rode down Rucker Canyon, driving about seventy horses. It took them almost two hours to cover fourteen miles, until they came out on the flat ground below Squaretop Hills. Once in the defile of the canyon, they passed two prospectors or miners, who backed against the rocks when the remuda came on them. The warriors blasted their rifles when they went by but did not slow down. They changed horses and took seven along for remounts, leaving the others at the mouth of the canyon.

They rode north along the west slope of the Chiricahua Mountains, looking for prey. They found two ranches, one on Turkey Creek, the other on Fivemile Creek, twelve miles apart, and burned buildings in both. They met no resistance and hurt no one. They turned southwest across the wide Sulphur Springs Valley toward the Dragoon Mountains, which rose pale blue into the deep blue sky. On the flats here and there grew clumps of beargrass and sotol plants, their flowering stalks reaching four feet above the rich midgrasses. Bunches of antelopes stood and watched them ride by. Even with a naked eye someone would have spotted the horsemen from many miles away. They wanted to be seen, but the land lay as still and remote as they had always known it, and whatever enemy eyes might have seen them caused no action against them. They found no trace of a military presence and wondered where the companies of Apache and Pima scouts and the cavalry regiments had gone.

They torched two empty huts below Sixmile Hill and turned south. Ten miles on they killed a solitary miner at Browns Peak and burned his log cabin. Another ten miles and they rode again among pale red Mexican cattle. They found a ranch on the east slope of the Mule Mountains, among the sycamores on Gadwell Creek, and hit it, taking nine horses and leaving two buildings afire. Here Galeana received a flesh wound in his right thigh. They searched for the hidden shooter but did not find him. In the clean air, under the cloudless sky, the smoke plumes in the valley behind them could be seen from forty miles away. They passed one ranch but circled it and, after six more miles, came to the mouth of Dixie Canyon.

Again Josanie marked them off against the dead, kneeling on the ground. Nalgee lanced a heifer, and they butchered it, taking the choicest pieces. They rode into the canyon and made camp below Potter Mountain, near potholes in the creekbed filled with good water and behind a curtain of pines and junipers.

At sunrise on the following morning, the horses saddled, they heard hoofbeats on the side of the creek, approaching slowly. Three riders. Silently Josanie and four men moved forward and crouched in the brush, while Galeana and Zele stayed with the horses. Two men and a boy, partly hidden by undergrowth, the first rider leaning from the saddle, studying the horse tracks. Twenty paces farther and they would see the horses if they had not already heard them. Josanie cocked the hammer of the Sharps and put the sights on the second rider, waiting for him to come clear. The first one came into the open, and Nalgee and Tisnol fired at the same time. The quiet exploded and the bullets struck with powerful slaps. Horse and rider disappeared with a crash. Josanie shot at the second man but missed. This one and the boy were gone in an instant, with a rush through the undergrowth and a wild staccato of hoofbeats.

The dead man lay partly buried under the horse, perhaps a rancher worried about rustlers. The man and the horse had been shot in the head. Josanie removed a red leather scabbard holding a shiny, engraved .44-40 Winchester. A silver nameplate was imbedded in the stock, reading E. B. Daniels. After looking at the engraving Josanie held scabbard and rifle toward the two who had killed the man, but they declined. When he offered the weapon to the others, Zele took it. They rode out with their herd of remounts. Josanie left last, sealing the trail between them and the dead man.

Now they went east and southeast, recrossing the valley. They reached the Perilla Mountains looming above the border with Mexico and rode through on a narrow, winding trail. They had wanted the cavalry to find them, but they found the cavalry instead.

Near midday, the horses hidden in the canyon below, they lay under junipers on a hogback above Silver Creek and studied the soldier camp on Astin Spring, seven miles away, near the Guadelupe Canyon road. They were careful to shield the glass of the binoculars with their hands so it would not reflect light like a mirror. Between the giant saguaros and ironwood shrubs they made out rows of white tents, wagons, horses, and mules. The camp seemed to have been in this location for at least a number of days. If the soldiers had patrols out, how could they not have seen the smoke of burning ranches?

"Maybe three troops of cavalry," Josanie said, "some scouts, too." He moved the binoculars. "No outriders, no guards. They feel real safe." He laughed. "They are not doing anything. They must be waiting for something."

In early afternoon two patrols left the camp. One went north, into San Simon Valley, the other northeast, toward the Peloncillo Mountains. Each was made up of a dozen troopers or more and some Apache scouts.

The warriors watched them ride through the towering saguaros and creosote and ironwood shrubs, often losing them from sight. "If that bunch goes far enough north, it will find our tracks going into the Chiricahua Mountains," Josanie said. "If they follow the tracks, they will send someone to tell the camp."

The sun climbed slowly toward the west. Black dots—turkey vultures—circled high in the sky. In early evening a single Apache scout galloped past and rode into the camp.

Josanie smiled. "They have gone into the mountains. I think they send soldiers west in the morning to close the Sulphur Springs Valley. They think we are still in there."

Later they watched the cooking fires go up, and after dark they saw them glow like so many angry eyes. There were no pickets. The second patrol did not seem to have returned either.

It was a quiet night, and the warriors were saddled at first light. A bugle sounded in the soldier camp, and at sunrise one troop of cavalry with about twenty Apache scouts and a mule train came out and rode west, passing eight miles below the watchers on their perch. A little later another troop with Apache scouts and pack mules rode out toward the southeast and the Guadelupe Canyon road. The camp seemed to be deserted but for a small guard.

Josanie looked at the sun rising radiantly above the Peloncillos. He pointed west where the column had disappeared behind ridges on the south slope of the Perilla Mountains. "If they turn north, about fifteen miles up, they will cut our trail from yesterday," he said.

He did not have to explain; the men with him knew what he was thinking. They had to wait until both columns were so far away that they would not be able to come back in time. They painted themselves and made ready. Time passed slowly, but they were patient. Finally Josanie raised his arm.

They rode at a walk down the arroyo through which Silver Creek ran south and into Mexico. Ironwood shrubs lined the sides of the creek and hid them from sight. Galeana and Zele rode point ahead of the herd of seven horses, and Josanie followed with the rest of the men. They rode on the sandy bottom, avoiding small pools of water sleeping under the yellow walls. When they were parallel with the soldier camp, they climbed out from the arroyo and rode into the arid flat around the spring, dotted with creosote bushes and a few saguaros. They rode slowly and kept their formation until they were close to the camp.

Josanie called out and the warriors loosened the war cry of the Chokonen, breaking into a dead run, fanning out. A small wave of horses rolled into camp and washed around the tents and wagons. Guns barked and soldiers were running and falling. Two made an escape on horses, but five lay dead.

Galeana and Zele rode after the horses. They had stampeded and were finally overtaken and brought in. The warriors sat their horses in the middle of the camp and looked stunned at the wealth around them. The dead men wore the insignia of the Fourth Cavalry; the Apaches did not touch them. Finally they searched the tents and the wagons. They found wooden boxes with about four thousand rounds of .45-70 ammunition, tons of food and equipment. Two mules and five cavalry horses were tethered behind a wagon and were loaded with ammunition boxes, the dead men's Springfield rifles, and useful pieces of equipment. One of the wagons was filled with blankets and uniforms, and each of the warriors took a cavalry jacket; Galeana, one with lieutenant's stripes. They took additional pieces of clothing and blankets and loaded their extra horses. Josanie found a pair of binoculars in a case in a captain's tent and a series of maps of the country on both sides of the border. They found cans with kerosene and dumped the liquid into the wagons and lit it with a torch. When they rode away, columns of smoke were rising behind them.

They rode as hard as the heavily loaded animals allowed. They took the Silver Creek road and crossed the border. There were no markers, and they did not know when they were across and did not care to know. They rode south for another twenty miles after they passed the Silver Creek ranch, leaving Guadelupe Canyon well to the rear and east. They turned east into the Sierra de San Luis and rode on an ancient and arduous Chokonen trail into the mountains. They passed through thickets of manzanita and chaparral and had to move slowly. They met no one. Zele covered the back trail. Red disk of the sun, yellow disk of the moon. They spent that night and the next in the high mountains, among pines and junipers, and then climbed down a canyon on the east side toward the meeting place with Chihuahua on the spring by the Sierra Enmedio.

They stayed hidden in a fold of the mountains with a clear view of the spring and the empty plain around it. They waited for what seemed a long time.

Two dots appeared to the north, a distance apart. They came closer, horsemen. Josanie and the men watched them through binoculars. The horsemen rode at a walk, scanning to the front and sides. When they came closer, they were recognized as Antonio and Cuchuta. They approached the spring and circled it wide on both sides. Antonio rode on when Cuchuta dismounted and searched the ground around the spring in the rocks. He mounted again, and both, a wide distance between them, rode on south for another half a mile. They circled again and rode quickly back toward the spring.

Four more horsemen appeared in the distance and approached at a fast clip. They surrounded the spring and sat their horses, waiting. And then a dark cluster of horses and riders because visible far away, the women with the packhorses and the remuda and a handful of men behind them, and they came on fast and reached the plain.

Josanie waited until they were gathered at the spring. He raised his arm, and they rode out into the open. Galeana and Zele rode point in front of the train of pack animals. Josanie and four warriors rode in a line behind them. They wore the blue cavalry jackets they had taken from Lawton's and Hatfield's camp, Galeana the one with the lieutenant's golden stripes. He had tied a white piece of cloth to the muzzle of the Winchester and waved it frantically in the air. Army scouts surrendering.

First there was a dead silence among the people around the spring; then they recognized the raiders. No one missed the irony of the uniforms and the length of the pack train. Among jubilant, unrestrained shouts the blue-jacketed raiders rode up laughing and yelling, waving the rifles high above their heads.

NINETEEN

Until I was about ten years old I did not know that people died except by violence. That is because I am an Apache, a Warm Springs Apache, whose first vivid memories are being driven from our reservation near Ojo Caliente with fire and sword.

As I tell this story, I am the sole survivor of the Massacre of Tres Castillos [October 15–16, 1880] in which our great leader, Chief Victorio, fired his last bullet before taking his own life, and in which his band of almost four hundred people was nearly exterminated. Among the seventeen who escaped death or slavery were my mother and myself. She managed to make her way to Nana, a chief whom I will call Grandfather but white men would call my great uncle. It was Nana about whom the survivors assembled before making their desperate flight to the Sierra Madre. Our warriors were away on a raid for ammunition when the attack occurred, but later they joined Nana, a few at a time.

Victorio had killed many people, but the count was small in comparison to the number of lives Nana exacted in retaliation for Victorio's death.

Statement of James Kaywaykla to Eve Ball.

TWENTY

The women, safe for the moment, sang the Chokonen victory song for the first time since they had fled the reservation. Their high-pitched voices ebbed and flowed over the plain and broke against the slopes of the mountains to the east and west. They had come into the *tierra despoblado* of northern Mexico, the deserted land, so called because centuries of Chokonen warfare with the Spanish and decades of warfare with their Mexican successors had left the country empty of people. During the sixteenth century the Spanish had called this place *una tierra de guerra*, a land of war—not the least because of resistance to their slave-hunting expeditions aimed at supplying labor to the mines of Santa Bárbara, Léon, and Monclova. A few military posts had been built to protect roads into what was later New Mexico and Arizona, but these roads were now abandoned.

The tierra despoblado lay on both sides of the boundary between the states of Sonora and Chihuahua—a vast stretch of land 200 wide and 180 miles long, reaching from the U.S. border south far into the high mountain and deep canyon country of the Sierra Madre, to the Aros, Sirupa, and Tuluaco Rivers. In the grasslands of northern Chihuahua a few large cattle ranches held out. There were about a dozen tiny towns in this land, alive, if barely, because they traded with marauders, Anglos from across the border, or Indians. The tierra despoblado was an empty quarter traversed by Anglo and Mexican rustlers; by scalp hunters looking for black hair, any black hair; and by military units, American and Mexican, searching for renegades.

And now a few Chokonen had returned.

The song ended and the raiders dismounted into outstretched arms. Josanie embraced Jaccali and the shy Ramona. Chihuahua waited, then put an arm around his brother.

"You have made us rich, Brother," he said. "Rich like some white people." He laughed. "We could sell some of it to the Mexicans, and they sell it back to the white eyes."

Josanie smiled. He looked worn from the exertion of the raid. "We keep the blue jackets, though. They might want to enlist us and fight Geronimo for them." He was serious again. "I wonder where he is, and Nana, Naiche. We saw nothing of them, no trace. Did you?"

"No," Chihuahua said, "nothing."

"You had any trouble getting here?"

"No," Chihuahua answered. "We rode through one ranch. It was nothing. We saw no one else. I don't know where the soldiers went. We crossed one big trail—soldier horses and ponies, a mule train. Six, seven days old, going west, into the Animas Mountains."

He paused. "Did you see them?"

"No. We only saw the big soldier camp by Guadelupe Canyon, the one we burned."

"You must tell us later," Chihuahua said. "We should leave here. This place holds bad memories."

He called out to the people, telling them to water the horses and fill canteens and water bags. Once these tasks were done, the band moved out, Galeana and Zele riding point half a mile ahead. The men had stripped to their breechclouts.

The Chokonen rode into a furnace, the sun burning from a merciless sky. The heat blurred the pale mountains and lay over the plain like a fiery, wafting, invisible cloud. Tsach led the rear guard. With three warriors Chihuahua and Josanie rode at the head of the column of women and pack animals. The brothers rode side by side.

They pressed to the southwest, across the dry, grassy plain dotted with sage and creosote bushes and yucca, whose sinewy stalks reached up like dead white arms holding flowers. They rode along the east slope of the Sierra de San Luis, alternating walk and lope to spare the horses. To the east lay the vast, haunted expanse of the Janos plain, and in it the killing place of the Arroyo a las Alisos, where they had been ambushed by eight hundred Mexican regulars in 1882. They made twenty miles and climbed into the foothills and followed their contour over high, broken ground until they reached a ragged opening in the mountain chain and a trail that led west into the high sierra. They followed it.

"Something happened when you were away," Chihuahua said. "Ramona is going to be White Painted Woman. She had her first blood."

He paused. "It happened during the first night you were away. Next morning I gave a little feast and told them. I wished we could have had fresh cooked food, but I didn't dare to make fires."

He paused again. "My wife is a prisoner somewhere. So I have asked your wife to make Ramona's dress. She has agreed."

Josanie nodded.

Chihuahua continued. "Ramona went to Chaddi's camp and asked his wife to take her through the ceremony. Chie accepted the eagle feather and will take care of her."

They rode in silence for a while. "I have asked Chaddi to be the singer," Chihuahua continued. "He knows the songs and everything. He said he would be pleased to do it."

He paused again. "Jaccali is already working on the dress. She went around the camps and got five deer skins she needs. I have not yet decided who will paint the mountain spirit dancers. We have two who have done this, you and Tsach. Should I ask you, or do you want me to ask Tsach?" Whomever he asked would hardly be able to refuse the request.

He looked at his brother. They rode slowly, watching the trail, letting the horses choose the way around rocks and fallen trees. Pines and junipers grew on the sides of the canyon, and ocotillos bloomed in scarlet fury on red, rocky hillsides between mesquites with long, yellow-flowered spikes.

"I think you should ask Tsach," Josanie said at last. "He is probably better at it than I am. I should be on watch when you have the ceremony, make sure no one comes in who doesn't belong."

"It is good," he continued. "I am happy for all of us. I am happy for Ramona. She is close to our hearts. We need the ceremony to remind us of who we are."

His voice was full of pent-up anger. "Too much fighting, killing. We are becoming like them, the whites. We are not anymore the way we used to be."

He fell silent, trying to control himself. Finally he said, "We must let the spirits see that we remember and still live by the laws they have given to us."

"That's what Chaddi said," Chihuahua said quietly.

Josanie looked up, searching the sky. "We'll help you. It will be good. When do you want this to take place?"

"After we get to the campsite in the Pinitos Mountains. There is good water and plenty of wood. I think we will be safe there, at least for some time. If we wait and go farther south, we will run into Geronimo. I don't want him with us. He hates the Mexicans so much, he fights them all the time. The Mexicans will tell the Americans, and their Apache scouts will find him. He is trouble."

He added, "I wish Nana would join us."

They camped for the night on a high meadow with a spring, near the watershed of the sierra. On the way up they had seen only trails of animals that lived in the mountains, including the pug marks of a jaguar, but no horse tracks. They removed packs and saddles and let the horses and the two mules graze. When Galena and Zele returned from exploring the head of the trail that led west and down toward the Bavispe River, and Ures and Antonio came up over the back trail, both parties reporting no enemy signs, the spoils of Josanie's raid were carried to a flat, grassy area and laid out. The people crowded around the piles of goods, laughing and joking. It looked as if the government stores on the San Carlos had been pilfered.

According to Chokonen law Josanie asked the band chief to distribute the unexpected wealth. What little the warriors on the raid had taken for themselves was theirs to keep or to give away if they so chose. The bulk of the spoils was for the chief to divide among the members of the band. Chihuahua obliged after thanking Josanie and the men who had been with him. Everything was faithfully dispersed, except the crates with the .45-70 ammunition. They were not touched, kept as a special store. Eight men, including Josanie and Chihuahua, used rifles with that caliber, but their cartridge belts were still full, and they carried extra boxes with ammunition in their saddlebags. The women were excited about bales of blue and white calico, bags of pinto beans and wheat flour. Fires went up quickly.

Beans were boiled and jerky added, and that evening the people ate tortillas until they could eat no more.

After dark some of the young men build a huge fire in the place where the booty had been divided. The flames burned high, casting a red shine on the irregular belt of pines surrounding the meadow. The eyes of the horses, looking in, glowed like red stars. Two older men, Tsach and Nitzin, moved near the fire, holding pottery drums.

Men joined and formed a line in front of them, their arms around each other's shoulders. Nitzin started a song and Tsach fell in, and the men began to dance sideways around the fire, clockwise. The women came forward and formed another circle, facing the fire, standing side by side. They started, following the male line of dancers. Both groups shuffled to the beat of the drums.

Chihuahua, Josanie, and Chaddi sat crossed-legged outside the circles and watched. They were the only ones not participating. Everyone else was dancing, even the smallest children, who were helped either by their mothers or their fathers. Once, when Jaccali passed, she made a gesture with her hand encouraging her husband to get up and join. Finally he rose and went to stand behind the drummers. Chihuahua came and stood next to him. With clear voices they joined in the songs.

On and on the dancers went. Slowly, dancers and singers lost themselves to the songs, the movements, the magic of the moment. They seemed lost in time, as if they were alone in the world, as if the world in which they were hunted was only a dream, and this night, this fire, the soft swishing of bodies and the thumping of moccasins in the grass, were the real world.

The round dance lasted until after midnight. The men rested and the women went back to their campfires and cooked once again. They ate and talked and laughed and joked with each other. The big fire was kept up.

And then the two drummers stood on the dance ground again, starting with a song different from the ones sung before. The men joined the drummers, forming a line beside them. The women formed a second line opposite them. With the second song the two lines moved toward each other until they were a few feet apart, stopped, and danced backward to where they had started. They went back and forth, the drummers dancing along with the line of men. This time everyone participated, wives dancing toward their husbands, boys toward their sisters. Jaccali winked at Josanie when they approached each other, and Ramona smiled at her father, taking her mother's position in the line.

After the fourth song by the drummers, Kezinne started a song and the men fell in. The two lines came close and separated, and when the song had ended, the women chorus took it up and repeated it, but changing the gender mentioned in it. So it went on and on. Twice they stopped and passed water jars. They danced and sang and both lines made up new songs and teased and frolicked to first light, the night turning ashen above the eastern rim of the sierra. Chaddi walked away from the dance ground and sang the morning song, facing east.

This ended it. Children who had long walked out of the line and lay asleep in the grass were picked up, and the adults made sleeping arrangements around the cold fireplaces. Josanie shook his head when Jaccali spread a blanket for him.

He took his rifle and walked through the bunches of grazing horses to the spot where the trail from the Janos plain came through the trees and into the meadow. The camp was slightly below him, and everyone seemed to have gone to sleep. The big fire had burned down, but there was a thin plume of smoke. He found a good place to sit, overlooking the head of the trail and the camp. He had the rifle on his knees and the thumb of his right hand around the hammer. There was something out there, he felt, something unseen, dangerous, but he did not know what. He was restless but sat for a long time, listening to the thunder of the sun's rays dueling with the chanting of the birds.

TWENTY-ONE

I could not lose sight of the fact that the Apache represents generations of warfare and bloodshed. From his earliest infancy he has had to defend himself against enemies as cruel as the beasts of the mountains and forests. In his brief moments of peace, he constantly looks for attack or ambuscade, and in his almost constant warfare no act of bloodshed is too cruel or unnatural. It is, therefore, unjust to punish him for violations of a code of war which he has never learned, and which he cannot understand. He has, in almost all of his combats with white men, found that his women and children were the first to suffer; that neither age nor sex is spared. In surprise attacks on camps women and children were killed in spite of every precaution; this cannot be prevented by any foresight or orders of the commander any more than shells fired into a beleaguered city can be prevented from killing innocent citizens or destroying private property.

Statement by General George Crook to Charles R. Lummis, correspondent for the Los Angeles Times, *April 1886.*

TWENTY-TWO

Sun and heat woke Josanie up in the early afternoon. He pushed the blankets away and looked around. Children were playing among baggage and saddles, and some of the men were still asleep, while others sat by the fireplaces talking softly with their wives. Ramona and Jaccali sat near him, but Chihuahua was nowhere to be seen.

Josanie watched his wife and listened to her. She sang in a barely audible voice. She sang to White Painted Woman and to the gown for Ramona she was working on, the gown considered a replica of the one the holy woman had worn when she had been with the people a long time ago. The cut was the same as for everyday women's leather dresses, but the decoration was different and specific, full of religious symbolism. For the upper part of the garment, made of two doeskins, the skin side faced out, the tail of the deer hanging down in the back. For the skirt the flesh side was out, without the tails. Josanie noticed that the four skins had already been prepared and stitched together and that his wife was absorbed in the process of cutting the fringes.

Ramona touched Jaccali's arm and pointed with puckered lips. She turned and saw that Josanie was awake and watching them.

"You did not wake me up," Josanie said. "It's already late."

"Yes," Jaccali said with a smile. "Chihuahua said we should let you sleep. He decided that we should stay here for a day."

Josanie stretched and lifted himself up into a sitting position. "Where is he? I don't see him."

"He went with two men over the back trail," Jaccali said.

Josanie rubbed his eyes. "Is anyone on the trail down to the river?"

"Yes. Galeana and Zele."

"You are almost done with the dress," he said.

Jaccali smiled. Josanie got up and went to relieve himself. In the greasewood brush he almost stepped on a snake but was warned in time by the rattling sound. He carefully retraced his steps. Chokonen religious concepts forbade the killing or even touching of snakes.

Whoever offended this taboo, even in self-defense, had to undergo ceremonial purification.

He washed in the channel of the rivulet below the spring and drank deeply from the sweet, cold water. He walked into the clearing where the horses grazed. Ures was guarding the herd. He squatted against the green skirt of pines and raised an arm, and Josanie did the same. Back in camp he sat next to Jaccali. She combed his raven hair and tied it with a blue calico headband. Ramona handed him a plate with cold tortillas and jerky.

"Eat, Husband," Jaccali said.

He ate slowly. Up high two golden eagles circled in the updraft rising from the west face of the sierra. He watched them for a while. Then his attention was drawn to the skillful hands of his wife as they guided the old, thin knife blade through the white deerskin, producing long, even fringes around the bottom of the skirt.

It was a lazy, unusual day. For the first time since the people had ridden away from Turkey Creek, they felt at ease. They were where they had planned to be.

But when the sun dipped below jagged crags to the west, the people heard quick hoofbeats from the head of the trail leading toward the Bavispe River valley, and Zele rode in on an exhausted horse. He looked around briefly and dismounted and walked up to Josanie.

They stood. Zele held the silver-plated rifle, the one they had taken from the dead man in Dixie Canyon, in the crook of his left arm. Body and face glistened with sweat.

"Lots of Apache scouts," he said. "One troop of cavalry, two pack trains half a mile long. Down there." He pointed to the head of the trail.

"Where?" Josanie asked, his voice harsh.

"By the river," Zele said, "where the creek from west of here runs into the river. They are making camp on this side of the river."

"Where is Galeana?"

"Down there, in the trees."

He paused.

"We were just coming out of the canyon. We wanted to look for tracks along the river. If we had gone there, they would have seen our tracks. But we saw the dust cloud coming from the north and stayed in the canyon. We watched them. They were making camp when I left Galeana. He told me to tell you."

Josanie called the men together, and Zele repeated what he had already said. Josanie, as Chihuahua's *segundo,* his second, was in charge of the band in the nantan's absence. He said he wanted to see for himself and told Tsach to be in command until Chihuahua came back. Josanie slipped the medicine cord over his chest and put a cartridge belt and bandolier on. Zilahe brought a chestnut mare and saddled it for him. Jaccali squeezed some food into one of the saddlebags and tied a blanket to the saddle. Tisnol led a bay up and removed the saddle from Zele's horse and put it on the fresh one. Jaccali handed her husband the rifle and the leather case with the binoculars he had taken from the soldier camp, and the two men mounted and rode off and were quickly swallowed by the pines.

They rode about four miles to where the rivulet ran into the creek, which had carved a canyon southwest and down into the sheer rock. A narrow trail snaked through pines and junipers and brush along the creek, which gushed and foamed heedlessly over rocks and twisted timber. Sometimes they had to dismount and lead the horses around obstacles. They rode another ten miles, and in early evening they came to the place where the canyon opened up above the flat along the river. Galeana's horse was hidden behind a group of junipers off the trail, and they tied their horses up. Zele led Josanie through the trees to a high point with a broad view of the valley where Galeana lay in cover, watching the enemy camp through binoculars.

Josanie and Zele crawled on their bellies to Galeana's position. Below them spread a treeless, dusty flat. Beyond it, four miles away, ran a thicket of tall cane that formed a nearly impenetrable yellow and green wall on the riverbank. Behind it lay the hidden river. In front of it were two camps, one on each side of the creek that joined the river through a gash in the cane wall. Josanie took the binoculars from the leather case and adjusted them for his eyes.

The camp on the south side of the creek was that of Apache scouts, the one on the north side that of a troop of cavalry and a bunch of civilians, probably the packers for the mule trains. In both camps the men were grouped around fires burning freely; they had no fear of being detected. When he counted the ponies feeding near the Apache camp, Josanie came to an estimate of between 130 and 150 scouts. They were the ones to worry about. The soldiers and civilians, perhaps 70 altogether, mattered little.

Josanie wriggled away from the lookout post and lay on his back, eyes wide open, staring through branches above him into the sky. Was this big camp what he had feared last night? Galeana and Zele came and sat opposite him.

"It looks like the army that came after us two years ago, with the general himself," Josanie said. "Maybe he's there this time, too. All this for sixteen warriors and thirty women and children." He grunted in derision and shook his head.

There was silence between them. They thought about what had happened two years before and after the surrender, the road to Turkey Creek.

"What do you plan to do?" Galeana asked at last.

"Wait. Watch what they do in the morning. I think they will go south along this river and try the high mountains where they found us last time."

He paused. "But we are not going there. Later maybe. We go across the river and into the mountains west of here. They go south and we stay north of them. If we are careful, they won't find us.

"This may not be the only army coming into the Blue Mountains after us—and after Nana and Geronimo and Naiche," he added thoughtfully.

Zele looked at the elegant Winchester that lay across his knee and caressed the smooth, finely grained walnut stock with his right hand. He said nothing, but the two men knew what he was thinking.

"Yes," Josanie nodded. "We'll find the whites when we want to."

They watched the camp again, but no scouting party came in; it seemed that none had been out. There were no sentries; they were secure in their numbers. Josanie, Galeana, and Zele rotated a watch throughout the night. In the gray morning a bugle blew and cook fires went up. The watchers observed that the Apache scouts went for a bath in the river, but none of the whites did. A little later the trumpet blared out reveille. The mules were loaded with packs and horses were saddled, and the column moved out south when the sun peeked over the rim of the sierra, the large body of scouts leading off. The troop of cavalry came next, with the colors of the Sixth Regiment, and the mule trains, led by a white bell horse, stretched out a long way behind it.

The enemy column moved past as on parade and eventually disappeared from view. Behind it four dozen fires were left smoldering, their smoke rising slowly in the still air. The three men stayed on the lookout for another hour, but the country before them remained what it was, a lonely, forbidding place. Josanie touched Zele's arm.

"I need you again," he said. "Ride to our camp and tell my brother that he should bring the people here. We can ride to the big trail the army has made and stay on it until we come to the place where we cross the river, a few miles south. We know the place. No one will discover our tracks on the army trail."

Slowly the sun climbed higher and the heat became oppressive. Five turkey vultures lay on the lazy air curls rising from the mountain slope and watched the empty flats under their wings. And then Zele brought Chihuahua up and Josanie explained to him what they had seen. Chihuahua listened and looked to the campsites by the river.

When Josanie ended, Chihuahua said: "Yes. We'll do as you say." And after a pause: "You know, if we had not had the dance last night, we would have crossed the river this morning, and the scouts would have seen our tracks."

He paused again. "We might still be fighting them right now."

Josanie nodded and touched his brother's arm. The warriors came out of the canyon with Josanie and seven men in the lead, the rest of the band following, and Chihuahua bringing up the rear. They rode down the south bank of the creek, straight for the cold camp of the Apache scouts. They did not linger and did not dismount. They looked in passing at the fireplaces and at where the scouts had bedded down for the night. They turned onto the wide, fresh trail cut by unshod ponies, the heavy mounts of the cavalry, and the mule trains and rode over it until they came to the hidden ford in the river. Josanie broke through the canes, with Galeana and Zele behind him.

He dismounted and knelt above the river's edge. He took four turquoise beads from a pouch and lowered them into the brown, silent waters. He prayed for a safe crossing, then mounted and rode into the first stream channel, the water reaching to just above the horse's wrists. There were two more channels between sand dunes and gravel bars in the wide riverbed, and he crossed and went through the cane thicket on the other side. Next the herd was pushed across, the horses shouldering their way haltingly at first and wide of eye. The women following with the heavily loaded packhorses and mules went through without incident, and on the even ground below the Hojade Eata Mountains the column formed up and turned north, moving leisurely in the cover of the canes. No human eye saw them; the turkey vultures still hanging in the sky would not tell.

TWENTY-THREE

Governor Pesquiera of Sonora has offered a bounty of $100 per scalp for Apaches, and a proportionate sum for animals retaken from them. This should be imitated by the Authorities of Arizona. The Pimos and Papago Indians would be most valuable auxiliaries in the pursuit of these "human wolves." They lately killed about sixty Apaches and took several prisoners in a single campaign. The children of the Apaches when taken young, make good servants and are sold by the Pimos in the Territory (Arizona) and in Sonora.

There is only one way to wage war against the Apaches. They must be surrounded, starved into coming in, surprised or inveigled—by white flags or any other method, human or divine—and then put to death.

If these ideas shock any weak-minded individual, who thinks himself a philanthropist, I can only say that I pity, without respecting, his sympathy. A man might as well have sympathy for a rattlesnake or a tiger.

Sylvester Mowry, The Geography and Resources of Arizona and Sonora; *as quoted by Arthur Woodward,* Side Lights on Fifty Years of Apache Warfare, 1865–1886.

TWENTY-FOUR

The Bavispe River came out of the high Sierra Madre and ran north on a long, winding course between mountains until it struck the outlying mesas of the Sierra Ojos Azules. There it was forced to edge west, and, after it was joined by the San Bernardino River from the north, the Bavispe turned south along the Teres Mountains, eventually, a hundred miles farther on, to become the Yaqui when it met the Aros River.

Chihuahua's band followed the wide curve of the river north, west, and south. It passed a couple of ancient Indian ruins, stone houses hundreds of years old, and two dilapidated Mexican adobe villages, abandoned a century ago, their tumbled roofs and walls overgrown with mesquite. After twenty-five miles, Josanie, riding ahead, came on the old trail that led southeast into the Pinitos Mountains. They had been over it often, the last time in 1883, before the surrender. It appeared that no one had used it since. Josanie let Galeana and Zele pass to ride point, and the column swung in behind them.

They climbed steadily. The slopes of the foothills were dotted with tall saguaros, jojoba shrubs, slender-branched ocotillos, and yuccas, their long flower stalks heavy with white bell-shaped flowers. On the sides of the canyon, between chaparral and agave, grew Christmas cactus plants. Sapphire-hued hummingbirds flitted among the bushes to drink from the small yellow flowers of the chaparral and the large yellow flowers of some of the agave. Twice the riders saw parrots, sparkling with red and blue plumage. Large yellow butter-flies fluttered back and forth across the trail.

Near the head of the canyon, about six thousand feet up, the trail left the canyon when the walls closed in and turned around a sharp ridge. It became a treacherous, uneven path, a mere fold along a smooth, rocky surface above a drop of three hundred feet.

The riders dismounted. Galeana's horse shied and refused to go on. He stroked its neck and talked to it, giving it time to overcome its fright. He led it slowly along the precipice, and when he was across, the others were made to follow one by one. The two mules went without fuss. One of the packhorses near the end of the line slipped and fell, almost taking Bish with it. It skidded over the sharp incline and crashed into boulders below, the packs flying high on impact. There was no chance to retrieve them. The screaming of the injured horse was unnerving, but the last animals were brought safely across.

Josanie walked back over the path and shot the horse in the head. It was a difficult shot downward at a small, shifting target, but the bullet hit, and the animal stretched and lay still. The report of the rifle rolled along the mountain slope; it could not be helped. From where he stood he could see far across the valley of the Bavispe River and into the Teres Mountains. He saw nothing suggesting humans. He took his place behind Galeana and Zele, and the column moved on and came into pine forest below eight thousand feet and went to an old campsite near a spring and a pond in a glade with good grass.

Circling the pond they saw countless prints of deer and mountain sheep, turkey, raccoon, wolf, bear, and puma superimposed over each other. During the cool night a light wind tugged at the pines. The fires burning down, Josanie and Jaccali lay close together, each wrapped in a blanket. Josanie felt his wife's body behind his back, and he wondered if time had come to a standstill.

The people stayed another day in this camp. They bathed in the pond, and three men went out with bows and brought in deer. The women worked on the hides and on new calico dresses for themselves and shirts for their husbands, and the men checked the hooves of the horses, cleaned their rifles, and worked on reatas and rawhide lariats, sitting in groups, talking. Scouts went a few miles over the trail that forked east of the camp. One branch wound south into the green valley between the Pinitos and Hojade Eata Mountains; the other went southeast through the Hojade Eatas and meandered down to the Mexican mud town of Bavispe, twenty-eight miles away. They returned at midmorning and reported that they had seen nothing suspicious.

For a while in the hot, restful afternoon Josanie sat with his back against a tree trunk, about fifteen feet away from Jaccali and Ramona. Around them was the sweet smell of pines and of grasses and herbs lying under the sun. The young girl was assisting the older woman as she worked on the ceremonial dress. Both sat in the shadow of the tree. Jaccali was singing ritual songs appropriate to the finishing of White Painted Woman's gown. She had done the fringes and had already dyed the gown with yellow ocher. At the moment she was threading deer hooves on a string of sinew to be sewed on the collar. In the song she gave thanks to the deer for the hooves they had contributed.

Josanie listened to his wife's singing and watched her. She rocked slightly back and forth, absorbed in singing and doing delicate work at the same time. He watched the movement of her slender body, the intense face framed by black hair. He was happy, watching her. He saw her breasts move under the blue calico blouse and the turquoise necklace. He would have liked to make love to her. They had not had sex since they had left Turkey Creek. They could not make love while they were still at war. In ancient times White Painted Woman and her spirit son, Child of the Water, had forbidden it. They had ruled that there was a time for killing, for taking life, and a time for making love, for making new life, and that the two could not be mixed.

Jaccali was forty-two years old. They had one child together, the boy Nachi, who was now a prisoner among the whites. They had been married fifteen years. Josanie remembered the first time he had seen her. She had been living with her parents in one of Cochise's subbands, a sad, lonely young woman. Her husband and a one-year-old son had been killed almost a year before in the Chiricahua Mountains in a fight with troops from Fort Bowie. Josanie's wife had been killed a year earlier, 1868, near the Enmedio Mountains by Mexican militia from Bavispe. He and most of the warriors had been absent on a raid to get ammunition.

He and Jaccali had liked each other immediately. They had come to love each other deeply, although Chokonen never put something like this into words. She was his fifth wife; the others before her had all been killed by either Mexicans or Americans.

He dropped his eyes and stared at a pinecone in the thin grass below his knee. He thought back to where he had been half a lifetime ago. It was not good to think about the past. He had married for the first time when he was twenty-two years old. His wife had been two years younger. Her face came into his memory. There was no child yet when she was killed one year later by Mexican troops in an ambush in the Pitaicache Mountains, twenty miles east of Fronteras, in the spring of 1849. His second wife and a daughter of seven years were captured by Mexican troops in an attack on their camp in the Otates Mountains near Fronteras, in 1858, when the warriors were out. They had never been heard of again. A third wife and a four-year-old son were killed in another attack on the camp, this time by American troops from Camp Mimbres, in the mountains north of the Gila River in Arizona in 1864. And his fourth wife was killed at Alamo Hueco, near the Enmedio Mountains, in 1868. It had been the woman's second marriage. Her first husband and two small boys had been killed in the Animas Mountains of New Mexico by Mexican troops from Fronteras in 1864.

A coldness settled over him. So many gone. They love to kill our women and children even more than they love to kill us, he thought. He shook his head and put the bad thoughts away. Jaccali was still here and singing, and the mountain and the spirits heard her, those with little hooves or claws, those of the earth, and those of the air and sky. The world was still here, and the mountains were the way they had always been. This was worth living for and dying for, on the path to the spirit world. He got up and walked over to where Chihuahua sat with Chaddi and a few of the men.

The brothers decided to stay three more days in the good camp by the pond. Then they were eager to move on. Nana would not find them where they were, and they wanted to see him and his band again. He knew the campsite on the east slope of the Pinitos Mountains where they had planned to be for a while, and he might search for them there after he left the Black Range. The wily old man knew how to evade the troops assembled along the border. Throughout his life he had passed through their hands like wind but had struck hard at them at places and times of his choosing.

Where the trail divided, they rode south. They descended into a green valley lying like a crater within rimmed mountains. From the

valley floor only one passage led west into the flatlands along the
Bavispe River, cut by a small mountain stream. The two forks of the
stream ran the length of the valley, one coming in from the north,
the other from the south. On the even ground along them stood tall
grasses with some yuccas, a few willows, rose and blackberry bushes,
and small stands of oak. Herds of deer were grazing out in the open,
watching the column go by without moving away. The crests of the
mountains around the valley were bare, but the slopes inside were
covered with junipers and pines.

Galeana and Zele, half a mile ahead, followed the southern fork of
the stream and by midmorning reached the campsite, which was on
a narrow hill that overlooked the valley. They circled the small area
and looked down on the hardened ashes of the old fireplaces and
the wickiup frames still standing under the pines. A few frayed
baskets and other camp refuse lay in the grass, along with horse and
deer bones. There were animal tracks but no trace of human visitors.
They dismounted and waited for the column to come up.

The people gathered around Chaddi. Despite a fiery sun, a cool
wind wafted down from the Hojade Eata Mountains. Chaddi spread
a few stones in a circle and knelt before it. He spoke a prayer to the
Master of Life. He got up slowly, his legs stiff from riding. Now he
sang to the chiefs of the mountain spirits, turning in the four
directions, holding a single eagle feather in his right hand. First he
addressed the black one of the east, then the blue one of the south,
the yellow one of the west, and the white one of the north.

He ended and the people walked away slowly. Chihuahua directed
them to a location a little south of the old campsite. Women selected
spots to put up wickiups, and horses were brought in and unloaded.
While Jaccali and Ramona measured a site for a wickiup to
accommodate the four of them, Chihuahua, Josanie, and half of the
men rode through the trees to the top of the hill. They looked down
into a horseshoe canyon with trees and grass and some potholes that
held water. The canyon was as they remembered it. The only access
was through a coulee running past the south side of the hill. A
natural corral. They rode back and through the camp and into the
coulee and the horseshoe canyon. They looked up at the rocky walls

and knew: a good place to shelter the horses, a trap if there was a surprise attack.

The horses were let loose to graze along the creek below the camp, with Zilahe guarding them. Men and women started to work on a dozen wickiups. The men cut limbs of young trees and tree branches and tied them together to form a circular, domed frame. They anchored it in the earth, and the women covered it with a thatch of grass and brush and closed it with skins of horse, cattle, elk, and deer. The doorway was a low opening on the east side. Inside bundles of grass were spread and covered with blankets for beds. In front of the wickiups stones were arranged for fireplaces. The individual camps were finished within a few hours. Parties of women carrying baskets, talking, and laughing went out to gather wild onions, prickly pear fruits, and berries from blackberry bushes. The season was too late to cut agave heads for steaming mescal in earth ovens. But there was plenty of food. Cooking fires were started only at dusk so that smoke could not be seen from a distance.

By nightfall the horses had been driven into the canyon and the arroyo passage closed with brush. A dozen low fires burned among the wickiups spread out on the hill. In Jaccali's camp Ramona had cooked the food while Jaccali was bend over the ceremonial gown. After they had eaten, Jaccali returned to her work. She sang in a low voice when she painted on the yellow-colored dress the rest of the sacred symbols, morning star, thunder, rainbow. On front and back the other symbols were already finished, sun, moon, and the triangle to represent both the ceremonial lodge and the mountain made holy because the holy woman lived there.

Chihuahua and Josanie watched her in silence for a long time. Twice they fed wood to the fire and then let it burn down. Jaccali finally stopped and sat quietly, her mind still under the spell of the powerful songs.

"You worked hard," Chihuahua said at last. "You are almost done."

"Tomorrow I'll finish," Jaccali said. She looked at Ramona and nodded to her. "Has Chie finished with you? Has she told you what you have to know?"

"Yes," Ramona answered shyly, her eyes cast down.

There was a pause, and then Chihuahua said: "Perhaps we should start preparing the dance ground tomorrow. Get everything ready. It will take three days, maybe. If the weather stays good, we could begin in four days."

Over the next three days a level place was prepared for the dance ground. *Ramadas*, brush arbors, were built, and the four poles for the sacred lodge were cut, cleaned, and brought in. One time scouts were sent out to make sure that the people were safe. Once the sacred ceremony had started, it should not be interrupted. Tsach had taken five men into seclusion to prepare under his direction the mountain spirit masks and horn headdresses. Four dancers represented the chiefs of the cardinal directions; one dancer was the clown.

Ures and Antonio, scouting west, went as far as Oputo, a squalid mud town on the Bavispe River. They had not been told to ride that far, and Josanie was angry with them when they reported to him.

During the night of the third day a thunderstorm struck. The dance ground flooded and the creek became a torrent. It continued to rain off and on for the next three days, and the people spent most of their time in the wickiups.

In the gray, misty morning the rain stopped. Jaccali was combing Josanie's hair when they heard a shout from nearby, followed by a single shot. It was answered with a volley from somewhere, and a rapid firing was kept up, bullets striking all over camp. Josanie and Chihuahua grabbed ammunition belts and rifles and dashed outside. Jaccali and Ramona went through the doorway after them and saw a skirmish line of their warriors forming at the edge of the camp and the powder smoke from many guns coming from rock outcrops on the opposite slope, five hundred yards away. Everywhere, it seemed, rifles boomed. Josanie stood in the open and shouted for the women to run and take cover on the top of the hill. Chihuahua knelt beside him, firing as fast at the distant flashes as he could aim.

Many of the women, dragging children along, ran up into the pines, but one group dodged the hail of bullets and dropped into the arroyo. Josanie called out to his men to abandon the camp and to withdraw behind the women. They retreated slowly, and then Josanie saw a bunch of Chiricahua and White Mountain Apaches herding women and children out of the arroyo and across the creek and onto the opposite slope. He shouted to stop firing, and the rifles of the band fell silent, the men watching in desperation as their wives and children were driven away among the enemy scouts.

A ghostly quiet settled over the mountain. They watched as the attackers climbed swiftly with their captives toward the crest of the Pinitos ridge and disappeared. Josanie followed them with most of the warriors when they were out of sight. When they reached the summit, they saw the enemy descending fast through the foothills and the big camp of the American army spread out on the flat by the river. They sat for a long time. Finally Josanie told the men to look for their families, or for who was left. He stayed up there and watched through binoculars. But the enemies did not come out in full force; they seemed satisfied to have caught some women and children.

TWENTY-FIVE

We had just finished burying the dead scout when his three relatives who had followed us came back from the direction of Oputo with the information that near Oputo they had struck the trail of some hostiles who had been in the outskirts of the town the night before, and the trail, which the scouts had followed a little distance, led toward the mountains east of the Bavispe River. Returning to camp at once with my news, the command was assembled and we started for Oputo to pick up the trail.

On the arrival of the command we camped on the river at a little distance from the town and were flooded with such delicacies as their poor village afforded; nor would the grateful people accept a cent in payment.

Crawford [Captain, Third Cavalry,] prepared at once to give the hostiles a surprise. To attempt to follow the trail with our troop of cavalry and pack trains would be folly, feeling sure, as we did, that the hostiles were not very far away. The question has often been asked me why we used cumbersome and useless cavalry in these expeditions when the cavalry only retarded the movements of the scouts and hardly ever got into action against the hostiles. The answer is that the cavalry was supposed to serve as a rallying point for the scouts, increasing their morale and protecting the pack trains. The danger of inadequate protection for camp equipage and supplies was exemplified in the disaster to Hatfield's [and Lawton's] camp. The disadvantages were, however, found to outweigh the advantages and the General abandoned the use of cavalry in Crawford's and Major Davis' second expedition.

Crawford detailed about thirty scouts, under Chato and a White Mountain sergeant we called Big Dave, to take the trail of the three hostiles who had been down to the town the night before and follow it as far as they could that afternoon. They were given two days' rations and were to try the next day to reach the hostile camp and surprise it. [Chief of Scouts] Sieber and I wanted to go along, but Crawford was afraid we would be an encumbrance rather than an aid and turned us down, much to our disgust.

About noon the next day, June 23, the scouts returned to camp with fifteen women and children prisoners. Among them was a little boy about four years old with a flesh wound in his arm. Chato reported that one woman had been killed in the fight but no men.

The only casualty among the scouts was Big Dave, who had been shot through the elbow. . . . He was aiming at one of the hostiles when the bullet struck him. From the scouts we learned that a little after daylight, when they had taken up the trail where they had left it the night before, it was raining. The trail led up a ridge that came down from the main Sierra Madre Mountain. Suddenly the rain ceased and the sun came out from behind the cloud. On account of the rain the scouts were proceeding rather incautiously, covering their heads with their blankets. As the rain ceased they saw the hostile camp on the ridge five or six hundred yards away. At the same moment one of the hostiles came out of a brush shelter they had erected, caught sight of the scouts, and gave the alarm. The Indian men, with most of the women and children, fled up the ridge, the men stopping now and then to fire back at the scouts to delay them.

From the memoir of Lieutenant Britton Davis, Third Cavalry.

TWENTY-SIX

A light wind stood in his face. The sun had returned to the great blue bowl of the sky with renewed strength after the thunderstorm and the rains. In the stillness of the mountain he heard a muffled sound behind and below him, a single stone rolling. He turned around. Galeana and Zele walked up quietly as deer. They stood next to him and gazed at the tent rows and the widespread camp near the river, five miles away. A dozen turkey vultures circled above it, black specks in the sky.

"They are waiting for you back there," Galeana said. He pointed with his thumb. "We packed everything and moved away. Chihuahua said we'll stay in the valley where the creek runs west into the canyon. We must find out what the army is going to do. He wants you to speak."

They stared at the big camp below, in the open, for everyone to see.

"They just sit there," Josanie said. "They know where we are, but they sit. They could have a fight with us, but they don't want that. I don't think they will come after us."

He paused. "How many were captured?"

"Fifteen," Galeana said. "My wife and my two girls, too."

"And my wife's mother," Zele said.

"How many died?"

"Cuchuta's wife." Galeana could no longer speak her name. "We buried her."

When Josanie walked down from the ridge, he saw the men and the remaining women and children standing among the horses readied for travel. Galeana's and Zele's horses were tethered to a small tree. Chaddi sat hunched before a small fire. He placed two stems of sage on the coals as Josanie approached. Josanie knelt and held his hands over the thin curl of smoke and rubbed them in it and brushed his arms, legs, chest, back, and head. He got up, and Chaddi covered the fire with sand. "Good," Chaddi said. "Now we are ready."

"Let's ride," Chihuahua said, mounting. Jaccali held the bridle of Josanie's horse out to him. They looked into each other's eyes, eyes so dark, and Josanie nodded. He boosted himself into the saddle, reined the horse about, and set off after his brother. The two rode side by side, the column forming behind them.

They rode a mere five miles on the valley floor through groves of oak trees and halted where the two forks of the creek came together and tumbled west through the Pinitos Mountains toward the Bavispe River. Josanie measured the canyon in his mind. Good places in there to hold against an army! Chihuahua pointed to a small prairie sheltered by stands of oak and pine, and they rode there and dismounted.

They sat next to each other as the horses came in. The warriors joined them in a circle, women and children at their backs. Josanie glanced at their faces. Faces of stone. He counted. Five grown women, including Jaccali; the girl Ramona; and six children. These were all who were left. Seventeen men, including Chihuahua, Chaddi, and himself, the boy Zilahe, Tsach's son, a dikohe, a warrior-to-be but not a warrior yet. Not one warrior lost, but so many women and children.

There was a heavy silence.

Finally Chihuahua spoke. "What will we do?" And after a pause: "Do we surrender to them?"

No one answered. With a low voice he continued: "We lost sixteen today, fifteen taken prisoner, one woman dead. The second time that they attacked our camp when we thought we were safe. They seem to find us wherever we go."

"Their Apache scouts found us," Josanie said quietly. "Our brothers."

"They'll find us again," Chihuahua said. "Why go on?"

Again there was silence. Insects hummed and the horses cropped grass. A bird called in the distance. These were the only sounds.

"We must have the ceremony," Chaddi said. "If we surrender, they will never let us have the ceremony. Ramona will never be a real woman. This time, when we surrender, they won't let us go back to Turkey Creek. They'll probably put the men in prison. They have done it."

There was a murmur of agreement.

"Chaddi is right," Galeana said. "My wife and my daughters are in their hands. If we give up, I might never see them again."

Again there was silence.

"We must finish what we have started," Tsach said. "First we must have the doings for Ramona. After that we go for our women and children, bring them back."

"What about the army?" Chihuahua asked.

"They won't come after us," Josanie said. "Not now. They would have come already if they wanted to. They know we are waiting for them. They won't come. They sit. They want us to give up."

And after a pause: "The soldiers don't want to fight us in these mountains. They brought the Apache scouts to do it for them."

Again they sat in silence. Jaccali watched her husband. She knew how he worked. He did not want to take the lead right away. He wanted others to speak first. Then he would speak and give direction to the talk, if necessary, and let Chihuahua sum it up.

"I brought them to us," Ures said bitterly. "I and Antonio. We should never have gone near that Mexican place, Oputo. The Mexicans told them. They came on our tracks."

He paused. "We were careful, but not careful enough."

Into the silence that lay on them like a mountain, Chihuahua spoke. "Yes," he said. "It happens that way. But when they found our camp a month ago, there were no tracks they could have followed, and they found us."

"Ures and Antonio lost their wives and children, too," Josanie said. "I should have watched over their tracks after they told me they had been near Oputo, but I didn't." He paused. "I say we go on, go way south into the mountains where they can never surprise us. I'll go after the women and children later. I'll bring them back."

"We must have the ceremony," Chaddi repeated. "Then you go after our women and children."

They sat in silence. Josanie bent forward and looked at Chaddi and nodded.

"Yes," Chihuahua said. "We will try that. I have heard what you said. Do we all agree?"

He looked from face to face. They nodded solemnly. No one spoke against it.

"It is agreed then," he said. "We let the army go away. We stay until they are gone."

They made a temporary camp and spent an unhappy night. Galeana and Zele went through the canyon and watched the army camp from the foothills. Zele reported early in the morning that the army was moving out, going south, and that the captured women and children were riding mules and were being taken north by an escort of forty Apache scouts.

In camp a brief discussion erupted about whether they should attempt a rescue. Josanie refused. "It is too dangerous," he said. "They will use our people as shields. It has happened before. We'll get all of them later when they don't expect us."

They stayed for two more days. They left the valley through the canyon the creek had clawed through the mountains, rode down through the foothills and the flats, and forded the swollen river eighteen miles north of Oputo without incident. They climbed into the mountains to the west and came down into the valley of the Moctezuma River.

They rode up to the dirt road that ran north to the desperate mud *colonia*, small colony, of Esqueda and beyond to Fronteras and the Arizona border. The road was empty. Wagon tracks on it were a week old. They swung south and followed the road along the river. Eight miles farther on, where a broad valley and a creek came in from the northwest, Galeana and Zele, a mile ahead of the column, came on six Anglo men starting a camp in a grove of cottonwood trees at the edge of the cane thicket where the creek joined the river.

Their horses were unsaddled and grazing nearby. The men stood motionless and watched the two warriors approach. Perhaps they were trying to figure out who these Indians were and what they wanted. They let them come too close and realized their mistake too late. When they went for their guns, the warriors shot four by the fireplace, then ran down the other two and took them alive.

When Josanie and the men at the head of the column arrived at a gallop, Zele was stooped over the wounded men. The two prisoners

stood in front of Galeana's rifle. One of them grinned at Josanie and
spat tobacco juice on the ground. The other man looked morosely at
the grass between his frayed boots, holding his injured right arm. Of
the four men on the ground one was dead and three were alive but
badly wounded.

These were hard, hungry men with bearded, sunburned faces.
Their smelly clothes were stained with grease, tobacco juice, and
sweat, but the tools of their profession, their weapons, were well
cared for. These were members of the lawless crowd that preyed on
victims on both sides of the border. They seemed to have come to
this place from the northwest, running from something or running
somewhere.

Josanie sat his horse and looked them over, wondering what to do
with them. There was a sudden outcry. Nitzin had been rummaging
through one of the bandits' saddlebags lying by the fireplace when
he touched human hair. He dumped the content on the ground, and
there were three scalps among dirty clothes and stolen trinkets.

Now the other saddlebags were emptied out, and more scalps
were found, a total of fourteen. Indian hair. The warriors poked at it
with sticks but did not touch it. Nitzin, who had, would have to be
purified.

They inspected the scalps closely but recognized none. Hair
ornaments might have identified them, but none was left attached, if
there had been any. Perhaps Chokonen hair. Perhaps Yaqui. Perhaps
someone else's. Chokonen or not, Indian people had been murdered
for their hair.

Josanie spoke one word. The hands of the two prisoners were
expertly bound behind their backs with rawhide. They would not be
able to loosen the thongs. They were pushed under a cottonwood
tree and were hung from one of the thick branches by their bare
feet, head down, with their own reatas. The other four were hung
the same way, the groaning wounded and the dead man. The turkey
vultures would find them soon enough. Nothing of their possessions
was touched after this, not their weapons and not the horses that
had run wild during the shooting and stood watching, a long way
off. Josanie drew a hoddentin line on the ground and ritually treated

Nitzin against ghost sickness by touching him with sage from head
to feet, each limb separately.

When the column and the remuda came up, the people saw
strange fruits on the cottonwood tree, but they hardly looked, and
Josanie and his warriors rode past and took the lead again. They saw
nothing alive for the next thirty miles. They went by the mud huts of
Cumpas and Moctezuma, where nothing moved, and camped for
the night by the dead lava field below the northern tongue of the
great black *malpaís*, badland, that reached for thirty miles along the
east bank of the Moctezuma River.

It was here that the mysterious boy, Child of the Water, the son of
White Painted Woman and Thunder, conceived when his mother
bathed in a creek, had killed a monster so frightful that its name
could not be mentioned. He had killed it on the eve of the arrival of
the ancestors of the Apaches from way north, making the new
country safe for them. The monster had been a terrible enemy, but
the boy had destroyed it with four lightning arrows given him by his
father, and its blood had covered the land and had hardened into
the broken black waves of lava stone.

In camp that night the full story of what had happened under the
cottonwood was told. The next day the Chokonen rode along the
river for forty miles, past Batuc, dead as a dead mule, to where it
joined the Yaqui, and turned east, upstream, and camped beside it,
towering mountains on both sides. One more day and they forded
the Yaqui River in high water, losing two of the horses, and climbed
east through canyons over the crest of a mountain range six
thousand feet high and dropped down into the valley of the Aros
River in the heart of the Sierra Madre. They went ten miles downstream
and made a permanent camp in a beautiful valley at the junction of
the Aros and a small mountain stream that ran in from the west.

A waterfall broke through a rocky ledge opposite the campsite and
gushed a sparkling band of water eighty feet straight down into an
emerald pool encircled by boulders and a dense green thicket of
scrub oak. Thick pine forests climbed the ranges all around. Just to
the east lay one of the major mountain chains of the Sierra Madre,
running north to south, rising to nine thousand feet and higher.

On the first day in this camp they built sweat lodges, and all of them went through the purifying heat, the men and the few women and children left, and cleansed themselves from the smell of death and a numbness ensuing from the loss of loved ones.

They had missed the American army, camped to the northwest, at the juncture of the Bavispe and Aros Rivers, by about twenty miles. At that moment in time neither camp knew where the other was.

Searching the area, they discovered remains of wickiups and camp debris on a site near the pool. They looked closely. Not Chokonen, perhaps Nednhi Apaches. They had been here a dozen years ago, or earlier. There were also some stone tools on surfaces near the creek, old-time artifacts of a much earlier people that might have liked this place also, but the Chokonen were careful not to touch them.

TWENTY-SEVEN

It happened a long time ago. Our ancestors came into this country from the north. We have always been a mountain people, and they came through the mountain chains and the high country. The places they had come from are in what you call southern Utah; there was our original homeland.

The first place in which our ancestors came together in this country was at the Hot Springs [Ojo Caliente, near the San Mateo Mountains, New Mexico], where the prairie branches out in four directions [the Plains of San Agustin], with mountains all around. It was a new country for them, and they did not know whether they were allowed to stay. All living things here were the same as they had been in the north, and the spirits were the same, those of the sky, the air, the mountains, and the lowlands, but still they did not know whether they could stay. There were other people here already, people who lived in stone houses and grew corn. They did not know what to do, and they were starving.

It was at the Hot Springs that the two spirits came to our people. They told them that they could stay, and taught them the ways of the country and how to live in it. These spirits were Iszánádle-sé, White Painted Woman, and her son, Tóbáshi-scinén, Child of the Water. Some spirits, Sun, Wind, Thunder, had watched our people and had felt pity. So they made the sacred woman for us as the spirit to watch over us and to give us life. They also made the mysterious boy to protect us against death. They must have thought that both were needed. It was Thunder who made the child through water when White Painted Woman bathed in a creek. Child of the Water made the new land safe for us by killing the monsters.

At the Hot Springs, White Painted Woman instructed us in the gotál ceremony through which a girl of our people about to become a woman is taught how to be a giver of life. And Child of the Water instructed us how to prepare ourselves to take life and how to protect ourselves against enemies.

After they had taught us they departed. White Painted Woman resides on the Yellow Mountain of the West (Mount Graham, Arizona), but she hears us when we mention her name, and she comes down whenever we hold the gotál ceremony. Child of the Water went to the sky to his father, Thunder. He hears us, too, when we mention his name, and he rides over our land in the rainclouds.

It was Thunder who set the boundary markers of our land a long time ago. By breathing he created four persons and sent them out in the four directions, as guardians. One lives on the Black Mountain of the East (Salinas Peak, San Andres Mountains, New Mexico). One lives on the Blue Mountain of the South (a peak in the Sierra Madre north of Madera, Chihuahua). One lives on the Yellow Mountain of the West (Mount Graham, Arizona). One lives on the White Mountain of the North (perhaps Cebollita Peak south of Grants, New Mexico).

From the Hot Springs, where we had been taught, our ancestors moved in bands to the east, south, and west. Sometimes we fought with the stone house people, and eventually they moved away to the south and west. When the Spanish came into our country, and the Americans much later, there were six divisions of our people, each with a number of larger and smaller bands.

The northern division people were called iyaaye. Their land was north of the Plains of San Agustin. Southeast of them were the chihenne, in the Black Range and near the Rio Grande. South of them were the chiquende, who ranged through the Mimbres Mountains into Chihuahua. West of them were the secotende, in the heart of the Mogollon Mountains. Farther west and southwest were the chokonen, in southwestern Arizona and northern Sonora. And the nednhi were south of all of these, in the northern Sierra Madre.

Once we were many. Centuries of war made us few. Our enemies were like grasshoppers, countless in numbers. At the end chokonen and chihenne were joined by the last people of the other divisions. The whites then called all of us Chiricahua—a word by other Indians (Opata) for one mountain range in Arizona. We came to call ourselves ndé, meaning, "the dead."

That was in the 1860s, 1870s, 1880s. But we did not die. Some of us are still here.

Statement to the author on Chokonen understanding of their history. Dragoon Mountains, Arizona, August 1995.

TWENTY-EIGHT

On a brilliant morning they were sitting against the rock wall above
the waterfall pool, six men and two women. They sat in a half circle,
facing the giant corridor of the valley. They gazed into the stark
beauty of the Sierra Madre, their Blue Mountains. From below and to
the right came the low rumble of the river, but the chattering of the
creek tumbling over boulders to merge with the stream was lost to
the splashing sounds of the waterfall. Above the triangle formed by
river and creek, under the pines, seven wickiups could be made out.
There were four more somewhere. Horses were grazing everywhere,
on the green flats along the river and under the trees.

They sat silently for a while, taking the view in, thinking. Finally
Chihuahua spoke. "Are we ready for the gotál?"

Seven heads nodded.

"We are ready," Chaddi said.

Chihuahua glanced at his brother, who sat with Jaccali.

"Yes," Josanie said. "We finished the camp and had four good days
of hunting. We killed enough deer and bighorn sheep to last us a
moon."

Chihuahua nodded. "Are we safe here?" He paused. "We thought
we were safe before, and they found us."

There was a pause, and then Josanie said, "We are safe."

He pointed with his lips at Galeana. "He'll close the valley
downstream." He pointed at Nitzin. "He'll close the valley
upstream." Both men nodded, looking at Chihuahua with open
faces, serious eyes.

"I'll watch over the camp," Josanie continued. "No one will come
through who doesn't belong here."

Chihuahua's blue-gray eyes searched their faces. "Yes," he said.

He addressed Jaccali. "You are taking Ramona through, then.
I'm grateful, sister." Jaccali had taken Chie's place after Chie had
been captured with the others in the attack on their camp east of
Oputo.

"Yes," she said. "I am sad that Chie is not here. She was the first asked. I wish her well wherever she is."

She paused. "I am happy to do this. I have done this before, two times."

Chihuahua nodded. "I know. Yes. When should we start?"

"I need two days to get ready," Tsach said. "I have five men for the mountain spirits. I have to prepare them. I have picked the place." He would be the instructor of the mountain spirit dancers.

Chihuahua looked at Manda, Cuchuta's mother-in-law, a widow, thirty-eight years old.

She saw. "Yes," she said. "I'll be ready then. I'll do the cooking." She laughed. "I have some help. But I need the ramada built." She looked at Josanie.

"We'll do it," he said.

Chihuahua turned to Chaddi. The medicine man would be the singer, the one in charge of the ceremony. He would be responsible for everything that happened inside the lodge; Tsach would be responsible for the dances outside the lodge.

"We could start the day after tomorrow," Chaddi said. He looked at Tsach. "That would give you the time you need."

They waited.

Chihuahua looked out into the valley, the incredible greenness. Sadly, they knew what he was thinking.

"Yes," he said finally. "Let's start the day after tomorrow."

With this decision the band chief passed authority to Chaddi. The camp had become a gotál camp, and the medicine man would direct the events of the six days, beginning with the close of the meeting. Chihuahua's obligations during this time would be that of the father of the girl who would be White Painted Woman.

Chaddi rose. It was his duty to give a formal address to explain and commemorate. He stepped forward and stood quietly for a long moment. He turned. He spoke slowly, carefully.

"It started a long time ago.

"It was not until Child of the Water was rid of all the monsters and evil things, until there were many people and the different tribes began to be seen, that the big lodge was known.

"There was a woman who had a daughter who was almost grown. It was time for her to have her first blood. Then Child of the Water and White Painted Woman showed them what to do; this good time was given to the people."

He paused.

"They gave a little feast this first day when she bled. Then, after this first day, the relatives of this girl went out and hunted and got everything together so that they could give a big feast. They did this in the fall when there was plenty of fruit and many good things of all kinds. They got a man to sing for her in the lodge. The best mountain spirit dancers were got ready. They made them, not in camp, but way off in the mountains where the spirits live. They led them in. Four spruce trees were cut down for the lodge.

"Then, when all was ready, they let many know, and they came from far places. All were invited. The celebration was held for four days. The people had a good time at the dancing.

"First came the mountain spirit dances. Child of the Water and White Painted Woman gave the people the round dance to enjoy, but this came after the mountain spirits. After that came the partner dances."

He paused.

"We are only a few this time. There used to be hundreds at a gotál. None of our people we can invite to join us and be with us and have a happy time." He swallowed. "We will be all right; we will do the best we can."

He paused again.

"I became a singer through experience. I was interested. Every chance I got I sat inside the big lodge and sang the songs. I went to the ceremony every time and learned the songs. I have been with this ceremony for over forty years and learned it from the ground up. There are many songs, but I learned them all. I went to one of the men who conducted the ceremony and asked for help. The one who is learning to become a singer gets instruction right at the ceremony. When he has enough experience, he conducts it himself. I have conducted it many times."

He paused.

"This is what I had to say."

There was a murmur of satisfaction, thankfulness, from those sitting. They had listened intently. They had felt a need. Now it had begun. The spirits were coming.

TWENTY-NINE

The gotál was in essence a new life ceremony, a ceremony of regeneration of the natural world through the medium of the pubescent girl. The four-post lodge in which the ceremony took place represented the Chiricahua world. The four posts symbolized the sacred guardians of the four corners whom Thunder had once created through his breath. The singer ritually represented Thunder himself, who, with other important spirits, had made White Painted Woman and who later had fathered with her Child of the Water. During the ceremony the pubescent girl was ritually transformed into White Painted Woman. Physically the girl wore White Painted Woman's dress and was painted white as she had been. With her, through the singer's (Thunder's) sacred songs, the natural world of plants, fruits, grasses, trees, was once again made new and plentiful as it had been in the beginning of Chiricahua time. The lodge essentially was a spirit lodge from which the miracle of transformation was enacted. Because Child of the Water had been present at the original giving of the gotál, a single warrior representing him sat on the north side of the lodge throughout the proceedings.

The mountain spirit part of the ceremony took place outside the lodge during the four nights. The mountain spirits were the protectors and keepers of animals. They represented in the gotál the animal world and themselves, a population of humanlike spirits who dwelt in the interior of mountains, dangerous but beneficial to Chiricahuas.

They appeared as masked and painted dancers, wearing elaborate crowns called "horns," reminiscent of horned game animals such as elk, deer, bighorn sheep, and antelope. Four of the dancers represented the mountain spirit chiefs in the directions east, south, west, and north and wore their specific colors; black, blue, yellow, white. The fifth dancer, the Gray One, acted as a clown who burlesqued the solemn dance movements of the mountain spirit chiefs. In Chiricahua tradition he represented a mountain spirit group that had sprung from an incestuous relationship at the beginning of the world. Evicted from the company of spirits devoted to the sacred, the clowns expressed a category of being that was opposed to the sacred structure of the universe. During ceremonies in which the gahé appeared, he made fun of the four somber representatives from the cardinal directions by burlesqueing their dances, acting toward them and the people attending with contrary behavior.

The mask of the clown inverted the normal: his face was depicted as unfinished, crazed, and ugly, with protruding eyes, ears, nose, and mouth. The face seemed to be turned inside out. As a spirit he was considered most powerful because he represented chaos standing, with a contemptuous smile, against the manifestations of sacred order. A clown's request could not be refused without serious consequences. For this reason the four gahé chiefs used the clown as go-between during their performances when they needed something from the people present.

Author's summary of the original meaning of the Chiricahua gotál ceremony. In the existing literature on the Chiricahua the gotál is usually put down as a "girl's puberty rite."

THIRTY

The morning came cold and clear. Smoke from the sweat lodges curled up and drifted along the valley with a light south wind. Before sunrise the people had all taken sweat baths, the women separately from the men. Glistening with sweat from the cleansing heat, they took dips in the icy water of the river. When the golden rim of the sun peered over the eastern mountain, and Chaddi ended the welcoming song, Jaccali returned with Ramona to Chihuahua's wickiup. There she washed the girl's hair in yucca root suds and dressed her with the special gown. They would wait there for Chaddi.

Manda went with the remaining three women to the ramada that had been built near the east bank of the river, a rectangular shelter covered on top with brush. It served as cooking shed during the ceremony. Tsach and the five men who were to represent the mountain spirits returned to the secret arbor in the pines. The men, excepting the guards upstream and downstream, gathered north of the ramada. They were unarmed and unpainted and wore no personal adornment. They were dressed in moccasin boots and clean calico breechclouts and shirts. Without headbands, their hair was hanging loosely.

Before them lay four young pine trees about thirty feet tall that had been cut the day before. The trunks lay side by side in the high grass. The lower branches had been trimmed off; only the small boughs near the top had been left on.

Chaddi walked down from his wickiup. Behind him came his seventeen-year-old grandson, Zilahe, who carried a tray basket. Both were dressed like the others but for a single eagle feather in Chaddi's hair. He held a deer-hoof rattle in his right hand. He nodded to the men when he arrived near the poles. He pointed with the rattle. The men moved; they knew what to do.

The poles were laid in clockwise fashion, butts the same distance from a central point, tops extending outward. First the east pole was

laid, then the second pole, the top pointing south. The west and
north poles followed. At the base of each a round piece of sod was
removed and a shallow hole dug.

The men stood with bowed heads when Chaddi walked to the
south side of the pole arrangement on the ground. The rattle made
clacking sounds when he shook it rhythmically in his hand. He
hummed to it briefly and stopped. Into the silence he spoke the
opening prayer of the gotál.

"When the earth had been created, there were four fir trees. When
fir trees of the four directions have been put together for me, only
then shall I go there.

"The White Painted Woman, on the earth today, her mind has
been created. Her words have been created.

"Of the four that will move together, that which lies stretched
toward the east, under it, there is good. All the people on earth share
in the good under it."

He walked to the east pole. Zilahe held the basket for him. Chaddi
sprinkled pollen over the pole from butt to top. He tied two eagle
feathers to the tip so that they would lie freely on the wind, and a
bundle of sage below them. About five feet farther down the trunk
he affixed a rawhide rope, and near the butt a bunch of grama
grass.

He walked to the south pole. "That which lies stretched toward
the south, under it, there is good. All the people on earth share in
the good under it." He sprinkled pollen along the pole's surface and
tied a bundle of sage near the top.

He repeated the procedure on the west and north poles.

He stepped away and finished the prayer. "From the east, a road
leads here. Right at the door, roads made of the rays of the sun go
out to the four directions. Long life! Its power is good.

"The White Painted Woman, on earth, her mind has been created.
This is how she breathes; this is her body; this is her strength. The
strength of all of us is made of that. Do not say that it is good for
only one day! On this earth which has become old, in the sky which
has become old, only in this place does power remain. We want it for
all of those who are children.

"White Painted Woman, do not push us toward that which is evil on the earth. White Painted Woman, all of us were created from you. Because this is so, you have brought to us the earth pollen which lies in the space between the earth and sky. This is good. We are still living in it."

The men looked to him when he ended. He nodded. The butt ends were slipped into the postholes, and the posts were swung up and held stiffly vertical.

To the sound of the deer-hoof rattle Chaddi started the first song of the ceremony, the one about the four poles of the lodge:

> Child of the Water and White Painted Woman
> have made them so.
> They have made the poles of the lodge so.
> For long life stands the black stallion.
>
> Here Child of the Water and White Painted Woman
> have made them so.
> They have made the poles of the lodge so.
> For long life stands the blue stallion.

The next stanzas were sung for the yellow pole, or stallion, of the west, and the white one of the north.

When he sang the second song, the poles were lowered until they crossed above the rawhide rope on the east pole.

> The home of the long-life lodge ceremony.
> It is the home of White Painted Woman.
> Of long life the home of White Painted Woman
> is made.
> Child of the Water has made it so.
> Child of the Water has made it so.

Chihuahua grabbed the rope hanging down and circled the conical frame, thus tying the poles together in the fork. He fastened the tail end of the rope to the west pole. The postholes were filled in.

With Chaddi's third chant oak boughs were brought up and lashed across the poles as a lodge cover. An opening was left to the east. As Chaddi stood singing and shaking the rattle, Chihuahua and Josanie, as kin closest to Ramona, dug the central firepit inside the lodge and took the sod and earth removed outside. Next the grass was trampled down and the floor of the lodge was covered with a dark green carpet of pine boughs. Wood was brought in. Chaddi knelt and placed four flat rocks painted red around the fireplace, in the cardinal directions. He lit a fire using a fire drill. He stood and sang the fire song for the sun. The ceremonial home of White Painted Woman was ready. The fire would be kept alive until the end of the ceremony.

The men stood in a row, in silence, as Chaddi walked slowly toward Chihuahua's wickiup, three hundred yards away. He was followed by Zilahe, his assistant, and by Zele, selected by Chaddi to represent Child of the Water. Because Zele impersonated the holy young man, he also wore a single eagle feather tied to his hair. Chaddi walked singing. He knelt when he reached the wickiup door. Josanie saw him reach inside, and then Ramona came out, followed by Jaccali. Slowly the five people made their way down, Chaddi leading, singing. Ramona was close behind him. The two were linked through an eagle tail feather, Chaddi holding the quill in his hand, while Ramona grasped the tip.

> They move her
> with the finest eagle feather.
> This is how White Painted Woman
> walks into her home.

Josanie watched with emotion when the slim, beautiful figure of Ramona approached. Yellow mocassin boots, a long, fringed yellow dress painted in front with the signs of sun and moon, mountains, stars, the rainbow, his wife's work. Downcast eyes in a face still that of a child but changing ever so slightly into that of a young woman, framed by shiny black hair crowned with an eagle plume. He glanced at Chihuahua by his side. A hard man, but there were tears in his eyes.

Chaddi stopped at the lodge entrance. Jaccali laid a deer hide on the grass on the southeast side, head facing east. Ramona knelt on it. Jaccali placed next to her a tray basket with ritual objects: bags with pollen, ocher, and other paints; a scratching stick; a cane-drinking tube; crystals; a bundle of grama grass.

Chaddi knelt in front of the girl. He opened a bag with pollen. He took a pinch of yellow dust and, after offering it to the four directions, painted a yellow line across Ramona's face, from cheek to cheek across the bridge of the nose. She painted Chaddi the same way. Next came Zele. She painted him, and he traced the line made by Chaddi with his right index finger across her face. With Zilahe and Jaccali it was the same. A line had formed. One by one the Chokonen stepped forward and knelt before the girl, from Ramona's father and uncle to the smallest child, Tuscas, a little over one year old. Aralos, Zele's wife, had to guide the baby's tiny index finger over Ramona's face. When Ramona painted her father and Josanie, her hand trembled a little, but her eyes smiled.

Josanie's eyes met Jaccali's when he stepped away. "You have been blessed," her eyes said. "All will be good. Watch over us."

"I watch over all of you," his eyes said to her. "All will be good."

He waited to observe the girl about to be White Painted Woman enter her lodge. Chaddi led the group in. Ramona came behind him, with Jaccali. Zilahe and Zele were next. He heard Chaddi direct Zele to the ceremonial position of Child of the Water, on the north side. Josanie knew that Chaddi would sit on the south side, near the fire. Ramona sat on the deer hide on the west side, facing the door and east. Jaccali's place was beside her. Zilahe was to the left and slightly behind his grandfather, as his helper.

Josanie heard Chaddi sing when he turned and walked away, climbing the slope toward his wickiup. He took the binocular case and one cartridge belt and unsheathed the Sharps-Borchardt. He chose a place in the shadow of an ancient oak that carried the dark furrow of a lightning strike down through the side of its weathered gray trunk. The tree had lived. From there he had a clear view of the ceremonial camp and much of the valley.

He sat at rest but alert, keen eyes missing nothing. Once, with a brief shifting of the wind, he heard Chaddi sing and knew that the chants of transformation had started, that the singer, Thunder, was making the girl Ramona over into White Painted Woman.

He listened to the sounds of the mountain and occasionally scanned the long rocky slope to the west with the binoculars. He saw some bighorn sheep and once a black bear lumbering along. Below, men stacked firewood next to the lodge, on the northeast side. In late afternoon women brought food from the ramada and took it into the lodge. Shortly thereafter the people gathered around the ramada for the first meal of the day. Magalena came up to him with a bowl of soup red and thick with venison, beans, and chile; a wooden spoon; and a canteen with cold water from the creek.

He ate and watched two men ride away with food for the sentinels. Silently the sun walked away over the sky. At dusk Tisnol and Antonio hazed the horses out of the trees and bunched them on the flat north of the creek for the night, along the overflow rivulet from the waterfall pool. He stayed in his spot until Chihuahua came, and they walked down the slope together to await the coming of the mountain spirits.

THIRTY-ONE

The black turkey gobbler, under the east,
the middle of his trail; toward us it is about to dawn.
The black turkey gobbler, the tips of his beautiful tail;
above us the dawn whitens.
The black turkey gobbler, the tips of his beautiful tail;
above us the dawn becomes yellow.
The sunbeams stream forward, dawn boys,
with shimmering shoes of yellow.
On top of the sunbeams that stream toward us
they are dancing.
At the east the rainbow moves forward;
dawn maidens
with shimmering shoes and shirts of yellow
dance over us.
Beautifully over us it is dawning.
Above us among the mountains
the herbs are becoming green.
Above us on the top of the mountains
the herbs are becoming yellow.
Above us among the mountains,
with shoes of yellow,
I go around the fruits and herbs that shimmer.
Above us among the mountains
the shimmering fruits
with shoes and shirts of yellow
are bent toward him.
On the beautiful mountains above it is daylight.

*Morning song. Fifty-third song of the gotál ceremony, recorded by
P. E. Goddard, circa 1908.*

THIRTY-TWO

The brothers went by the ramada, where Josanie left the empty bowl, the canteen, and the spoon. Men, women, and children were gathered around a fire northeast of the lodge, waiting in silence. They listened to the sounds coming from the lodge and for the sounds that would announce the coming of the mountain spirits. The fire had been made with enough wood to last until shortly after midnight. When the mountain spirits came, they would stay as long as the fire was alive. On this first night they would stay only for a few hours.

When Josanie and Chihuahua approached the lodge, they heard Chaddi singing in a low voice to the rhythmic beat of the deer-hoof rattle. There was a shuffling sound, and when they passed the entrance, they caught a glimpse of the sacred woman dancing slowly, as in a trance or a dream, the slender figure illuminated by the yellow light of the fire, looking unearthly before the dark shadows of the lodge in the yellow gown, her face and lower arms below the sleeves painted white.

No one was allowed to close the lodge opening from the direction east, but they stood transfixed for a moment and watched, caught up in the magic of the encounter, then moved quickly toward the knot of people around the fire. They stayed aside, by themselves, Josanie holding his rifle in the crook of his right arm.

Darkness fell like a curtain. From end to end the sky came ablaze with the fiery light of the stars. The burning wood crackled and threw sparks, and in the quiet Chaddi's muffled voice was heard from the lodge. Night birds called from far away. All of the people waited.

Out of the night, from the north, came a sharp, drawn-out cry. Another, closer. Chaddi's song ended. The lodge stood mute. Two more cries, closer still. From out there a clear voice spoke the arrival prayer for the gahé, the mountain spirits:

The Big Black Mountain Spirits.
The Big Blue Mountain Spirits.
The Big Yellow Mountain Spirits.
The Big White Mountain Spirits.
Their homes are in the east.
Their homes are in the south.
Their homes are in the west.
Their homes are in the north.

The thump thump of a drum, approaching from the east. The
people stepped away from the fire and formed two half circles
around it to the north and south. Three men with drums took up
positions on the west side. The clanging of wooden pendants from
the gahé horns, the swishing of moccasins in the grass. They came
into the light of the fire, Tsach leading them in, beating the drum.
He was dressed like other men, unpainted, hair hanging loosely. The
mountain spirits came one behind the other. Their crowns reached
high above Tsach, the tallest man in the band. He walked around the
fire and stood with the drummers, who fell in with their small,
handheld instruments.

Josanie and Chihuahua watched the entrance of the gahé.

The one representing the gahé of the east was the leader, followed
by those of the cardinal directions south, west, and north. They wore
moccasin boots and fringed buckskin kilts painted yellow. Their
bodies had an undercoating of greenish brown. A yellow snake was
painted on each arm. Each of the gahé had a cross painted on his
chest in the color of the direction he belonged to, black, blue,
yellow, white. Each had a white zigzag design for lightning on his
back. Long strips of red flannel were tied to their arms above the
elbows.

Each held a bow in his left hand and four arrows tipped with stone
points in his right hand. They wore yellow buckskin hoods, tied
under the chin, with the symbol for mountains, four triangles,
painted across the forehead, in the directional colors. Below it, above
the small openings for eyes and mouth, a piece of abalone shell was

suspended, to give strength and endurance. Green junipers covered the tops of the hoods where the crowns, or horns, were fastened to the hidden frames underneath.

The headdresses were essentially horizontal bars made of yucca to which vertical slats, about two feet high, were attached at both ends, with a shorter piece in the middle. From the ends of the horizontal bars four short lengths of wood painted green, the "earrings," hung down. Downy eagle feathers floated from the points of the horns and the tips of the pieces in the middle. The horns, with attached prongs, were painted with the sacred colors. On the horns the signs for mountain, sun, moon, stars, lightning, hail, and raindrops were displayed.

Fifth and last of the gahé was the clown. He came into view when the horned chiefs had begun to circle the fire. He approached with a marching step, shouldering a stick as a white soldier would a rifle on a parade ground. He wore one of the blue cavalry jackets taken in the attack on the soldier camp at Astin Spring. Underneath it he was naked but for a strip of white calico that barely covered his genitals. His body was painted white with black dots. The buckskin mask was modeled into a face with long nose and ears and a protruding mouth. It was colored white and topped with a bunch of owl feathers. He wore no crown and was barefoot.

There were bursts of laughter from the onlookers about his antics. Chihuahua elbowed his brother and smiled. The clown marched up and down, now strutting as a soldier on guard, now standing at ease, now at attention, now falling backward as if hit by a bullet, sprawling in the grass and shaking violently, rising up and running, trying to bayonet an invisible enemy but turning in fear and kneeling and begging for mercy, staging the lewd movements of a rape, drinking from an imagined bottle and acting out drunkenness. His caricature of a white soldier was vivid and bitter, but also hilarious.

The clown acted by himself and ignored the solemn dance of the gahé chiefs. They made a low whistling noise, bent slowly to the left, then to the front, then backward, until their heads were level with their waists. They spun round in full circle on the left foot, back again in a reverse circle to the right, making thrusts with bows and arrows in their hands. The crowns on their heads nodded and bobbed with their body movements, and the green earrings clanged and chattered.

Beyond the dance circle of the gahé, Tsach sang the opening song to the rhythm of the drums:

> When the earth was made,
> when the sky was made,
> when my songs were first heard,
> the holy mountain
> was standing toward me with life.

Josanie and a few of the men who knew the pitch and the texts of the song cycle hummed along with the singer:

> At the center of the sky
> the holy boy walks four ways with life.
> Just mine, my mountain became,
> standing toward me with life.
> Gahé children became,
> standing toward me with life.
>
> When the sun goes down to the earth,
> where Black Mountain lies
> with its head toward the sunrise,
> black spruce became,
> standing up with me.

This was the song for the black gahé. The songs for the other chiefs followed. There was no song for the clown. Four times the four dancers circled the fire. They moved in single file toward the lodge of White Painted Woman. First the black gahé, then the others, clasped the east pole of the structure and blessed it. They moved in clockwise fashion, touching each of the four poles and praying. When they finished on the north side, they walked past the fire and the people standing there and vanished in the darkness, the clown remaining behind, looking puzzled, frightened, more and more agitated, and finally rushing after them.

The stiff lines of the attending people broke up. There was talking with hushed voices. The two little children, Chino and Tuscas, were wrapped in blankets and bedded down in the grass by Aralos, Tuscas's mother. Chino's mother had been captured by soldiers in the attack on Chihuahua's camp in the Mogollon Mountains on May 24.

"That clown is good," Chihuahua remarked.

"Yes," Josanie said, "I've not seen anyone do it that way before. It is good."

They sat down in the grass and waited. After some time the drums called out again and the gahé returned. The clown went on with his mime as before, adding new sketches to his frolic, never uttering a sound, oblivious to the drums and the songs. Four times cycles of four songs were sung, with alternating tempo to which the gahé responded by changing their dance steps. In between were periods without songs during which only the drums inspired and guided the dancers.

The performances, spaced with intervals to let the dancers rest somewhere in the darkness, continued until after midnight, when the fire burned down. There was a parting song, and with it the five colorful figures were swallowed by the night. Four cries, as the ones that had announced the coming, came through the dark from farther and farther away, announcing the leaving. Suddenly the night air felt cold. Tsach had disappeared after the parting song, and people walked away to their wickiups.

Chihuahua looked at the silent lodge. The weak yellow glow of the fire inside cast no shadow.

"They are asleep," he said. "The day went well."

Josanie touched his arm. He thought of Jaccali. Nearby, yet in another world.

THIRTY-THREE

In the east,
the White Painted Woman,
she is walking with the pollen
of dawn.
In the south,
she is walking with
the sun's tassels.
Long life!
From this there is goodness.
In the west,
when the pollen of abalone shell
moves with her,
there is goodness.
Long life!
In the north,
the White Painted Woman,
she is looking at us.
She is happy.

*Song of the gotál ceremony, recorded by Jules Henry
in 1930.*

THIRTY-FOUR

The fifth morning, the last morning of the gotál, came. The gahé had danced the night through, transferring their power to White Painted Woman in the lodge. In the pale gray of first light the fire flickered and died and the mountain spirits left. The people were gathered in a tight group southeast of the lodge.

This was the coming out. There was a final song inside, and then White Painted Woman stepped out and stood, facing east. Jaccali placed the deer hide on the ground, its head to the east, about thirty feet from the lodge. The sacred woman went forward and stood on it. She was still painted white, although some of the paint had been sweated off in the dancing. Chaddi came to stand on her right. The white hair on top of his head, around the eagle feather, had been sprinkled with yellow pollen. Jaccali took her place on the left. Behind them were Zele, representing Child of the Water, and Zilahe. These two and Jaccali had been painted with a yellow and a red line across their cheekbones and bridge of the nose.

They stood in silence as the eastern sky became light. Chaddi turned to Zilahe, and he came forward, holding the tray basket. Chaddi handed him the rattle and dipped his right index finger in red paint, holding it up. He drew a sun symbol on the palm of his left hand in red ocher and yellow pollen and started the "red paint song" with a low voice:

> Now I will make long life
> with the sun's rays.
> Now I will make long life
> with the sun's pointed rays.
> I will make peaks extending outward.
> The rays of the sun and long life
> are made of pollen.
> The points of the sun and long life
> are made of pollen.

> The rays of the sun and long life
> are made of red paint.

The first shafts of sunlight heaved over the mountain rim. Chaddi greeted them by holding the palm of his right hand high. He stepped in front of the sacred woman. He touched the painted palm to her body, pressing it on, circling her head clockwise and rubbing it over her head as the rays of the sun shone upon them. He sang:

> The sun, rising,
> says, my grandchild.

The White Painted Woman knelt before him. With a grama grass brush he painted her with white clay for the last time, first the right side, then the left side of her face, next her right arm below the sleeve of the yellow gown, and her left arm. She rose and stepped to the left of the deer hide.

The people formed in a single line. Chihuahua came first, then Josanie, Ramona's kin, then all Chokonen present, down to the smallest child. Each was marked by Chaddi with a single white dot on the forehead. Little Tuscas, on his mother's arm at the end of the line, started to cry when Chaddi touched his head with the brush. Aralos held him close and calmed him quickly. She smiled shyly and moved away.

Chaddi knelt and painted a trail on the deer hide with red ocher and pollen, four footprints, west to east. He stood up and took the rattle from Zilahe. Jaccali led White Painted Woman around the deer hide and pointed to her right foot. She placed it on the first footprint. There were four steps, and for each Chaddi sang the closing songs of the ceremony, shaking the rattle. There were about three hundred songs to the gotál, and these were the last ones.

> I come to White Painted Woman.
> Through a long life I come to her.
> I come to her through her blessing.
> I come to her through her help.
> I come to her through all her different fruits.
> Through the long life she grants

I come to her.
Through this holy truth she lives.

I am about to sing this song of yours,
the song of long life.
Sun, I stand here on earth with your song.
Moon, I have come in with your song.

White Painted Woman's power emerges.
Her power for sleep.
White Painted Woman carries this woman.
She carries her through long life.
She carries her through abundance.
She carries her to old age.
She carries her to peaceful sleep.

You have started out on the good earth.
You have started out with good moccasins.
With moccasin strings of the rainbow
you have started out.
With moccasin strings of the sun's rays
you have started out.
In the midst of plenty
you have started out.

He stood still when he ended, tears streaming down his face.
Jaccali gently took the sacred woman by her hand and nudged her.
She ran out toward the east, her arms flung wide. She was
embracing the world, letting the power of White Painted Woman
flow out of her to make the world new again. Next she ran south,
west, and north. She returned to Chaddi's side. The old man was still
wiping his eyes, but he smiled at her.

He brushed Zele and Zilahe off with sage, releasing them from the
condition of having been touched by the sacred. He moved off,
followed by the two women. He returned them to Chihuahua's
wickiup, where they would remain for another four days. The White

Painted Woman would live in this Chokonen camp in person, surrounded by everyday life, and bless it through her presence. After the four days Chaddi would brush both women off and Jaccali would strip Ramona of the ceremonial gown and wash her in yucca root suds to clean off the gotál paint.

After the three had left the site of the ceremony, men removed the oak boughs from the lodge frame but left the four poles standing. The people gathered around the ramada and waited for Chaddi. He came and blessed food and water containers with a pollen cross, and the people ate. Food was brought up to Chihuahua's wickiup for the two women. They broke their fast. They had not eaten during the last two days of the ceremony, although they had been allowed to take water through the cane-drinking tube.

Thunderheads moved up in the afternoon. In the evening heavy rainfall pounded the camp, male rain. It confirmed that the gotál had been done right, that the spirits were pleased.

THIRTY-FIVE

The four troops 4th Cavalry from Fort Huachuca left on the fifth (of July) for their stations on the border and will be placed at Copper Canyon, Song Mountain, Solomon's Springs and Mud Springs. I expect on the ninth to send four more troops of the 4th. Cavalry from here, to be stationed at Willow Springs, San Bernardino, Skeleton Canyon and Guadelupe Canyon. Two companies of the 10th. Infantry are en-route to San Luis Pass. Three troops 6th. Cavalry left Separ today for the line in New Mexico. The stations have been selected with the greatest care so as to not only cover all known watering places, but also to give open country between these stations and the line. With each detachment of troops there will be stationed (five) Indian scouts who are to be used exclusively in watching and scouting in advance of line to prevent as nearly as possible the approach of any hostiles without the troops being notified. The dispositions will cover the line as thoroughly as possible from the Rio Grande as far west as it is thought probable the Indians will attempt to recross into the United States.

In rear of the advance line I shall place the troops of the 10th. Cavalry . . . to intercept parties should they succeed in sneaking through the first line. . . . These dispositions are the best that can be made, in my judgment. . . . I have given orders for the search in the Sierra Madre to be most vigorous and to pursue any party which may attempt to return so closely as to endeavor to drive them towards the troops and force them to cross in daylight.

Report on the dispositions of troops along the border. General George Crook, commanding officer of the Department of Arizona, July 7, 1885.

THIRTY-SIX

On a morning when the rains let up Zele walked to Chaddi's wickiup and sat down in front of the entrance. He sat quietly. The cool air was sweet with the smell of pines and grasses and flowers. From inside the wickiup came the sound of a blanket being tossed aside. Chaddi emerged, his white hair tussled from sleep, and stood and looked at the warrior with probing eyes.

Zele did not stir. His eyes were cast down. The precious rifle he had taken in Dixie Canyon lay across his knees, with a tan cartridge belt full of shells.

Chaddi sat down opposite him. He waited. Finally he spoke.

"You want to see me? Tell me; I hear."

"This ceremony," Zele began haltingly. "You did me and my family great honor by putting me in the place of Child of the Water. I did not deserve it. There were others more qualified."

He paused. "I am grateful. I am happy that the gotál turned out good. I did nothing. You did everything, you and the girl. And Jaccali."

Chaddi smiled. "The gahé, they were good, too."

He paused. "Everyone did well."

"I want to give you this rifle," Zele said. "I got it on the raid west. It is a good rifle. I want you to have it."

He held the rifle out to Chaddi with both hands, looking for the first time into the medicine man's eyes.

"Please take it."

Chaddi was puzzled. He raised his eyebrows in a silent question. Now it burst out of Zele.

"I lost no one. My wife, Aralos, my little boy, Tuscas . . . they are still with me. Everyone else lost someone killed or taken prisoner. My mother is safe at Turkey Creek. My younger brother is there, too. Aralos's parents, her sister. I still have my family. No one else has. I am not a witch."

Chaddi sat straight up, surprised. He plucked a leaf of grass and stretched it around his left index finger.

"No, you are not," he said slowly, gently. "You have nothing to do with these bad things. They happened that way. We have too many enemies. They come at us from everywhere. You did what you could. We all did. Don't feel bad. I lost my wife, a prisoner. It's not your fault; it's not my fault."

There was a silence. A big yellow tiger swallowtail butterfly circled around them and rested for a moment on a stick protruding from above the wickiup door.

"You lost a sister in that fight in the arroyo with the Mexicans, three years ago, didn't you? I lost a son there. They cut him up badly."

Chaddi shook his head. "We cold not help it. No one can say otherwise."

He swallowed. "We all have lost people. It doesn't matter how hard we fight."

"I still want you to have the rifle," Zele said. "For everything. I ask you to pray for me."

Chaddi looked at the young man, twenty years old, already a known warrior. He understood. He nodded. He reached out and accepted the rifle. He cradled it. He looked at the shiny Winchester, the silver nameplate, the smooth stock of deeply grained wood, the scroll engraving on the blue metal. He stroked the length of the rifle with his right hand, feeling the expert fit of metal and wood. This was a gift that hurt giving, the only gift that counts.

He cleared his throat.

"I thank you. I take your gift. This is a real good thing you are doing. I will pray for you and the ones in your family."

He paused.

"I am not a warrior anymore. I was one, like you are. But for many years now I have been listening to the voices of the spirits more than I have listened to the voices of men. I am not like Nana. He is older than I and still a great man of war. I have concerned myself with the spirit world. Sometimes I don't know if I'm still here or in the spirit world."

He paused.

"But then the soldiers remind me that I am still here."

A brief smile came over his face.

"Chihuahua, Josanie . . . they wanted to give me things. Much. But I don't need anything. I said so. What I did worked out good. I am happy for that. I did it for Ramona and for all of us, for myself, too. For the ones who were not here . . . and for the ones who can never be with us again. Not in this place."

He paused.

"What I did wasn't much. There are many who could have done this. You are one of the men who kept us alive. I know about you. Without you we would not be here, in this valley."

He looked toward the east edge of the valley where the great fiery ball of the sun began sliding over the crags.

"You gave me this rifle. I give it back to you with my blessing. The spirits be with you! You will do much with it that I can no longer do."

He paused.

"I am grateful for the gift. You have made my heart feel happy. The spirits have seen you, heard you. Take the rifle again and protect us with it."

He handed the rifle to Zele, who hesitated but then gripped it firmly.

Chaddi touched his arm. "I am pleased that I can say: that great rifle of Zele's—I owned it once. It was mine." He paused. "That is enough for me."

He looked toward the river and the empty ramada and the four-post frame of the gotál lodge.

"There is something you could do for me. My grandson, Zilahe. He is dikohe. You know. He has been on one war trail but on none since we left Turkey Creek."

He paused.

"He has to go on the war trail three more times before he is a warrior and a man. You know all about that. I want you to prepare him and take him with you on the next three raids, teach him what he must know, watch over him."

They looked at each other, the young man and the old medicine man.

"There are so many others knowing more. . . ." Zele stuttered. Chaddi made a gesture to cut him off. He tried to get up and was helped by Zele. Finally he stood, rubbing his knees.

"You I want," Chaddi said. "Go and see Zilahe. Tell him." He turned slowly and bent down and slipped back into the wickiup.

THIRTY-SEVEN

General Crook sent two columns into Mexico to destroy or capture the Chiricahua and Warms Springs Apaches in the Sierra Madre. The first, under Captain Emmet Crawford, was ordered south on June 11; the second, under Captain Wirt Davis, was ordered south on July 13.

Roster of Troops, Department of Arizona. Operating Against Hostile Chiricahuas July 14, 1885, In the Sierra Madre: Captain Emmet Crawford, Troop G, 3rd Cavalry, commanding. Captain H. M. Kendall, Troop A, 6th Cavalry, commanding troop. First Lieutenant Robert Hanna, Troop A, 6th Cavalry, with troop. First Lieutenant C. P. Egan, assistant surgeon, medical officer. Second Lieutenant Britton Davis, Troop L, 3rd Cavalry, commanding Indian scouts. Second Lieutenant C. P. Elliott, Troop H, 4th Cavalry, commanding Indian scouts. Troop A, 6th Cavalry. 92 Indian scouts. Two pack trains. Al Sieber, Chief of Scouts. Mickey Free, interpreter.

Captain Wirt Davis, Troop F, 4th Cavalry, commanding. First Lieutenant H. P. Birmingham, assistant surgeon, medical officer. First Lieutenant M. W. Day, 9th Cavalry, commanding Indian scouts. Second Lieutenant R. D. Walsh, Troop B, 4th Cavalry, commanding Indian scouts. Troop F, 4th Cavalry. 100 Indian scouts. Two pack trains. G. B. Roberts, Chief of Scouts. Frank Leslie, Chief of Scouts.

THIRTY-EIGHT

Chihuahua had a new ramada built on a stretch of flat ground at the edge of the camp. It was covered on top and on the south and west sides with hides and canvas to keep it relatively dry from the monsoon rains coming through the mountains on their way north. There were only six women left, including Ramona, and they cooked in the ramada twice a day for seventeen men and eight children. They ate their meals together, sitting on logs around the fires. In the evenings they stayed there until dark, talking, the captured women and children heavy on their minds. It was not yet time to go north to Fort Apache to bring them back. The ground was soggy everywhere, and they would leave a trail as easy to follow as a railroad track.

After breakfast one morning on a clear day, as white clouds drifted slowly, unthreateningly across the deep blue of the sky, Josanie went to the river and brought two horses up. He had tied a soft hobble over their lower jaws by an ordinary double knot and held the makeshift bridle for Jaccali. She mounted the second horse, and they rode bareback toward the creek and the waterfall, guiding the horses with their thighs. Josanie had his weapons with him, constant companions. They rode slowly, letting the horses pick their way among boulders and around bracken and scrub oak.

The creek ran high from the rains, gushing through its rocky bed. The horses shied and refused to cross, but the riders gave them time and encouraged them with soft, reassuring voices, stroking their necks, and finally they went into the discolored waters and bucked through and up to the higher ground on the other side. They went into the scrub oak thicket on a narrow game trail. The amount of water falling in from the high rock wall had doubled, and the overflow from the pool ran swiftly through the boulder screen. The emerald color of the pool had changed to a light brown. Josanie and Jaccali dismounted and led the horses to a patch of grass and tied the long rawhide bridles loosely to tree branches.

Josanie walked around the pool, looking down, searching for signs. Doing so had become part of life. A brown and light brown banded gopher snake slipped across his path and disappeared. He stopped and spoke the ancient phrase of respect. "My mother's father, don't bother us. Go where we can see you. Keep out of our paths." He stepped carefully over the snake's trail and went on. In soft gravel and sand near the rock wall, on the east side of the pool, he found the pug marks of a jaguar. He knelt and measured them. Most probably they had been made by a young female. He looked around. From the number of tracks in this spot it appeared that she came here often to drink. No one in camp had yet seen her, so it was clear that she kept away from people and the horse herd.

Josanie took pollen from the pouch on his belt and put four pinches in one of the pug marks. Again he used a kinship term, speaking in the secret language of Chokonen hunters. "My mother's mother, don't bother us. Go your way in peace. We mean no harm." He moved on and came across the remains of an old deer kill and tracks of deer, turkey, and raccoon.

Jaccali had watched him. He walked up and touched her shoulder. "We are safe here." She nodded with a smile. He laid the cartridge belt on the cusp of a boulder and propped the rifle against it. He turned and undressed and made a neat pile of his clothing and the moccasin boots. He climbed over the boulder and slid into the cold water. He felt his way over gravel and around two boulders hidden beneath the surface and reached the deep part of the pool where the falling waters struck.

He swam on his back in front of the transparent curtain of water and saw Jaccali undress but turned his face when she stepped naked into the pool. He looked at her when she was in the water and pointed to the hidden obstacles. She moved toward him and swam, the shiny black hair flowing behind her. "Medicine woman of mine," he thought, his eyes laughing. He dove until he touched the bottom, then circled underwater to the back of the waterfall curtain and came up to the surface. He trod water and looked but did not see her. Suddenly he felt her hand on his right leg, and she came up beside him. Laughing, she blew water in his face, and he lunged and put his arms around her.

They played in the pool as if they were alone in the world, their bodies touching, wheeling free and touching again, diving, splashing. They felt their flesh come together and the surge of a sexual drive that had been forced to lie dormant for months, for all the time since the breakout.

Josanie fumbled with his erection, but Jaccali shook her head and led the way to the boulder ring and the green thicket behind it. They found a grassy place hidden among the oaks, near the horses, and there they made love. One hummingbird with a black throat and one with a rufous back saw them, as did the horses and a parrot with red and blue feathers. Perhaps the spirits, too, saw them, but no one else did. Afterward they lay on their backs, happy and still, side by side, looking through branches above them into the sparkling sky. The valley was awash in sunlight, the sun's golden disk edging toward midday.

Josanie had his eyes closed.

"You want to sleep?" Jaccali asked.

He shook his head. "No. I am tired, but I don't want to sleep."

He lay quiet for a while. "I am tired of the constant war. It is not over. Maybe it will never be over, or it will be over when we are dead."

He paused.

"I have to go up and bring the women and children back. And our son. We can't stay here without them."

Jaccali turned and bent over him, her right breast resting on the side of his chest. She stroked his hard, brown body over belly and chest, softly, with her fingernails.

"Soon. Not today," she said. "I know you will bring them to us. Perhaps we can live here for all time. There are many places in these mountains where they will never find us."

She feared for him. How would she live without him? She knew she was speaking a lie born from a desperate hope, but this was not the time to face the truth.

THIRTY-NINE

In the little town of Nacori I met a curious state of affairs. The population was 313 souls; but of these only fifteen were adult males. Every family had lost one or more members at the hands of the Apache.

Here also I first heard the legend of Toyopa. This mine was said to have been of such wonderful richness that blocks of silver taken from it had to be cut into several pieces so that mules could carry them to the seacoast for shipment to Spain. My informant, the white-haired Presidente, a man of over eighty years of age, told me that his grandfather, who also had lived to be a very old man, had worked in the mine as a boy, and that it was in a mountain range the Presidente pointed out to the east of Nacori.

The Apache attacked the place one day when the men were nearly all away at a fiesta in one of the river towns, killed everyone in the camp, destroyed the buildings, and blew up the entrance to the mine. A hundred years went by with no force in the country strong enough to conquer the Apache and the mine had never been found.

Those who would seek, as have hundreds before them, the lost mine of Toyopa, should bear in mind the statement of the old Presidente's grandfather: "Here in Nacori, where we stand, on a still night one could hear the dogs bark and the church bell ring in Toyopa."

Finding no sign of hostiles in the vicinity of Nacori, we moved north again along the Bavispe River bottom until Crawford decided to try the main Sierra Madre range to the east of us. Another expedition, similarly constituted of a small troop of cavalry, a pack train, and about thirty Apache scouts, was now in Mexico and supposed to be operating east of us; the whole under Major Wirt Davis, with Lieutenant M. W. Day in command of the scouts; but we had seen nothing of them.

Climbing to the crest of the Sierra Madre was no picnic. It took two days from daylight to dark each day. Mules fell and rolled down the mountain slopes, killing themselves and destroying their loads.

A week on the crest and eastern slopes of the Sierra Madre brought no results except to exhaust our rations. Returning to the range of hills in the bend of the Bavispe, where there was much better grass than on the main mountain, we went into camp and sent the trains back for more supplies. During the two weeks' wait for the return of the trains Sieber and I with a dozen or fifteen scouts went south again to the Aros River above its junction with the Bavispe. Here we sent some of the scouts as far south of the Aros as they would go in fear of meeting Mexican troops, but no trail of the hostiles was found.

From the memoir of Lieutenant Britton Davis, Third Cavalry.

FORTY

After another week, near the end of July, the wind currents shifted and the stream of the monsoon clouds took a more westerly course, passing north well west of the Sierra Madre. In camp the Chokonen waited a few more days for the sun to dry the land. Josanie decided the Chokonen would visit Nacori to trade for vegetable food supplies and to see about the American army. The little stone and adobe town on the Arroyo Nacori Chico, tucked away in the western vastness of the Sierra Madre, had survived a century of conflict by trading with Chiricahuas and trading information on them to Mexican authorities. No love was lost between the two parties, but there was a truce; the Chiricahuas needed trade, and the town had to accommodate them or die.

Josanie led the party of ten. They took two horses to trade and two mules with pack saddles, *aparejos*, to carry loads back. They left at sunup on August 2. They rode single file. Half a mile ahead of Josanie and the rest of the men rode Galeana and Zele, and with them was Zilahe. This was not a raid, and Zilahe was not along as a dikohe. Since Zele had agreed to be responsible for Zilahe, the boy had hardly left his side. Josanie was followed by Tuerto, Nalgee, Nitzin, Kezinne, Bish, and Tisnol, the latter two bringing up the rear with the two spare horses and the mules. The men, as always, were heavily armed but not painted. War paint would throw the people of Nacori into a tizzy. Tuerto was chosen to be with the party because he spoke Spanish fluently.

He had been captured in an attack on one of Cochise's Chokonen bands at Espia Hill, near Janos, in 1866, during which his parents had been killed. Twelve years old, his life was spared, and he was sold to a hacienda south of Chihuahua City. He became a vaquero, and when his patron's mother, who had been good to him, died, he rode away. He was twenty-four and met up with Juh's band of Nednhi in the Sierra Madre. When Juh surrendered to American authorities in January 1880, Tuerto went with the Nednhi to the San Carlos

Reservation, where he met the girl Naqui of Chihuahua's band. He married her and remained with the band when the Nednhi fled the reservation six months later. His wife and their little son, Balin, were among those captured on June 23. He was a mature and experienced man.

The Aros River, swift and aquamarine, ran north through green mountains to meet, forty miles northwest of the camp, with the Bavispe River coming south. There the two streams became the Yaqui River, which ran south through the rugged mountains of the Yaqui people and emptied into the Gulf of California. The Yaquis fought the Spanish and Mexicans through the centuries as relentlessly as the Apaches did farther north and east. The greatest fear of the intruders had always been that the two would join forces, but it never happened; the two cultures were too different.

Josanie's party rode silently along the Aros, sometimes crossing and crossing back, staying on the trail, barely visible, made by the advance riders. They evaded stretches of sand and soft gravel but looked them over in passing, searching for tracks. Imprinted there were the marks of the animal life of the mountains. Over a distance of ten miles, to the mouth of the Arroyo El Riito, they saw among many tracks the prints of black bears, of a male grizzly, a wolf pack, two ocelots, and two pumas. There were antlers on the sand and white bones, twice the rib cage and vertebrae of deer. Seven miles farther on they found the advance riders dismounted and walking slowly, searching the ground.

"Ponies," Galeana said. "A small bunch, ten, maybe twelve."

Josanie dismounted and studied the hoofprints.

"Five days ago, maybe," Galeana said. "After the rains. They came up the river. We checked already. They went there." He pointed. "An old camp. They didn't go farther than that. They went back downriver."

"Nednhi camp, Juh's," Tuerto said. "I have been here with them a couple of years ago. We camped here in the summer before Juh went to the San Carlos."

Two hundred yards away above the riverbed, on a section of flat ground below the mountain slope, were the remains of a *ranchería*, a camp, partly hidden by brush and small pines. The horse tracks led there, and the men followed them. Few of the fragile wickiup frames were still standing. Most had been torn by wind, snow, and rains, the poles and limbs tossed around. On a sandbar below the camp horses had been bunched and tethered while the party had searched the area and rested.

"A scouting party," Josanie said. "If they had gone on, they would have found our camp."

There was a silence.

"They are not Tarahumara," Tuerto said. "The Tarahumaras are way south and have few horses."

"Yes," Galeana said. "They are Apache scouts with the army, or they are Geronimo's men."

Josanie nodded.

"Yes. We haven't seen anything of Geronimo and Naiche and the others. They must be around here somewhere. We'll find out in Nacori."

They went back to their horses and mounted and rode on. Galeana, Zele, and Zilahe took the point again, now only two hundred yards ahead of the main body. The tracks left by the unknown party were easy to follow. Eight miles more and they reached the gash in the mountains that was the Arroyo Nacori Chico, east of the Aros, and the small stream running down through it. The horse tracks passed it and continued downstream. But now they found the trail of the American army. It had come upstream on the Aros and entered the arroyo toward Nacori.

The trail was deep and wide, made by many horses and mules. It had been only partly washed away by the heavy rains of the previous weeks. They sat their horses and looked at it.

"They have come before the rains," Galeana said.

"When we were holding the gotál," Josanie said bitterly.

"Yes," Galeana said. "But they could not have taken us by surprise this time."

Josanie nodded. "They have gone up to Nacori but not come back." Then he added, "They are either at Nacori, or they went from Nacori into the mountains."

He paused.

"Who, then, are these other men? They ignored the army trail. They must know more than we do. Has the army circled back, or are they Geronimo's men?"

He paused again.

"Let's ride to Nacori. Then we will know."

They turned into the arroyo and rode on the cold army trail. They discovered no sign that anyone had come this way since. They rode slowly on the upward slope of the valley to spare the horses and made the eighteen miles from the river to Nacori in three hours. They halted close to a mile outside the town and took the horses and mules to a safe place by a pothole in a dry creekbed behind a pine-covered ridge.

From the height of the ridge they scanned the town through binoculars. In the afternoon sun sat a little stone church with two towers on a rise in the middle of a cluster of houses. The stream ran along the edge of it. Sheds, *carretas*, a number of pole corrals for cattle, sheep, and mules, fences that did not seem to keep anything in. Huts distances away from the town, gardens with tall corn and low greens and ditches sucking water from the creek. But for two men working outside on something, the town looked deserted or asleep, the way it had always looked. There was no hint of an army camp.

They made a cold camp in the pines behind the ridge and rode out before sunrise. Galeana, Zele, and Zilahe circled the town and rode in from the north when Josanie and his men entered from the south. They rode slowly through the narrow streets, weary, rifles ready, and halted in the dusty little plaza in front of the church. It looked as if it had been crumbling for a long time. There was a *penitente* cross above the stairs that led to the portal. The community was too poor to afford a permanent priest, so the penitente brotherhood had taken over Catholic services. Half the warriors watched the windows and roofs of houses.

Josanie signaled Tuerto and he called out for the presidente, the mayor, to come forward. An old white-haired man stepped from one of the stone houses, a rainbow-hued serape flung over his shoulders, a black wooden staff with a silver knob in his right hand. He was sharp-eyed and bore himself with dignity. He approached Josanie without hesitation. Slowly people began to gather in the streets. Most of the women and children squatted on the flat roofs of adobe houses, the women covering themselves with serapes so that only their eyes showed.

"Ask him if he knows who I am," Josanie said.

Tuerto spoke in Spanish and the old man nodded three times. "Ulzanna," he said.

Josanie smiled. "Yes, some call me by that name."

With Tuerto interpreting, Josanie continued: "We know each other. I have been in this town many times, always in peace. I have come in peace again. I'm not taking from you. I have come to trade two horses for supplies. We need cornmeal, beans, chile."

He signaled to Bish and Tisnol, and they rode forward and dropped the halters of the spare horses at the old man's feet. He bent and took hold of them, the horses shifting sullenly from foot to foot in the dust, lifting and ducking their heads, and the old man called and two men edged forward and tied the horses to the rail of the stairs leading to the church.

The old man waited, staring at the ground. Finally he gave orders with a calm voice, and some of the Mexican men ran and returned with bags over their shoulders and sat them on the ground. They hastened away and the old man pointed to the pile. "Cornmeal," Tuerto interpreted. "Pinto beans. Chile."

He stepped forward and grabbed Josanie's stirrup, looking up, searching the warrior's face. There was a note of fear in his voice when he spoke.

"He says they are short of food themselves. The Americans took some of their food away. He says he can give you no more. The new harvest is not ready yet."

Josanie made a comforting gesture with his right hand. The old man stepped back and stood, waiting.

"It is good," Josanie said. The bags held about three hundred pounds of food.

The old man called out, and some Mexican men came forward and divided the bags and expertly packed the mules' aparejos and walked clear.

"Ask him about the American army," Josanie said.

Tuerto talked in Spanish and the old man answered at length, pointing north once.

"He says they came here three to four weeks ago, looking for you," Tuerto said. "They stayed for a few days. They went north into the mountains. He has not heard of them since then."

After a pause, Tuerto added, "I think he speaks the truth."

"Ask him if he has seen any Apaches or heard of Apaches near here," Josanie asked.

Tuerto again spoke to the old man, but he shook his head. He spoke and shrugged his shoulders.

"He has not seen Apaches and has not heard of them," Tuerto said. "The Americans did not know, either. They were looking but knew nothing."

Josanie nodded. He looked into the old man's eyes. He raised his hand in greeting. He turned the horse and rode out from the plaza, the warriors following, the mules lumbering behind. He knew that the old man would report their visit if he could, if anyone was eager to listen. It could not be helped.

They made forty miles and camped for the night. When the stars came out, they heard wolves call on the mountain to the northeast. They reached their camp by the waterfall before noon the following day. They still wondered who the mysterious riders were who had come as far south as Juh's old ranchería and turned back.

FORTY-ONE

Late in July a band of ten or twelve Indians, who had been hiding in the New Mexico mountains, swooped on the border from the north, driving forty or more head of stolen horses. [Captains] Charles Hatfield's and Leonard Wood's command took up the chase. A citizen named Tevis went with them some distance, leaving the column sixty miles deep in old Mexico on July 28 and reporting, on his return, that the command was traveling swiftly on a fresh trail and had forced the enemy to drop the stolen horses, some broken down and ruined. Wood's scouts played out and came back. Fortunately Hatfield's were mounted and are with the command.

Dan L. Thrapp, from a report by Lieutenant Colonel George Alexander Forsyth, Fort Huachuca, to General George Crook, July 30, 1885.

FORTY-TWO

On his post underneath a twisted pine Galeana closed his eyes for a moment, and when he opened them again, two riders were there. They had appeared around a bend of the narrow valley and were coming upstream along the river on the tracks Josanie's party had left on the visit to Nacori four days before.

Galeana raised the binoculars to his eyes. Two men with white headbands and white calico shirts and breechclouts, high moccasin boots. Their hair was long, uncut; they were not in mourning. They were not painted and held Winchesters in the crooks of their left arms. On the right sides of the horses, behind the saddles, hung Springfield carbines in leather sockets. They led the horses with knees and thighs, lariats hanging loose. They rode slowly, watching the ground and the rocky slopes before them.

He looked, and when they were four hundred yards away and he could see their faces clearly, he recognized them. The first rider was Horache, Nana's son-in-law. The second one was Chaha, his brother. Galeana got up from his hiding place and stepped into the open on a wide boulder fifteen feet above the sandbars of the river. He raised his arm and shouted the Chokonen war cry. The two Chihenne reined their hoses in and looked. Finally Horache raised his rifle and the riders continued, watchful, always concerned about a trap.

Galeana climbed down behind the screen of a ridge and went to his horse, hidden by another bend of the river. He mounted and rode out to meet them. They recognized him and came up and brought the horses to a halt. The three men briefly raised their hands, looking each other over.

"We are glad you came," Galeana said. "Where is Nana?"

Horache, a slim, muscular man with a strong face, thirty-eight years old, pointed over his shoulder with a flick of his thumb. "Behind us." And after a pause: "Where is your camp?"

"Two miles this way," Galeana said. He turned his head sideways. "We wondered where you were."

"We wondered where you were, too," Horache said. "We tried Nacori and found your trail. Then it was easy."

"You went to Nacori?" Galeana asked.

"No, we rode around it. We came through the mountains and found the army trail. We caught a Mexican who was in a hurry. We shot him. Before he died, he told us that you had been in Nacori."

He paused.

"We think he was going to tell someone about you. He sure would have told about us. We couldn't let him get away. We went around Nacori and came on your trail."

"Have you seen Naiche and Geronimo and them?" Galeana asked.

"No. We know nothing of them. We had a rough time getting here. There are American armies all over. You better move your camp. Someone will come looking for you, and for us, too."

"We have come from the Black Range ten days ago," Chaha said. Six years younger than his brother, he was slightly heavier, with a bullet scar across his left cheekbone. "There was one army behind us all the way to Casas Grandes. They had plenty of Apache scouts. We lost them in the mountains."

There was a pause, and then Galeana pointed with his chin. The two Chihenne turned around in their saddles. Way down around the bend came a bunch of horses and riders, the horses yellow and brown, the riders white dots.

"My father-in-law," Horache said with a rare smile. "The old man of the mountains, the wizard."

The three horsemen watched as the little band approached unhurriedly. Nana and the warrior Nalze were in the lead. Behind rode six women leading a number of packhorses. Three older children were also mounted. About a dozen spare horses followed, one warrior riding drag. Nana wore a blue army captain's jacket over his shirt and his old beaded war cap. The women looked pretty, long black hair floating over long white skirts and blouses, necklaces of turquoise and beads.

Nana's wrinkled face showed a broad smile, the obsidian eyes sharp as a fox's. He shifted the Springfield rifle that lay across his saddle and greeted Galeana with a raised hand. Nana looked fondly at Galeana's hard face and observed that his hair was cut short; Nana knew then that Galeana had suffered a personal loss.

Next to him, Nalze had a long lance tucked under his left leg along the horse's flank, a Henry repeater across his left elbow, and a Springfield carbine in a leather socket hanging down behind his right leg. The men, with the exception of Nana, wore double cartridge belts. Nana carried a leather box with shells tied to his belt under the jacket. Four of the women wore gun belts with holstered handguns over their blouses.

Nana drew rein and the little column behind him halted, horses nickering, moving their heads.

"I said I would find you." He nodded. "It's good to see you, Galeana. Where is your camp?"

Galeana pointed with his thumb upstream. "Two miles."

"Good," Nana said casually. "Let's get there. You lead us in."

The sun was resting on the mountain crest to the west. They sat near the ramada, the men on the inside of the circle, the women and children behind them. The Chihenne sat together on the east side, Nana in the center. The happiness of the arrival was past. They had eaten the food Jaccali and the Chokonen women had cooked. The mood was somber. Chihuahua had recounted what had happened to the band. There was a silence. They waited for Nana to speak.

The old man cleared his throat.

"We knew that you had been hit in the Mogollons two months ago. We visited the old place, the hot springs by the San Mateo Mountains. The hot springs run no more; they have given up. The whites messed it all up. They are running cattle there now. It's a dead place."

He made a forlorn gesture with his hands.

"The Mexican trader in Monticello, the one we know well, he told us. He had heard about the attack on you. He also knew that you had make it into Mexico. He knew nothing about the attack near Oputo. Bad town, Oputo. We always had trouble there."

He paused.

"He told us that two armies had gone into these mountains looking for you and the others. He said the Americans brought in hundreds of Apache scouts from Fort Apache, many of our own people, Chato with them. That traitor knows all the places where we were safe in the past. We should have killed him before we left Turkey Creek."

There was a murmur of agreement from around the circle.

"It was Chato who led the attack on our camp east of Oputo," Chihuahua said darkly. "It was Apaches who surprised us, took our wives and children. The whites would never have made it up the mountains."

Nana nodded. "Yes." He looked at Josanie. "You bring them back."

Josanie nodded. "I will," he said. "Soon."

Nana shook his head. "You better wait a little. When we came south, another army followed us. Lots of Apache scouts with that army, too. We got away from them. But they are still in Mexico, searching everywhere. There are also Mexican troops out looking. They don't like the Americans in here. They dislike the Apache scouts even more."

"We saw tracks coming from the west," Josanie said. "They went as far as Juh's old camp. Was that you or someone else?"

"It wasn't us," Nana said. "We saw those tracks, too. We don't know who made them. We came from Casas Grandes through the mountains. We hit that army trail and came south by Nacori. We made a circle around the town. That Mexican messenger from Nacori we killed told us about you. That's how we got here."

"We should move the camp," Josanie said, looking at his brother next to him. "Go farther south on this river. Now there are two sets of tracks from Nacori to this camp, ours and Nana's."

Chihuahua nodded. "Yes. We should move tomorrow. South."

There was a silence.

"You have lots of horses and plenty of supplies," Nana said. "We brought some horses and supplies, too. We have plenty of ammunition. We can stay away for a long time. During that time you can go north and get your women and children." He looked at Josanie.

"Did you have trouble in the Black Range?" Chihuahua asked.

"No," Nana said. "We stayed in Black Canyon, way up there. We didn't move around much. Someone was fattening tame sheep up there. We made sure no one reported on us. We ate a lot of mutton." He chuckled.

There was a pause. He was serious again. "We felt like prisoners, though. Too many white people. Mining towns, ranches, sheepherders, railroads. White people everywhere. It's our country, but they live in it now."

He paused, swallowing hard. "Maybe we have lost it. They won't let us live there again."

There was a heavy silence. "We decided to join you." He nodded. "We went to Monticello for news. Then we went south on the east slope of the Black Range, past Kingston and Hillsboro. We hit some freight wagons and took some dry goods and weapons. We hit two ranches near Lake Valley for horses. We got about sixty head and went south in a hurry. The army picked up our trail when we crossed the railroad near Deming. They were waiting there, I guess. After that it was a race."

He chuckled again.

"We rode hard, changing horses. The army scouts never got close. We left them there, somewhere."

He paused.

"When we came west from Casas Grandes, in the mountains, we came across a place with dead mules, where army mules had fallen into a canyon. The soldiers never tried to get to the packs. We did. We got some boxes with .45-70 shells and some other things pretty good."

Some of the men nodded. Everyone knew that American soldiers had too much of everything.

"Did you hear anything about Naiche, Mangus, Geronimo?" Chihuahua asked.

"Nothing," Nana said thoughtfully. "Nothing."

"The Mexicans in Nacori knew nothing either," Josanie said. "What about Mexican troops?"

"Once we thought we saw something, way off. But we were not sure."

Nana stretched, opening his hands, palms up. "I'm happy we found you."

He looked away into the green slopes. "This is our country, too. Always was. That's what the old people said long ago. Maybe it's the only one left to us now. Perhaps we can be safe here—if we are careful," he added.

FORTY-THREE

Child of the Water was the quintessential Chiricahua warrior. He was given to his mother, the custodian of Chiricahua life, as the killer of enemies. He instructed Chiricahua males on how to feed their people through hunting and on how to protect their people in war. Whereas his mother introduced the ceremony of new life, he introduced the rituals of taking life.

A boy still, he destroyed the monsters, spirits in giant humanlike or animal forms. He did this with great courage, skill, and supernatural help given by his father, Thunder. Child of the Water taught that these attributes were essential for a man to be successful in hunting and in war, although the supernatural help a Chiricahua warrior acquired might come from a wide range of sources, from animal spirits or the gahé or such powers as rain, clouds, wind, lightning, stars.

Although the gahé were the keepers of animals, they allowed game taken for genuine need, with proper rules observed. These rules had been made by Child of the Water in agreement with the keepers. Included in these rules were the respectful treatment of game and a conscientious behavior, physically and spiritually, toward animals. He introduced a secret language for hunting and rituals preceding hunting. After animal life had been taken, the spirits of the slain had to be propitiated.

He also introduced a secret language to be used in war. The process of killing itself, whether animals or humans, was considered an act that could contaminate the killer. To protect against ghost sickness inflicted as punishment by the dead, a special ritual was required. The purpose of the secret language was not to dupe an enemy but to prevent contamination of the normal language with terms related to death. Child of the Water set rules for behavior toward enemies alive or dead. Scalping or the taking of other body parts of enemies was not permitted. The spirits of slain enemies were not propitiated but were made harmless through ritual.

For a Chiricahua adolescent boy, years of hard training, both physical and mental, culminated in the condition of dikohe. The role model for the dikohe boy was Child of the Water, and during the dikohe time the novice, in the process of becoming a man, was called by the name of the supernatural.

As dikohe the adolescent boy underwent warfare training, which included participation in four military actions. Whereas spiritual concerns were addressed by a medicine man, time in the field and the learning of the secret language were supervised by a distinguished warrior. Like the girl in the gotál ceremony, the dikohe boy, on the four raids, took water through a cane tube and carried a prayer stick. Water, which was spiritually associated with Thunder, was not allowed to touch the novice's lips, otherwise an unwanted thunderstorm might result.

On these raids the dikohe wore a buckskin war cap in commemoration of the headgear Child of the Water had worn when he slew the monsters. On the war cap were painted lightnings in the colors of the directions, black, blue, yellow, white. Lightning arrows were regarded as main weapons in the arsenal of the mysterious boy. After the fourth raid, if the novice had carried himself in a manner worthy of his namesake, he was formally accepted as a warrior and an adult and again called by his nickname. His real Chiricahua name could be spoken only in life-threatening situations when the spirit world was addressed or in other religious contexts.

Author's note.

FORTY-FOUR

The bands broke camp early the following morning and moved south for fifteen miles around one of the great bends of the river and built a new camp above the west bank in a strong defensive position. Four days later Galeana and Zele, with Zilahe, went over the back trail as far as the entrance of the Arroyo Nacori Chico, and there, in the early afternoon, they found Mexican cavalry coming their way.

First they saw a dozen Tarahumaras trailing tracks barefooted, their dark brown bodies naked but for short white cotton kilts. They wore red headbands and were armed only with bows and arrows. Behind them came one cavalry troop. The light uniforms stood out, and through binoculars the three Chokonen saw in the distance a whole column of white-clad horsemen.

They were able to retreat undetected. Zele immediately sent Zilahe to alert the camp. He and Galeana decided to stay behind to cover the troop movement. This would be difficult because the Tarahumaras were excellent trackers and would not be fooled. They would read correctly the slightest disturbance imprinted on the ground. When they came to the place where the three Chokonen had spotted them and turned back, they stopped and one waved to an officer. He rode up to them and dismounted. They showed him the fresh hoofprints, and after a brief conversation he mounted and rode swiftly to the main force, apparently to inform the commander.

"They are coming on our old trail and on Nana's trail. Now they found our new tracks and know that we have seen them," Galeana said. "If they have come to fight, they will hurry now, hoping to catch our camp on the move."

He had guessed right. As the two watched, the officer galloped back and the whole column was set in forceful motion. The Tarahumaras, great runners, effortlessly loped ahead.

"You tell the chiefs," Galeana said. "They must either move camp or pick a place for a fight. I'll stay in front of them as long as I can."

After Zele galloped away, Galeana used the many bends of the Aros valley to his advantage, moving from one to the next before the keen-eyed runners ahead of the cavalry came in sight. They did not see him, but he was sure that they knew of his presence and that he was alone and that two riders had sped away. Through the runners the Mexican officers would know; they might conclude that the Chiricahua camp was within striking distance.

Twice the cavalry halted briefly to rest the horses and to adjust equipment. It covered ground fast, alternating walk, trot, and a slow gallop. In late afternoon it was five miles away from the recently abandoned campsite.

Galeana rode past it, and nearly a mile farther south he was joined by Josanie and Zele. Together, from cover, they watched through binoculars as the cavalry came through the narrows and into the valley by the creek and the waterfall and saw the ramadas and wickiups.

A bugle blew and the first troop raced past the camp to block an escape route upriver. Three more troops came in sight and quickly formed a broad line opposite the camp, preparing the charge across the river. But the charge was halted. The trackers had found the trail leading from the camp and knew that the site was empty. They stood in a group and talked with some officers behind the center of the line of troopers. Through the binoculars the watchers saw that they pointed south.

"The Tarahumaras are telling them where we have gone," Josanie said.

He looked along the lines of white uniforms. "One hundred fifty soldiers, maybe. Maybe more." Judging Mexican and American military units correctly had become a matter of life and death.

"Look," Galeana said. "Downriver."

From the narrows a mule supply train emerged, with civilian packers on horseback. It was halted. The three troops rode through the river, and two dismounted on the flat ground around the empty frame of the gotál lodge and the first ramada, unbit the horses, and led them to water. One troop spread out and rode upslope toward the wickiups and circled them, riders disappearing and reappearing under the pines.

"I wonder if they give up and turn back or come on," Josanie said. "This is unusual. Mexican soldiers have never come this far into the Blue Mountains." He shook his head. "They have always tried to overwhelm us with great numbers in open country where they could choose the place. They want us where they can see us."

"If they come on, what have you planned?" Galeana asked.

"There is a good place for an ambush eight miles south of here. When Zilahe came, we got ready. After Zele came, we went up to that place. All our men are there, waiting. We are not running."

"It looks as if they are going to camp there," Zele said.

The troop that held the position south of the campsite turned in formation and moved downriver toward the group of officers and the Tarahumaras. It halted there. After a white the watchers saw the Tarahumaras start running toward them on the trail the camp had made upstream. The first troop followed, riding by twos.

"They are coming on a scout," Galeana said.

"Yes," Josanie said. "Let's ride."

They slipped away and went to their horses and mounted and rode off. They rode in silence, leaving clear tracks to follow. When they neared the ambush site, Josanie slowed the horse and gestured for the others to do the same.

"There's that crack in the rocks before us, to the right," he said. "I and Galeana get off the horses there and climb up through it. You take our horses with you. Our men are waiting around the next bend. Tell Chihuahua and Nana that the Mexicans are coming. Let them come into the trap. Make sure none of the Tarahumaras comes out alive. I and Galeana will catch those that got away."

There was a vertical rock shelf, twenty feet high, above the gravels on the west side of the streambed. They rode close to it, and when they were parallel to the crevice that angled upward through its face, the two men smoothly stepped from the stirrups while Zele held the bridles of their horses and then rode on with them without changing gait. He waved once with his left arm and was gone. The crevice was deeper than was visible from the outside, with horizontal ledges that gave good handholds. Rifles on their backs, they edged upward until they came out and reached the flat top of the shelf, a dozen feet wide, behind which the mountain slope swung high.

They sat and painted themselves with a white line across nose and cheekbones. They put the paint pouches away and eyed their position. Three hundred yards to the right the river curved to the west and disappeared behind a steep rocky ledge covered with pines. There the warriors were waiting. About the same distance to the left the river swung east around another rock wall. There was a clear field of fire for about six hundred yards. They laid down on their stomachs so that they could not be seen from downriver and from below. Above the sun fell toward the western rim; there would be long shadows across the valley soon.

For a while there was no sound but the hum and chatter of the river running between sand flats and gravel stretches on a valley floor only about two hundred yards wide. Then—another sound, faintly, and suddenly, when the cavalry rounded the bend, there were the clatter of many horses moving fast over gravel and rocks and the clanking of saddles. Before the Mexicans passed below, the two warriors heard the patter of the Tarahumaras' naked feet and knew that they would be the first to suffer the waiting guns.

Josanie and Galeana raised themselves to a sitting position and laid out rows of cartridges. It did not take long before they heard the crashing of many rifles, a terrific noise in the narrow space, echoing among the mountains. There were distant screams from men and horses, but the rifles went on without mercy. Josanie trained the sights of the Sharps on the curve of the streambed upriver around which survivors would appear.

First came three horses with empty saddles, wide-eyed, utterly frightened. They raced and splashed through the winding waters and passed by. Next was a trooper hanging low in the saddle, obviously wounded, trying to keep from falling. Josanie left him to Galeana's .44-40 repeater. Two more riderless horses, another, another, and then a single trooper, then two more, riding hard to get away. Josanie shot the first one and saw him plunge from the saddle. He missed the second one, then caught him with a second round. Josanie got the third one a hundred yards away and then there were more panicked, riderless horses. On the other side of the river bend the rifles were relentless.

Galeana shot the wounded trooper from his horse when he was passing. A bunch of horses came with three Mexicans among them, and Josanie shot one after another with his heavy, long-range rifle. After this they saw only two horses, walking slowly, then standing still, badly injured. The rifle fire slackened and died. Nothing more came.

They refitted the cartridges to their belts and climbed through the crevice to the valley floor. They walked by the troopers flung down by the bullets, two of them face down in the green water, and saw that they were dead. When they came near the bend, they heard a sudden burst of gunfire. No war cry, but a deadly silence.

The site of the ambush was a place of carnage. Dead and crippled horses, soldiers in blood-splattered white uniforms, thirty of them, the crumpled dark bodies of the Tarahumara trackers. Warriors were moving among the fallen; two shots rang out as two wounded troopers were killed. A cluster of men stood near a brush-lined hollow in a patch of gravel. Josanie and Galeana approached and saw one of their men on the ground, Ures. He had been shot through the stomach by two soldiers who had made a stand in the hollow before they were killed. Tsach was bend over him, inspecting the wound. It was mortal. He looked up at Chihuahua and shook his head. Ures moaned, blood running from his mouth. His eyes turned in their sockets and showed white.

Josanie looked at Chihuahua and Nana, and Chihuahua said, "These are all dead." He made a sweeping gesture with his hand. "But Ures is dying. He is worth more than all of these."

And after a pause: "Did any get away?"

Josanie shook his head. "No. No one."

Chihuahua nodded.

"We should leave here," Nana said dryly. "The troops down there, they must have heard us."

Josanie called out to the warriors, and they shot the sick horses and walked away. They took the sheathed sabers of the two officers, two sets of field glasses, and the bugler's trumpet. They did not touch the dead and took neither their rifles nor their ammunition; they had no use for the .50 caliber of the Mexicans. Josanie stayed behind and knelt and prayed with hoddentin, asking forgiveness from the spirits of the slain, and marked the line of separation on the ground. Ures was carried between four men until they reached the horses. He died there, and they laid him across the saddle of his mount and led it back to the camp.

They got there when the last light of the sun lay golden on the eastern lip of the mountain, leaving the camp in dark blue shadows. There was no victory celebration. Ures was buried under a rock overhang behind a wall of stones. Chaddi led the proceedings.

Galeana, Zele, and Zilahe kept a watch on the killing place from a distance. The Mexicans sent a patrol of five men. They inspected the ambush site and quickly withdrew. No effort was made to bury the dead; they must have feared another ambush. Another day and the cavalry was gone. The three scouts followed its trail beyond the mouth of the Arroyo Nacori Chico.

Zilahe had gone through his second war experience. The warriors had been faithful in the presence of Child of the Water in the physical being of the dikohe.

FORTY-FIVE

The whole city turned out—all classes and conditions. The housetops were covered, the balconies were alive, and banners were flying from all the masts. The bands played, and from the church and cathedral towers the bells rang out in tuneful clamor. . . . Beyond the city we could discover some black objects against the sky like waving plumes of the knights of old. The signal is given and the column moves forward, and behold! these waving plumes are the ghastly scalps of the fallen enemy, held aloft to the gazing crowd, who yell and cry, and follow along perfectly wild with excitement. They are on poles about ten feet long, carried by the victors four abreast. We count them, seventy-eight in number, sixteen of which are women and children. I had of course expected to see some scalps, but there I saw a long black line of terrible looking objects worse by far than I had supposed. The whole head of hair had been in most cases taken.

First came an immense throng of people, men, women, and children, pushing each other to and fro, mad with excitement. Then came a band whose music was drowned from time to time by the plaudits of the populace. Then came Colonel Terrazas and his staff of officers, looking worn and travel-stained. Immediately after came the prisoners mounted upon ponies and mules. They were all women and children, from old age to infancy. After the prisoners came the scalp bearers and pack trains. The men were bloody and dirty in the extreme, as a natural consequence; but they could not equal the Apaches, who for filth, dirt, and mean looks surpassed anything I ever saw or could imagine. . . . This campaign will cost the state not less than $50,000 cash outlay [for scalps and prisoners]. The scalp of Victorio, tinged visibly with gray, was carried by the man who was given the credit of shooting him. . . .

About 1 o'clock the procession halted before one of the large prisons or camp yards, and the prisoners dismounted and passed in. The next day all the smaller children, up to girls of 13 years of age, were given away, and, strange as it may seem, they have been taken into the best and wealthiest families in the city. Governor Luis Terrazas took two, a boy and a girl. One gentleman took three. They have been cleaned up, and are much improved in appearance. The women are all confined in the city prison. . . .

The slayer of Victorio has been presented with a suit that is neat and not gaudy, either. The short jacket is of crimson broadcloth; the vest and pants of black doeskin, trimmed with silver face; the hat magnificent white fur broadtrim, and covered with spangles. He is a peaceful Tarahumara Indian, and bears his honors quietly.

On October 15, 1880, a Mexican militia force under Colonel Joaquin Terrazas ambushed Victorio's band of Warm Springs (Chihenne) Apaches and Mescaleros at Tres Castillos in eastern Chihuahua. A Chicago Times *correspondent was an eyewitness to the entry of Terrazas's forces into Chihuahua City after the massacre. He wrote under the pseudonym, "Consular," and his account was reprinted by the* Daily New *Mexican (Santa Fe), on December 2, 1880.*

Author's comments: This account contains two errors the correspondent was not aware of. According to statements by survivors of the Tres Castillos massacre, the number of warriors trapped with the column of women and children was twenty-five, fourteen of whom were Mescaleros. What little ammunition they had they spent in repulsing the first attack of the Mexicans; then, by command, the warriors stood up and raised their arms in surrender. They were shot down, as were many women and children. Therefore, of the seventy-eight scalps carried in Terrazas's triumphal march, fifty-three were those of women and children, not the sixteen listed in the official report, which the correspondent repeated. Historians, without exception, have copied Terrazas's self-complimentary lies as statements of truth and perpetuated them in the literature. The number of women and children captured and sold into slavery was sixty-eight, thirty of whom were Mescaleros.

The man decorated with a new suit for the slaying of Victorio was Mauricio Corredor, captain of the Tarahumara contingent of Terrazas's forces. He could not possibly have killed the chief because Victorio and three of the Chihenne warriors next to him had committed suicide after running out of ammunition.

FORTY-SIX

Ures was the nickname of the man who had died in the ambush. His wife, Maria, and their young son, Eskinyah, had been captured by Apache scouts near Oputo on June 23. Ures had got his nickname from a town in Sonora, below the western slope of the Sierra Madre. It had been the capital city of the state of Sonora for many years and was often the target of Chiricahua raids. During the last raid, that of 1883, Ures had been instrumental in capturing a mule train outside the city limits.

Galeana was the nickname of one of the most trusted scouts of Chokonen and Chihenne bands. His wife, Escani, and their little girls, Chinaca and Elisa, had also been captured on June 23. His nickname came from the small town of Galeana in the state of Chihuahua, located thirty miles southeast of Casas Grandes, on the northeastern edge of the Sierra Madre. It was situated on a hill and consisted of one-story mud houses grouped around a small plaza and a chapel.

Here is a story to be told.

The most prominent citizen of Galeana was Juan Mata Ortiz. After May 25, 1849, when the state of Chihuahua adopted the so-called Fifth Law, which encouraged the slaughter of Apaches by bounty hunters, Ortiz mixed the cattle business with scalp hunting, as did Joaquin Terrazas. Bounties were fixed at 200 pesos for each warrior killed, 250 pesos for each warrior captured, and 150 pesos for each female or any male Indians under fourteen captured.

The mother of the warrior Galeana was Chihenne; his father, Chokonen. His father had been killed on a raid in the Mogollon Mountains in May 1880. With his mother, younger brother, and sister, Galeana had been with Victorio on his excursion into western Texas and the return to northeastern Mexico. Two days before the Tres Castillos massacre, he joined a raid for horses and ammunition led by Blanco. Two more raiding parties were out, one with Lozen, Victorio's sister, and one composed of Mescalero warriors. None of these was close enough to come to Victorio's rescue; neither was the rear guard of ten warriors led by Nana.

Nana gathered the few who had escaped the massacre, seventeen women and children, and one day later was joined by Blanco's raiders. They went over the south hill of Tres Castillos where it had happened and searched the site and buried as many of the dead as possible. They found the bodies of twenty-five warriors, fourteen of whom were Mescaleros. They piled rocks on the bodies of Victorio and the three Chihenne with him who had killed themselves with their knives. Fifty-three bodies were those of women and children, sixteen Mescaleros among them. All the dead had been scalped. Galeana found the body of his mother but no trace of his younger siblings; they were among the captured. He was never to see them again. On the following day Nana led the remnant of the band north, consisting at that time of twenty-five warriors and seventeen women and children. They reached the Black Range in New Mexico safely.

On their ride north, near the mud town of Carrizal, they came on nine militia men. They shot five and took the others prisoner. When searching their baggage, the warriors discovered that these men had been at the Tres Castillos and that one had in his possession the saddle and personal effects of Victorio. The warriors made the Mexicans die hard. Before they died, they revealed that the governor had announced before the ambush that the state would pay rewards for Apache scalps and captured women and children, according to the law, and 2,000 pesos for Victorio, dead or alive. They also revealed that the militia had been led by Joaquin Terrazas, cousin of the governor of the state of Chihuahua, and by Mata Ortiz, of the town of Galeana.

The time for Mata Ortiz to pay for Tres Castillos and other acts of treachery committed against Apaches came on November 13, 1882. Three warriors on fast horses were sent to the town of Galeana. They were to take horses from a small ranch at the outskirts of town in broad daylight and to drive them on the road to Casas Grandes. The three were decoys for an ambush. Galeana was the leader of the decoys.

The plan worked. Mata Ortiz should have known better, but he clattered out from the town with twenty-one men and had been chasing the decoys almost fifteen miles when he suddenly saw warriors emerge in his front and rear. He led his force to the top of a pointed hill, since known as Cerrito Mata Ortiz. There the desperate men tried to dig rifle pits, but the stony soil refused them. In the effort to get Mata Ortiz alive, then a heavy-set, sixty-two-year-old man who had taken part in expeditions against Chiricahuas for forty years, the Chiracahuas lost two warriors. Twenty Mexicans were killed; the Apaches let one escape to bring reenforcements, who would be destroyed at the same place, an old Chiricahua trick; and Mata Ortiz was taken alive. He was made to suffer for a long record of evil perpetrated against Chiricahuas, and he died on the hill.

Joaquin Terrazas was careful to stay out of Chiricahua reach. He died peacefully on October 8, 1901.

In honor of his service in luring Mata Ortiz and his men into the trap, the young warrior who had led the decoys was nicknamed Galeana.

FORTY-SEVEN

Headquarters Department of Arizona,
In the Field, Fort Bowie, A. T. September 17, 1885
The Adjutant General,
Division of the Pacific.

Sir:

It has been my intention to turn over to the civil authorities any hostile bucks captured, for trial under the provisions of Sec. 9, of the Act of Congress, approved March 3, 1885, with reference to jurisdiction of the courts over certain offenses committed by Indians. But upon consultation with several prominent lawyers on the subject, I am assured that it will be impossible to secure conviction in the civil courts, owing to the impossibility of obtaining evidence against individual Indians, and that the same difficulty will be experienced in obtaining proof should the Indians be indicted for conspiracy. Unless aided by a stroke of good fortune, it will take years to kill all these hostiles situated as they are, and so long as any of them remain out in the mountains, life and property will be unsafe within their reach and it will be impossible to prevent their depredations.

It is desirable to have them surrender and this they will not do if they think they are to be killed, or what they believe is worse, turned over to the civil authorities.

It is believed they could be induced to surrender after a little more hammering, if they are assured that their lives would not be forfeited and that they would simply be transported. Please give decision by telegraph.

It is important that this matter should not gain publicity, so as to get to the ears of the Indians.

Very respectfully,
Your obedient servant,
(Sgd.) George Crook,
Brigadier General,
Commanding.

FORTY-EIGHT

It rained for two days, a thin, steady, benevolent drizzle from a gray sky, female rain. On the third day the sky cleared and Josanie called a meeting. No one was surprised. All knew what it would be about. They came and sat and waited for him to speak. He sat next to Chihuahua. Jaccali and Ramona sat behind them.

"It is the time," Josanie said. "It is the time to ride and bring them back, the ones they have taken from us. We miss them. We cannot live here without them, not for a long time."

He paused. "I have been patient. We have been patient. We had to be. It is the time now."

There was a loud murmur of agreement. Faces turned toward him with shining eyes.

"Yes," Chihuahua said quietly. "It is the time. When will you leave?"

"Tomorrow. At sunrise," Josanie said.

"How many will you take?"

"Ten," Josanie said. "Not more. We have to ride fast. Ten are enough."

"Whom do you want?"

"I want everyone here," Josanie said. "But I can't take everyone. Ten."

He looked along the circle of men. "Galeana," he said. Galeana nodded. He named nine more, and they gestured that they would ride with him. "Zele. Zilahe. Tsach. Kezinne. Bish. Tisnol. Nalgee. Nitzin. Tsana. The others must protect this place with you, nantan," he smiled at Chihuahua and added seriously, "and with Nana, so that we still have a place when we come back. Where would we go when we came back and you were gone?"

There was a pause, and then Nana spoke.

"You are right, Josanie. There is no reason to wait longer. Bring them back and who else wants to come. There are some at Turkey Creek who now would like to join us. Let them come with you."

He cleared his throat. Ever the great tactician, he asked the important question: "Which route north do you plan to take?"

"I think west," Josanie said. "I think it is too difficult to get through on the eastern route. Since you came over it and surprised them, there are probably army scouts and troops everywhere, looking in both directions." He smiled. "They think there are more of us in the Black Range waiting to come south."

"There are three American armies here in Mexico," Nana said thoughtfully. "There are more north of the border, waiting for you. And there are Mexican troops around. We saw some recently." His mouth twisted briefly into a smile, but his eyes were hard as flint. "If we don't give them a chance to surprise us, we can forget them. But the Mexicans resent that American armies are running through the country. They are eager to show them that they can fight us, too. If we let them."

He smiled again. "It's the American armies we have to watch out for. The whites in there are not a danger, but the Apache scouts are. There are hundreds of them. They know how we think and how we fight. They are the same as us. How will you evade them?"

"Perhaps I can't. But we will ride. I'll try to pass them on the west. Stay on high ground wherever we can. Cross roads and open valleys at night. We just had a full moon. That can be done. If they find us, we must make it look as if we were hitting places in Arizona for ammunition and horses. If they would know that we are making for Fort Apache, they would surround it with guns."

He paused.

"We must ride hard and hit hard when we have to. Stop only for fresh horses, confuse the Apache scouts, force the Americans to protect places we aren't going to, circle, and circle again, and loose whoever follows us. We have to outsmart our brothers." And after a pause he added, "It will be hard to do."

He paused again. "Now, that's the plan."

There was a strong murmur of approval from the warriors.

"It is good," Chihuahua said, touching his brother's arm.

"Yes, it is good," Nana added. "I would do it like that. If you run into too many enemies, come back and try somewhere else. There must be a hole somewhere."

So it was decided.

That evening, lying side by side in their wickiup, Jaccali and Josanie spoke little. They listened to the murmur of the wind coming down the mountain. They enjoyed being close to each other. Jaccali wanted their son, Nachi, back, but was afraid for her husband. Thousands and thousands of eyes would be hunting for him, peasants and townspeople, vaqueros and cattlemen, white scouts and Indian scouts, soldiers and miners and railroad men, everywhere. And at Fort Apache were hostile Indian police and soldiers, and among their own Chokonen and Chihenne at Turkey Creek there were those who would betray him because doing so would get them trinkets, or because they were jealous of him, or afraid of him, or because they were the way they were.

She did not tell him how afraid she was for him and for herself. At last they fell asleep and the night turned toward morning. It was past mid-September; the cold of early fall was in the air, and the sounds of a rising camp woke them. They dressed quickly and embraced before they left the wickiup. Men and women began to assemble below the camp; everyone seemed to be moving. The best horses were cut from the herd and ridden in, thirteen, two extras for an emergency. The raiders had brought saddles, bedrolls, and packs that included food for a week or longer.

Each man carried on his person objects that contained spirit power for protection. Some wore painted shirts and feathered or plain buckskin caps with beaded or painted figures and signs of the spirit universe. Some wore medicine cords with sacred objects, or necklaces. Nearly all had amulet strings tied to their hair and paint and pollen pouches on bandoliers above the cartridge belts. Zilahe wore his cap with the painted lightnings in the colors of the four directions, the headgear of Child of the Water. On his blue shirt dangled the drinking tube from a string around his neck.

Most men wore eagle, owl, or hawk feathers singly or in a bunch, according to the individual's interpretation and purpose. Each man quietly painted himself with a white horizontal line below the eyes, the paint for war, as Child of the Water had once instructed them. White was the Chokonen paint, red the Chihenne paint that had given them their name, Red Paint People.

Chaddi conducted a brief prayer ceremony. The warriors bent before him, and he sprinkled them with sacred pollen. He prayed with a loud voice. There were no farewell and no command when he was done. They mounted. Josanie looked at his brother, at Jaccali, at Ramona. He burned the sight into his memory. Jaccali saw him as she had seen him for the first time when they were young: the sharp, intense face, the lean, strong body. Now his eyes smiled under the feathered war cap. He carried his rifle on the back of the fringed buckskin shirt she had made for him, the four lightning zigzags on it Chaddi had painted. Josanie raised his arm. They all did. He turned his horse, and the raiders rode off in single file, the sounds made by the horses and leather saddles quickly swallowed by the river.

They were a colorful sight. Nitzin's and Nalgee's feathered lances waved over them. They did not look back. Eleven men riding against the monsters, Jaccali thought, with Child of the Water among them, once again to clean the world and bring happiness to ndé, our people. She prayed silently: "Go with them, White Painted Woman. Hold your hands over them. Bring them back—with those who belong to us." But even before they reached the great bend of the river, they had already disappeared among the pines and boulders, as if the deep mountains had opened their secret places and the mountain spirits themselves were riding.

Half a mile upstream from the place of ambush the raiders began the climb of the western mountain, slowly angling upward. Josanie let Galeana, Zele, and Zilahe pass and take the point. On the valley floor, among the used-up cadavers of men and horses, a few ravens and turkey vultures walked and hopped among the strips of torn horsehide and scattered pieces of uniforms, bones, skulls, hair, the red hollows of rib cages. They rode on, and after climbing along the slope for seven miles, they reached the western slope and went down. They came to a creekbed and dismounted. They walked the horses over the hard gravels through the trickle of water downstream, found better footing, and cut across the slope and circled. After twenty miles they came to a river that ran north into the Yaqui.

They rested the horses and let them graze, hidden from all but a bird's view by a belt of tall canes on the riverbank. After an hour they mounted again and searched upstream for a game crossing. They found a thin break in the canes and went across, the cold water in the stream channel reaching to the horses' bellies. They rode south on the other side of the river until they came to an old trail that led west across another mountain ridge to another river that ran north. After climbing and descending fifteen miles, they reached the river by midafternoon, went along it a little ways, and stopped well south of where it gushed into the Yaqui. The only tracks they had seen were those of the animals of the mountains, none of horses and no human footprints.

They halted in a glade with good grass screened by tall pines. The horses were unsaddled and turned out to graze.

"We'll wait here until the moon is up," Josanie said. "We better eat and sleep some. It will be a long night."

When the great white face of the moon came over the mountain to the east, they rode out again. In the silver light they went along the river to the broad floodplain of the Yaqui. Josanie dismounted and gave turquoise beads to the river, and they crossed without difficulty, although they had to swim the horses through the last part of the channel, below the northern bank.

They clambered up and went west beside the big river for thirteen miles through stands of sycamores, oaks, and cottonwoods to where a creek ran in from the north, eight miles east of the mouth of the Moctezuma and the dirt road to Fronteras. They followed the creek into the foothills of the mountain chain that stretched north to the Teres Mountains and kept in the foothills until they reached the eastern corner of the bulge of the great black malpaís. There, when the shadows grew long and the moon dimmed in the west, they reached a campsite, surrounded by tongues of black lava, that they had used before. They quickly built three small fires to warm food. They ate and extinguished the fires just before the first light came white and cold. One man on guard, the others rolled themselves in their blankets and slept.

They spent the afternoon under a bright sun, taking dips in the creek, lying around, talking. There were small, hopeful laughs. When night fell, they made small fires again and prepared food. When the moon came out, they rode again, passing along the dips and rises of the foothills like ghosts come from the other world. Somewhere to the west in the silent whiteness lay the mud town of Moctezuma, and they went on without hurry until the moon began to fade. They made camp in the hills twelve miles east of the colonia of Cumpas, a stopping place by the river and the road. There was a creek with good cover and grass and with artificial hills of flat stones all but overgrown with jojoba and creosote bushes, ruins of a town of Indian people long gone.

During the following night, under the waning moon, they rode twenty-five miles over sloping, rocky ground before they made camp. Earlier a bad accident had occurred. In the shadows Nalgee's horse stepped on a rattlesnake and was bitten on the forearm of the right front leg. The horse bucked and almost threw him, but two riders quickly surrounded him and pulled him off. They inspected the horse where it stood in pain; the forearm above the punctures was beginning to swell. Perhaps the snakebite was a bad omen, or perhaps it had no special meaning. Nalgee took one of the spare horses, and they moved on, leaving the sick animal behind.

Their camp was eight miles below the notch through which they had come after the attack on their camp in June. They crossed the area during the next night, remembering the despair they had felt at losing so many women and children. There was no trace of their passing; it was as if they had never been there. They rode another eighteen miles and made camp in the high hills below the southern end of the Teres Mountains, among pines and scrub oak by a dry creek with some deep waterholes. They were ten miles east of the road to Fronteras. When the dark turned gray in the east, they drowned the fires and went to sleep. They had not seen any tracks associated with humans since leaving the Aros River and doubted that they had been seen by human eyes.

Kezinne was the sentinel late that morning. He sat in the pines above the camp, hidden by an algerita shrub, the high mountains at his back. He could look over some of the broken ground to the west and north and over part of the trail to the south. He saw six horsemen, coming over the back trail and riding slowly, when they were less than a mile away. He brought Josanie's binoculars to his eyes. The horsemen disappeared and reappeared behind ground rises and stands of trees, but were approaching steadily. White headbands, white shirts, cavalry horses. Apache scouts.

He slipped away unseen. "Wake up," he called softly in camp. "They are coming."

The men were up in an instant and took arms and ammunition belts. "Where?" Josanie asked. "How many?"

Kezinne spread his fingers. "Six. On our trail. Apache scouts." "How far away?"

"Half a mile, maybe a little more. They are coming slowly."

"Get the horses," Josanie said. "Make them ready. Quick. No noise. Get your horse ready, too, Kezinne. Then go back and keep watch. Let us know if there are more behind them."

The men went for the horses, saddled them, and put their packs on. They worked fast.

"You stay with the horses," Josanie said. He pointed with his chin at Bish, Tisnol, Tsana. They bunched the horses up and took the bridles. "The others come with me."

They hurried silently and spread out behind a low ridge line a hundred yards south of the camp, on both sides of the trail. The cover was good for some quick shooting but dangerous in case of an engagement with a large force. Through the broken ground to the west an enemy could circle around them and cut off retreat north.

Hidden, they waited. Under the full sun the only sounds were the humming of insects. Then, from a distance, came the low thumping sound made by horse hooves on soft ground and the clinking sound of hooves on hard surfaces striking stones. Josanie lay on his back in a shallow depression, the rifle on his chest. Two of his men were nearby; the other four lay somewhere in the trees on the other side of the trail. The horses came on, and once, a faint sound, a saddle creaked. Then they seemed thirty yards away. Josanie turned onto his side and gathered his legs under him, ready to spring up. Suddenly the silence was pierced by a yell and the crash of a rifle followed by two, three more reports, powerful and close, and yells. Horses squealed, hooves hammered the ground, and when he stood up, the rifle butt at his shoulder, horses were galloping away and he saw through trees and brush that three bodies were lying on the trail. Climbing out and walking toward them, he heard Kezinne call out. "Three got away. I see no one else. One is badly hurt. The others are holding him up."

The men gathered around the bodies. "Who shot first?" Josanie asked.

"Me," Nalgee said. "One of them saw me."

Josanie nodded. "We should have let them pass and shot them in the back. No one would have escaped."

He paused. "Now they are going to tell that we are here. They will bring those American armies on us. They will sure try."

He sought Nalgee's eyes, but the man looked down, distressed.

"It's not your fault," Josanie said. "It had to happen. Sooner or later they would have found us. There are so many of them; they can search everywhere."

He looked at the bodies.

"White Mountain," Tsach said. "I know this one." He touched a body with the muzzle of his Henry repeater. The man lay face down in a puddle of blood oozing out from a head shot with a fist-sized exit wound. "Chino." And after a pause: "He lived on East Fork."

"I have seen him," Josanie said. "He should have stayed there." He turned to Galeana. "Take those two and follow them." He pointed with his chin at Zele and Zilahe. The boy gripped his Winchester .44-40 repeater so hard his knuckles had turned white. This was the second time that he had shot at men and killed. He looked wretched, as if he were close to vomiting.

"Go," Josanie told Galeana. "Follow them a few miles, not more. See where they go. Don't get close! Don't let them ambush you! We will wait for you in camp."

The three left and Josanie turned back toward the bodies and the men around them. "Who are the others?"

"Belinte and White Boy," Nitzin said. "They ran with the Fat Boy, the officer Davis. Scratched his back for him." He laughed. "Always eager to please the white man."

Galeana raised his arm as the three riders passed and went down the trail. The men with Josanie gathered the dead men's Springfield rifles and cartridge belts and belt knives. They turned the bodies over so that their faces were up, broken eyes staring into the sun. "Leave them," Josanie said. "They might come back and bury them, or the animals will use them." The men walked away, and he knelt and prayed, placed hoddentin on the ground, and drew the lines of separation in the sand. He walked back and joined the men who sat by the horses. No one spoke. They thought that within a few days the enemies would gather behind them, perhaps try to drive them north against troops stationed on the border. It would be hard to get through.

After an hour Kezinne came down from his observation post. "Galeana and them are coming," he said. He handed the binoculars to Josanie. They were ready to ride when Galeana came up. His horse snorted and stepped nervously. Behind him Zele and Zilahe each held the reins of one of the White Mountain scouts' horses. They were big boned cavalry horses, their saddles and packs intact.

"We found these on the trail," Galeana said with a laugh. He added: "The scouts have gone east toward the Bavispe. I guess that's where their army is. We could not stop them."

Josanie nodded. "Yes," he said. "You did well. Let's ride. They found us. But we have something important we must do."

The men nodded and grunted in agreement. He mounted and turned the horse north and they followed.

Southeast of the mud town of Esqueda they came to the pass that went through the Teres Mountains and connected the Moctezuma Valley with the Bavispe Valley. They rode in and upward but turned away to the north before reaching the summit. They took a slippery game trail among the rocks that wound into the high mountains. They walked the horses and tried to obliterate their tracks where they left the pass, knowing that White Mountain Apache eyes were as good and as practiced as theirs. They made camp under the great red sky of evening near a small lake below the highest north-south trending ridge of the Teres. This was old Chokonen country, and they knew all the secret places in it.

That night, around a low burning fire made from dry wood, they spoke about their concerns. The moon rose late in the west. The call of an owl came through the darkness, three times, four.

"Perhaps we should ride fast," Tsach said carefully, "before they come up behind us and drive us north."

There was a brief murmur of agreement.

"They can only drive us if we let them," Galeana said. "We know this country better than they. We can work around them."

"We have to know where they are," Zele said. "But if we go looking for them, we leave tracks, and they might find them. Then they come after us."

There was a heavy silence.

"If they think we are going south, they will try to push us," Josanie said finally. "If they think we have given up and circle back, they will stay where they are, spread out, try to keep us from going south. And if we got through them, they would look for our trail and try to find our camp by the river."

He paused.

"I think we should confuse them by staying here, moving slowly through these mountains. Make sure they don't find us again. Make them wait wherever they are."

And after a pause he added, "Then, when we are close to the border, we ride fast." He gestured with his right hand.

There was another silence.

"It is true that we are between their armies in Mexico and their armies north. It happened before, and we knew it would happen this time. But they don't know where we are and why we are here. We'll get through where they don't expect it."

So it was decided.

For three days they traveled through the roughest part of the Teres Mountains, high up in the country of bighorn sheep and eagles. They walked on narrow game trails through thick pine forests and over barren slopes and screes of loose sheets of rock, climbing and descending and climbing, pulling the horses with them. On the first day they went down and crossed the pass that led west to Fronteras and made sure that they left nothing to see. On the evening of the third day they came to the northern edge of the Teres and overlooked the high plateau with the canyon of the White River in it and behind it, pale blue in the distance, the Perilla Mountains that reached into southeastern Arizona.

At sunrise, from a high point, they scanned the wide, open expanse of high desert before them with binoculars but saw nothing move. They rode down into the sandy flats, straight north, careful not to raise dust flags that could be seen from a distance. When they came into the canyon of the river on an old trail, they saw two bunches of desert bighorn living by the waterholes in the dry river bottom. The country might have looked dead, but it wasn't. The riders went by and climbed out of the canyon and went on, eleven more miles, to the southernmost edge of the Perillas. There they paused and searched with binoculars along their back trail and all around, but the desert lay empty and silent under the sun. Finally they rode on into the mountains, keeping to the high country.

In late afternoon they came on the gap where one of the trenches of Guadelupe Canyon cut through the mountains, coming in from the east. It was one of the major travel routes for outlaws and Apache refugees between the United States and Mexico and was constantly guarded farther east where the canyon snaked through the borders of Arizona, New Mexico, and Mexico.

They watched for some time but saw no signs of humans. They waited. The red sky of sundown passed, and darkness came slowly. When the diminishing face of the moon appeared and cast its eerie light, they rode into the canyon and followed it for a few miles and climbed out and went northeast into the Perillas of Arizona. On a trail known only to Chokonen, bighorn sheep, and pumas, they rode another six miles and made camp behind the cliffs by a waterhole in Hog Canyon. They butchered one of the cavalry horses taken from the scouts and roasted meat on wooden spits for a meal and a three-day food supply. Coyotes howled and yelped below the canyon mouth but fell silent before first light.

In late morning Josanie climbed with Galeana and Tsach to the first level of the hog-nose ridge above the canyon mouth. Before them, straight east across the level plain of San Bernardino Valley, rose the blue back of the southern Peloncillo Mountains. In the north, its peaks shrouded by white clouds, lay the giant turtleback of the Chiricahua Mountains. Along its east slopes San Bernardino Valley merged with the grasslands of San Simon Valley that ran north and north to the green valley of the Gila River.

They surveyed the open country methodically through binoculars, paying much attention to stretches where breaks and arroyos were hidden from sight. Having lived and fought in these valleys and mountains for much of their lives, they knew nearly every foot of ground and all the good and bad hiding places. They saw three herds of antelopes but no trace of humans.

"This looks suspicious," Josanie said. "We know there are lots of troops along the border. There are supposed to be troops and scouts everywhere, south and north. We have seen nothing of them since we killed the scouts, and we see nothing here."

"The armies in Mexico," Tsach said, "we left them behind. Maybe they thought we would turn back, as you said. And maybe we passed the others when we went through these mountains." He pointed south.

There was a silence.

Galeana nodded. "Yes, I think so, too."

Josanie still gazed through the field glasses, searching for what could not be seen. "Maybe," he said. "But I have a bad feeling. This is too quiet."

They went down to the camp. The horses were unsaddled, but the men were ready and looked expectantly at Josanie. He sat down among them.

"Last time we came through the big valley, three months ago, we wanted attention so my brother and our people could get safely into Mexico. We didn't get any, although we burned places on both sides of the Chiricahuas. Now we don't want any attention."

He paused.

"I and Tsach and Galeana looked up and down the big valley for fifty miles. We looked at the Peloncillos and across the face of the Chiricahuas. Nothing but antelopes. Some cattle. It looks quiet like last time, but I don't think it is. Not from what Nana told us."

He paused again.

"The big valley—it's too open. I have a bad feeling about it. It could be a trap. It's when I don't see them that I am afraid of them." Another pause.

"I say we go west, along the Chiricahuas, then through them, cross the valley in the northeast to the Peloncillos. That's what I think now."

He looked at the men. He saw serious faces, probing eyes. They nodded. No one spoke or asked a question. They were experienced warriors. They knew that a bad feeling better be respected; it usually was a warning from somewhere with a truth behind it.

They saddled up and rode out after they had filled canteens and water bags. They rode at a walk along the east slope of the Perillas, mindful not to raise dust swirls, and after four miles they reached the pass between the Perillas and the southern spur of the Chiricahuas, the Pedregosa Mountains. In the pass, leading northwest, they let the horses run at a lope, and when they came to the dry ground of the Poverty Flat, they turned north toward Castle Dome, the towering crag blanking a trail behind it that led north between the Swisshelm Mountains in the west and Packsaddle Mountain of the Chiricahuas to the east.

Passing Bald Knob above the Mud Springs, they at last came on the enemy. Galeana, riding point with Zele and Zilahe, flashed a signal with the hand mirror, twice: three men. When Josanie came up with the others, they had already been spotted. There were four shots in the distance, fired into the air, and they saw three Apache scouts cut across the trail nearly a mile away and gallop west, then southwest, toward the springs.

Josanie called out, and they urged the horses to a gallop. They made straight for Castle Rock, two miles away, and when they came to the sharp lower slope, they rode beneath the red rocks and toward the opening of the trail below the northwestern walls. Josanie halted at its mouth, looking back. He did not have to wait long. A dust cloud was rising due south and coming their way. He raised the binoculars. Blue horsemen and a bunch of white-clad Apache scouts. He smiled grimly. Finally the enemy had a face. He turned the horse and followed his men on the high trail between the mountains.

They rode ten miles under a warm afternoon sun, slowing the horses down often but always staying in sight of the cavalry. When they arrived at the opening of Rucker Canyon that came down from the high Chiricahuas, they rode in. This canyon was as familiar to them as their canyon wickiups. There were many good places for an ambush in it. They wished the cavalry would continue after them, but someone there knew better. They saw through field glasses that the troopers and the scouts had halted outside. After milling around for some time, the column withdrew a short distance and appeared to make camp beside Rucker Creek. Josanie nodded with satisfaction. It was good to know where this bunch of enemies was.

Letting the horses walk leisurely up the canyon, the raiders met with three prospectors near where they had killed the two in June. Three bearded white men were coming toward them with five mules loaded high with wooden boxes and heavy bags and equipment. They were the kind of men who drew hundreds of white men after them, despoiling land that belonged to ndé and the animals and the spirits. Now they stood in utter terror, limp, muttering incoherently when they realized that the dreaded Chiricahua Apaches, said to be masters of torture, were on them. They were shot down quickly. The warriors caught the bellowing mules, unhooked the cinches of the aparejos, and pulled covers and loads off. They chased the mules up the trail, smashed the boxes and searched the prospector's possessions, but took only water bags and three Winchester .44-40 repeaters, some boxes with ammunition, and one Colt 1873 model revolver with a gun belt.

They left the bodies where they had fallen, for the animals of the mountains, and rode another five miles and made camp east of where Tex Canyon ran in from the south. They recaptured one of the mules when night fell, and Nalgee lanced it for food. They roasted fresh meat once again, this time over a blazing fire. They ate and laughed and ate and were happy. During the night, like last time, a wolf pack howled to the north. Where they would go.

The white dawn came cold and clear. These were the last days of September. The aspen leaves were turning yellow; soon aspen stands along the high slopes would dazzle with golden fury. In the canyon a thin veil of fog lay over the creek and evaporated after sunrise. The raiders broke camp and rode northeast, higher and higher into the Chiricahuas. From the last campsite to Sentinel Peak, rising to a height of nine thousand feet, was a distance of nine miles as the raven flew. Walking on slippery, dangerous game trails, pulling the horses with them, the warriors took most of the morning to get around the peak. By the time they reached South Fork Canyon, it was late afternoon. Josanie decided to make camp among the towering walls of red and yellow stone to rest the horses. He sent Galeana and his two companions to reconnoiter two miles down the canyon, but not to go any farther. They reported back that there were animal tracks, as they had seen them all day, but no hoofprints.

That night, sitting around a fire that could not be seen from more than three hundred yards away, and not smelled from another hundred, the men talked about the day to come. They were close to the far eastern edge of the Chiricahua Mountains. Four miles down the canyon merged with the small area of open ground around Cave Creek and the wide gap, three miles on, to San Simon Valley. From there the distance to the Peloncillos of New Mexico was a mere twelve miles of level plain, with ranches in it that they had sacked in June. There they hoped to remount and leave their trail-worn horses behind. Josanie summarized what was said. "This is what we will do." He added cryptically, "If we can get through."

But they could not. When they came near Cave Creek at first light the following morning, they heard a trumpet blaring for reveille and saw a big soldier camp come alive. They watched from cover through field glasses as troopers tumbled from rows of white tents on the company streets and assembled for roll call. There were a hundred horses or more picketed behind the wagons and a like number of mules, teamsters walking between them.

"Negro soldiers," Josanie said. "The same ones who attacked our camp back in New Mexico in May. The ones who killed my mother and took my son and my brother's son and wife and others prisoner. The same ones."

From east of the soldier camp came a shot, another, and when Josanie turned the field glasses to the area the shots had come from, he saw two mounted Apache scouts, gesturing wildly to their rear. Two more joined them, more, until they were about a dozen, and they came straight for Josanie's group. They were nearly a mile away and came fast at first, then slowed down, approaching at a walk, waiting for the troopers to arrive. Out in the open these scouts were of no danger, and they would not rush the hidden guns, Josanie knew. He looked again at the soldier camp, now in great confusion, a trumpet sounding again. He saw men struggle with nervous horses. He walked to where Tsana and Zilahe held the horses, and they all mounted and rode back the way they had come.

They stopped once in a place where they had a good field of fire for about five hundred yards, and Josanie taught the enemy a quick and discouraging lesson. With Nitzin, Bish, Tisnol, and Tsana, each of whom carried a single-shot long-range rifle, as he did, they waited until the cautious column of blue-clad black soldiers, urged on by white officers, came into range. The scouts had disappeared; they must have known what was coming. With the booming of the guns the column broke up and scurried to safety behind the twisting stone walls. Even so, the heavy bullets left a couple of men sprawled out on the rocks and a few horses standing motionless. When the shooters went back to where the others waited, Josanie said: "This will keep them away from us. If they ever come close again . . ." He did not finish the sentence. They went back up the trail, but below Sentinel Peak they took another trail leading northwest.

FORTY-NINE

In the north, a white cloud stands upright.
There, his home is made of white clouds.
The Great White Mountain Spirit in the north,
He is happy over me.
My songs have been created.
He sings the ceremony into my mouth.
My songs have been created.
The cross made of turquoise,
The tips of his horns are covered with yellow
Pollen.
Now we can see in all directions,
Drive evil and sickness away.
My songs will go out into the world.

*Gahé song. Song of the mountain spirits, recorded by
Jules Henry in 1930.*

FIFTY

After two days of hard climbing up and down through the heart of the mountain massif, the raiders reached one of its western doors, the canyon of Turkey Creek. They camped near its mouth after they had surveyed the adjacent plain of Sulphur Springs Valley. They desperately needed fresh horses. They clambered out into the big valley in the morning and struck two ranches in succession, taking seven good horses on the first ranch, six on the second one, leaving their own exhausted mounts there. At both ranches white people did not resist but seemed to eye the exchange with a sort of stony, impersonal interest. Perhaps they were petrified with fear. No shot was fired and no harm was done.

After the second ranch they turned east and then north along the west slope of the Chiricahuas. After a few miles they saw a number of small dots come over a little rise on the plain, perhaps five miles away. Galeana stopped and looked through his field glasses. Josanie and the men with him rode up; they sat their horses in a tight group.

"Apache scouts," Galeana said.

Josanie searched with the binoculars past the line of dots but saw nothing behind them. "Eight," he said. "No cavalry."

"They haven't seen us yet," Tsach said. "We could take them."

There was a pause.

"Yes," Josanie said. "we could. But I think I want to talk to them if I can. We might have to fight them. Let's get ready."

They slid off the horses and walked them in cover to a little draw. The men took their shirts off and prepared themselves for battle. They waited. Josanie, lying flat on his stomach behind a creosote bush, watched the scouts approach. He came down when they were a little more than half a mile away and motioned to the men to mount. They rode out in single file, at a trot, straight west into the plain, across the scouts' path. They formed a skirmish line, turned the horses, and rode toward the scouts at a walk.

The scouts had stopped. When they saw Josanie's men ride forward, they also formed a skirmish line and rode on. Two hundred yards apart the lines halted. The men in both lines held rifles ready.

Josanie raised his right arm and rode forward, alone. Slowly from the other side a single rider rode up. The two met between the lines. Josanie knew the man well, Manuel, a subchief in Loco's Chihenne band. He looked along the line of scouts. They were all from Loco's band, and Josanie knew them.

"Greetings," Manuel said with a smile. He was a sturdy man in his forties, a proved warrior, holding a government-issued Springfield across his saddle. Above his dark, lined face a white headband struggled against uncut black hair that reached to his belt. His glittering eyes took in Josanie and the skirmish line behind him. He noted that the men were painted for war; he and his men were not.

"My respect, Josanie," he said, bowing his head briefly. "We didn't think we would run into you."

"You did," Josanie said. "Why are you doing this?"

There was a silence.

"You know about that," Manuel said. "We made a contract with the Americans. We are supposed to bring you in."

"You are doing what they can't do. They are using Chokonen and Chihenne to hunt Chokonen down. They would never get to us without you."

"Yes," Manuel said simply. "That is true. They want this war to be over. We want it over, too."

There was a pause.

"You are making a lot of hardship for all of us," he added. "We want peace. We are sick of this fighting."

"We didn't start this war or all the other wars before," Josanie said angrily.

"Yes," Manuel said. "But look how many of us have been killed in these wars, women and children, too. You know what the Mexicans did to our women and children. The Americans, they just killed them." He paused. "So few of us left. We can't fight them anymore. The whites are like grasshoppers. They keep coming, more and more."

"If we give up, there will be even more," Josanie said. "They dig up the mountains, build their dirty towns, and trample everything under their boots. Our land. Your land, too."

There was a pause.

"What have you gotten for helping the Americans?" he continued. "You live in a big prison camp. They have taken away everything. You can only leave that prison when you enlist in the army as a scout. Then they give you a rifle and a horse to hunt us and some money. When it is over, they take the rifle and the horse away from you and force you to live where they want you to live, where they run your life for you. If we," he pointed over his shoulder, "were not still free, you would never have seen these mountains again. They wouldn't let you. They let the white miners in to dig everywhere, the white sheep men, the cattlemen."

He paused. "These mountains. These valleys. Ours, yours. Of the spirits. You help them take it all away from us," he said angrily. "You even kill our women and children for them."

"Not us," Manuel said. "Chato did. We don't. We only want you to give up."

He paused. "It is true what you say. We live in a prison at Fort Apache. And we wouldn't be here if you were not here."

"Chihenne you are," Josanie said. "Ndé, our people. Why don't you join us in the Blue Mountains? We can hold it against the Mexicans. We can be free there, together."

There was a silence.

Sadly, Manuel said finally: "We have done that, I and you and others. So many of them gone, women and children slaves in Mexico. We could do that, yes, but they would hunt us with bigger and bigger armies, American and Mexican. These people are crazy. They are scared of us. That's why they would kill us all. They would never leave us by ourselves."

He paused. "I don't want my wife and children killed or sent away as slaves. I want to keep the little we have. That's why I enlisted. I wanted to tell you to give up so that what little is left to us comes together. Work together on the reservation. To let our people live."

There was a pause.

"To live in a prison, in a place where we are treated like children, in a place that was never our country," Josanie said. "We tried that. Surrounded by spies who tell lies about us to the white officials and officers, by missionaries who spit on our ceremonies. Thieves for agents who talk about a book and let us starve. They keep us shackled while they run over our land. It that where you want us to be?"

"No," Manuel said. "I want to go with you to the Blue Mountains. Kill me a few more Mexicans. That's what I want."

He paused. "But the time for that is gone. Everything is changing. If we want our women and children to live, we have to give in. I, for myself, would rather die beside you than do this." He tapped the government rifle.

"You and Nana are the best war captains we have left," he continued. "If you give up, Geronimo and them give up, too. You get wives and children back. Loco and you and Nana and your brother and Mangus could speak for all of us on the reservation, Chokonen, Chihenne. Work together." He made a gesture with his right hand. "No more killing."

There was a silence.

"I can't," Josanie said. "If we give up, they'll put us in irons, maybe hang us or send us away." He paused. "We would rather all be dead in our own country."

The two men looked into each other's eyes.

Josanie nodded and turned his horse.

"Wait," Manuel said. "I want to tell you what I know. No one expected you to get this far."

He pointed south. "The two outfits searching for you in Mexico, Crawford, Davis, all them scouts, too, they have come back. They are worn out, no danger to you. But there are troops of Fourth Cavalry at San Bernardino Spring, Mud Springs, Skeleton Canyon, Guadelupe Canyon. You went through them already. There are more at Copper Canyon, Song Mountain," he pointed southwest. "East there is the Tenth Cavalry, at Cave Creek in these mountains and all along the railroad east. There are foot soldiers at San Luis Pass. And behind us is the Third Cavalry from Fort Bowie, across this valley, north of here. That is all I know."

He paused.

"We won't tell them that we saw you. There are some white trackers who can read signs, too. Siebert is not around, though."

"We ran into Negro soldiers in the mountains," Josanie said. "There were some Apache scouts with them. Who were they?"

Manuel chuckled. "Navajos. They make themselves look like Chokonen."

"Where are you riding to?" Josanie asked.

"Mud Springs, along this side of the Chiricahuas. Then report back to Fort Bowie if we saw any sign of you." He smiled.

"We have met with these soldiers from the springs. Who are the scouts?"

"White Mountain. Over from Canyon Day and Slim Rock."

He raised his hand and Josanie did the same. They rode back to their men. Josanie pointed toward the Chiricahua Mountains, and his men followed him and opened a path for the scouts, who continued to ride south, past them. They all raised their arms briefly.

They made camp behind a ridge that gave them a good view of much of the valley, clear to the big, pale blue hump of the Dragoon Mountains in the west, twenty-five miles across the plain. Josanie told about his talk with Manuel and what he had learned about troop deployments. The warriors were quiet, mulling over in their minds what they had heard.

Finally Tsach broke the silence. "First we have to get our wives and children back." He paused. "It is right what you said to him. I say the same." There was a murmur of approval from the men, and then Tsach added, "How do we continue?"

Josanie nodded. "I think we should wait until dark and cross over to the Dragoons. If they don't find out about us, we stay in the mountains in the west all the way to the San Carlos."

So it was decided.

Night came. The waning moon was just a carved white blade in the middle of the sky, but the dark tent of heaven was ablaze with the glitter of myriad stars. It was beautiful, but a track-obliterating rain would have been more welcome. There would be none. Josanie took point, and they rode into the dry arroyo of Turkey Creek west to where it flattened itself against the Sulphur Hills, fifteen miles on. It was easy riding. They passed between the hills, and Josanie turned southwest toward the Dragoons and the old trail that ran up toward Cochise Peak. After another ten miles they reached the lower tablelands on the east slope of the mountains and rode in. For five miles they rode on a dry creekbed that snaked through the tumble of great round boulders and then came to one of the old campsites that had served Chokonen bands for many centuries. There were still some tattered frames of wickiups visible in the tall grass. No one had been here for years. In the white dawn coming over the eastern sky Josanie knelt and prayed and blessed the place. There was a spring. They watered the horses and turned them loose to graze. The men chewed some cold meat they had roasted days ago and went to sleep.

Josanie woke up in full sunlight three hours later. Something nagged at him, made him uneasy. He took the field glasses, climbed a few hundred yards up the mountain, and sat down on a huge boulder with a view in all directions but to the north and northwest. He looked south along the spine of the Dragoons, to South Pass, and southwest, toward the filthy cow town of Tombstone, and saw nothing. A faint sound of moccasin boots came from behind him. Galeana walked up and, with a nod, sat beside him, the binoculars dangling on leather strings on his chest. They scanned Sulphur Springs Valley from the south end up along the Chiricahua Mountains, and finally they saw it.

East of Willcox Playa, about eighteen miles away, a dust fan rose lazily in the haze lying on the plain. They watched as it moved steadily south, and finally they recognized a column of cavalry, two troops, riding by twos, and a widely spread out screen of Apache scouts in front.

"The ranches yesterday," Josanie said. "Someone must have told Fort Bowie."

While they watched, the command split up, one troop continuing south, the other turning southeast, past Sulphur Hills, each with a handful of scouts.

"They'll find our tracks," Galeana said. "They can't miss them."

Josanie nodded. "Yes." The scouts of the troop nearest to the Dragoons were the first to notice. They dismounted and went over the ground on foot, looking down. When the column came up, an officer dismounted and talked with them. The column halted and soon two troopers were seen racing off, one east to call the other column, one north.

"This one, the one going north . . . he will tell Fort Bowie that we made it into Cochise's mountains," Josanie said. "He will be there by midday." He paused. "They'll talk through the telegraph wire, alert every town along the railroad, Willcox, Benson, every white man who can lift a gun, every soldier to Fort Grant and the San Carlos."

They kept watching and saw the second troop ride over and join the other. The scouts went ahead, and the column formed behind them on Josanie's trail toward the Dragoons, the swallowtail guidon of Third Cavalry troops flapping over them.

"We should go," Josanie said. They climbed down and Josanie threw a heavy stone to the side down the slope. It clattered and bounced among the rocks, and when he and Galeana reached the campsite, the men were standing ready, rifles in their hands.

"Two troops of cavalry," Josanie said. "Apache scouts. They saw our tracks and are coming."

There was a silence.

"Get the horses ready," he said. "Get water. We must ride."

"Where?" Zele asked.

"South. We won't be able to go north and cross the railroad. They sent a rider to Bowie, and they'll use the telegraph line to bring everyone down on us."

"Are we going back?" Tsach asked.

"No," Josanie said. "We don't want them to trap us in these mountains. Here they could surround us easily. We get out of their way first."

They saddled up and rode out, first south, then west, and when they came out of the Dragoons, they turned south along the southern spur of the range. They rode slowly at first, trying to preserve the strength of the horses. They went by South Pass on the west and, from a distance, passed Tombstone on the east, making for the Mule Mountains. They rode harder when they approached the mountains, thinking about Dixie Canyon. They had ridden twenty miles, but they did not get there. There was a dust cloud in the southwest, the direction of Fort Huachuca, and one from the southeast, coming up from the bottom of Sulphur Springs Valley.

Josanie called out and they came to a halt. There was nothing yet to see from where they had come; the cavalry there was probably still moving in the Dragoons. But the immediate danger was from the southwest and the southeast.

"East," Josanie said, and the race began. They were at Hay Mountain when they turned. They went straight east across the valley, making once again for the Swisshelm Mountains in front of the southern Chiricahuas, twenty miles away. When they had covered half the distance, they saw a new dust flag rise from the Mud Springs area, a little more to the southeast than the other and closer.

They halted for a few moments to rest the horses. Josanie looked through the binoculars at the new danger. "The same people we left at Rucker Canyon days ago," he said. He searched briefly for the other column and noted its quick advance.

"They closed the valley in the south," he said. "They closed it in the west, too. They can't close the Chiricahuas. I think they are trying to." He paused. "I am sure now that they have another outfit in the north they try to push us against."

He put the field glasses away. "We must ride fast to get as far north as we can."

They turned northeast and rode at a fast gallop. They went by two ranches and through rust-colored cattle resting or feeding calmly in the afternoon sun. From one ranch a couple of rifles fired at them, but they ignored the bullets as they whistled past. One of the spare horses was hit in the left hind leg and fell behind. They rode eight miles and changed gait, letting the horses walk. But the soldiers from Mud Springs came on strong, and when they were three miles behind them, the warriors resumed full speed again. The second column stayed farther west, about eight miles away, but continued on its course.

They passed Squaretop Hills, rising sharply from the plain, and saw the column again that had followed them into the Dragoons in the morning. It had finally negotiated South Pass and joined the race, but came too late to cut them off. Now there were three different enemy outfits charging after them.

"When does the force from the north show itself?" Josanie mused. He was certain that there was one. But they went across the arroyos of the creeks now called Pridham, Ash, Turkey, and Rock, snaking down from the Chiricahuas, and their horses were nearing the end of their endurance. They were covered with sweat and foam, and the enemy closest, the one from Mud Springs, was gaining on them. And the expected happened: a dust cloud in the north signaled the appearance of the new enemy. It would arrive too late.

Josanie called out, and they urged the horses to give their last. They rode toward the Chiricahuas and reached Fivemile Creek, the horses stumbling, and went upward and came to the gate of the mountains as the blue men from Mud Springs began to close in. The warriors jumped off the staggering mounts, and Josanie and the men with long-range rifles sprayed the head of the column with bullets, while the rest of the warriors dragged the horses to safety behind a sheltering rock wall.

Josanie and his riflemen stood in the open, firing with reckless fury. The cavalry had dismounted, and the soldiers took to the ground and formed a firing line. Bullets began to fall fast among the five warriors, but they stood and shot round after round, seeing the enemies' horses wither under their guns. Finally Josanie raised his rifle high and yelled the haunting war cry of the Chokonen, the men following his example. They stood for a moment in the rain of bullets, then turned and ran to safety, balls whirring past and raising small fountains of dust around them.

They reached safety and Josanie looked to the men who had been with him. He and the four had minor cuts from flying stones, but no one was hurt. A ball had shattered the stock of Bish's Springfield and made it useless. No matter; he would take one of the extra Winchesters. Josanie nodded to them and smiled, touching them on the shoulder. He took his horse's bridle and led the staggering animal gently, slowly, up the canyon. The men followed. They walked less than a mile, unsaddled the horses, and tried to rub their foam-coated bodies dry with grass bundles. They stood, shivering on wobbly legs.

"They are ruined," Tsach said matter-of-factly.

"Yes," Josanie said. "But they can walk with us and help us to get fresh ones. They need a long rest, though."

Galeana and his two companions were sent to watch the enemy. Zilahe reported later that four columns of cavalry had congregated before the entrance of the canyon for a time. Three had moved away, one south, two north. One troop stayed and was encamped.

"They just keep the door closed," Josanie said with a shrug. "They won't try to come in."

They made camp and cared for the horses. They left at noon on the following day, walking one mile to Pine Canyon, four more miles to where a short trail led north into Pinery Canyon and made camp on Pinery Creek. They were among tall Ponderosa pines and juniper and blue oak. Scattered among the evergreens and red-leaved oaks were the golden paints of aspen stands, as if the mountain spirits had emblazoned their haunts with magic colors to conciliate the dejected warriors. Tsach shot with arrows two deer that walked into the camp as if sent by a beneficial power. The warriors took it for that and feasted and opened their eyes wide to the beauty around them. On the following day they walked north for seven miles and camped east of Sugarloaf Mountain of the high Chiricahuas, at the head of a trail that ran east to Whitetail Creek.

That evening Tsach came to talk with Josanie. He sat down opposite him. He smoothened the front strip of his breechclout and folded it neatly over his crossed legs. He held an eagle tail feather in his right hand. He touched it lightly against his chin and looked into Josanie's eyes. Something serious was about to be said.

"Tomorrow morning," Tsach said, "I want to call the mountain spirits. Before sunrise." He paused. "I want to call on Child of the Water for help. I want the dikohe to assist me."

Both men thought about this; it was an important matter.

"Yes," Josanie said. He nodded. "That is good. You do that." He paused. "Do you need anything from me, from us?"

"No. What I need I have."

"I will tell the men," Josanie said. "Thank you for doing this."

When first light intensified in the eastern sky, the men followed Tsach and Zilahe a little way up the trail. The dikohe and his father wore a single eagle feather in their hair. Tsach held another eagle feather in his left hand and a deer-hoof rattle in his right. There was a sandy place in a nook below boulders. Tsach knelt and removed a few pebbles and made the surface even with a twig. He had an old-time stone-tipped arrow stuck in his belt. He pulled it out and laid it aside. His son stepped next to him, while the men formed a half circle behind the two.

Tsach knelt and took yellow pollen paste from a pouch. He offered it to the four directions and painted a line across Zilahe's face below the eyes, from cheekbone to cheekbone. They reversed positions and Zilahe painted Tsach the same way. Tsach motioned to the men and they passed Zilahe, who painted them. They went by one by one and stood back.

Tsach nodded. He knelt in front of the sandy place. He touched the ground four times with both hands, praying in a barely audible voice. He bent forward and molded with his hands a small mound on the east side, three more, each a yard apart, in the remaining cardinal directions, south, west, north. He took paint bags from his belt and sprinkled the mounds with paint: charcoal, east; dust of ground turquoise, south; yellow ocher, west; white clay powder, north. With yellow pollen he drew a line from the eastern mound to the western one, from the southern to the northern. The earth painting showed the four sacred mountains and the center.

He moved to the east side. With the obsidian point of the arrow he scratched the pug marks of the four feet of a puma into the sand, each half a yard apart, going east. Mountain lion the stalker, the hunter. He dubbed the tracks with charcoal. He got up and moved below the blue mountain. He took Zilahe's arm and made him walk into the center of the earth painting to stand on the cross of yellow pollen. He stood there with bowed head. Tsach stepped back. The tail feather in his left hand, the rattle in his right, he started the first song to Child of the Water, slayer of enemies, and the gahé.

Right at the center of the sky the holy boy
With life walks in four directions.
Lightning with life in four colors
Comes down four times.
The place which is called black spot with life.
The place which is called blue spot with life.
The place which is called yellow spot with life.
The place which is called white spot with life.
They have heard about me.
The black gahé dance in four places.
The sun starts down toward the earth.

Josanie and his men stood stiffly, looking at the ground, listening to the song and the sound of the rattle. Once they heard the delicate tap-tap-tap of deer hooves nearby, someone come to listen. There were four songs. Tsach sang with a low, clear voice, and when he finished, he stood crying.

He waited a moment. He tool Zilahe's hand and guided him out of the center, east across the puma tracks, making him step on each of the pug marks. He motioned for Josanie to follow, and he walked through from the west side and over the tracks. The men followed one by one. Tsach walked last. He brushed the men off with the eagle feather to release them from the touch of the sacred. Zilahe brushed him off. Then he went back to the earth painting and wiped it gently away with a twig, leaving no trace on the sand.

They returned to their camp and saddled the horses. They waited for the first rays of the sun to appear. Tsach sang the morning song, and they rode at a walk down the trail, the dikohe, Child of the Water, at the point. They wore the regalia they had started with, painted shirts and medicine cords and amulet strings and war caps and feathers of owl and eagle and hawk. They still wore the yellow face paint, the sign of the puma.

After three miles they came to the canyon of Whitetail Creek. They drank deeply from the cold, clear water and let the horses drink and filled canteens and water bags. They followed the creek to where it left the mountains and ran into the wide, grassy plain of San Simon Valley. They pulled back hard when they got there.

Whitetail Creek, running northeast, had carved an arroyo where it met the plain that curved three miles on around Blue Mountain, an isolated butte in front of the Chiricahuas. They arroyo was about forty feet wide, with banks three to four feet high, although they had in places eroded to creek level. There were natural water tanks in the creekbed. Above the northern bank, a mile away, sat a group of wooden ranch buildings, sheds, and pole corrals behind a two-story main lodge with a veranda. It had not been there when the warriors had come through in 1882.

Josanie whistled and they turned back into the shelter of the canyon. They hobbled the horses on a stretch of ground with some grass and went back to survey the ranch and the country beyond. The ranch and the open valley to the east lay in the full, clear light of the cold early October morning. They watched from cover as activities unfolded before them. Josanie's and Galeana's binoculars were passed around so that everyone could see and remember details of the setting.

A knot of men gathered at one of the corrals, and soon cowhands rode out, three passing south below the watchers. Riders were coming and going. From midday on buckboards and other carriages were coming in with women and children and supplies, each with a few riders beside them. They counted six vehicles until late afternoon. These were probably from smaller ranches in the area.

"What are they doing?" Galeana asked.

"It's what they call a roundup," Josanie said. "They gather the cows in the valley and drive them to the railroad. I've seen them do this. They load them into railroad wagons and take them away." He grinned. "There must be many good horses there, better horses than the army has."

Next to the large lodge a big fire was built in the open and tables were set up. Some women in long dresses started cooking, and children ran in and out of the arroyo. Three large dogs were with them. In the early evening riders drove small herds of red-colored cattle toward the plain behind Blue Mountain. Later they came and lariated horses to a rail around the main lodge. They stashed the saddles on the veranda and fed the horses with grain.

Galeana counted them. "There must be about thirty."

"They put the wagon horses in the corrals," Josanie said. "Those around the big house—they want them close by. Perhaps they have been warned about us." He paused. "It's easier for us if they leave them there for the night."

They watched the white people eat and chat around the big fire. Dusk came and the chimneys of houses blew smoke into the air. Night fell and the tables around the big fire emptied, and it slowly burned itself out. And the cow horses were still lariated around the big house.

The raiders waited until midnight. Under a moonless, starry sky they walked their worn mounts into the arroyo for about two hundred yards. Tsana and Tisnol held them, while Josanie and the men went on. The sand was soft under their moccasined feet, and they walked without a sound. But the wind was coming from the south, and the dogs caught their smell when they were three hundred yards from the ranch. The dogs ran up and stood on the bank above them, huge and black and threatening, howling with rage.

Tsach and Kezinne were prepared. The strings of their mulberry wood bows hummed, and two of the dogs died with gurgling sounds, arrows in their throats. The third dog ran wildly a circle in the dark and was shot when he reappeared on the bank. In the silence that followed Nitzin, Nalgee, and Bish quickly woofed and barked and yip-howled like a pack of coyotes, mixing long-distance threat calls with alarm calls because they made for impressive sounds; fellow Apaches would have known that something was wrong. But the whites would not know the difference. After a little while the three men stopped, and the raiders moved silently toward the big house.

Nothing stirred there or anywhere else. The men slipped out of the arroyo. Three with underlever repeaters took up positions at the front and sides of the house, covering door and windows. Josanie and the others walked slowly among the horses, letting their hands brush along the horses' bodies, keeping them calm. They cut the lariats with knives and gently led the horses away. Well-trained cow horses as they were, they came along without a fuss.

These were the most dangerous moments. Would the white men in the house not hear the soft thud-thud of hooves moving, the sighing noises made by horses moving away? Would doors and windows burst open and explode with gunfire? But they did not. All thirty horses were led into the arroyo and away. Last to leave were Tsach, Nalgee, and Kezinne, who had guarded against a probable onslaught coming from the house or from some other building on the ranch. They melted away once the horses were secure.

At the place where their broken mounts had been held, the warriors put their saddles and small packs and the arms captured from the scouts and the prospectors on eleven cow horses and moved out, each man taking one or two extra horses on lariats. They took only the horses from the ranch and left the others behind; perhaps they would recover. The three miles to Harris Mountain, another butte rising before the Chiricahuas, they rode at a walk, but when they had gone around it, they let the horses run east at a space-consuming lope that these horses could keep up for hours. But the raiders rode only seven miles to the San Simon River. Under golden-leafed cottonwoods they let the horses drink and rest. Then they moved northeast into the foothills of the Peloncillos. They had ridden through cattle lying asleep or still grazing under the starlit sky but had seen nothing to the west, where they had come from, no lights, only a dark silence. They rode by Antelope Pass, took a well-watered draw above the forty-five-hundred-foot level, and made camp among junipers before dawn spread its chalky sheen across the eastern sky.

They were eight miles south of the small railroad town of Steins and near where they had come through in early June after the posse had botched its ambush at the mouth of Doubtful Canyon. They slept a few hours, and then Josanie sent Galeana, Zele, and Zilahe to scout Steins and the railroad and see if there was still a chance to ride north. Before they left, Tsach arranged a little circle of stones as an altar and prayed and thanked the gahé and Child of the Water for the gift of horses. The three scouts returned at midmorning to report a soldier camp at the railroad east of the town; they had seen Apache scouts coming in and a bunch of six leaving, perhaps going out to search for tracks.

The men sat and listened with heavy hearts. Finally Josanie gave voice to what they all knew.

"It's no use. We could get through, yes. But even if we get through without being seen, our ndé brothers find our trail and bring everyone down on us. If we make it to Fort Apache, they'll have surrounded our women and children with so many rifles that we can't get to them." He paused. "We could fight our way in. Even so, we would not get them out without some getting killed." He waited and finally said, "We have to give up for now and go back to our camp in Mexico."

There was silence. The men sat with stony faces.

"Are we coming back for them?" Nalgee asked.

"Yes." Josanie paused. "The whites don't know yet that we intended to go to Fort Apache to rescue our people. But they would suspect that if we crossed the railroad. Until now they think that we made a raid for horses and ammunition. I want them to think that way. We wait until they are tired of waiting. Next time we go east, through the Black Range, go way north before we hit Fort Apache. We hit it from the east. They won't expect that."

He looked at the faces around him.

"I think we should go on," Nalgee said stubbornly.

Two men nodded in agreement.

"I understand you," Josanie said patiently. "I feel the same. But it would get some of us killed, and we still wouldn't get our people back."

He paused. "It is not good now, and we cannot afford to lose anyone. To die is easy for us. That doesn't help the prisoners. We must be smarter than the whites."

He paused again. "We'll get our people."

"How long do we wait?" Tsach asked after a moment.

"Maybe a few weeks. The whites tire out and go back to their posts. That's when we work around them."

"We tried that this time," Nalgee said.

Josanie nodded. "Yes. But we didn't know how many troops and Apache scouts they had sitting on both sides of the Chiricahuas." He waited. "Is it agreed?"

The men looked into his eyes, and one by one they nodded.

They broke camp and loose-herded the horses over a trail east into the Animas Valley of New Mexico, Kezinne riding point, Tisnol and Tsana along the flank, Josanie with four men riding drag, and Galeana, Zele, and Zilahe a mile ahead of the remuda. They rode south along the east slope of the Peloncillos and had made eighteen miles at a leisurely pace when they saw a column of cavalry emerge from Antelope Pass and aim straight at them. They veered sharply southeast toward Playas Valley and crossed the northern foothills of the Animas Mountains to the first of the playa lakes. They let the horses run, and the cavalry fell back.

Josanie halted and looked through the field glasses. He saw two troops riding by twos, with a swallowtail guidon of the Tenth Cavalry, three officers and a few civilians at the head, a bunch of Indian scouts off to the side.

"Negro soldiers," he said to Tsach, who sat his horse next to him. "The ones we ran into in the Chiricahuas. White officers, some other white men, Navajo scouts, I believe." He passed the field glasses to Tsach.

"Yes," Tsach said. "They won't catch us."

They rode on southeast for another twenty miles and crossed the southern playa lake, a narrow basin eight miles long and less than a mile wide. There was water on the flats, and in it were some restless flocks of ducks and geese. The raiders rode slowly on the clay bottom, the water reaching no higher than the pastern of the horses, and off the lake and continued through the grassy plain to the rift between the Big Hatchet and the Alamo Hueco Mountains. They held at a spring and let the horses drink and graze. It was nearly evening, and after a while they saw the cavalry coming on their trail, ten miles distant. It came slowly but crossed the playa and made camp on the east bank.

They waited until a red dusk filled the sky and rode on unnoticed for another five miles. They looked for a good campsite and found one in the shelter of mesquite and juniper and boulders, near water, and built a series of big fires that would burn for a long time and could be smelled from far off. They put some branches together that could be taken for wickiups when the fires faded and rode another eight miles and headed the remuda to a glade by a waterhole on the northeast slope of the Alamo Huecos. They ate cold meat and had two guards out all night. Shortly after midnight they heard reports of heavy rifle fire from the direction of the fake camp. Silence again. The enemy's surprise night attack had been an embarrassing blunder.

At sunrise they saddled fresh mounts from the remuda and rode on in the formation of the day before, Josanie and four men riding drag behind the haze of dust drifting off the trail, back of the sleek, muscular bodies of the horses. They saw nothing more of the blue-clad cavalry and took their time and knew that they were over the border when they passed the abandoned rancho Las Palmas by midmorning. They went on south through a short grass steppe with tobosas and cresote bushes toward the Janos plain and the Sierra Madre, pale blue and high and beckoning behind it.

Two days later they passed Casas Grandes to the west and went into the Sierra Madre along and up the Rio Piedras Verdes. They had been seen twice by vaqueros and by some travelers on mules and carretas on dusty country roads, but they had gone by without paying attention to them, and the Mexicans were grateful for it. The cow horses were steeds of the plains, great runners of the flat country, but not nimble on mountain trails. For another seven days, patiently working to protect the horses, on trails only known to the gahé and Nednhi and Chokonen and Chihenne and bighorns and bobcats and grizzlies and eagles and birds and clouds, they crossed the high sierras and finally rode into their camp on the river Aros.

FIFTY-ONE

In view of the outbreak in May, and as a precautionary measure against any collusion or combination that might be made between those off and those remaining on the reservation, as well as to assure quiet and peace to citizens, it has been deemed advisable to place all the Apaches temporarily under the charges of the War Department, that Department to have full authority to prescribe and enforce such regulations for their management as may be deemed proper. To this end United States Indian Agent Ford was relieved of his duties as agent, on September 1st, and Capt. F. E. Pierce, of the United States Army, was placed in charge.

This office heartily sympathizes with the effort of the War Department to control the rebellious and warlike spirit of the Chiricahua outlaws, and to prevent a recurrence of their raids upon white settlements, and I trust that the military will be able to capture the murderous band now skulking in the Sierra Madre Mountains and to bring them to condign punishment. It has been suggested that the less guilty and responsible of those captured might be transported to an island in the Pacific Ocean, where they could be safely guarded without material expense to the Government, and where the products of the fisheries and the native flocks could be made to furnish a living; or, perhaps, it would be more practicable to place them on the farm belonging to the military prison near Fort Leavenworth, Kans., where, under guard, they could be forced to make a living for themselves by manual labor.

Report of the secretary of the interior on the San Carlos Apaches, for 1885–1886.

FIFTY-TWO

The sun was sinking, casting a red glow over the high eastern slopes of the Aros River valley. There was a cold wind from the southwest. A large fire had been built. The flames licked along the logs laid crosswise, ends pointing in the four cardinal directions. Sparks flew sometimes as if to underscore something that was said.

The people sat around the fire, the Chihenne warriors around Nana on the east side, women and children behind them, the Chokonen warriors filling the remainder of the circle, with Josanie and Chihuahua side by side on the west side. Jaccali and Ramona sat behind the brothers, and the few women and children left in their band sat with their husbands and fathers. They sat quietly, wrapped in blankets against the wind, wrapped in thoughts about what had been told.

First Chaddi had spoken a prayer to the Master of Life. Then he had thanked the spirits, White Painted Woman, Child of the Water, and the gahé for helping to bring the men back unharmed. After Chaddi, Josanie had explained what had happened on the raid. He had spoken softly, carefully measuring each word. All eyes had been on him. When he had stopped speaking, there had been a strong murmur of approval.

Now there was silence but for the sounds made by the fire and the wind. The prisoners at Fort Apache lay heavily on their minds.

Chihuahua touched his brother's arm. "You did well, all of you. You did what you could. No one could have done more."

"Yes," old Nana said, his eyes glowing in the light of the fire. The lines in his face showed up sharply, as if carved by a sculptor's knife. His hands played with a prayer stick. "Yes." He nodded. "You could not have done more. You also taught the whites a lesson. Regardless of how many soldiers and scouts they put against us, they can never feel safe from us."

Josanie stared into the fire, watching the flames and restless curls of smoke running along the logs.

"There is something else I must say." He paused for a moment. "The dikohe, Child of the Water." He pointed with his chin toward Zilahe, who sat between Tsach and Zele. "He proved himself to be a Chokonen warrior. He did everything right." He paused. "He scouted ahead with Zele and Galeana most of the time. He led us to the horses we took from that ranch . . . he and Tsach. He made us proud."

He nodded to the young man, who sat with downcast eyes in the circle of famous fighting men. "These are hard times, and we have much to think about," Josanie continued, "but we must celebrate a new warrior's accomplishments."

He paused again. "I have thought about it. I want to give him a Chokonen warrior's name. Ndóí bikèh, Mountain Lion Is His Power. It is to be his real name. We'll still call him Zilahe most of the time." He grinned.

Once again there was a strong murmur of approval from the men and women.

"We are happy for you, Ndóí bikèh," Chihuahua said. "I speak this name this time in public. Everyone will know it. We are glad you are with us."

"His father and I thank Zele, who was his guide," Chaddi said. "And Galeana, and Josanie, all of you. We thank Josanie for the name. It is an honor for us. I speak for my grandson, too. You helped him to become a man."

The silent circle burst into a flurry of sound. From the women came a series of high-pitched cries, from the men raucous acclamations. All faces were turned to Zilahe, who sat hunched, trying to make himself invisible. Finally Tsach nudged him and he looked up and sat straight and looked around, smiling shyly.

The din ended. "We will go back in a few days," Josanie said quietly. "This time we'll go up east and through the Black Range. This time we'll get to Fort Apache and get our people."

He looked briefly around the circle of men. All nodded agreement.

"We should bring the gahé before you leave," Chaddi said. "They will take you through the mountains. They will."

"Yes," Chihuahua said, "that is good. But before that we'll move camp farther up the river, deeper into the mountains, prepare for winter. Make sure that no one surprises us."

Across the fire Nana cleared his throat. "If you go through the Black Range, you should take one of my men with you. We know that country better than anyone."

"Yes," Josanie said. "I would like that."

"I'll go with you, if you want me," Horache said. "I want to be there when you hit the fort from where they don't expect it." He laughed.

"Yes," Josanie said. "I want you with me."

After a pause he asked, "Where are the cows from that we saw when we came in?"

Nana smiled and pointed with his chin at Chihuahua. "Ask him."

Chihuahua grinned at his brother. "I went down this river to the river they call Yaqui. Five of us. Tuerto knows places there from the time he was with Juh." He paused. "It was nothing. We took twenty-two cows and drove them here. Chokonen cowboys. No one followed us. We checked." He made a gesture with his right hand. "It's getting cold. We need plenty of food. Winter is hard here."

Night was coming on and darkness seemed to creep up out of the ground. Women with children left for the wickiups, but the men stayed longer. There was some small talk, even laughter. Life was hard, but the sky turned and life went on; they felt safe where they were.

"Josanie." Nana's voice came through, and the small talk ended. "I'm wondering about what Manuel said to you." He paused. "Do you think that what he said is also what Loco, Bonito, and the others up at Fort Apache would say?"

Josanie stared into the fire, a face of stone. His answer came slowly. "Up there they are under the white man's gun. They lie to them-selves. They say they want this war to end, but without this war they would not be allowed to leave the reservation. Without us to hunt they would not even have rifles to hunt elk and deer. They would dig in the ground to live, like the crazy white farmers."

He paused. "We give them life. Without us they would be sitting around dreaming of old times. They are not allowed to raise horses and cows. White men do, but they can't."

He looked beyond the fire into the darkness.

"I don't know," he continued. "I think they get tired of this kind of life. If the Americans would give up and leave us alone in these mountains, maybe many of our people at the fort would run and join us."

There was a silence.

Finally Nana said, "Do you think the Americans would leave us alone?"

"I don't know," Josanie said. "This here is not their country. Perhaps they would be happy to leave it alone." He paused. "I think we should try to make a treaty with them when the time comes. We would have to agree that we won't go back across the border anymore. Stay here. Maybe they would agree to leave us where we are. We would lose all our country in the north, though."

"We lost it already," Chihuahua said. "When we are up there, we have to fight all the time. The whites are everywhere."

There was another silence.

"First we have to get our families back," Josanie said. "After that we can try to make a treaty with the Americans, if we want that."

"They are good at making treaties," Nana said. "They made many with us. They broke every single one."

"Yes," Josanie said. "They did. This time we must make them see that it is good for them what we have in mind."

There was a silence again. "How?" Chihuahua asked.

"By punishing them next time we go up, show them again what we can do. Make them see that it is best for their people to make a treaty with us. They leave us alone in this country; we leave them alone." He had almost said, "in theirs," and recognized it.

"This is the only way, I think. We make the Blue Mountains our only home. Close them against anyone else. We can do this if most of our people on the reservation join us."

"There are some up there we don't want here," Chihuahua said. "Chato and them, the ones who helped to kill our women and children."

"Yes," Josanie nodded.

"The people would be split in two," Nana remarked. "One bunch up there, we here. Some would go back and forth and make trouble. How can we prevent that?"

"I don't know," Josanie answered. "I know it would be difficult, but what else can we do? Even if we kill a hundred of them for each one they kill of us, they would still run over us."

Chaha, Horache's brother, spoke: "I don't want to give up going to places up there, in the Black Range, on the Gila, other places, places our hearts know. I can live here, but I want to go up there some time."

Some of the men voiced their agreement.

"I want that, too," Josanie said. "We could have that written into the treaty that we have a right to see places up there."

"It won't do," Chaha said. "The army there might agree, but the other white people will not: miners, cow people, sheep people. They would not. They would get together and try to kill us, no matter how friendly we would try to be. They done it before."

"They were trying to do that last time we were there, two moons ago," Nana said. "What do you think we should do, Chaha?"

"I don't know," the warrior answered glumly. "I don't know."

"Josanie is right," Nana said. "Something has to happen. We can't wait here until one army or another finds us. There will be a time when we can't fight our way out of it anymore. Remember Victorio."

He paused. "This is hard. If we surrender now, we might never see these places again either. They might shut us in for a long time. We don't know. We must do something, like what Josanie said."

He paused again. "I'm an old man. I will be gone soon. It is not for me to decide. But I want my grandchildren to live, live as I used to live, as our ancestors lived. Not in that jailhouse they call reservation. Let them live free, Chihenne, like old times. For that we can sacrifice something."

Again there was silence.

"I don't trust white people," Nana continued. "They broke every promise, every treaty they ever made with us. Perhaps they could keep this one if we agree to live in Mexico, away from the border, in these mountains."

Silence again.

Finally Chihuahua spoke. "We must talk about this more. We must do something different. I don't think we have much time." He paused. "We must discuss this with Naiche and Mangus and Geronimo, too. They are part of this and must be included. We don't even know where they are. We all have to agree on what we want to tell the Americans—if anything."

He paused again.

"I know one thing. We can't go on like this."

Around the fire they sat in silence, with bowed heads. No one spoke; they all listened to themselves. At last Josanie said: "First we have to get our women and children back. Then we decide on these matters." He paused. "We'll leave after the gahé have come into our camp."

People nodded. Then the meeting broke up and people walked away.

Later, in the darkness of the wickiup, Josanie and Jaccali lay side by side under a covering of blankets. They lay in silence, their bodies touching. Once Jaccali delicately brushed the side of Josanie's face, like a mother caressing a small child. She was happy that he was there, and he knew, and nothing needed to be said.

It rained during the night, and toward morning the rain turned to snow. Huge flakes, wet snow. The sun came briefly in the morning but disappeared quickly and a drizzling rain continued, soft and thin and steady, female rain. In camp they waited, and on the third day the gray cloud curtain washed away and the sky showed brilliant and blue from end to end.

They waited three more days to let the swollen river level off, and on the morning of the seventh day after the raiders' return the camp moved upstream, higher into the mountains. They made nineteen miles to a site where the Aros ran south and turned sharply north. At the bend it was met by two rivers running in from the west and south. Between and around the three rivers were flats with good grasses, enough for the 140 horses of the Chokonen and Chihenne camps and the remaining 20 steers of the herd that Chihuahua had brought in. Thick forests of oak, autumn colored red and yellow, and of pine, climbing the mountain slopes, were rich in deer, bighorn sheep, and turkey. The mountaintops all around were inaccessible, impossible to cross. An enemy could approach upstream only along the Aros River, a direction that could be guarded.

FIFTY-THREE

Headquarters Division Pacific,
Presidio, San Francisco, October 8, 1885.
General Crook,
Fort Bowie, A. T.

The following dispatch is repeated for your information and action. Please acknowledge receipt.

By Command of Major General Pope:

(Sgd.) Taylor, Aide-de-Camp.

Referring to General Crook's application, dated September seventeenth, inquiring whether promise can be made to hostile Chiricahuas that their lives shall not be forfeited if they surrender, the Secretary of War approves a recommendation of the Lieutenant General, that General Crook be authorized to secure the surrender of the Chiricahuas now at large upon terms of their being held as prisoners of war, but it must be understood that any negotiation looking to their surrender must include all hostile Chiricahuas, and that as soon as the surrender is made that they at once be sent under suitable guard for confinement at Fort Marion, Fla. Please so inform General Crook by telegraph and direct him to acknowledge receipt. No publicity must be given as to the intentions of the Government in this matter beyond what is absolutely necessary in communicating with the Indians.

(Sgd.) R. C. Drum,
Adjutant General.

FIFTY-FOUR

The thump thump thump of a small, handheld drum five hundred yards away. So tiny a sound but a sound like the rumbling of thunder to those waiting and listening. A torch—a small eye of bright light in the dark, coming down the mountain, appearing and disappearing among trees and slanted ridges, coming. The crackling of the fire-eaten wood where people stood in a circle, illuminated by yellow light, casting tall shadows. And the small distant drum, the ball of light, walking. First the gahé came straight down, as if moving toward the fire and the people, but then they turned east, circling Nana's camp.

There was a piercing call, and they moved on, to the south and west, circling Chihuahua's camp, and from each direction one call was made, and they went north, around the last of the wickiups. Another call stabbed the night. Above the sound of the drum, the swishing of moccasins and the clanging of "earrings" were heard as they passed. And when they had completed the sacred walk around the camp and the fire, they approached from the east side.

It was Chaddi's voice and the drum that led them in. Tsach, behind his father, carried the torch. When they approached the radius of light, Tsach stepped forward and placed the torch on the burning logs. He joined Chaddi and both walked around to the west side, where they stood with Nitzin and Nalgee, both holding small drums and curved drumsticks. Josanie, Chihuahua, and Nana sat on the ground beside the drummers, a deer hide before them, and beat it rhythmically to the sound of the drums with straight sticks.

People on the east side of the circle had opened a lane. The mountain spirits burst through at a trot, in single file. The gahé of the south was the leader, followed by the gahé of the west, north, east, and the clown. They sounded their call, "Hoo-hoo-hoo!" and circled the fire. They were greeted with high-pitched cries by the women, and when these ebbed away, the "Eyá-eyá-eyá" of the singers kept on. The gahé circled the fire four times, then worshiped it from the four directions, stopping at the south side first, making their call, and completing the circle by stopping and calling from the west, the north, and the east. The clown did not participate in this ritual but trotted around the fire in the opposite direction of that taken by the gahé chiefs. The singers fell silent, and the four chiefs lined up on a row on the east side, facing Chaddi.

He sang:

> In the middle of the Holy Mountain,
> in the middle of its body stands a lodge.
> Brush-built it is, for the Blue Mountain Spirit.
> White lightning flashes from his moccasins.
> White lightning streaks on an angular path.
> I am the lightning flashing and streaking.
> My headdress lives. Its earrings
> sound and are heard.
> My song shall surround these dancers.

This was a prayer song for the blue gahé. Songs for the other three followed. The drummers beat their instruments to the rhythm of Chaddi's singing, and the mountain spirits danced slowly around the fire, making low whistling sounds.

This was a free-step starting song, allowing the gahé dancers much freedom of movement. They bent and stretched and spun around and twisted and stomped the ground, the horned headdresses turning and shaking with the head and body movements. After the fourth song, the one for the black gahé, the tempo changed and Chaddi sang a cycle of four short-step songs, which required rigid body movements and short, tense steps.

Chaddi was the singer for this ceremony. Tsach had painted the gahé according to the designs his father owned. Both men were *diyin*, medicine men, who had been granted *diyi*, supernatural power, from the spirit world. Every diyin's power was personal and differed from anyone else's. A diyin who served another diyin as painter in a ceremony painted the other one's designs under his instruction but by doing so did not earn the right to use them for himself. For the gotál ceremony Tsach had painted the gahé with his own designs. This time he had painted them for his father, and thus they looked slightly different.

The four gahé chiefs wore the usual moccasin boots and the fringed, yellow buckskin kilts. Bodies and arms had been given an undercoating of greenish brown. Each had a cross painted on his chest in the color of the direction he represented, blue, yellow, white, black. But instead of snakes each had a white zigzag sign of lightning painted on his arms, from the shoulder to the wrist. On the blue chief's back the outline of a jaguar was drawn in white; on the yellow chief's, that of a wolf in black; on the white chief's, that of a grizzly in black; and on the back of the black chief, the outline of a puma in yellow. The animal spirit depictions were between eight and ten inches wide. Strips of red flannel were tied to the arms above the elbows, to which four eagle feathers were attached, each a few inches from the next.

In their hands the gahé chiefs carried bows and stone-tipped arrows, and for masks they wore yellow buckskin hoods, tied under the chin, with four blue triangles, the mountain sign, painted across the forehead. Pieces of turquoise were tied above the small openings for eyes and mouth—sacred stones to call on the spirits for assistance. The tops of the hoods were covered with green juniper to hide the frames of the crowns, or horns.

The horned headdresses, about two feet high, were painted in the ceremonial colors of the direction of the gahé wearer. Here the "earrings," dangling from the ends of the horizontal bars, were clusters of four pieces of white bone about six inches long. Eagle, turkey, and owl feathers were attached to the points of the horns, and sacred symbols were painted on the middle sections of the horns in white and yellow.

The Gray One, the clown, was barefoot, his body painted the usual way, white with black dots. He was naked underneath the blue cavalry jacket but for a g-string that gave him a rather obscene appearance. The buckskin mask, modeled into a distorted face, was not white but painted light brown, with a thick black line below the eyes, extending from ear to ear. He wore a white headband but no feathers. He carried a stick for a rifle.

Tsach's clown during the gotál had imitated a white soldier. Chaddi's clown in this gahé performance imitated an Apache government scout.

While the gahé chiefs danced, the clown pretended to read tracks, bent to the ground, actually lying down with an ear to the earth, jumping and running, then standing still, presenting his stick as a rifle on a parade ground, now crouching fearfully, now crawling on his stomach, spying on an invisible target. Then, again, he was hit by a bullet and thrown to the ground to lie sprawled, in great pain. He rolled to the side and got up slowly, offering his stick in surrender, passing along the line of onlookers, peering into faces. There was laughter at times, but some of his antics were watched in silence, perhaps because they were too close to the real activities of Apache scouts working for the government.

After the four short-step songs Chaddi sang four high-step songs. With the first line of the first song the gahé chiefs formed a circle around the fire, facing away from it. Each stood in the position of his cardinal direction, south, west, north, east. They danced in place, throwing first one leg and then the other forward and upward, bodies bent and twisting, arms moving to the beat of the drums. Twice the clown stood next to one of the dancers and imitated his movements, distorting them, falling down, and crawling away.

After the last song the gahé chiefs walked around the fire and disappeared in the night. The clown stood alone for a while, as if listening for something, then ran after the others. The drums were silent. The tight circle of the onlookers shifted slightly, people stretching their legs or rearranging blankets. The wind whistled in the dry leaves of an oak tree nearby.

Time passed slowly until the gahé returned. They came in single file, with measured steps, the blue chief leading, the clown last. Josanie heard his wife pray in a low voice. "Men of the mountains," she whispered, "I ask you to protect us. If anyone comes to hurt us, me and my husband, stand in front of us and help us." They came into the circle and walked around the fire, the clown running again.

There was a sudden movement among the attendants, a ripple going through their line. Men and women who had been sitting were getting up, tilting their heads in one direction. Josanie heard Jaccali breathe in deeply and hold the air back. In the lane on the east side a figure not seen before appeared.

This gahé approached slowly. He was painted black and wore a black buckskin hood without a crown, but with owl feathers tied in a bunch to the top. He wore a skirt of woven yucca that reached almost to the ground. He carried juniper branches in his left hand and an obsidian stone knife in his right hand. He had juniper tied to each arm.

"He has come," Jaccali whispered in Josanie's ear. "The Black One. He has come to protect us."

Josanie turned his head and nodded to his wife. "Yes. It is good."

The Black One came into the circle and stood on the southeast side. He would not dance or move from where he stood. He projected an awesome presence. The gahé chiefs would be careful not to touch him when they later danced past him. The clown, who poked fun at everything and anyone else, was careful to avoid him.

The Black One was the great gahé Killer of Enemies, the final protector of ndé, the people, called up only in extreme situations, as occurred when epidemics of deadly diseases ran through the camps, threatening extinction, or when human enemies seemed over-powering. He was the most dangerous of the gahé, deadly even to ndé if they abused him. He could be called only by very careful and powerful diyin; there were adults present who had never seen him.

He stood motionless in his place, all eyes on him. Then Chaddi started the first of the free-step songs, and the gahé chiefs danced to the drum and the song.

> At the place called "Home in the center of the Sky,"
> inside is the home's holiness.
> The door to the home is of white clouds.
> There all the Gray Mountain Spirits
> rejoice over me,
> kneel in the four directions with me.

When first my power was created,
pollen's body, speaking my words,
brought my power into being.
So I have come here.

There were three more free-step songs, and the gahé chiefs
danced and whistled, and the clown did his mime. Then came four
short-step songs and four high-step songs. There was a final song,
addressed to the Black One. Men and women around the circle
stood stiffly, looking at the ground. The gahé chiefs, even the clown,
stood still. It was a haunting spirit song, sung by Chaddi alone, with
a low voice, without a drum. It was short and powerful. The dance
was over.

Chaddi prayed to the Master of Life and spoke to the Black One,
the Gray One, and the gahé chiefs, thanking them for coming and
begging them for help. Tears were streaming down his face when he
ended.

The fire was nearly burned out when the gahé left. First to walk
away was the Black One. The chiefs gave him space, then moved
out, too, the blue chief leading. The clown went last. For some time
the clicking sounds of the "earrings" could be heard, and then the
night became still, as if waiting. There were four piercing cries as the
gahé walked toward their mountain home. The night stirred and
sounds came back, wind brushing dead leaves, night bird calling. An
owl hooted. Toward the west one wolf sang, another, then a whole
pack, melodious sounds intertwined, rising and falling, sweet on the
air.

FIFTY-FIVE

When first my songs became,
when the sky was made,
when the earth was made,
the breath of the gahé on me
was made of down.
When they heard about my life,
where they got their life,
when they heard about me:
it stands.

The day broke with female rain.
The place called "lightning's water stands,"
the place called "where the dawn strikes,"
four places where it is called "it dawns with life,"
I arrive there.
The sky boys, I go among them.
He came to me with long life.
When he talked over my body
with the longest life
the voice of thunder
spoke well four times.
Holy sky boy spoke to me four times.
When he talked to me my breath became.

*Gahé song. Song of the mountain spirits, recorded by
P. E. Goddard, circa 1908.*

FIFTY-SIX

The war party left at sunrise on the cold morning of October 23 under a red sky. The men were dressed for mountain winter weather, wearing leather pants tucked tightly into moccasin boots, and leather shirts. Six of them, Zele, Galeana, Nitzin, Nalgee, Kezinne, and Bish, wore the blue cavalry jackets they had taken in the sacking of the soldier camp in Arizona on June 8; Galeana sported the one with the lieutenant's yellow shoulder stripes. Josanie and the remaining four, Tsach, Zilahe, Tuerto, and Horache, wore fringed buckskin jackets. Each man took additional pairs of moccasins and clothing in saddlebags and a canvas poncho strapped to the top of the blanket roll behind the saddle. Nitzin's and Nalgee's lances were tied below the saddles along the left sides of their horses.

Tuerto rode at point with Galeana because of his intimate knowledge of trails in the high sierra. Josanie followed a short distance behind, leading the single file of warriors. Zele and Zilahe brought up the rear, each with two extra horses on lariats. Three men, Josanie, Tsach, and Nalgee, wore feathered war caps. The others had their hair tied with blue headbands, Zilahe, too, no longer a dikohe but a new warrior. The Chokonen had painted their faces with a white line. Horache, the Chihenne, had painted the line with red. From a distance the party could be taken for a detachment of government scouts.

Eleven riding out, a trail of two thousand miles waiting for them. They rode from the camp and upstream along the Aros, the shining river, and quickly vanished from the sight of anxious people secretly watching them go.

The horses, well fed and rested, were eager to run, but Josanie ordered them held back. For eighteen miles they rode slowly on sandy benches and gravel bars by the river until they struck a trail Tuerto knew that led north-northwest. They climbed for nearly three hours and reached a narrow plateau at six thousand feet and walked on it north, sometimes in fields of fresh snow, then east, downslope to where a creek ran into the Rio Sirupa. They got there in late afternoon and made camp for the night.

On the second day they went north through the canyon the creek had carved out of the mountain, then climbed up to another plateau on the trail that led north-northeast, broke through a ridge over seven thousand feet high, and camped in a snowy gorge ten miles west of the great Mesa del Huracan. There was no water, so the men gave to the horses from the water bags and ate snow for liquid themselves.

On the third day the trail led east around a snow-capped mountain, down into the canyon of one of the tributaries of the Rio del Gavilan, and up the east side and onto the great mesa. Its flat surface was covered with short, thin grass, yellow and brown in autumn colors, dotted with junipers and pines and some silk tassel evergreen shrubs. Swept by winds, snow held on in ravines under tall, straight cypresses. Here the men let the horses run a little, past the abandoned mining towns of Chuhuichupa and Huracan, prosperous once in Spanish times, now dead and part of the tierra despoblado. Once they crossed a big trail two months old, made by perhaps two hundred horses and mule trains. It came in from the northeast and continued west. The men held the horses and looked it over. Josanie surmised that it had been made by one of the American armies searching for them. That night they camped among junipers on a creek north of Huracan.

For the next two days they rode north on another mesa of great expanse that stretched north between two snow-covered mountain ranges. On the sixth day they cut through the eastern range and went down its slope and by evening reached the Rio Casas Grandes, eight miles below the gate of the mountains. They had seen birds of many kinds, deer and bighorn sheep, and a few black bears, but no humans. Under the gold-flecked cottonwoods by the river they found the army's old campsite and rutted tracks going upstream, south, the same they had cut earlier on the Mesa del Huracan.

By midmorning on the seventh day they had come out of the mountains and ridden into the rolling plain that stretched north to the border of New Mexico, 110 miles away. They passed the adobe ruins of the great ancient Indian city of Paquime, lying silently before the backdrop of a cottonwood bosque by the river, and swung northeast, bypassing the mud town of Casas Grandes, for over a century a site where trade alternated with treachery and murder. Behind them the snow-packed peaks of the Sierra Madre faded away, but to the east the Sierra de la Escondida sparkled with the splendor of new snow. They camped in a draw on the lower slope of the range.

On the morning of the eighth day the sun stood unblinking in a cloudless sky. Now the war party rode north along the edge of the mountain slope. Once the men saw wolves running antelopes in the plain, but no other sign of life. Near midday they noticed a thin curl of smoke ahead. Then there were flashes made with a hand mirror. Galeana. Josanie, in the lead, raised his right arm and the men behind him halted. Three men, the signal said, watch out! It was repeated twice. Josanie checked his rifle and let the horse walk forward, cautiously choosing the ground. Galeana and Tuerto waited at the foot of a low ridge.

"Three men, Mexicans. They are sitting by a fire, eating," Galeana said. He pointed behind him.

"Vaqueros," Tuerto added.

"How far?" Josanie asked.

"Three hundred yards," Galeana said.

Josanie nodded. He turned and pointed to his left. Five men rode along the foot of the ridge, got their horses in line, and stopped, waiting for his sign. He brought his right arm up and forward, and the riders flooded over the ridge and raced toward the little camp. The riders to the left fanned out and caught three horses bucking away and came up behind the men sitting on the ground. They had been eating beans and tortillas from tin plates and stood up slowly.

Josanie, with Tuerto, Galeana, and Tsach, held in front of them. He looked them over. Dark brown faces, black eyes squinting at him. Colorful but tattered clothes, worn boots. They had only one poor rifle and a revolver between them. He saw that they were frightened and shook his head.

"Ask them where they come from."

Tuerto repeated the question in Spanish.

One man pointed to the northwest. "Corralitos."

"The big hacienda by the river," Tuerto said. "Maybe twenty miles from here." Heavily fortified, it was the only cattle ranch in all of northern Sonora and Chihuahua that had operated through the wars.

Had they seen any soldiers?

No.

Had they heard of any soldiers?

No.

Josanie nodded. "Tell them we have to take their horses. Nothing else."

Tuerto translated and the vaqueros nodded and bowed emphatically, jabbering incoherent words. The warriors who held the vaqueros' horses untied the latigos and let saddles and saddle blankets fall and took bridles and reins off. Josanie called out and they rode away at a lope, loose-herding the three horses between them. They went straight north, passing through some groups of red-colored cattle, and once, looking back, Josanie saw the three men still standing there, as if frozen to the ground, staring after them. Death had visited but had not stayed.

When they were out of sight, the warriors turned straight east and rode to the low saddle between the Sierra de la Escondida, south, and the Sierra del Capulin, north. Among the last of the Corralitos cattle Nitzin lanced a young steer. They butchered it and packed the meat, rode on to the east slope of the saddle, camped in a ravine with water, built a good fire after dark, and feasted.

On the next day they moved on north along the winding east slope of the sierra. The land lay quiet under the October sun. They saw black bears and bighorn sheep in the pines and junipers of the mountain slopes and saw antelopes play in the yellow- and russet-colored grass of the plain below. It seemed as if humans had become a memory. From higher ground they caught glimpses of the great white playa toward the east, forty miles away, and the white and dark clouds of migratory birds circling above them. That evening they camped on the east slope of the Sierra del Fresnal and until dark

watched the waterfowl rise and fall above a small playa two miles
below the camp.

Morning came with a red dawn and they continued north, passing
well west of Laguna de Guzman, a great blue lake in the midst of
wide belts of cane and swampgrass, with thousands of birds above it.
The warriors went on along another playa and its feathered hosts
and to the end of the Rio Casas Grandes, where it loosed itself in the
northernmost nook of the playa. They made camp fifteen miles
below the New Mexico border. They searched with field glasses but
saw nothing of humans. They knew they were close. It had taken
them ten days to get there.

At first light they were on their way. They rode west, upstream
near the river for ten miles, then turned straight north into a gap
between two escarpments and toward the Tres Hermanas Mountains,
rising pale blue in the distance. They thought that they had crossed
the line. And then, around a nose of the escarpment, they came on a
patrol of four government Indian scouts. They were dismounted,
studying something on the ground. They heard the hoofbeat of the
war party and stood stiffly erect, looking. Galeana and Horache were
riding point fifty yards ahead of Josanie and the men.

The war party approached calmly at a slow lope, showing neither
surprise nor any indication of hostile intentions. Perhaps the scouts
were fooled by the cavalry jackets Galeana and five of the warriors
wore. They waited too long. When the point riders had bridged the
distance to about two hundred yards, one of the scouts shouted and
the four men mounted their horses on the run and whipped them
into a gallop.

Behind Josanie his men fanned out, and the wild chase was on.
Galeana and Horache were ahead and slowly gained on the scouts.
Both held their Winchesters out. A race of six hundred yards and they
closed in on the last three. Yells, a series of shots, and two were
down and one was hanging low in the saddle, trying to hold on, but
could not. He raised a fountain of dust when he fell. There were
more shots when warriors passed the downed riders. The last scout's
horse gave out, and the man dismounted and faced his pursuers,
firing the Springfield single shot from a kneeling position. He got

three shots off, one hitting Kezinne's horse; then he was brought down by three or four rifles and lay still.

"I know this one," Josanie said.

"Yes. White Mountain. Cut-Face. Carrizo band from White River," Tsach said.

"Brave man," Josanie said. "I'm glad he didn't hit anyone."

"He hit my horse," Kezinne said. He stood with his arm around the neck of the dun mare, trying to hold the excited animal still. The bullet had gone through the upper neck below the artery, leaving an ugly exit wound.

Tsach looked at it. "I have some medicine for this," he said. "But you shouldn't ride her."

"We have no time for this," Josanie said. "Take one of the other horses."

Kezinne opened the latigo and pulled saddle and saddle blanket and the pack attached to the saddle from the dun's back, dropped them into the grass, and untied the double knot of the bridle under the lower jaw. He leaned the Henry repeater against the saddle and embraced the mare's neck with both arms. He buried his face in the long hair of her mane for a moment. He let go and the mare backed off, snorting, nervous from the smell of blood, and he went for a chestnut mare among the lariated horses Zilahe brought up to him.

Nitzin took the dead man's cartridge belt and rifle and tied them to the pack of one of the spare horses. Josanie and the others were riding back to look at the three dead scouts. The first one they came to was White Mountain, but the last two, the ones to die first, were not Apache. Brown buckskin boots with white soles, silver-buttoned trousers, concho belts, leather pouches with silver ornaments, copper bracelets.

"Navajos," Josanie said grimly. "Come to serve the white eyes."

They rounded up the scouts' horses, collected their government-issued Springfields and ammunition belts, and rode on north. Past the last of the dead Josanie stayed back and cut the line of separation in the sand, asking their spirits to forgive the bad deeds of the living. Turkey vultures were already gathering in the sky. Horache led the small column around the east face of the Tres Hermanas and finally up toward the highest of the three peaks in the northeastern corner of the mountains. There, at its base, an ancient spring was hidden. They camped there for the night. They had glassed the flat, dry plain all around but seen nothing of danger.

Before they drank water from the shaded pool among the rocks, Horache knelt and gave turquoise beads to it. He prayed briefly, the men standing behind him, wondering. He turned around.

"This is a special place," he said, "the one they tell stories about, the one in the Three Mountains. Here. You may have heard them."

"Yes," Josanie said. "I have. Most of us have, maybe all of us. But I have never been here myself."

The men around him nodded. "None of us has," Tsach said.

"We may take water from this pool," Horache said. "But we must remember who lives here. Her story must be told at this place. She hears us when we mention her."

Later, after men and horses had tasted the sweet, cold water, horses now grazing on a grassy bench, and the men sitting around a small fire below a rock wall near the pool, in the dark, Horache told the story.

"She was a very, very pretty girl. She was dressed in buckskin. They told her, 'Go to the spring and get water.' They waited for her. She didn't come back. The spring was just a little way from her camp. They went over to look for her after a while and found only the water jar. They discovered her trail and followed it. They saw she had walked to 'Three Mountains.' They didn't know where she was. The couldn't follow her any farther. They lived there a year and hunted all over for her. They had good diyin. They asked some who were good at finding lost objects to look for her. Finally they got the best one. He got all the people together. He sang and sang to find out where she was.

"Then the singer said, 'She's right there in 'Three Mountains.'

"That was the place where this man had obtained his power. He told the people to come with him in that mountain. My great-grandmother went with him; my great-grandfather, too, and others who were living in those days. He ordered those people who were going in there with him to cover themselves with pollen.

"All at once, after they had worshiped at the rock wall . . ." Horache pointed with his chin, "it might have been this one, a place opened and a door appeared where there had been none before. Bears and other fierce animals, the worst they had ever seen, were right there in front. But they worshiped just as the diyin told them to do, and they were all allowed to enter. Inside was a fine level bench of sand, very beautiful, and a big opening.

"Those inside told them, 'Go ahead, the leader is there. Go and see him.'

"They traveled ahead. They saw fierce animals but were not bothered. The bear told them, 'Your girl is married to the son of the power of this place. I don't believe she can leave this place even if she wants to. There is her camp.' He pointed to a camp.

"So they saw her in there. They urged her to go home with them. She was as pretty as could be, and the man she had married in that holy cave was just as good-looking as she was. She didn't want to go back with her relatives. 'I want to stay here. I don't want to go back to earth any more,' she said.

"The son-in-law said, 'You people go back. But stay around this holy place. I'll watch you. You'll have plenty. Have no fear. Don't leave this region no matter how many enemies you see.'

"So they went out. The girl wouldn't go back with them. She also told them, 'You stay around this holy place and you will increase in numbers. I'll be with you. You'll have plenty of horses, and the enemy will not bother you.'

"But the people disobeyed. They went back west. They all got killed. That's the way the old people used to tell it. The power of this place belonged to the father of the young man who married the girl. They don't say how the girl got in there, who led her into this place. It might have been Water Monster who took her there."

Horache had ended and cried. He did not wipe off the tears. "This place," he said, "holy, it makes me cry."

The men sat in silence, moved by the story and the place. It was still all here, they thought, the spring and the pool and the rock walls. Which one hid the door? There was no answer.

"We honor them," Josanie said. "Those who live in the earth, the gahé, Water Monster, spirits of places, some of our own people, ndé. We honor them. I ask them to help us."

It was a quiet night and they made gifts of turquoise to the pool when they left in the morning. They rode north, through a flat country of short, yellow grasses dotted with yucca, toward the Florida Mountains, ten miles away. They could see a long way all around. After a dozen miles, below the southeast slope of the mountain range, they rode through some small bunches of red-colored cattle and saw a dead she-wolf lying on her left side, amber eyes half open, the upper lip drawn back in a contorted grimace. There was no bullet mark, and they wondered how she had died. They found three more dead wolves farther up before they came to the partly eaten cadaver of a steer, most of the hide stripped neatly away.

The men sat their horses around the cadaver. Sharp eyes saw where some knife cuts had been made through the hide. There were hoofprints of two horses in the soft ground, perhaps two days old, coming from the north and going back.

Josanie knew what had happened. "Poison," he said. "They call it arsenic. Two men came here after wolves had killed the cow and eaten from it. They put poison on what was left. They stripped part of the hide down so they could smear the poison on better."

He paused. "I have seen it before, in the mountains. White men, trappers, poisoned skinned-out beavers and left the whole bodies for wolves. But foxes and coyotes and birds ate, too. They killed many animals that way."

He paused again. "Now they are killing wolves for their cows."

When they rode away from the site of a new and fiendish kind of death, Zele called out. They halted and looked. He pointed south. A light flag of dust stood over the plain, a few dark dots below it, about a dozen miles away. Josanie and Galeana watched through field glasses.

"Soldiers," Josanie said. "A dozen maybe. Two civilians, white scouts perhaps. One Indian. They are riding fast."

"They found the scouts we killed," Galeana said.

The field glasses were passed around.

"We have to stop them," Josanie said. "We can't drag them with us. We find an arroyo to ambush them. Five," he pointed with his chin at Galeana, Nitzin, Nalgee, Kezinne, and Bish, "stay with me." He looked at Tsach. "You take the others and go on with the horses. Make enough dust so they think we are running away."

He paused. "Let's ride."

They rode on with an easy lope. The pursuers kept coming, getting closer. Josanie's party crossed three arroyos, but these were still in full view of the enemy. In the gap between the Florida Mountains and the Little Florida Mountains they turned west, and, out of sight, Josanie and five men slipped off the horses when another arroyo was crossed, while Tsach and the others rode on, following the curved outline of the slope leading southwest.

In the arroyo the men spaced themselves twenty paces apart and sat down. They checked their rifles and waited. At last there was the sound of hoofbeats approaching fast. The men looked to Josanie. He shook his head. Not yet! A few more minutes. It seemed the horses were on them. Now! He signaled.

The warriors rose above the edge of the arroyo. Josanie saw the Indian scout to the left of their trail, two civilians to the right, about a hundred yards away, and half a troop of cavalry three hundred yards behind them. He fired at the Indian scout and heard the whack of the bullet when it hit him in the chest. Rifles crashed along the arroyo, and when he aimed the Sharps at the cavalry in the distance, he saw from the corner of his eye that the two civilians had been shot down. Horses ran wildly in front of their rifles, and when he had a free field of fire, he saw that the cavalry had turned to the side and was frantically galloping away. He and Nitzin got a few shots off with their long-range rifles, but without causing visible damage. The dust settled and hoofbeats from behind them announced Tsach's return. Zele and Zilahe fanned out to round up the horses of the dead. Those of the civilians, one injured, had Winchester repeaters slung in leather cases below the saddles.

They walked around and looked at the bodies. The Indian was a Navajo. The two white men had multiple bullet wounds. These were men in their thirties with hard, suntanned faces; they looked like professional hunters. No one knew any of them. They were quickly stripped of cartridge belts with .44-40 shells, and Kezinne turned them to lie face down. The warriors did the same with the Navajo. One of the horses was still good, and they took it with them when they rode away, north again. Josanie once more talked to the spirits of the dead and, with Horache, took the lead of the little column.

They passed the Little Florida Mountains and crossed the tracks of the Southern Pacific Railroad twelve miles east of Deming. They veered to the northeast and rode for twenty-four miles through a grass country of low, rolling hills, seeing no one but antelopes and occasionally small herds of pale red cattle. They crossed the tracks of another railroad east of Nutt, where the northern spur of the Santa Fe ran north to the silver mining town of Lake Valley, and slipped into the hills to the north. They camped for the night in a draw on Ricketson Creek where Horache had found water. At dusk they spied with field glasses from a point high above their camp. To the east they saw the silver sheen bends of the Rio Grande; to the northwest, the dark, ragged massif of the Black Range; to the west, the Mimbres Mountains and Crooks Range. They looked and looked and felt that they had come home.

FIFTY-SEVEN

In the west, a yellow cloud stands upright.
There, his home is made of yellow clouds.
The Great Yellow Mountain Spirit in the west,
He is happy over me.
My songs have been created.
He sings the ceremony into my mouth.
My songs have been created.
The cross made of turquoise,
The tips of his horns are covered with yellow
Pollen.
Now we can see in all directions,
Drive evil and sickness away.
My songs will go out into the world.

*Gahé song. Song of the mountain spirits, recorded by
Jules Henry in 1930.*

FIFTY-EIGHT

At sunrise, horses saddled and ready, the warriors stood in a group. "There are many white people on the east slope of these mountains now," Horache said. "More coming all the time. Mostly miners and those who live off the miners. There," he pointed northwest, "is Lake Valley, where the railroad goes. There are silver mines, tents, and wooden houses. Almost a thousand people, including white women who sleep with men for money."

He paused. "Worse is Hillsboro, fifteen miles farther. Mines all around the town. And Kingston, just west of Hillsboro. Together maybe two thousand people. A few years ago, with Nana and others no longer with us, we tried many times to drive them out. We couldn't. That gold and silver they dig up make them crazy. These people rather die for it than give it up."

He paused again. "We tried to drive them away. It is our country, but they have driven us away. We killed many, but it was for nothing."

He made a gesture of futility with his hand. "There are wagon roads from Hillsboro to the railroad at Lake Valley and east to the Rio Grande. Wagon trains with things from the mines going out, wagon trains with supplies for the mines going in. And north of these are two more bad towns, Winston and Chloride. Mining towns, too. A thousand people together there. Maybe more."

He shook his head. "And there are ranches all through the great plain in the mountains they now call San Agustin, and west to the San Francisco River. It was all our country, Chihenne, and yours, Chokonen. Now there is a railroad at Magdalena, and they drive cows there from all over. There are three cow towns on the San Francisco River, close together, west of the Tularosa Mountains. And there is the sheep town of Luna, from where they run sheep all through the San Francisco Mountains and the Mogollons."

He shook his head. "When I and Nana and our band came through last summer, we watched some of it. We talked with people we knew in Monticello, and they told us. It is true."

The men had listened in silence.

"Someone is going to see us," Horache said.

Josanie thought for a moment. "Yes. Let them see us. We let them think we are scouts for the government."

He paused. "The army has Indian scouts of many tribes. Whites don't know one Indian from another. They know nothing of us. We pose as Navajo scouts if we run into whites here."

He laughed. Serious again: "No shooting if we can help it! Let's ride."

He took the lead with Horache, and they rode out of the draw and turned north. They stayed on the wide shelf that extended all along the Black Range below five thousand feet. They kept well east of the railroad to Lake Valley and the Hillsboro wagon road. Sometimes they could see the great river ten miles to the east, meandering through the dense cottonwood bosque of its floodplain. The golden autumn leaves of the gnarled, ancient trees had turned a dusty brown. Sandhill cranes cruised and dipped along the river. Before them, to the northwest, the crest of the Black Range, ten thousand feet high, showed fields of glittering snow on alpine meadows surrounded by dark Douglas fir forests. There they would go.

They rode through black grama grass sprinkled with tobosa and creosote bushes, which sometimes formed thickets they had to circle around. They crossed the dry, gravelly beds of seven creeks and in the eighth, on Percha Creek, four miles east of Hillsboro, they came on an elderly white man on a good horse. He had halted and coolly watched the warriors approach. His clothing and the horse's accoutrement suggested a cattleman, his bearing that he was not a cowhand. Quizzical eyes in a suntanned face under a black hat. He wore a gun belt and a holstered revolver on his left. A left-handed man, Josanie saw. He raised his right hand when Josanie and Horache were thirty paces away. Josanie did the same. Behind him the little column halted. He and Horache rode forward.

"Howdy," the man said. He looked into Josanie's eyes. Josanie nodded. The man glanced along the faces of the warriors. "Where are you going?"

Josanie pointed north. "Horse Springs."

"Oh. The Eighth Cavalry camp?"

Josanie nodded.

"Where are you from?"

"Up north, Navajo land."

"You are Navajo?" the man asked.

Josanie nodded and smiled.

"You been hunting Geronimo?"

Josanie nodded. "We look for him."

"You been to old Mexico?"

"Yes."

"Who's your officer?"

"Davis. Crawford."

"Yeah," the man said. "I heard that Crawford is back from old Mexico putting a new force together. Are you with this force?"

Josanie nodded. He smiled. "We go now."

He clicked his tongue and squeezed the horse's left flank lightly with his thigh. He touched its neck on the right side with the bridle, and the horse turned left and away from the cattleman. Josanie urged it into a lope up a low bench and out of the dry creekbed. His men followed, and Zele and Zilahe waved at the man when they passed him with the spare horses, the captured rifles sticking out from the packs. He touched the brim of his hat with his right index finger and watched them pass.

They had ridden twenty miles that morning. Two miles farther north they crossed the wagon road that led from Hillsboro down to the Rio Grande. After another four miles they came to Las Animas Creek and climbed down into its dry bed and followed it upstream toward the peaks of the mountains.

It was easy riding, although the gravels were hard on the horse's hooves. They took their time to spare the horses. After they climbed slowly but steadily for over twenty miles, they came near the head of the Las Animas below McKnight Mountain. Riding through a gorge, they came to a mass of scattered horse bones.

Horache, who was riding point, dismounted. Behind him, Josanie and the men also dismounted.

"This is the place where we, Chihenne, had a battle with soldiers six years ago, after we came from Mescalero," Horache said.

"Yes, we heard about it," Josanie said.

"This was the first battle, September 1879. We had three more in the same month, all on the headwaters of creeks on this side of the Black Range. One up on the north fork, Palomas, one on the south fork of Cuchillo Negro, one on the north fork. We moved north this high up, and different troops of soldiers followed us, fresh troops all the time, lots of San Carlos and Navajo scouts, other white men. We defeated them, killing many of their men, many horses."

He paused. "They tried to break through in this place. We shot them down."

"Where did you go from these mountains?" Josanie asked.

"North, into the San Mateo Mountains." He laughed. "Then we circled back and came through here again. Went south to the Florida Mountains and into Mexico, to the Candelaria Mountains. We had to fight all the way, but they couldn't stop us."

The men looked around in silence. A good place to defend, a bad place to attack. Nana had chosen the right location.

Josanie touched Horache's arm and pointed forward with his chin. Horache nodded, and they walked the horses through the gorge. Beyond it the main stream channel switched to the left and a small rivulet ran in from the north. Horache followed it and led the way into a series of high meadows, partly covered with fresh snow. There were stands of aspen, their empty branches stiff and forlorn in the wind, and firs and pines standing like a wall around the clearings. The raiders went by a few beaver ponds and made camp behind a windbreak of fallen trees on ground free of snow.

"This is where our camp was when the soldiers came," Horache said. He pointed to a number of torn wickiup frames still visible. "We stopped them in the gorge."

They let the horses graze and built a good fire. Galeana had kept watch over their back trail at the gorge. He saw nothing and came in when dark settled.

On the next day they traveled north below the spine of the Black Range to the headwaters of the north fork of Palomas Creek under

Diamond Peak. The distance was twelve miles as the raven flew, but criss-crossing on the eight- to nine-thousand-foot level, often in snow and on passages slick with ice, took them most of the day.

They climbed over the top of the mountains on the following day and down into the canyon of South Diamond Creek that ran its water into the east fork of the Gila. So they came into the great triangle of the Gila basin, surrounded on its three sides by mountain chains that scratched the clouds. The basin was still free of snow. From the pine and Douglas fir forest they had come into juniper and piñon woodland, grassy plateaus, and wide, grassy slopes around streams with oak thickets. Where Diamond Creek turned west, Horache took a trail north to Whitewater Creek, where they made camp.

They stayed in this camp for eight days, rested the horses, and hunted elk. The large herds had come into the basin from the high mountains. Tsach and Kezinne did the shooting with their bows; the other men helped sometimes by driving the game. They killed thirteen hinds, ate well, and dried meat for provisions. It was like old times. Tracks of many species were everywhere, including grizzly, wolf, and puma, and perhaps even jaguar, and sometimes at night they heard the howling of a wolf pack. They wanted to be forgotten by the world but not by ndé, their own, and by gahé and the spirits. Tsach had built a small shrine to the gahé, a simple circular arrangement of pebbles, and put some turquoise on the ground inside.

But the men got restless. They wanted to get their families, and Josanie had difficulties holding them back. He finally yielded, concerned that some might leave on their own. The party started out again on the morning of November 15, Horache and Josanie riding point. They cut north across a low saddle and into the flats along Beaver Creek and went upstream to where the canyon now called O Bar O Canyon came in from the northwest. They followed it for about fifteen miles and made camp in a wooded draw with water below the east face of Elk Mountain.

For the next four days they went west through the northern edge of the Mogollon Mountains, then through the Kelly Mountains, and across the San Francisco River below the Saliz Mountains. They rode through these and the San Francisco Mountains behind them and reached the headwaters of the Blue River. This had become tame sheep country, and they killed two ewes with arrows and stayed for the night. In the mountains on both banks of the San Francisco and in its wide floodplain they had seen cattle and once had hid to let three cowhands pass, who went by without noticing them. On the day following they went straight west along the headwaters of the San Francisco and crossed a high saddle and, finally, came into the narrow valley of the East Fork of Black River, northwest of Tenney Mountain.

For hours they had ridden in snow, their and the horses' breath as white clouds before them. The snow-capped peaks of the White Mountains to the west, rising above eleven thousand feet, glittering in the evening sun, beckoned and urged them on, and they knew that they would be on Turkey Creek and among their people very soon.

They found a place where the snow cover was light and brushed it away for a campsite. They knew that no one would see them there, so they built a roaring fire and kept it up all through the cold night. With Galeana at point they rode on after sunup, the snow sometimes reaching to the bellies of the horses. They rode south throughout the day, along the curving stream, criss-crossing often, evading ice bridges and fallen trees. They were forced to move slowly and made only twenty-five miles. They stopped to camp when they came down to below six thousand feet and left the snow zone behind. It was in one of the many bends of Black River, below Poker Mountain, where there was dry grass for the horses. They made a cold camp because they were no more than twenty miles from the mouth of Turkey Creek, near where they expected Chokonen and Chihenne camps to be. They had to be careful. If they were spied by White Mountain Apache eyes, surely the garrison of Fort Apache and Apache police would be brought on them.

In the morning Josanie let Galeana and Zele ride to scout through the deep canyon of Black River to the mouth of Turkey Creek and upstream into the hills below Fort Apache. He stayed in camp with the rest of the men. The two scouts returned in the early afternoon.

They had seen no one in the canyon and for eight miles only one abandoned camp by the creek. Through field glasses they had seen one camp on the creek below Corn Creek Plateau and one more farther east on Bonito Creek. The first one seemed to be Loco's camp; whose the other was they did not know. It seemed that camps had been moved north to Fort Apache. They had not dared to get closer. They had seen two riders looking like Indian police briefly visit Loco's camp—if it was his.

"I'm not sure," Galeana shrugged, and Zele nodded with a pensive look.

They stayed in their camp for a second, restless night. Throughout the following day they waited for daylight to pass, but the sun rolled on its invisible track without hurry.

Finally dusk came and they mounted and rode, Galeana and Zele at point again. A dark night, the moon a thin sickle in the eastern sky. The bottom of Black River Canyon, foreboding in daytime, was shrouded in darkness, and progress was slow. Finally they reached the mouth of Turkey Creek, a cut in the north wall of the canyon. They led the horses up on foot and mounted again when the creekbed flattened out. They rode along the slopes of the hills east of the creek, slowly, until they could smell campfires and came to a horse herd near the first camp under Corn Creek Plateau.

Josanie sent Galeana and Zele out to find out whose camp it was. The two wound their mounts slowly through the nervous herd and were swallowed by the dark. Josanie and the men around him readied the rifles. It seemed to take a long time. A dark shadow reached out to them.

Zele. "Loco's camp," he said. "He says to come in."

He turned his horse, and Josanie and the men followed him. They passed through horses, which had been grazing but now stood watching, came to a low basin, and saw the many glimmering campfires of the Chihenne camp. The fires lit dimly an irregularly spaced group of about thirty wickiups. The Chihenne chief stood behind a fire in an open area between the lodges.

He was wrapped in a trade blanket and watched Josanie and his men approach. Behind him men began to gather, and women with a few children hastily formed a circle around the open space. They were covered with blankets, only eyes showing, glittering in the light of the fire. Galeana stood beside the chief.

Wearily Josanie and the men dismounted. Loco looked at their wild, haggard faces; hollow eyes; the ready weapons; the paint and war regalia. He stretched his right hand before him. Josanie did the same.

"Come, brother," Loco said gently. "I am glad you came. You are safe with us. You and your men, sit down."

He turned and spoke to two of his men, and they vanished between the wickiups.

"We'll have guards out tonight," he said. "No one is going to come in."

He spoke to his wife behind him, and she called out softly and was joined by a few women, and they went to prepare food. Wood was brought in and fed to the fire.

They sat down, forming a circle around the fire. It crackled and threw sparks and new flames began to leap, casting a bright light.

Wolves they are, Loco mused, cornered grizzlies. His broad, deeply lined face showed sorrow.

"We thought you would come," he said. "When Manuel told us that he ran into you near the mountains, south, we thought that you would try to come here."

He paused. "Too many soldiers, I know. We didn't tell anyone what we were thinking."

Josanie looked at the man who had fought beside him for half a lifetime. So many good people lost around them.

"I am glad we met you," Josanie said. His eyes under the feathered war cap shone like sparks in the firelight. "You know why we have come. We want our women and children."

"Yes," Loco said sadly. "I know." He looked into the fire, his eyelids closed to slits. "I know."

He paused.

"I have to tell you something bad." He looked up into Josanie's eyes. "They are not here. They are prisoners in Fort Bowie. Down there. They were never brought back here."

The men sat stunned, their faces blank. Someone groaned.

"I am sad to tell you this," Loco said. "There is more. Your son, he died on the way to Fort Bowie."

Josanie nodded. There was a long silence. "Yes," he finally said. No one spoke. They stared into the fire.

Finally Loco broke the silence. "What will you do?"

Josanie swallowed hard. "We go back tomorrow."

He looked into the fire without seeing. He removed the war cap and put it over his right knee. He stroked the eagle feathers.

"Whose camp is that on the creek east of here?"

"Bonito's."

Josanie nodded. "Bonito. Chokonen little chief, the one who lets his men guide the soldiers to our camps. A man like Chato."

He paused.

"Who is north of here?"

"One White Mountain camp south of the fort. The others are north of there; Chato's, too."

Josanie nodded. Women brought food in tin cups, a thin broth with a few scraps of fatty meat. It was hot, and the raiders sipped slowly.

"We don't have much," Loco said. "Much of the time we go hungry. The army doesn't let us hunt. We depend on government rations. It is poor meat, and the flour is full of worms." He laughed scornfully. "They like to starve us."

After the men had eaten, they unsaddled the horses. They took them to water and hobbled them by the creek. They stashed saddles and saddlebags and rifles and blankets in two wickiups that Loco had ordered emptied. They would sleep there for the night. They sat for another hour around the fire, Loco and his men making serious efforts to talk, but the raiders remained aloof and distant.

The fire was beginning to burn down, and Josanie got up. "Thank you for your kindness, brother," he said. "You can't come with us, and we can't stay. We ride early."

They spent a fretful night and saddled up long before first light. Hoarfrost lay whitish on the grass. It was November 24. The stars were bright in the black tent of the night. Orion, the hunter, stood brilliantly in the eastern sky. Loco walked up and saw that they were painted and held the rifles ready. He knew what was about to happen. He held out his hand, palm forward, and Josanie held his against it.

They looked into each other's eyes. They remembered what they had shared, where they had been, everything. There was no need to talk. They nodded briefly to each other, and Josanie moved the horse sideways and rode off into the dark, the men in a loose bunch behind him. They had left two of the captured Springfields and some ammunition as a gift in one of the places where they had slept.

A mile from Loco's camp they halted. Josanie told them his plan. The men eagerly agreed. They rode slowly through the low, barren hills they knew so well, through the short, yellow grass. They had less than ten miles to cover to Fort Apache. They passed the widely spaced buildings and corrals on the south side, riding west near the White River, sometimes in full view of the post, and came out on the flats at first light. There they came up on the cattle herd of the fort, guarded by two night riders, white men, cowhands, not soldiers. The raiders shot both without slowing the horses and galloped toward the White Mountain camp by the river.

They rode with a cold fury and yelled and fanned out and circled white canvas tents and a few wickiups. They rode through the camp, driving women and children before them, their rifles searching for men. Heavy gunfire exploded, people running wildly before the horses. Eight men, young and old, were shot down. Women and children were bunched and held outside the camp. Tsach, Kezinne, and Galeana went through the tents and shot three more men who had been hiding. Nothing was taken, and the raiders did not bother about a small horse herd downriver. They grabbed five women, one with a six-year-old girl, and put them on the spare horses, two women riding double. They made sure that the White Mountain men were dead. Two shots rang out, and they rode off, driving the hostages before them. Tuerto and Bish raced downriver and, out of sight, cut the telegraph line to San Carlos. The soldiers would find the cut and restore it, but the war party might gain a few hours' time.

They joined the band again when it swerved to the southeast, away from the river, and rode across the Bonito Prairie, and on upper Turkey Creek they hit Bonito's horse herd. They yelled and waved blankets and hazed the herd into motion and drove it off toward Eagle Creek Trail. The people of Bonito's camp gathered quietly in front of their wickiups and watched the party race away with their horses. No shot was fired. Kezinne took the point, and Bish and Nalgee rode as flankers of the remuda of about fifty horses. Behind the herd rode the women hostages, followed by Josanie and most of the men. Galeana, Zele, and Zilahe held back behind the main body to watch for the certain pursuit.

They rode east six miles until they reached Willow Creek, then followed it down for another five miles to Black River Canyon. They went into the canyon and upstream through its dark, towering walls for eleven miles to the mouth of Freezeout Creek, which ran in from the east. Here they climbed out and onto the high plateau north of Willow Mountain and after another fifteen miles reached Eagle Creek, and the old trail that led south to the Gila, the one they had traveled over in May. It was near midmorning, and they rested the horses for the first time.

Josanie walked over to the women, who sat huddled together in a tight group. Their dark faces showed no emotion, but he know that they were angry and vengeful.

"You know who we are?" he asked.

The women did not stir. Finally one said, "Ndé-ndà-i."

Josanie nodded. "What band do you belong to?"

"Black Water People," the woman said. "By the river." She pointed.

"You know who I am?"

"Josanie," the woman said.

He nodded. "Yes." He paused. "We expected more men in your camp. Where are they?"

No one spoke. Finally the woman said proudly: "My husband, Carrizol, he is with the officer Crawford in Fort Bowie, getting ready to go after you. He and our men there, they'll find you."

Josanie nodded. "We are angry, too. Our women and children were taken from us. Some were killed." He looked at the sullen faces.

"We will not harm you. I want to exchange you for our women and children." He waited. "Don't try to run away or slow us down. If you do, we'll shoot you. That's what your men did to us."

He looked from face to face and walked away.

After the rest they changed horses, taking the best mounts of Bonito's herd for themselves and the hostages, along with three spare horses, and left the others there, including the faithful but exhausted companions that had brought them from the Aros to this place. They took three colts on lariats and rode on more slowly, but made thirty-five more miles and camped for the night behind a bend of the creek seven miles above the Gila. There Nalgee lanced the colts, and they handed knives to the White Mountain women to butcher and prepare the meat. Galeana and Zele remained ten miles behind to watch over the back trail.

FIFTY-NINE

In your issue of Oct. 30 is an article by "L". He asks "Where are the men who some months ago were offering to subscribe hundreds of dollars to outfit a force to raid the reservation? Their ardor seems to have cooled until next spring's outbreak again revives it." I submitted a proposition to the citizens of Grand and Sierra counties. I saw no other. Mine is still submitted, and if "L" and eight of his friends will "ante" I will meet them in Silver City. I will give "L" $500 if he will deliver Geronimo dead or alive, at Silver City, N.M. I had no "ardor" in the permises [*sic*]. I asserted a business proposition to accomplish a certain object. With "L" I think the reservation should be raided—K. K. K. them.

    H. W. Elliot

A letter from Hillsboro, New Mexico, published in the Silver City Enterprise, *November 4, 1885.*

Citizens Meeting. Yesterday afternoon a citizen's meeting was called to devise means for immediate relief from the present Indian troubles. As an initiative step it was moved that a meeting of the Grant County stock association be called. . . . A motion was put and carried that the board of county commissioners be requested to offer a reward of $250 for the scalps of marauding Indians. To this amount Lyons and Campbell offered an additional reward of $500 for Geronimo's scalp.

News item in the Silver City Enterprise, *December 23, 1885.*

SIXTY

The night over the canyon of Eagle Creek turned toward morning. A southwest wind dragged across the sky a screen of clouds that hid the stars. A feeling of moisture was in the air, of rain or snow. Through the dark came the sounds of horses moving slowly, feeding on dry grass, the murmur of the creek. Two fires still burned brightly under the bony, lifeless-looking cottonwoods. Near one, their feet close to it, the women and the child lay, tightly squeezed together for warmth and comfort. They were covered with three blankets they had been able to snatch before being hoisted on horses and driven from their camp. The men lay asleep around the second fire.

Josanie awoke from the hoofbeat of a single horse slowly searching its way downstream. He pushed the blanket aside, got up, and walked toward the horse and rider coming into the light of the fire. Zele. It has happened this way before, Josanie thought, in May, at almost the same place. He thought that the message would be the same. It was.

Zele slowly dismounted and let the bridle drop. The horse stood for a moment, then backed away. He let the chestnut mare walk. His face under the blue headband was tired. The white war paint across his cheekbones had largely worn off.

He nodded to Josanie. "They are coming."

"Where are they? How many?"

"We think between twenty and thirty. We don't know who they are." Zele paused. "They have rested for some time, but now they are coming again. They are maybe eight miles behind me. Galeana is in front of them."

Josanie nodded. Men began to gather around them. "We better saddle up and go." He called out to Tsach, who was getting up, to wake the women and tell them to hurry.

"Which way do we go?" Tuerto asked.

Josanie looked into the hard, attentive faces around him. "I think to that long canyon in the Peloncillos. We stop them there, the ones who are behind us. Then we go west, where they don't expect us to go. When they come after us, we circle back." He paused. "We can't go east now. They are waiting for us up on the San Francisco. They remember last time." He paused again. "We can't go south now. By morning they are putting soldiers everywhere on the railroad. We'll go east and south when they have gotten tired of waiting for us."

He looked around, waiting for a question or a disagreement. None came. The group broke up, and men went to gather the horses. Water bags and canteens had already been filled, and food distributed among all, before the camp had gone to sleep last night. Now men and women, in separate places, relieved themselves, drank from the creek, and splashed water in their faces. They mounted. Josanie took point when they rode out.

They wound their way slowly through the canyon to the Gila. Before they crossed it, Josanie gave turquoise beads to the spirit of the river. On the south side they rode upstream between towering red rock walls for another four miles until they came out on the flats, where they let the horses run a little. Under a leaden sky they crossed the Hot Springs trail and the Safford road and paused to let Galeana come up behind them.

"They are coming," he said. Josanie waved to him, and they rode on southeast through the rolling plain toward the tracks of the Arizona and New Mexico Railroad where they emerged from the narrows of the Gila. They rode alongside the embankment, pausing long enough to cut the telegraph line five times that connected Clifton with Duncan and Lordsburg. When they reached the mouth of the canyon now called Tollhouse, leading northwest into and through the northernmost part of the Peloncillos, Josanie rode in and up for about six miles.

He halted and dismounted behind a good place for an ambush. Two men stayed to guard the horses and the women. Josanie sent Galeana once again over the back trail to report on the pursuers and took the rest of the men into the rocks above a passage where the canyon walls tapered to a winding corridor.

Daylight had come, a gray day under gray and dark clouds. The men waited patiently. After a while a single rider came around a bend and approached briskly over the red sands. Galeana. He rode through the passage and halted, searching for Josanie's face above him. He shrugged.

"They have stopped outside. They are not coming anymore!"

"How do you know?" Josanie asked.

"I saw them through the glass. The soldiers wanted to follow us, but the Apache scouts said no. They had an argument. I saw it. When I left, the scouts were sitting by themselves, away from the soldiers."

"Who are they?"

"Ten soldiers and one officer. I think fifteen to twenty Apache scouts. I think I saw Chato."

Josanie nodded. "Chato." He paused. "He's clever. He knows." He paused again. "Let them sit there! We ride!"

They rode up toward Thumb Butte and down into Tollgate Wash and, fifteen miles later, came out on a high bench above the broad valley of the San Simon River. With fieldglasses they swept the wooded stretch of the Gila valley around Solomon to the northwest and the grassy valley before them to the west and south. They saw no movement. Behind the valley lay the brooding massif of the Pinaleno Mountains. The highest of its peaks was the holy Chokonen mountain of the west, now Mount Graham, the place where she had lived since leaving the people, White Painted Woman. Although her seat was hidden by clouds, Tsach stretched out his arms and sang from horseback one of the sky songs of the gotál to it:

> White Painted Woman
> commands that which lies above.
> Child of the Water commands.
> Through long life they command.
> From the mouth of the chief bird
> yellowness emerges.
> Yellow pollen emerges from your mouth.

The men listened in silence, holding the horses still. When he finished, two of the White Mountain women wept softly, rocking in their saddles. Perhaps they had not seen this place, holy to them also, for a long time.

Josanie waited for a moment, then clicked his tongue and urged the horse on. The cavalcade followed and they rode down to the little river, through the tall dry grass dotted with dwarf shrubs and yucca, and went along it south to Oak Draw, which led southwest and up into a gap in the Pinalenos. The draw was deep enough to shield them from view.

Now they rode slowly to spare the horses. They climbed steadily and crossed a saddle to the west face of the mountains. In late afternoon they reached the spring at the head of Hog Canyon and made camp in dense chaparral. Seven miles to the northwest lay Fort Grant, and below it, due west, the huge Sierra Bonita ranch, largest in Sulphur Springs Valley. From their aerie they scanned the long valley, from the narrows of Avaraipa Canyon in the northwest to Willcox by the Southern Pacific Railroad, twenty miles away to the south. Once they saw a single rider moving toward the ranch, but no one else. They wondered where the soldiers of Fort Grant had gone.

That night they talked for the first time about their families imprisoned in Fort Bowie. The moment they had heard the terrible news from Loco, they knew that everything had changed. They realized that their hopes had been mere fantasies, that their struggles had been in vain. There were hundreds of soldiers and civilian white men in Fort Bowie, and the few Chokonen warriors would not be able to force their way in.

The men stared into the fire with empty faces.

"Do you really think the white men will exchange our women and children for the White Mountain women?" Tsach asked.

He spoke in the special Chokonen language known only to men and used only on war expeditions. The discussion continued in this language so that the women hostages could not understand what was said.

Josanie swallowed. "I don't know. I hope they do."

"I don't believe it," Nitzin said bitterly. "For them ndé women are all the same. They don't care about these White Mountain women. They would like us to kill them. The fewer Apaches, the better for the whites."

"I don't believe it either," Kezinne said. "They won't trade them for our families."

There was a heavy silence.

Finally Galeana spoke. "I don't think they'll trade for these here." He paused. "Maybe we must trade them something else, or someone else."

"Who?" Josanie asked.

Galeana gestured with his right hand. "If we had the nantan lupan, Crook, the general, we could trade him for our people, couldn't we?"

Faces turned to Galeana. Tsach smiled sarcastically. "How do we get him?"

There was a long silence.

Finally Josanie spoke quietly. "We have to think about it. If we would get him, the whites would trade. Galeana is right."

"How?" Tsach insisted.

"I don't know," Galeana said.

"Crook wants us to give up. He wants to make peace with us," Josanie said. "We know that. Only he wants a peace that is good for them, bad for us."

He laughed angrily.

"If we agreed to meet with him, we could grab him and make him our prisoner."

He paused. "They have done the same thing to us, over and over again. They took many of our chiefs that way in the past, arrested them at a peace meeting and killed them. You know that. They have always done that when they could not win in war."

"How can we make him our prisoner when there are always so many soldiers and scouts around him?" Tsach asked.

Some of the men nodded.

Josanie broke a twig and threw it into the fire.

"We agree to meet him at a place where we can do this. We pick the place. Make a condition. Tell him not to bring soldiers."

He waited. "Is it not strange? He trusts us, trusts our promise, yet he and all those others, from long time ago, they have always lied to us, betrayed us."

He paused. "He would come to us when we ask him to talk peace. He is a brave man. We can arrange it."

There was a murmur of agreement around the fire.

"He would only come if we promise him that he is safe," Tuerto said.

There was a silence.

"Yes," Josanie said. "We lie to him. How often have they lied to us?" He looked from face to face. "We don't kill him. We want to trade him."

"If we do that, they'll search everywhere for us, turn every stone to find us," Tuerto said.

Josanie nodded. "They are doing that already. We are still here." He paused. "We must think about it. In our camp, when we are back with the others, we must talk about it."

Again there was agreement. The men's faces no longer looked as empty and forlorn as before. Some looked thoughtful, some skeptical but interested, others hopeful. It did not matter that the clouds finally opened and released a snow flurry. Big, watery flakes came down in a dense, tumbling cascade of white. It was too late to build shelters. They endured the onslaught wrapped in blankets. The flurry ended as abruptly as it had started, and men and women built up the fires and went to sleep around them.

Over the next three days they made a wide sweep through Sulphur Springs Valley into Aravaipa Canyon, out past the northwestern edge of the Pinaleno Mountains, and into the San Carlos Reservation. In Black Rock Wash, southwest of Fort Thomas, they shot a white man who crossed their path. They circled southeast again and during the night of November 28 camped in Marijilda Canyon southeast of Mount Graham. There they sang to White Painted Woman. The women hostages, as expected, had ridden the many miles as well as the warriors. No one had tracked them; white and Apache hunters had to be searching elsewhere. But the horses were worn out, and in the morning the raiders rode out to collect fresh mounts.

They swooped out of the canyon toward the Gila, rode east past Solomon, hit two ranches by the river, and took the horses they needed. On the first ranch they killed two cowhands who had foolishly resisted, but on the second ranch the man and his family stood by when they took nine horses from the corral, and were not harmed. The war party turned southeast, toward Ash Peak in the Peloncillos, and to Ash Canyon, which led to Duncan on the Gila. When they reached Slick Rock Wash, they became aware that they were being followed by a posse. They rode on and found a good place for an ambush.

It happened as it had happened so many times before. Josanie and seven men formed a half circle across their back trail. They sat hidden in a shallow draw. When the hoofbeats of the eager posse thundered uncomfortably close, the eight Chokonen stood up and fired their rifles into the densely packed horsemen. The head of the column collapsed under the hail of bullets from Henry and Winchester repeaters, and the riders following plunged into the melee of falling horses and thrown riders. Screaming horses and men, the hard, slapping sounds of bullets striking flesh. Riders farther down the line tried to extricate themselves from the confusion and the raking fire and swerved to the side and raced away.

The warriors shouted the Chokonen war cry and raised the empty rifles high above their heads. They reloaded the weapons and went to the place of carnage. They shot badly injured horses and found two white men dead, seven wounded, lying still, with huge eyes. They took rifles and gun belts and let the wounded be. Nitzin, Tuerto, and Zilahe brought the horses up from behind a ridge, with the mounted women, and the warriors stashed arms and rode away. Josanie stayed behind to propitiate the spirits of the dead. This he had done so many times before. When he finished and looked up, he saw three men of the posse sitting their horses out of rifle range, watching. He mounted and followed his men on the trail to Duncan.

They reached the railroad and the Gila and crossed both after cutting the telegraph wire again. They turned south, upstream, and passed Duncan, a small railroad town above the west bank of the river, and rode on, through the wide floodplain under ancient cottonwoods still decked out in yellow leaves. Sometimes they had to cross the stream channel that meandered between dry bars of gravel and yellow and red sand. Below Black Mountain the river valley turned northeast, and they followed it and came to the mouth of Blue Creek, running in from the mountains of the north.

On the twenty-mile ride from Duncan they passed two ranches but stopped only once to kill two heifers with lances and let the women butcher them, while white men from the ranch looked on. They rested and watched the women work, and when it was finished and the meat divided, they moved on and into the wide draw of Blue Creek and up for another five miles before they made camp. It was early evening. They had ridden sixty-eight miles since leaving Marijilda Canyon at dawn.

"What do you have in mind?" Tsach asked. "Why are we going back north?"

"I want to hit some places up on the mining road," Josanie said grimly. "We talked about it one evening in camp, with my brother and Nana. Make the whites bleed, show them that they are not safe from us, that we can reach them whenever we want to. They can only be safe if they leave us alone."

Over the next one and a half day they made only eighteen miles, climbing until they cut their old trail from Bear Valley where it crossed Blue Creek, northeast of the Summit Mountains. While Bish, Kezinne, and Nitzin moved with the women east over the trail to the Bircher Flats for an early camp, Josanie and the others stayed back and searched for a place to cache the booty of weapons and ammunition they had taken from the enemy. They found a crevice under a rock overhang, filled it, and closed and camouflaged it.

On the next day they rode north down the winding trail for about eight miles and came into the "Valley of Mother's Sibling," the valley of the grizzly below Bear Mountain, where they had camped for four days in late May. In this valley Tsach's grandmother and Chihuahua's wife had been born. They found tracks of one large grizzly in a number of places, always the same animal, but they never saw it. Snow was rare in this part of the Mule Mountains, between five and six thousand feet, and the bear probably lived through the winter by killing game and cattle. Elk and deer were plentiful, and Josanie decided to stay for four days. In the early mornings hoarfrost covered the tall, dry grass along the creek, but a powerful sun warmed the mountain world during the day. They hunted a little and enjoyed the interlude. Scouts went out through Buckhorn Creek and over the back trail and saw game, but no trace of humans.

On the fifth day they rode out north through the canyons and camped on a spring below the bend of the San Francisco River where it came from the north and turned west. They made this a cold camp because the dusty road to Silver City passed two miles away to the east.

The morning of December 7 dawned cold and clear. The warriors painted themselves and checked the rifles. They drank from the spring and chewed jerky and rode into the wide floodplain of the river. The women were troubled but tried to hide it; they knew that something was about to happen. They were placed between Josanie and seven warriors, the main attacking force, and three warriors at the tail end with the lariated spare horses. The floodplain was half a mile wide in parts, adorned with stands of ancient cottonwoods, and the stream channel, carrying little water, wound through low benches and sand bars. They passed the hot springs, the mouth of Whitewater Creek, and a small ranch nestled in the hills and came to the outskirts of Alma.

The small town sat above the eastern edge of the floodplain, its wooden cabins and houses lined along both sides of the road that connected Silver City with the San Francisco Plazas farther up the river and Horse Springs, Datil, and Magdalena in the north. It was a hub for local cattlemen and the gold and silver mines on Mineral and Silver Creeks eight miles away in the Mogollon Mountains.

Josanie waved the drag riders on, and they continued with the women through the floodplain. There were some irrigation ditches, and they slowed down and rode around them. Josanie swung east with his party, climbed the slope, and rode into the town between closely spaced log cabins. The rutted street was nearly empty under the rising sun. But outside a store two men were harnessing mule teams to a freight wagon, and the Apaches killed both and emptied their rifles into windows facing the street, sweeping through on a slow lope. They yelled and were out of the town. They rode into the floodplain and overtook the three warriors with the women, reloading their weapons while they spurred the horses into a gallop. Across from the mouth of Keller Canyon they came upon a ranch and stopped briefly to set the main building on fire after they had pushed a woman and three children out. They did not harm them and did not bother about some horses in a corral.

The wooden building burned fast. A rising plume of smoke behind them, they crossed the San Francisco and rode up Keller Canyon toward the low saddle of Alma Mesa and the Little Blue. They set an ambush and waited for a posse, but none came. They turned south and rode through the twisting canyons under Maple Peak for thirteen miles and turned east again and crossed the river at the mouth of Whitewater Creek. They rode into the deep draw and under the barren sycamores into the cut of Little Whitewater Creek. They halted near the place where they had camped in May.

For this day and the next they watched the road but saw only a mail rider once and let him pass. They waited for bigger game, and when it came, it came to them.

At sunup on December 9 the quiet was shattered by gunfire from below the camp, a little glade where they had left the horses. Bish and Nitzin, who had guarded them during the night, escaped the attack and joined the men around Josanie.

"Soldiers," Nitzin said. "Indian scouts."

The horses were lost. Josanie spoke to the women. "Wait for the soldiers. They'll take you back to your people."

The soldiers were slow in climbing up to the camp. The warriors took their weapons, blankets, and saddle bags and walked away, leaving saddles and other equipment behind. They went over the same trail they had taken in May, and after two miles of climbing they halted and prepared an ambush. But no one followed. Later, from the high slope of Nabours Mountain, they scanned the area of the road visible among rolling hills and evergreen shrubs and finally saw them. The White Mountain women were riding with a detachment of Indian scouts, probably Navajos, who drove the captured horses along. Behind came a column of blue horsemen. Through fieldglasses they saw the swallowtail guidon of Troop C of the Eighth Cavalry. The column went north toward Alma.

"We walk through the mountains into the basin," Josanie said calmly. No one had asked, but everyone had wondered. "There are ranches on the west side. We take their horses and come back."

He slid the fieldglasses into the leather case and got up. They had been in situations worse than this before; there was no cause for alarm. He threw the saddlebags over his shoulder, wrapped a blanket around his rifle, and started out on the trail. Nitzin had lost his lance in the skirmish for the horses; it was the only loss truly regretted. That night they camped at Rock Spring, at eight thousand feet. For food they had a few slices of jerked venison every man carried in a belt pouch for emergencies.

On the next day they walked on snow below Black Mountain and Center Baldy, passing the white peaks at nine thousand feet, often slipping on ice, and went over a saddle and dropped into the high basin along the West Fork of the Gila. The snow gave way, but the basin was frigid when the sun dipped below the crest behind them. Kezinne managed to kill an elk hind with his bow, and they camped under pines where Turkeyfeather Creek ran into the West Fork from the north. Josanie had been born eleven miles farther east, on the Middle Fork of the Gila, as had Chihuahua. It seemed to him an endless time ago.

On the next day they searched for cattle and horse tracks along the Gila headwaters and tributaries. They found two small bunches of heifers on springs below Lilley Mountain and a horse trail leading east toward a high parkland. Galeana and Zele followed the horse trail and came on a ranch surrounded by tall pines: three log cabins, a shed, and a corral. Horses were grazing under the trees. They watched for a while and reported they had seen only two white men. Nalgee lanced a heifer, and after dark the warriors roasted a supply of meat around a fire three miles below the ranch. The wind came out of the southwest and carried the smoke away.

They went up at first light and killed the two men with rifles. More men had been there some time ago, but now there was no one else. The horses had been corraled during the night, sixteen of them. The warriors went through the buildings. They did not touch everything but took a few things, among them four saddles, two rifle scabbards, a Sharps .45-70 and a Winchester .44 rimfire, boxes of shells for both, some clothing, rawhide ropes, a water bag, a small saw, a couple of woolen blankets, two Navajo horse blankets, a couple of tanned elk hides, boxes with matches, two hatchets, and a whiskey bottle filled with elk teeth. They burned nothing, bridled the horses, and put saddles and blankets on their backs. They mounted and watched Josanie speak to the spirits of the dead men and draw a line on the ground. He took the lead, and they rode south for a mile and slipped into Lilley Canyon and went down to the Gila West Fork, where they turned upstream to White Creek. They climbed out south to the Diablo Range and into Mogollon Creek.

They moved slowly. It took them this day and four more days to come out of the Mogollons, but near midday of December 17 they were once again near the Silver City road, four miles southwest of the great bend of the San Francisco. At the place where the ruts of the dirt road crossed the dry gravel bed of Little Dry Creek, they surprised two freight wagons pulled by mule teams. The two drivers were mounted on animals on the left-hand side of the teams, maintaining control by means of a check line.

The warriors rode down on them and killed one driver but let the other escape to bring reinforcements. They unhitched the mules and loosened the chains of the doubletrees. The frightened animals scattered, but the warriors saw the man catch one on the road ahead, where it ran up the hill. This they had hoped for. They saw him swing himself on the mule's back and race toward Alma, fifteen miles to the north. They checked the wagons but found only mining equipment. They piled dry brush under the boards and burned them, making sure that the smoke rolled heavy and dark.

They tied the horses up in a draw by the creek half a mile west of the road and left Bish to guard them. Tuerto was sent south on horseback, with Josanie's fieldglasses, to watch the road toward Silver City. Josanie walked with the remaining eight men into the hills to where the road dipped toward Dry Creek. He split them into two parties and let them position themselves in cover on both sides of the road. He told Tsach to come with him, and the two men walked north, parallel to the road, for about five hundred yards. Josanie searched cuts and dips in the red earth for clayey soil. He found something close to it, dug with his knife, took his jacket off, put chunks of grayish soil in it, and walked toward the road.

Tsach had watched in wonder first, but then he understood. "I know what you are doing," he said.

Josanie nodded. "I know you would." He grinned.

Close to the road Josanie prepared the soil. There was no water, so Josanie put the chunks on the surface of the ground and urinated on them. He kneaded them thoroughly with his hands.

"There," Tsach said with a hushed voice.

Josanie looked up and followed the direction of his eyes. There was a movement between junipers in a hollow on the east side of the road, and the head of a large male grizzly emerged. He walked out and up onto the road and, thirty feet away, caught the men's scent. He stood still, swinging his broad head from side to side, his mouth half open, the brown eyes on them. They sun lay shiny on the rough, reddish mat of his fur.

Tsach opened his hands wide and softly sang to the bear with closed eyes. The grizzly listened. They could almost feel his breath. He shook his head and moved on, crossed the road and walked past them, and vanished in a draw leading west.

"Mother's sibling," Tsach said. "The great one. Perhaps he wants to tell us something."

Josanie nodded. He walked up to the road and placed the softened mass of soil squarely on one of the grizzly's pug marks. He knelt and started modeling it, shaping it into the figure of an owl sitting on the ground, facing in the direction in which the warriors were waiting. He stepped back and looked at it. He nodded; it would do.

"If a posse comes, they will run over it," he said. "But if Navajo or Apache scouts come with soldiers, they will know." He paused. "They won't go on; they know that death waits for them up there."

He sang a short song to the owl, and they wiped their moccasin prints away and circled back to their men. They joined them there. Behind the hill to the south smoke still billowed.

They lay on the ground, patiently, and finally they saw dust and horsemen come over the Alma road down the long hill to Dry Creek. They approached with good speed.

"Navajo scouts," Galeana said. He shielded the fieldglasses with his hands to keep the oculars from reflecting the sun's light. "Soldiers behind them." He waited, watching. "I think the ones who took our horses." He paused. "Yes. It's the same little flag."

They came closer and the warriors saw a small group of Navajo scouts in front and a troop of cavalry behind, the soldiers riding by twos, a guidon wafting over them. But then the Navajos stopped, and Josanie knew that they had seen the owl. They bunched up and the troopers almost rode into them. Horses milled around in a swirl of dust. Finally the Navajos rode to the side of the road, and the cavalry came on. The troopers picked up speed, and when they were between the jaws of the trap, Josanie stood up and fired the Sharps at one of the four officers at the head of the column. With the bucking of the rifle he saw the man thrown out of the saddle. He opened the breech and reloaded. His men were standing and discharged their weapons into the soldiers' ranks. The head of the column withered under the punishing guns, but behind it troopers swerved away from the road, dismounted, took cover, and began a noisy but ineffective fire with their carbines. Once the warriors shouted the Chokonen and Chihenne war cries. There were blue-clad bodies lying on and near the road among crippled and screaming horses, crawling and sitting wounded men, and horses galloping away.

Josanie saw the Navajo scouts sit their horses in the distance, unmoving. The grizzly had come, the owl had blinked its affecting eyes, and death had struck. With his few men he could not destroy the surviving troopers without losing men. But his men had families to regain, women and children to free. He would have liked to finish the soldiers off, men on pay without a cause, but he resisted and called out and the warriors walked away. Behind them, after a while, the rifle fire slackened and died. No one followed them.

SIXTY-ONE

Red is the color of war.
Red is the color of witches.
Red wind is the wind that brings death.
Owl is the messenger.

Chiricahua witching song.

SIXTY-TWO

Tuerto rode up when they reached the horses.

"No one on the road south," he said. He looked to where the men were untying the horses. No one was missing; no one seemed injured.

"I heard you," he continued. He handed the leather case with the fieldglasses to Josanie. In his eyes was an unspoken question.

"Yes," Josanie said. "It went good. We killed some and wounded some." He nodded to Tuerto. Josanie turned and walked to his horse. He untied it. He let the horse breathe out, pulled the rawhide that held the blanket instead of a saddle, and fastened it. He mounted and rode down the creekbed on the dry gravels toward the San Francisco River. The men fell in behind him. They rode for about a mile to where Burnt Stump Canyon came in from the southwest. Josanie rode into the canyon and up to Pine Cienega Creek and followed it south, between wide, grassy slopes, all the way to the pine forest below Tillie Hall Peak. They arrived in early evening. They were on the high ridge near the Arizona–New Mexico line, from where the dry creekbeds and canyons ran down in every direction, a rocky, pine-clad, labyrinthic vastness hostile to white invaders but a shelter to its native denizens.

Josanie decided to stay for a few days to let the enemy exhaust himself searching. They moved camp only twice, and only a few miles, once to the headwaters of the creek named after them, Apache Creek, the second time past the peaks of the Summit Mountains to the head of Carlisle Canyon. They had come near the cache of arms they had made earlier, but left it alone; they might need it later. There was a little snow up there, but hunting was good. They killed a bighorn and an elk hind with arrows but were careful to burn fires only after dark. No one came after them.

In the Carlisle Canyon camp Josanie said that they should start out for the Sierra Madre in the morning. The men agreed. In the soft black night the fire was burning cheerfully, but the men looked glumly into the flames.

"We need better horses than these," Tsach said. "They are good enough for the mountains, but we need horses that can run in the flat country."

"Yes," Josanie said. "Those two ranches on the Gila we came by when we came up the river—we take horses from them. If they don't have enough horses, we hit Duncan for horses."

"I wonder why no one has followed us," Galeana said.

There was a silence.

"They are afraid of a trap, I think," Josanie said finally. "They'll probably wait for us on the railroad, from Bowie Station to Lordsburg and Deming. They know we have to go south. When we cross the open country, we need fast horses. Tsach is right."

When first light crawled leaden over the eastern sky, they broke camp and rode down the canyon ten miles to its mouth. The day was December 25. Before them opened the floodplain of the Gila. Beyond lay the Animas Valley, a flat grassy plain ten to fifteen miles wide, bordered in the west by the chain of the Peloncillos, in the east first by the high bench of the Big Burro Mountains, later by the Pyramid and Animas Mountains. The valley ran ninety miles straight south to the Mexican border, where it butted against the Sierra de San Luis. The Southern Pacific Railroad crossed it thirty-two miles south of the mouth of Carlisle Canyon, between the railroad towns of Steins and Lordsburg.

They rode upriver and struck the two ranches that lay by the Gila seven miles apart. From the first they took eight, from the second six horses, good cow ponies all. At both ranches white people looked on but did not resist; no one was harmed. They left the horses they had taken in the Mogollons and rode south into the Animas Valley.

They saw herds of antelopes dance in the plain and flocks of sandcranes, geese, and ducks whirl over the three playas to the south. They rode in a loose bunch, the three spare horses lariated by the drag riders. Josanie was in the lead, and ten miles into the valley he turned southwest toward the Peloncillos. They crossed the embankment of the Arizona and New Mexico Railroad that came out of Clifton via Duncan and ran in a nearly straight line from a high point in the plain to Lordsburg. They stopped to cut the telegraph wire. They hugged the eastern slope of the mountains and continued south, past Horseshoe and Doubtful Canyons, gates in the Peloncillos toward San Simon Valley. Both canyons were notorious sites for ambushes and had been used by the combatants for decades. Josanie expected soldiers to be stationed there. Under a warm December sun they rode by the alkali flats and the restless bird flocks over its playas, slipped into the mountains four miles north of Steins, and went through them to where they could sweep the town and the railroad with binoculars. At least one troop, perhaps two troops of cavalry were camped at the eastern edge of town, with a contingent of Indian scouts. Horses and mules were picketed behind tent rows, and there were wagons on side tracks held ready, it seemed, for quick transportation of soldiers.

They watched until dusk, when a cavalry patrol with four Indian scouts came in from the east and six Indian scouts returned from the west. The scouts seemed to be Navajos. When they were gone toward the camp, the war party mounted and rode west for another mile and crossed the railroad out of sight. Under a waning moon, with a sharp wind out of the southwest in their faces, they made ten more miles and settled for a cold camp in a draw on the east slope of the Peloncillos.

During the night clouds drifted in, and morning came dark and cold, with a hint of moisture in the air. When they readied the horses, Tsach spoke to Josanie, but everyone heard him.

"I had a bad dream," he said. "It woke me up during the night. I saw soldiers, many foot soldiers, in the mountains on both sides of the valley, there, where it narrows in the south. And I saw horse soldiers in between, hidden in a canyon. They were all waiting for us. And there was a man, I think a Navajo chief. He came riding toward me on a yellow horse. He had an owl. The owl sat on his shoulder, looking back, away from me. The Navajo smiled and waved to me."

He paused. "This is all. I woke up." He paused again. "Oh yes, I remember I turned my head and there were soldiers behind us. I saw Chato, too."

The men had listened in silence. They looked at each other, holding the bridles of their horses.

"It is a bad dream," Josanie said slowly. "But it helps us. It tells us something important."

He stepped in front of Tsach. "Chaddi would do this, but he is not here. I do it. I will take the dream away. It is not ghost sickness. It is a dream."

Tsach stood stiffly erect, arms hanging limp. Josanie took a small bundle of white male sage from a pouch on his bandolier. He bent and touched the earth with it and, starting at Tsach's right shoulder, led it along the right side of his body to the tip of his moccasin boot. He did the same on Tsach's left side. He held the bundle on Tsach's head and prayed in a barely audible voice. He was finished and stepped back.

"It is done," he said.

"Thank you," Tsach answered. Both men stretched the palms of their right hands toward each other. Josanie nodded and put the sage bundle away.

"It is good," he said. "We learned something. We won't ride south. It is better this way. We go through Cochise's mountains, the Chiricahuas. We will visit that mining town again when we go in."

They rode south for a mile, came to a low saddle, and crossed it west to the San Simon River. Under the cottonwoods they let the horses drink and drank themselves and filled water bags and canteens. Before them lay the great turtleback massif of the mountains that bore their name. They rode in on the same trail on which they had left in October. The cattle were gone, but there were antelopes in the grass. They aimed for Harris Mountain, ten miles southwest of the little river, and rode fast and passed it. Instead of going up on Whitetail Creek, they went in on Turkey Creek.

On the west side of Davis Mountain they halted and painted themselves. The mining town of Galeyville was two miles ahead on the creek, a rough hive of tents and cabins and tunnels and tailings and waste and rotting machinery they had attacked a couple of times since its beginnings in 1880. About four hundred people lived there.

They rode on, following a dirt road deeply furrowed from wagon wheels. Snow began to fall, thin, cold flakes that would last on the ground. Before they reached the first cabins along the main street, they surprised two men working in a ditch. The two men did not notice the Chokonen, and Tsach and Kezinne had time to brace their bows. The two warriors rode forward and shot the men with arrows. They dismounted and finished them with knives and retrieved the arrows. They relaxed the bows and slipped them with the arrows into the hide quivers. They mounted and checked their .44 rimfire Henrys. They nodded to Josanie; they were ready.

Josanie looked along the faces of his men, hard faces under the war paint. He turned his horse and rode into the gathering snowstorm. They rode at a trot in single file and came to the first cabins. Josanie shot a man who carried a load of firewood and rode on, reloading. Behind him doors were flung open, and men rushed into the rutted road that was already turning muddy. There were shouts and shots and screams and the steady, relentless firing by the war party as it moved down the main street. Ahead Josanie saw a man with a raised rifle and shot him in the chest, reloaded the Sharps, and put a bullet through a window that had been thrown open. He shot at another man who ran up the slope where the tailings formed hills of yellow earth below the tunnels and saw him hit in the upper leg. Another shot at a shadow in a door frame and he was through the town. He halted and held the excited horse and let his men pass, bullets whizzing around them. Behind Zilahe, the last of the drag riders, he closed in, and they came out miraculously unscathed.

He took point again and continued upstream, now in a driving snowstorm, and four miles beyond Galeyville he took a trail south that led to the headwaters of Cave Creek and to a park by Anita Spring below Chiricahua Peak. They made six miles after the turnoff, walking, leading the horses, and found shelter under an overhang of red, rain-streaked rock. Outside the snow gathered in drifts. The hardy cow ponies stood under Ponderosa pines with their docks and hindquarters turned into the storm, while a white blanket formed on their backs.

The storm howled on with a rare, undiminished fury, and they stayed for another two days and nights, their only worry the horses.

The men cleared areas of snow for them to get to the grasses beneath and cut branches from the undergrowth and from some blue oak for edible bark.

When the storm relented, they waited a little and moved on, south over Raspberry Ridge Trail and into Bear Creek Canyon to the wide, pine-covered head of Rucker Canyon. They walked the horses through snow sometimes waist-deep but found shelter after a mere seven miles of traveling.

Another day and the snowfall ended. They walked the horses three miles west through Rucker Canyon and hit the mouth of Tex Canyon, the one they knew like the contents of their saddlebags, and followed it southeast and came out on the high ground above San Simon Valley. They scanned it from end to end and saw nothing but delicate antelopes frolicking in the white fuzz of the snow-covered valley and a few hungry ravens. They rode out and south toward the Mexican border, twenty-five miles away. The snow was only half a foot deep south of the Chiricahuas. They felt awkward themselves in the white wilderness, with frosted yuccas standing around like ghosts.

No one disputed their passage. Black Draw and Astin Spring, where they had sacked the soldier camp in early June, lay deserted, the saguaros rising pale green, startled giants, from the shining whiteness. Josanie and his men dropped into Guadelupe Canyon, went southeast and crossed the border, and came out among the mesas and high ridges of the Sierra de San Luis. Where they had been so many times before.

They came out and rode along the San Bernardino River, in the great quiet of the tierra despoblado. The snow gave out and they rode slowly through the brown grass and stubborn manzanitas, sparing the horses. Where the river from the north joined the Bavispe River on its course south they went along it, by the reed thickets on the west bank, and on past Oputo, mud town of ancient enemies, and passed it in broad daylight. There were two American armies in northern Mexico looking for them, but they saw no trace of one or the other. They passed the colonia Huasabas and came into the Sierra Madre, white peaks glinting in the sun, and to the Aros River.

They had been seen but did not care much anymore. They had nothing to lose, their families having been imprisoned in Fort Bowie, out of reach. They did not fear for themselves. They knew that their tracks would be pointed out and studied. So many eyes searching. They rode upstream on the great river and reached their camp on January 7, 1886.

The raid to free their people had lasted seventy-seven days. They had punished their enemies, white and Indian, but they had come back with empty hands. They knew that they would be found. They would fight, but the end was before them.

SIXTY-THREE

In the south, a blue cloud stands upright.
There, his home is made of blue clouds.
The Great Blue Mountain Spirit in the south,
He is happy over me.
My songs have been created.
He sings the ceremony into my mouth.
My songs have been created.
The cross made of turquoise,
The tips of his horns are covered with yellow
Pollen.
Now we can see in all directions,
Drive evil and sickness away.
My songs will go out into the world.

*Gahé song. Song of the mountain spirits, recorded by
Jules Henry in 1930.*

SIXTY-FOUR

Josanie would always remember how they came back to their camp.

The trail. It wound along the emerald river over rocky screes and soft earth embankments, sometimes fording the cool waters on white gravels. The horse herd. Light and dark dots showing in the distance, the animals grazing along the flats of the river that ran into the Aros from the south. The stark beauty of the Blue Mountains. Green, green slopes—evergreen forests climbing up toward the rock walls. Vertical cliffs in colors gray, rosy red, and yellow, with green tufts of shrubs and stunted trees in clefts and on narrow ramparts. And beyond, pale blue peaks lifting immobile snowy caps into the incredible blueness of the sky. The smoke. He could smell the wood fires before the war party rounded the last bend of the Aros. The camp. About fifteen wickiups spread out over a rocky knoll above the river, smoke curling up from some and drifting down the valley before a soft south wind. The people of the two bands. The ones left had gathered across the trail, so small a group, bright colors of the women, somber colors of the men. The women standing in a tight cluster in front.

They rode up in single file. Josanie honored Galeana, Horache, and Tuerto by letting them ride point, the ones who had guided them faithfully. He rode next. Behind him came Nalgee, the lance riding on his right moccasin boot, the shaft standing straight, the long steel blade glinting in the sun, feathers lying limp along the shaft below it—the guidon of an ndé warrior party. Tsach followed, then Kezinne, Nitzin, Bish, Zele, and Zilahe, the last three with the lariated spare horses.

Before they reached the women, they were stopped by a piercing cry. Jaccali. She stood with her head thrown back. She called four times, the high sounds breaking against the mountains. There was a pause, and then the thirteen women sang the ndé victory song. It was the second time since the spring of 1883. They sang four lines four times repeated, their high-pitched voices rising and falling. They ended with a piercing cry, defiant and jubilant.

The men of the war party sat on their horses, trying to hold the jittery animals still. They felt shamed, unworthy of the reception. They had been victorious but unsuccessful in their quest. The women had formed two lines. The warriors rode slowly through them, touched by outstretched arms. They dismounted behind the lines.

There was Jaccali. She embraced him quickly. They stood for a long moment, pressed against each other; then Josanie tore himself free and looked into her eyes. She was crying. "Our son . . . ," he started to say, but Jaccali put her hand over his mouth. "I know," she said. "We all know."

Josanie tried to step back, but now Ramona put her arms around him. Chihuahua was there also, smiling. He put a hand on his shoulder.

"What is it you know?" Josanie asked.

"We know they were not at Fort Apache," Chihuahua said. "You could not get them. We found out that they are in Fort Bowie."

"How did you find out?"

"They told us," Chihuahua said. He half turned and pointed with his chin.

Josanie looked. Two riders had come up behind them, familiar figures. One muscular, square-shouldered, a war cap above the broad face. Geronimo. The other tall and slender, a more delicate face with a strong nose, wearing a blue headband. Naiche, second son of Cochise. They saw him look at them and raised their right hands in greeting, palms forward, and he did the same.

"When did they come in?" he asked.

Chihuahua shrugged. "Shortly after you had gone. They found your tracks and trailed you here. They are camped half a mile up the river." He paused. "Their camp had been attacked, and some women and children were captured. Geronimo went to Fort Apache and got a wife and daughter back, but found out that our families were in Bowie."

Nana put his hand on Josanie's shoulder. His furrowed face lit up in a quick smile, the eyes sharp as an eagle's. "We are happy you and all the men are back. No one lost. It must have been a good raid. You must tell us."

Chihuahua took the bridle of Josanie's horse, and they walked up the trail to the camp. The men of the war party followed, Nalgee with his wife, Shanta, and their little son, Boca; Zele and his wife Aralos, and little Tuscas; and Nitzin with his boy, Chee. Chaddi walked between Tsach and Zilahe. Horache came with Nana and the people of the Chihenne band and his wife, Lucia, and daughter, Kazhe. Four men walked by themselves, Galeana, Kezinne, Bish, and Tuerto; their families were prisoners in Fort Bowie.

"How many men have they left, Geronimo and Naiche?" Josanie asked.

"Geronimo, five. He lost one man. Naiche, four." Chihuahua shrugged. "Between them they lost fifteen women and children captured, and two killed. Naiche, two captured, but Geronimo, thirteen."

Josanie nodded. There was a pause. "Mangus, where is he?"

"No one knows," Chihuahua said. "Somewhere here, maybe. Some say he is in the Black Range."

"We went through there," Josanie said. "We saw nothing of him."

They had reached the top of the knoll, and Jaccali steered Josanie through gnarled pines toward their wickiup, next to Chihuahua's. She had her arm around his waist, pushing her body against his. He had difficulty walking. He suddenly felt vaguely unsure of himself, uneasy, distant, overwhelmed. He wanted to be away with his men, somewhere on an empty trail. But Jaccali looked into his face. She saw the brown skin stretched tightly over the cheekbones; the wide, thin mouth; the shaded, unsmiling eyes; and she smiled at him.

In the afternoon the four bands met in Chihuahua's camp. They sat there in a circle around a bright fire, sheltered from a light southeastern wind. There was little smoke from the dry wood, and it drifted away without touching them. The men formed the inner circle facing the fire, their wives and children behind them. All were wrapped tightly in blankets.

They sat in clockwise fashion according to the ancient spatial distribution of Chiricahua bands. Nana and his people, representing the Chihenne, sat in the northeastern position. Geronimo and his band, representing the Bedonkohe division of the Chokonen and the Nednhi, held the southeast and south of the circle. Among them was Lozen, the Chihenne warrior woman, sister of the dead chief, Victorio. Naiche and his band, representing Cochise's, his father's Chokonen division, sat in the southwest, and Chihuahua's band of northern Chokonen, the largest present, closed the circle between Naiche and Nana, from the southwest to the northeast. The brothers sat together, Ramona behind Chihuahua, Jaccali behind Josanie, her knees touching his back. All together they numbered thirty-two warriors, including the chiefs; Chaddi; five boys counted as riflemen in emergencies; and forty-six women and children.

After they had assembled, Chaddi spoke a prayer of thanks to Bikego I'ndan, the Master of Life, and sang songs to White Painted Woman and Child of the Water and to the gahé. The people listened with bowed heads. He especially thanked the blue chief of the gahé, who had given them shelter in the Blue Mountains.

Next Chihuahua spoke briefly. And then Josanie described the raid. Three men who had been with him, Tsach, Horache, and Tuerto, spoke briefly after him. There was a clamorous response after the last speaker had finished.

And then there was silence. Finally Nana spoke. He turned to Josanie. "Josanie, before you left you said that we should make a treaty with the Americans. We would promise to stay in these mountains. If they left us alone, we would leave them alone."

He paused. "We talked it over with them," he pointed with his chin at Naiche and Geronimo. "We could not agree on this. We must talk more about it."

"I don't give up anything that belongs to us up north," Geronimo said. "We fought for it. Many died for it. From the Rio Grande across the Gila to the mountain of White Painted Woman—that is ours. I don't give it up."

Again there was a silence. Some of the men nodded.

"You have already given it up," Josanie said calmly. "You would not be sitting here if you had not given it up."

"This is only for now." There was an angry undertone in Geronimo's voice. "I'll be going north soon."

"Yes," Josanie said. "I know. But you know that the moment you leave a track, they'll be after you, trying to hunt you down. They'll take you alive or dead. They put money on your scalp; we heard that in Loco's camp." He shook his head. "That's no good. They have taken it all away from us, and we can't take it back anymore."

He moved his right hand clockwise, pointing along the circle of people. "Who is going to take it back? Count us, one by one. The few of us take it back?"

Chihuahua looked at his brother sideways and nodded. He touched his arm and turned to Geronimo. "What else can we do? They find us when we go north. They'll find us here, too. We must do something. We must have our families back. We must have a plan, a new plan, a good plan."

Naiche cleared his throat. "There is something in what you say, Josanie. But even if we agreed to give up our country in the north, would the Americans agree to leave us alone in these mountains? I don't think so."

Darkness came with clouds that pulled a curtain across the sky. In Geronimo's band a baby cried but was quickly stilled.

"There is a way, I think," Josanie said. "We talked about it when we were north." He looked into Naiche's eyes. "Galeana thought of it. We had these White Mountain women with us and thought to trade them for our people. But later we thought that the whites would never do that. So we came up with something else." He paused. "It is this: if we take Crook prisoner, the general, the Americans will talk with us. We can trade him for our families. How often have they done that to us? They asked our chiefs to come to a meeting and arrested them there, forcing bands to make a treaty to get them back. We can do the same to them. We have never tried that."

There was a murmur of agreement. "Josanie is right," Nana said. "Crook would meet with us if we asked for it. He would. He came to us three years ago into these mountains." He laughed. "We should have taken him then." He paused. "I don't know if the Americans would make the treaty Josanie thinks about if he were our prisoner."

Josanie broke a twig and threw it into the fire. "They would if he and some officers with him were our prisoners," he said. "We would tell Washington that we would kill him if no treaty is made the way we want it. We tell them to stop the war against us and let us have our families back. And leave us alone here and let others come and join us who want to."

"He is one general," Geronimo said. "Washington has many. They send another general to replace him. And another if they need to. They won't rest until we are dead."

"Yes," Josanie said. "That's why we must do something."

"We can take him and see what comes from that," Chihuahua said. "We talk with him first. If he threatens us and makes conditions we cannot accept, we take him and his party prisoner. Maybe Washington listens to us then."

"Yes," Naiche said. "It is good. We should hear him first. If he gives us nothing we want, we take him."

There was a murmur of agreement.

"If we do that, we must know what we want," Tsach said. "What kind of treaty we want. It is not enough to take him prisoner."

"We have to give up something to get something," Josanie said. "We have already lost our country in the north. More and more whites are coming, like grasshoppers. But as it is now, no one there is safe from us. We have shown that to them. Even with all the soldiers around, we can hit them where we want to. It is so. Perhaps we can make them agree to make peace and leave us alone."

"What about the Mexicans?" Naiche asked.

"We can keep them away," Josanie said. "We can keep them out of these mountains."

"Perhaps we can bring Loco and Bonito to come and join us," Nana said.

"Some we don't want." Geronimo's voice was harsh. "Like Chato and those who help the whites to find us."

There was a silence.

Then Chaddi spoke quietly. "We cannot exclude anyone from coming to be with us. They are still our people, ndé, our kin. Our fathers and theirs, they always fought side by side. It is the white man who has made them crazy, turned some of them against us."

He paused. "Some of them have done wrong, I know. Some of us have done wrong, too. We need everyone if we are going to stay here."

"We must make up our mind," Tsach said.

There was a silence.

"I have heard what has been said," Geronimo said. "You have heard what I said. I don't know if I agree with a treaty that gives away our country in the north. There are places I want to see when I want to. I don't want anyone to tell me I can't."

"Many things I want, too," Chaddi said gently. "I want to be buried up there in our country where the old ones are buried. But I have to think of the living. I don't want my grandchildren and great-grandchildren to live in the white man's prison they call reservation."

There was a murmur of agreement.

Geronimo nodded to Chaddi and looked at Josanie. "I understand what you are saying. There is truth in it. I respect you. We should talk with Crook first. If we don't like what he wants, we take him prisoner with every officer who is with him. Maybe Washington trades with us."

"How do we make him come to us?" Naiche asked.

"We make contact with some scouts and talk with an officer," Josanie said. "Tell him we want peace, that we want a meeting with Crook, but without any soldiers present. He can't bring any."

There was a strong murmur of agreement around the circle.

Close by in the dark a horned owl called. Women and children wrapped themselves more tightly in their blankets. After a short while the meeting broke up. The matter of discussion was left where Josanie had ended.

Contact was made sooner than anyone had expected. At first light two days later the camps awoke to the rapid firing of a single Winchester .44-40 from the direction of Chihuahua's and Nana's horse herd, one and a half miles away to the southwest.

SIXTY-SIX

Josanie rolled out from under the blankets and grabbed his clothes. He dressed hurriedly and counted the shots. Six, seven. Silence. "Tisnol," he said, "guarding the horses."

He slipped his moccasin boots on. Jaccali held the leather jacket for him. He put one ammunition belt around his waist and slung another over his shoulder. Suddenly the quiet was split by the crashing of an irregular salvo of rifle fire from north of the knoll, followed quickly by another from the west and one from the south. Bullets whistled over the wickiup and smacked into the pines. A heavy thud came from the outside. Silence.

"Stay low," Josanie hissed to Jaccali. "Don't move around."

She stood and smiled and nodded and held the rifle out to him.

He burst through the low entrance and stumbled against the body of his horse, one of the few animals they had kept in the camp. The bay mare lay on the side, stone dead, shot through the head. He bent low and rushed toward the edge of the knoll. He saw other warriors dash to defense positions. He heard panting behind him. Chihuahua crouched behind a boulder ten feet away.

Josanie peered through a crack in the rocky outcrop of his cover. About twenty feet below him the slope of the knoll merged with the valley floor. There were rocky seams in the grass, with some ironwood and creosote bushes. In the back a series of pine-colored ridges rose slowly toward the height of the mountain. The first of these was about three hundred yards away. From there the shots had come.

A figure appeared on the crest of the ridge. Blue shirt, brown army trousers, long black hair, a white headband. Ndé, Apache government scout. The man raised both arms and hollered across.

"Alchisay. I am Alchisay! You know me!" He paused. "You are surrounded. You can't escape. We ask you to give yourselves up! We don't want to kill anyone."

Chihuahua stepped out and stood in the open. "I am Chihuahua! Who is your white chief?"

SIXTY-FIVE

Captain Emmet Crawford's force of four companies of Apache scouts, Lieutenants Maus and Shipp, Tom Horn as chief of scouts, and two mule trains with civilian packers cut Josanie's trail near Oputo and followed it south to the Aros River, into a region "rugged almost beyond description." They located the Chokonen and Chihenne camp on January 9, 1886. In his report, Lieutenant Marion Maus wrote:

Captain Crawford now decided to continue our march and attack the hostile camp at daylight the next morning. A hard day's march had already been made, but there was a chance we might be discovered and our present opportunity lost. The scouts requested the officers to take off their shoes and put on moccasins—this to avoid all noise if possible.

All night the command toiled over the mountains and down into canyons so dark on this moonless night, that they seemed bottomless. However an hour before daylight, after an eighteen hour march, within a mile and a half of the hostile camp, tired and foot sore, many bruised from falling during the night's march, the four companies were disposed of as near as possible, so as to attack the camp on all sides at the same time.

"Nantan Crawford."

"Tell him to stop the shooting! We want to talk with him."

Alchisay bent sideways. He appeared to speak with someone. He turned and shouted: "Crawford says no talk. You must give up. You can't get away."

A shot was fired from Josanie's right, and Alchisay ducked and disappeared behind the crest. Chihuahua scrambled for cover. About sixty rifles roared all along the ridge, and from the south and west of the knoll many rifles joined in. Deafening sounds rolled through the valley and echoed among the mountain walls. The defenders lay still under the torrent of bullets. Most whined harmlessly overhead; others splattered against the rocks; some found gaps and ricocheted through the camp. They could hear Chaddi's voice. Unmoved by the din of battle, the medicine man sat in the middle of the camp and sang spirit songs.

Josanie looked toward his brother. Chihuahua lay flat on his stomach, the rifle beside him.

"They found us again," Chihuahua said. "I've been careless again."

"My fault, too," Josanie said grimly. "They must have found my tracks." He paused. "They don't know about the second camp. And they don't know where our horses are. Tisnol has not fired again." He paused. "Geronimo and Naiche will get behind them."

Through the crack above his head he looked at the muzzle flashes in the powder smoke that enveloped the ridge. He opened the breech of the Sharps and checked the cartridge. He half raised himself and fired quickly and sat down, reloading. Chihuahua got up and fired four shots from a Winchester .44-40, furiously working the lever; sat down briefly; and made four more shots. Josanie fired again and again, and they waited. On the knoll around the camp warriors answered the fusillade at intervals with quick shots.

The enemy fire in front of Josanie's and Chihuahua's position slackened, then died altogether. Now rapid rifle fire could be heard from the northeast, from behind the enemy line. Josanie stood up and saw Apache scouts spill west over the ridge, some turning and shooting at targets behind them that could not be seen from the knoll.

With Josanie and Chihuahua four warriors stood and fired at the retreating scouts as fast as they could reload their weapons. They did not notice that the enemy rifles south of the river and to the west had also fallen silent. Nana was suddenly behind them. He put his hand on Josanie's arm. "Let them go, Brother," he said. "They are running. Naiche came up behind those on the other side of the river. They are moving away downriver."

Josanie and Chihuahua and the men with them took their rifles down and watched. The Apache scouts disappeared. A single rider came through the bushes of the flat below and waived and rode on slowly, the rifle leveled. Lozen, the warrior woman. Two riders came down the ridge from where the enemy line had fired its salvoes and joined her, one of them Geronimo. Both waved and went on.

"Let's get the horses," Josanie said.

"My men are bringing them in," Nana said.

They walked west where the trail left the knoll. They saw two more dead horses among the wickiups. A few women stood quietly, looking around. Limbs and twigs shot off the pines and the tops of wickiups lay around. Jaccali and Ramona were there and waved. Josanie waved back, and they went down the knoll. Horses had been driven up, and the men jumped on their bare backs and rode out, guiding the mounts with their leg muscles.

Chihuahua rode beside Josanie and six warriors, and Nana and seven warriors came on behind. Eight warriors were ahead and waited for them to come up. Josanie pointed with his hands to both sides, and the warriors formed a skirmish line across the valley floor, skillfully using depressions in the ground. Geronimo and Lozen and seven men rode in from the mountain slope to the north, and Naiche and his men came in from the south and joined the line. They rode slowly, rifles ready, but the enemy had moved rapidly down the Aros. Behind the big bend of the river, where it turned north, the valley narrowed. The warriors rode in four separate bunches, Josanie with his brother and his men first, then Nana and the Chihenne, then Naiche and Geronimo, each with his men.

They rode downstream for about five miles and finally came to Crawford's camp. They got a glimpse of horses and mules and white tents and were fired on once by a bunch of Apache scouts spread out among the rocks in front of the camp. Josanie halted and they sat their horses quietly for a while, not firing a shot and not making an aggressive move. Finally Josanie called out, and they turned and rode away, leaving the enemy camp alone.

"We could finish them today or tomorrow morning," Geronimo said, moving his horse close to Josanie's.

"We don't want that," Josanie said coldly. "We want to talk with Crawford so we can talk with Crook. Crawford decides nothing. It is Crook we want. If we finish Crawford and this bunch, Crook is not going to talk with us."

Above the big bend of the Aros, where the valley narrowed to a canyon, Josanie left Galeana, Zele, and Zilahe to watch over the approach to Chihuahua's camp. The horse herd had been driven up to a fold in the mountain slope northeast of camp, close by.

"How did Crawford and the scouts get here?" Chihuahua asked the question that was on everyone's mind when they reached the knoll. "They didn't come up the river," he mused. "They must have come over the mountains."

"Yes," Josanie said. "We didn't think that could be done. I think they must have climbed up from their camp and come down the mountain north of us. If Tisnol had not seen them and warned us with his rifle, they would have taken us in our camp." He paused. "Without Geronimo and Naiche we might not have been able to drive them away."

"They didn't want to die for the white man," Nana said. "They went away when it became dangerous for them. It seems they are tired of fighting, too."

Later the three dead horses were butchered, and the Geronimo and Naiche camp was invited to share in the feast. The people sat around a big bonfire in Chihuahua's camp. They gorged themselves on red meat. Later wooden spits with slabs of meat were still lined around the fire, but stomachs were full, and finally women collected them before they burned up.

Chihuahua rose to his feet, dropping the trade blanket he had wrapped himself in. He stood silently for a moment, looking into the flames. The noisy circle fell silent.

"Today," he said, "we were once again attacked in our camp. It happened before. It was my fault. We should have had guards out, but we didn't." He paused. "We felt safe here. But we were not safe. It can happen again. We should learn from this." He paused again. "We must make some kind of a peace with Washington. One we can live with. One that gives us our families back. One that leaves us in peace. Here, in these mountains."

There was a murmur of agreement.

"Today Geronimo and Naiche came to save us." He searched for the two men around the circle, found them, and nodded to them. "I thank them! We thank them! We would have done the same. Ndé. We belong together; we are the same blood. We have to help each other."

He paused again. "We should send someone to that white chief, Crawford, tell him we want to talk with the general, Crook. That is all I want to say."

He looked around the circle, lastly to his brother, who sat next to him. He sat down. There was a silence.

Nana spoke. "Chihuahua is right. We send someone to tell Crawford. Crawford tells Crook." He paused. "Whom should we send to deliver the message?" He paused again. "I could go."

"I go," Geronimo said.

Jaccali stood up from behind her husband's back. "I'll go," she said. "If one of the chiefs goes, Crawford could take him prisoner. They have done this often. They would not take me prisoner. I bring the message. That is all."

She looked from her husband to Chihuahua and Nana and along the circle. The fire crackled and sparks flew. "What should I tell? When do we want to meet with Crook? In two moons? Three moons?" She stood there, her eyes blazing. Josanie looked up at her and their eyes met. He smiled as he had not smiled in a long time.

"Two moons," Chihuahua said.

"Two moons is enough." This was Nana.

"Yes," Geronimo said. Naiche nodded. "Yes. Two moons." The chiefs looked around the circle. Warriors and women nodded in agreement.

So it was decided.

At sunup the following morning Jaccali prepared for the ride to Crawford's camp. She and her husband had taken a dip in the river and brushed each other's hair. She wore leather trousers and moccasin boots under a long, blue calico dress, and a colorful, patterned blouse over it, held by a broad belt. Below her delicate throat dangled a turquoise necklace. Josanie saddled the horse for her, a feisty chestnut mare, and held the bridle. Chihuahua, Ramona, and most people of the band were standing around them. But before Jaccali could mount, they heard heavy gunfire from the northwest, downriver. They stood and listened. Sounds of a vicious battle continued for a while, then died. Silence.

They waited. A single rider came up the trail. He rode in as fast as the slithering trail allowed. Zele. He brought the horse to a halt. The young face showed excitement.

"Mexicans," he said. "Mexican soldiers. They are attacking the camp of the scouts. They have Tarahumara scouts with them. We saw it through the glass."

"Where did they come from?" Josanie asked.

"They came from the north, along the river."

Geronimo and Naiche rode up with their warriors. "What is happening?" Geronimo asked, looking at Josanie. He pointed with his chin to Zele.

"Mexican soldiers have a battle with Crawford," Zele said.

"Who is winning?" Geronimo asked.

Zele shrugged. "I don't know."

"The Mexicans cannot win against ndé scouts," Josanie said.

"What do we do?" Naiche wondered.

"Nothing," Chihuahua said. "Let them fight. They are both our enemies." He paused. "We still must talk with Crawford. We have to wait."

They left it there. Zele rode back to the canyon, and Geronimo and Naiche and their men tied their horses up below the knoll and walked to Chihuahua's camp. They built a small fire and sat in the same place as the evening before. They talked and waited.

Zele returned around midday.

"We had a talk with Alchisay," he said. "Crawford was shot in the head. He's still alive but cannot live. The Mexicans are still there. They had some killed, many wounded."

"Who is in Crawford's place?" Josanie asked.

"A little chief, a lieutenant. Maus."

"We don't know him. Does anyone?" Josanie looked around the circle of faces, but there were only shrugs.

No more information came that day. But on the next day Zele reported that Maus had given the Mexicans half of his mules to move their wounded. They moved out shortly afterward, going back north. In the afternoon Maus moved his camp a few miles farther north on the Aros, to a location in which he could not be surprised by another Mexican force. It seemed that he was certain that he was in no danger from the people Crawford and the scouts had attacked two days earlier. Galeana and the watchers in the canyon learned that Crawford had made a bad mistake. He had believed the Tarahumara scouts with the Mexicans to be Apaches, the advance guard of the American army under Captain Wirt Davis, who had been moving around the state of Chihuahua with a Fourth Cavalry unit and a handful of Apache scouts. The Mexican commander had started the battle when Tarahumaras reported hostile Apaches encamped in front of them.

Zele also reported that Maus wanted to talk. The chiefs decided to send two women at sunup on the following morning, Jaccali and Lozen.

Morning came clear and cold. Once again Josanie had saddled Jaccali's horse and held the bridle for her. Lozen was already mounted. She was of medium size, with a slender but strong body. Black hair framed a round, energetic face with high cheekbones, a wide mouth, and keen eyes. She was dressed much like Jaccali, a patterned blouse over a full skirt of blue calico, moccasin boots, a broad, beaded belt. Both women wore their belt knives, but carried no other weapon.

Jaccali took the bridle from Josanie's hand and mounted quickly. They looked into each other's eyes. "I will be with you," Josanie's eyes said. "You won't see me, but I will stand behind your left shoulder."

"I know you," Jaccali's eyes said. "I will do right. I will be safe. We will always be together." She nodded and smiled, turned the mare quickly, and pushed her forward into a trot, then a lope, with Lozen behind her. The two women rode out on the trail. They did not look back.

They passed above the great bend and rode north along the narrowing canyon walls. Twice they crossed the river and came by the outpost where the three warriors kept guard on the scout army. They waved as they rode by, and Galeana followed them with the binoculars. He saw that they were stopped by ndé sentries at the edge of the enemy camp and let through; they disappeared among white canvas tents, milling horses, and a large gathering of ndé scouts streaming toward a place he could not see.

Broad ndé faces looked up to the women when the ndé men took the bridles of their horses and led them to a white tent set apart from a row of others. The two women sat their horses until two officers emerged from the tent, followed by a white civilian. They had brought folding chairs and sat down. Jaccali and Lozen dismounted. The horses were held behind them. Two white men, probably mule packers, brought chairs forward, but the women declined. They stood facing the officers. A great, tight ring of men surrounded them, over a hundred ndé scouts, perhaps thirty white civilians, mule skinners. Three more men joined the officers, two of them Chiricahuas, one a slim white man who was dressed and looked like ndé but for his gray eyes.

The two women stood proudly, if arrogantly. Jaccali looked at the group before them and glanced at the tight triple circle of ndé faces.

"I am Jaccali," she said. "I am Chokonen. Josanie is my husband. I speak for Chihuahua's band and for Nana's band."

She had spoken in Chiricahua. The white man who looked like an Apache, the interpreter, Mickey Free, translated. He spoke into Maus's ear.

"I am Lozen," the woman warrior said. "I am Chihenne. I speak for Geronimo's band and Naiche's band."

Again Mickey Free translated.

Lieutenant Maus cleared his throat. He stood up. He pointed with his right index finger to the officer sitting on his left. "This is Lieutenant Shipp." He pointed to the civilian behind him. The man's left arm was in a sling. Blood had seeped through the bandages. "Horn, Tom Horn, chief of scouts." He pointed to the interpreter, but Jaccali interrupted him.

"We know him," she said in Chiricahua. "Mickey Free. A liar. He has caused much trouble. We don't want him to translate for us."

She pointed with her chin to another of the interpreters. "Yellow Dog we call him. You call him Peaches. A liar, too. A liar and a coward. He cannot translate for us."

"We want him to translate." She pointed to Alchisay.

Mickey Free tried to speak to the lieutenant, but Jaccali cut him off.

"We have been sent to give you a message." She paused to let Alchisay translate. Lieutenant Maus looked disturbed but listened carefully.

"We want to talk with nantan Crook to make peace. No more war." She paused and Alchisay translated. The circles of Apache scouts stirred.

"We want to meet with him. But he cannot bring any soldiers. No soldiers."

She looked into the sky when Alchisay spoke in the foreign language to the lieutenant. Nachi, my son, she thought. Gone ahead of me, killed by these men. Maybe you look on from the spirit world.

She waited.

"When? Where?" Alchisay asked.

"Two moons from today. At the place the Mexicans call Canyon de los Embudos, way north of here." The Spanish, another foreign language, was not good, but Alchisay understood. "Yes, I know where it is," he said in Chiricahua. He turned to Maus and told him in his uneven English, repeating it to be certain that the white man understood.

Lozen spoke. "This is what the chiefs told us to tell you."

There was a long pause.

"You want to meet the general at the Canyon de los Embudos?" Maus asked in English. "In two months?"

"Two moons," Alchisay said in Chiricahua.

Jaccali nodded. "Yes."

"The chiefs all agreed on this," Lozen said.

Alchisay bent toward Maus. He translated correctly, but then he added something of his own. "They mean it. They want to talk with the general. You should say yes. The general wants it, too."

Maus sat very still. So many things to think of. Crawford still alive but unconscious, sure to die. The whole Sierra Madre operation— was it over? Was the war over? Had it ended at last?

He looked at the two haughty women before him. Wild as the mountains, untamed as the wind. He wondered if he could get away with it, if Crook, another madman, would endorse it. What he said was: "I will inform the general, and we will move out tomorrow. Perhaps this war is over."

Alchisay translated and Jaccali and Lozen looked at each other and nodded. Yes, there was a way.

SIXTY-SEVEN

The living sky black-spotted.
The living sky blue-spotted.
The living sky yellow-spotted.
The living sky white-spotted.
The young spruce as girls stood up
for their dance in the way of life.
When my songs first were,
they made my songs with words of jet.
Earth when it was made.
Sky when it was made.
Earth to the end.
Sky to the end.
Black gahé, black thunder,
when they came toward each other
the bad things vanished.
The bad wishes
which were in the world vanished.
The lightning of black thunder
struck four times for them.
It struck four times for me.

Gahé song. Song of the mountain spirits, recorded by
P. E. Goddard, circa 1908.

EPILOGUE

The four bands rode out of the Sierra Madre in early March 1886. Josanie and his men rode point; Geronimo's men formed the rear guard. They traveled slowly, looking at the familiar landmarks as if knowing that they might not return. They met with General Crook and his small party at the place agreed to, the Canyon de los Embudos, twenty miles below the border, on March 25 through 27. The bands encamped in a location, Crook wrote, "that a thousand men could not have surrounded them with any possibility of capturing them." The general had kept his word and not brought troops. Lieutenant Maus and his Apache scouts were in the vicinity but in no position to intervene in case of trouble. The general was in Josanie's hands if the hostiles could have agreed to take him hostage.

It is historical fact that they did not. Perhaps it was still unthinkable to them to break a serious promise they had made. Perhaps the choice the general offered to them, unaware of his personal danger, appeared more acceptable to them. He formally agreed that after surrender, in the words of the agreement, "they should be sent east for not exceeding two years, taking with them such of the families as so desired." After two years of exile, it was agreed, they would be returned to the Fort Apache Reservation.

The general could not anticipate that President Grover Cleveland, on receiving Crook's wire on March 30, would annul the surrender agreement and order a permanent exile. Thus both parties to the agreement were betrayed, an issue over which Crook resigned a week later.

Chihuahua's, Nana's, Naiche's, and Geronimo's bands surrendered to Crook on March 27. They started with him (he had no troops) on the road to Fort Bowie, where the first two bands were reunited with their families and put on a train to Florida. Josanie's war was over.

Geronimo's and Naiche's bands followed the other two but near the border met an American bootlegger and gun runner, a "white rascal named Bob Tribolett," who told them that certain death awaited them once they crossed the line. Both bands bolted and fled to the Sierra Madre once again. They finally surrendered to General Nelson A. Miles, who had replaced Crook, on September 3, 1886, still under the agreement made with Crook in March. Mangus's tiny band, which had remained aloof from the others, surrendered to a troop of Tenth Cavalry at the edge of the Black Range on October 15, 1886.

A few members of the five bands never surrendered. Their descendants are said to be still in the Sierra Madre today.

In a rare act of treachery, probably initiated by President Cleveland, on September 7, 1886, Miles ordered all Chiricahua and Warm Springs Apaches on the Fort Apache Reservation arrested and sent into exile in Florida, where they were imprisoned with the former hostile bands in Fort Marion, St. Augustine. Some of them had served the army loyally against their own kin. Having surrendered at different times, the bands were transported to Florida by train in April, September, and November 1886. Naiche, Geronimo, Mangus, and their warriors were confined in the dungeons of Fort Pickens in Pensacola Bay, while their families were in Fort Marion. Even then they did not know that the president, ignoring surrender terms, had insisted on a permanent exile for all of them.

Of the 498 Chiricahua and Warm Springs Apaches sent to Florida, 119 died before the end of 1889 from exposure and various diseases, especially tuberculosis. Only in 1913 was freedom restored to them. That year they were given the choice of accepting land near Fort Sill, Oklahoma, or going to the Mescalero Reservation in New Mexico. Of the 271 people the prisoners had been reduced to, 187 elected to go to Mescalero, and 84 chose to stay near Fort Sill. Their descendants are in these locations today.

Undefeated in the field, the bands surrendered to be reunited with their families under a formal agreement that they would return to Arizona. In Florida prisons, later in an Alabama prison, the Mount Vernon Barracks near Mobile, they were finally defeated by white people's diseases and by a cruel government that let them suffer.